CRITICAL  P9-DFY-347
AWARD-WINNING AUTHOR
JILL GREGORY AND HER NOVELS

ALWAYS YOU

"*ALWAYS YOU* HAS IT ALL. . . . Jill Gregory's inventive imagination and sprightly prose combine for another bell ringer."   —*Rendezvous*

WHEN THE HEART BECKONS

"Jill Gregory combines all the drama of a gritty western with the aura of a homespun romance in this beautifully rendered tale. The wonderful characters are sure to win readers' hearts."   —*Romantic Times*

DAISIES IN THE WIND

"Jill Gregory paints a true portrait of small-town America through her carefully crafted characterizations, wonderful descriptions, and snappy dialogue. . . . There might just be a tear or two in your eyes by the end."
—*Romantic Times*

FOREVER AFTER

"A colorful, exciting story . . . The characters are realistic and interesting. Spectacular writing makes this book a must on your reading list."   —*Rendezvous*

Dell Books by Jill Gregory

Just This Once

※※※※※※※※

Jill Gregory

A Dell Book

Published by
Dell Publishing
a division of
Bantam Doubleday Dell Publishing Group, Inc.
1540 Broadway
New York, New York 10036

ISBN: 0-440-22235-4

Printed in the United States of America

Published simultaneously in Canada

June 1997

10   9   8   7   6   5   4   3   2

OPM

To my family—with love!

Chapter One

~~~~~~~

Abilene, Kansas

He's the one.

Josie peeked out from the saloon's back stairs as the tall, handsome cowboy dressed all in black shoved his chair back from the poker table. He rose up to a magnificent and most impressive height and scooped up his winnings. Carelessly he stuck a few bills in his shirt pocket, tucked the rest into a leather wallet, and then dropped the wallet into his vest pocket with a series of easy motions that hypnotized her. Actually, it was the sight of all that money that hypnotized her.

She fairly quivered as she eyed the slightly bulging vest pocket that nestled against his lean, solid torso.

My, my, she thought, her mouth nearly watering. *What I couldn't do with all that lovely money.*

First off, she could buy a train ticket to New York City—possibly even a first-class ticket—and then steamship passage to England ... and even send some extra to the Magnolia Sisters United Orphanage in Savannah.

But there was a tiny problem, she conceded, biting her lip as she crouched unseen in the dimness of the stairs.

She had no doubt from observing the tall cowboy with the silver belt buckle that he was a gunslinger.

Why, Lord, why does he have to be a gunslinger?

She watched him carefully, holding her breath, wondering if she dared, if she really dared to try to pick his pocket.

You must, she told herself. You need that cash to get out of this pesthole of a town and far away from Snake.

You can't, a wise, warning voice squeaked inside her ear. He's not a man to be caught dozing.

He was most definitely a gunslinger, she decided on a sigh as his glance skimmed coolly, indifferently, over the other men at the poker table. There was something mean and hungry about him, something cold. She noted his lean bronzed cheeks, the hard arrogant face, the simple but elegantly cut dark clothes he wore upon his strapping form. Then there was the leonine way he moved and the easy way he wore his guns, as if he'd been born with them.

Oh, yes. A gunslinger. A deadly one, at that.

Anxiety rippled through her as she weighed her choices.

The miner at the table still had a pocketful of coins, she knew, but he looked down on his luck. Her conscience wouldn't let her pick the pocket of a man who looked as if he needed every last dime.

But *this man* was another story.

This man appeared as if he could spare some cash, a great deal of cash. And if he was a gun for hire, well, when his wallet was gone, he'd still have his guns. He could always hire himself out and earn himself more blood money, or win it in the next poker game.

So follow him and get it over with. What are you waiting for?

She crept down the steps, and peeked around the door as he shouldered his way through the double saloon doors and out into glittering Kansas sunshine.

Josie figured he was going to get some shut-eye at last or was on his way to watch the hanging along with everyone else in town. Either way, she'd better follow close behind, and find a chance to pluck that stash from his pocket.

"Jo, no, don't! I know what you're thinking, and it's a big mistake!"

Josie whirled as Rose MacEwen clutched desperately at her sleeve. Rose was whispering at her furiously.

"Honey, I know you want to get out of town, but you'll get caught. You'll land in jail. You can't just—"

"Shhh," Josie hissed. She peered frantically over her shoulder to the double doors through which the gunslinger had disappeared. "Rose, let me go."

"But, honey—"

"I have to do this!"

"No, you don't!"

It was hard to believe that she'd only known Rose MacEwen for two weeks, since she'd arrived in Abilene and taken a job in the kitchen of the Golden Pistol Saloon and Dance Hall. Rose, who'd been thrown out of her family's farmhouse when she was thirteen, had had a hard life—almost as hard as Josie's own. That realization had formed a bond between the two young women immediately. "He's got a fat purse, Rose, and that's all I care about," she whispered fiercely as the skinny, pale-haired saloon girl in the low-cut pink dress opened her mouth to speak again. "It'll be all right. Now let me go."

But Rose's grip tightened. "I'll give you all the money I've got—six dollars, maybe seven . . . and I'm sure Liza can spare something, too."

"I don't take money from my friends, Rose. Go on upstairs, and don't you worry. I'll be fine. All I need is enough cash to get out of town."

"But why, Jo, why do you have to leave?" Plaintively, Rose stared into Josie's eyes. "First Penny and now you. Can't you stay a while longer? I know Judd pays lousy, but you're the best cook he's ever had and business has picked up in the dance hall since you started fixing the meals—and it's good steady work." As Josie shook her head Rose plunged on. "And there's a lot of men who come through the Golden Pistol. If you started dancing with us more regular, too, instead of just filling in, you might find some feller who wants to marry you—"

"I've been married, Rose, and I'm never making that mistake again!" Impatiently, Josie shook free of the girl's grasp. "Look, the less you know about my leaving town the better," she added in a low tone. "If anyone asks, you never saw me. I'll say good-bye before I leave, don't you worry. But now I have to go and catch that hombre."

There was no mistaking her determination. Rose sighed in defeat and shook her head as Josie squeezed her hand, then dodged past her, rushing through the rear door.

She darted around the alleyway and scanned the main street. It was now teeming noisily with excited men, women, and children come to watch the hanging, but to Josie's relief, she spotted the tall gunslinger almost immediately. He had paused at the edge of the crowd, a little apart, definitely aloof.

*All right, mister. That's it. You're not getting away so
easily. Josephine Cooper always gets her man.*

A grim smile curled her lips as she started forward in
the hazy sunshine, her gingham skirt rustling. She'd
dressed "respectable" for the occasion—her plain blue
gingham gown buttoned up to the throat, tiny dangly jet
earrings, her unruly mane of brown hair tamed in a neat,
prim coil with not a wisp out of place. On her feet were
her good sturdy shoes, not the wicked rhinestone-studded
slippers she wore onstage whenever she filled in for one
of the dance hall girls who couldn't perform. She was
certain no one would recognize the Golden Pistol's prac-
tically invisible cook or the sometime dance hall girl with
the wild brown curls as the demure, respectable creature
making her way through the crowded street.

The necessity of leaving Abilene tomorrow weighed
heavily on her mind. Instinct told her Snake and his boys
were closing in. Her skin had been prickling all day each
time she looked out the window. Josie's "feelings" about
such things were never wrong. Snake would be here
soon. If she stayed, he'd catch her and then . . .

Then she'd be as good as dead. Because if her dear
outlaw husband and his cutthroat gang got their hands on
her, they'd show her no more mercy than these townsfolk
would show Rusty Innes, who was going to be hanged
today from the gallows in the center of town. Innes had
killed a teller and a customer when he'd robbed the bank
a month ago, and now he was going to pay for what
he'd done.

If Snake and the boys catch up with me, I'll pay, too,
Josie thought, swallowing down the metallic taste of fear.
I'll pay dear for what I did to them.

But she didn't regret it one whit.

❦❦❦❦

All of Abilene seemed to have gathered in the street—farmers and ranchers and merchants and gamblers and miners and drifters mingling elbow to elbow. Women called to one another, men smoked cigars and squinted through the sun, dogs barked and horses stamped at their tethering posts.

It was a beautiful day for a hanging.

The stranger remained on the fringes of the murmuring, restless crowd. He seemed oblivious to the heat and nervous energy vibrating all around him. Though heat poured down from a molten July sun, and women fanned themselves furiously, he looked cool and unperturbed.

Josie, on the other hand, felt sweat beading on her delicate brow as she slipped nimbly past a farmer in a checkered shirt, two boys tussling over a stick of licorice, a woman nudging forward for a better view. She spotted Judd Stickley, the slender, mustachioed owner of the Golden Pistol, standing on the boardwalk, studying his gold pocket watch, and as he glanced up she hunched her shoulders and ducked into the crowd.

It wouldn't do for Judd to spot her. Not at all. Her boss was none too happy that she'd befriended Penny Callahan, one of the other dance hall girls she'd met since coming to Abilene. He didn't like Josie's fearless attitude, the way she'd taken Penny under her wing. Stickley wanted to keep poor snub-nosed Penny in his bed—he was like a vulture that preyed on all those he sensed were weaker than he. And Penny had feared him too much to refuse.

Unable to bear watching Stickley keep Penny under his thumb, Josie had only today persuaded the girl to take the last of Josie's own stash of money and had sneaked her onto the noon stage bound for Missouri. Stickley would be livid when he found out she'd left town for good.

But Josie was leaving too, quick as she could. And she wasn't nearly as afraid of Stickley as she was of Snake. So now, though she hated pickpocketing, she'd have to do it to raise some quick cash and get out of town before all hell caught up with her.

Too bad all the stolen loot she'd taken from Snake and the gang when she ran away was gone. Of course, she still had her "treasure," but she wouldn't sell that. Never. Josie averted her face as she slipped past fat, balding Elmer Mills, who owned the general store, and peppery Sally Klemp, who ran the apothecary with her husband, Fred. Jo knew that money always just seemed to slip through her fingers. She'd never had more than a dollar or two to her name at any one time—until the night she ran out on Snake Barker, the night he'd beaten her senseless.

Her face bloody and bruised, she'd come to on the floor, every limb aching as if she'd been knocked over a cliff. She'd crawled to her knees and found Snake passed out beside the stove with the empty whiskey bottle next to him.

Her mind was blurred with pain and shock, but Josie'd known one thing. Snake had nearly killed her. First he'd forced her to marry him, imagining in a liquored haze of infatuation after he'd first set eyes on her that he wanted to settle down, have a passel of kids, and have someone cook and clean for him when he wasn't holding up stagecoaches or banks—and then, as if that hadn't been bad enough, he'd nearly killed her. If the liquor hadn't ren-

dered him unconscious when it had, he probably would
have beaten her to death.

She'd staggered across the room, grabbed up his
saddlebag containing the loot from the most recent stage
holdup, taken his fastest horse, and hightailed it out of
there.

He and the boys had been hot on her trail ever since.

The crowd in Abilene was growing restless. "Bring 'im
out, Sheriff."

"It's noon. Let's hang him and git back to work."

Josie threw one quick pitying glance at the gray-faced
man being led to the gallows by Sheriff Mills. What he'd
done was wrong, and he deserved to die for it, but she
had no intention of watching. While everyone else was
immersed in the process of justice being served, she
would dip her fingers into that gunslinger's pocket and,
with any luck, come up with enough money to buy a
ticket on tomorrow's eastbound train.

The stranger was less than ten feet away, his hat pulled
low across his eyes to block the sun. Josie sidled closer,
ignoring the flutter of nervousness in the pit of her
stomach.

Don't let him catch you, Jo, she warned herself,
wishing she could turn back somehow, but knowing it
was impossible at this point. She needed that money a
damned sight more than he did at this moment.

Growing up in orphanages and foster homes, Josie had
been taught over and over that you had to look out for
yourself. She always seemed to end up worrying more
about others who seemed somehow more unfortunate
than she—people like Penny Callahan, or the other children at the Magnolia Sisters Orphanage, the ones who

had nightmares and stomachaches and trouble learning to spell.

Old Pete Thompson and his gray-haired stick of a wife, Em, had tried to break her of this habit when they'd adopted her at the age of twelve, not because they'd wanted a child to love and care for, but because they'd desired an extra pair of hands to do chores on their Kansas farm.

They'd taken turns shouting at her whenever she sneaked extra scraps of table food to the dogs, or put a blanket out in the barn for the cats during the winter.

"The Lord helps those who help themselves!" they'd yelled, and slapped her hands, and pinched her arms, and sent her off to bed without supper. But Josie had never seemed able to get this idea into her head.

She had a feeling that Pete and Em, who worked their barren little Kansas farm from dawn till dusk, never smiled or spoke a kind word to anyone, who attended church and sneaked coins from the collection plate when no one was looking, didn't know as much as they thought they did about the Lord.

Anyway, she couldn't help herself. In the orphanage the younger children, whose clothes she mended and whose tears she'd wiped with the hem of her own ragged dress, had called her Ma. She'd been touched by this, since her own mother must have died shortly after she was born and she'd never known her, at least, not as she could remember.

Josie knew almost nothing about her own background, except that since the first orphanage she could remember was the Magnolia Sisters United Orphanage in Savannah, she guessed she was from the South. And she knew she'd been wrapped in a satin blanket when she'd come there, and most importantly, right from the beginning, she had the brooch.

The brooch had been pinned to her swaddling clothes—along with a note that had the words *Baby Josephine* scrawled upon it—and nothing else. The rest had been torn off, lost forever. Mrs. Guntherson, the kindly and honest woman who'd run the Magnolia Sisters United Orphanage, where Josie had lived until the age of seven, had kept it for her until the day she left, when her first family, the Coopers, had adopted her. On that day, Mrs. Guntherson had shown Josie the brooch, and advised her to keep it close.

From that moment on, Josie kept the brooch with her at all times—it was her one link with her past, the main clue she hoped would eventually help her discover her real name, and who she really was. It was exquisite. The centerpiece was the opal, a great pale, shimmering stone that flashed with blue fire. It was set in lustrous gold, surrounded by four creamy pearls. It looked to be an heirloom, a magnificent, treasured heirloom.

A family heirloom.

Josie had grown up wondering how it had come to belong to her. Who had pinned it to her swaddling clothes? Perhaps her true family had never wanted her, perhaps they might all be dead by now, or wish never to be found by the child they'd given up to strangers. Whatever the answer, she needed to know.

Knowing would be enough, she'd told herself many times over as she clasped the brooch in her palm, eyes closed, trying to conjure up an image from the heat and shape of it, trying to discern the dark curtain of her origin, the secret of her past.

She'd been trying for years to find out who'd brought

her—and the brooch—to the orphanage, who her family had been, where they'd lived, and why they had abandoned her. She'd searched near and far, written letters, asked questions, studied the faces and jewelry worn by strangers. Always she scanned for resemblances, wondering if she'd "know" her mother or father if they came face-to-face in a chance encounter, and dreaming endlessly of a joyous, glorious reunion.

All to no avail.

But now, thanks to Snake, in addition to the brooch there was the ring. The ring had given her new hope. It had suggested a place to look.

And that place was England.

So don't let that scowl the man's wearing scare you off, she urged herself. She straightened her spine. If there's one thing you learned from Pop Watson, it was how to pick pockets and not get caught, so just go ahead and do it.

The crowd was jostling, moving. Perfect. She reached his side, turned toward the gallows, but kept her eyes lowered so she would not see the men standing on the platform, what they were doing with Innes and the rope.

She peeked quickly up at the tall man beside her. The top of her head just reached his shoulder. His wavy hair was the color of midnight, worn long beneath his dusty black hat. Close up, she saw that he hadn't shaved in at least a day, perhaps several; coarse black stubble added to the harshness of his uncompromisingly masculine face, a handsome face of hard planes and shadows, the face of a dangerous man.

The crowd was starting to shout. To jeer. They were probably coiling the rope around Innes's neck. Then the moment she'd been waiting for, the slight surge as people inched forward as one, the jostling.

Josie swayed against the gunslinger.

"Ohhhh . . ." she whispered, hoping she sounded faint.

A hand caught her elbow, steadied her. She leaned into him, her body staggering against his, her free hand brushing with seeming haphazardness against his torso.

For an instant she clung weakly, then her hand fell away.

"I'm sorry," she murmured, blinking dizzily. "For a moment I felt so strange. . . ."

She let her voice trail weakly off. She had it. She had the wallet, she was nestling it securely in her pocket—but suddenly the tall man moved so swiftly, she didn't even have time to flinch. Iron fingers clamped over her wrist as he yanked it into the air, the wallet still clenched between her fingers.

"Ouch!" Josie squeaked.

A slight gasp, and then a cheer went up as the hanging commenced. But she was paying no attention to the crowd or to Innes's fate. Josie's gaze was locked onto the coolest, deadliest pair of gray eyes she'd ever seen.

Her stomach tumbled down to her kneecaps.

"Mister," she tried, as firmly as she could, "let me go!"

"The hell I will."

"How dare you! Let me go this instant!" She yanked her wrist back, trying to break free, but succeeded only in inducing him to dig his fingers in even tighter. Josie braced herself against the pain—and against a rising panic. "You're hurting me!"

"That's what you get, lady, for trying to pick my pocket."

"I didn't! Why, I never . . . !"

"Then why is my wallet clasped in your pretty little fingers?"

"Your wallet?" All around them rose the chatter of the crowd as it began to disperse and people returned to their homes or businesses. For the moment no one had noticed them, but Josie knew someone would soon, and then her goose would be cooked.

"Your wallet?" she repeated desperately. Somehow, with her eyes still locked on the gunslinger's fierce gray gaze, she managed to unclench her fingers. The wallet slipped from her grasp and hit the dirt with a solid plop.

"You mean that thing lying there on the ground?"

"Nice try." He hauled her toward him, one long arm snaking around her to imprison her waist, his other hand still crushing her wrist. But Josie scarcely noticed for as she hurtled forward into his chest, hitting a wall of solid muscle, she caught a glimpse over his shoulder of the grotesque vision hanging from the gallows.

"Oooooh!" There was no false faintness in her tone this time. Josie closed her eyes, swallowing back a hideous rush of nausea. "Oooooh. Aaaagh. . . ."

Her skin had turned a sickly green. The gunslinger scowled. "Women," he muttered. He spun her around to face the opposite direction. "Give it up," he said roughly. "You just tried, not very skillfully, to pick my pocket."

Eyes still closed, Josie automatically shook her head. "You're loco, mister. It fell out of your pocket, that's all. Please, I feel sick."

"Yeah? Well, you look like hell. But that doesn't change the fact that you're a thief."

She opened her eyes, swallowed hard, and as the nausea faded, realized she was being held hard and fast and indecently close by a man who could be a dead ringer for the devil. A man far stronger than she, with an icy hard gleam in his eyes, and a face so handsome, she ached looking at him, a man who would turn her over to the sheriff in a heartbeat.

"I'm not."

"Let's ask the sheriff."

"No!" She began to struggle frantically in his arms. "Hey, don't blame me if you can't hang on to what's yours. It's not my fault if—"

"Lady, I can hang on all right." With a lightning movement he scooped the wallet up, then, before Josie could break away, he dragged her swiftly into the alley, out of sight of those in the street.

"I'm hanging on to you until you're locked in jail."

Chapter Two

⋙⋘

The gunslinger shoved Josie up against the crumbling rear wall of the apothecary, pinning her wrists above her head and holding her there. "Admit it. You're a damned no-good little thief."

She fought back panic, trying to think. The alley was deserted except for a stray cat who'd been exploring the garbage piled in back of the apothecary. It sprinted off at the rough sound of the gunslinger's voice.

"They hang thieves in some of these here parts, you know," he snarled, watching the fear, worry, and dismay flit across her face, and edging closer. "And in others, they just send 'em to prison. There's some question among convicts as to which is worse."

"I'm not a thief! You can't prove anything!"

"I caught you red-handed."

"You're wrong. You're loco. I'm going to scream for help if you don't let me go right now."

"Lady, you just scream away."

Josie opened her mouth, then clamped it shut again. She couldn't risk attracting a crowd, or the notice of the sheriff. She couldn't risk questions, delays, complications.

And the man staring down at her with dark, glittering triumph in his eyes knew it.

He actually laughed as she set her lips together and gulped. It was a mirthless, unpleasant sound, Josie decided, squirming again in another useless attempt to get free. She hated him. *Hated him.* There was no pity in his ice-gray eyes. No hint of softness or compassion. And even though she knew he'd been up the entire night playing poker, he didn't look the least bit weary. He looked keenly alert, furious, and as if he was enjoying the fact that struggle as she might, she couldn't break his grip.

Damn him. Handsome as sin, and every bit as ruthless. She cursed her own foolishness for not having chosen an easier and less dangerous target.

"Look," she said, a blush staining up her neck and into her cheeks as she heard the genuine quaver in her own voice.

"I'm ... sorry. I did ... take your wallet. It was a stupid thing to do and it was wrong. But my father is ill, and needs to go east to a hospital right away for treatment, and we're about to lose our farm, and all I need is enough for train fare for the two of us."

The stranger's lip curled. She had a glimpse of flashing white teeth in that violently handsome face. "Lady, I've a mind to turn you over to the sheriff right now, faster'n you can blink those pretty long eyelashes of yours. I don't believe a word you just said."

"It's all true."

"And I'm half coyote."

"Please. Let me go." She might as well beg. Things couldn't get much worse, Josie thought, biting back a sob as the ache in her imprisoned wrists grew more intense. And then, suddenly, things did get worse.

Much worse.

From the corner of her eye Josie caught sight of someone riding up the street. Someone familiar. Dreadfully, terrifyingly familiar. She jerked forward to see better, then lunged backward so sharply, she banged her head against the wall. Red stars splattered before her vision.

Snake!

Instinctively she tried to squeeze herself as far back against the wall as she could, trying to melt into it, to disappear. She prayed Snake wouldn't turn his head, wouldn't see her here in this alley.

"What the hell is wrong with you?" The stranger's eyes were narrowed on her as he held her captive against the wall.

"Nothing," she croaked, her voice barely audible.

"Something sure spooked you just now. What was it?" The gunslinger glanced curiously toward the street, but Snake was gone.

"Nothing. I—"

"You got a lawman after you? Or a bounty hunter?"

No. A husband who's an outlaw, who'll kill me because I stole his loot when I ran away from him, she thought, fighting through her terror of Snake, a terror that threatened to surge up and engulf her in hysteria. Aloud, to the invincible dark-haired stranger with his muscles of iron, who probably had never known a moment's fear in his life, she spoke with all the calm she could muster under the circumstances—and that wasn't much.

"Please, I'm begging you. Let me go. I won't bother you again. Or anyone else. But I can't be found here. I've got to get out of town . . . I . . . ."

"All right. You can quit your bellyachin'." He released

her and stepped back. She saw no softening in his eyes as she began to rub her bruised wrists. His jaw was taut, and the only expression he wore was one of contempt. Josie guessed it was the same derisive way he looked at an enemy the moment before he shot him dead. It was a wonder that look alone didn't kill his prey for him.

"I don't give a damn about you or any of your stories, lady," he went on, shoving his hat back on his head, glaring at her from beneath a dark thatch of hair. "And luckily for you, I don't shoot women. But hear this. Woman or no, you're a thief, and the next time you try to steal from me, you're landing in a jail cell. Got that?"

She nodded. She started to sidle sideways, but the stranger seized her again, making her gasp. He hauled her up close against his powerful frame and the color drained from Josie's face. For a long moment he stared down at her, his eyes glinting in the sunlit alley.

"You caught me on a day when I'm in a good mood. So just this once I'm giving you a break. But don't press your luck."

"I won't." Josie moistened her lips with her tongue. "I won't," she repeated as he continued to stare menacingly into her eyes. She wondered what he was like on a day when he *wasn't* in a good mood. And knew she didn't want to find out. She was stunned by the strength of him as he held her, the solid, overwhelming power emanating from every bone and muscle of his being. But there was something else too. A seething heat beneath the icy surface. A black, restless energy infused with danger. After being married to Snake, Josie'd had her fill of danger.

Then why, she wondered, did this man's keenly dangerous eyes fascinate her as much as frighten her? Why this sudden heat burning her skin from within?

Strangely, the dark-haired man seemed to draw her in, to drag at something in her soul. She gulped, fighting the pull, fighting the flaring heat that scorched her. Something about those eyes enthralled as much as frightened her.

What had she been thinking when she'd started this? Why had she tangled with a man like him?

"I won't bother you again," she promised in a whisper that caught in her throat.

He let her go. Her skin still burned where his hands had touched.

"Get the hell out of my sight."

Josie gulped at the hardness of his eyes. She turned nimbly and fled through the tumbleweed-strewn alley.

Not once did she look back.

She kept close to the buildings, praying she wouldn't run into Snake. Her heart was hammering double time as her feet skimmed along the dirt. She slipped and stumbled in her haste, nearly falling once as she staggered into a trash can, but she never slowed for an instant. Her mind raced even faster than her feet, flashing with questions about Snake, trying to put the encounter with the gunslinger out of her mind for good.

Was Snake alone? Was the whole gang with him—Spooner and Deck and Noah? Did they already know she was here?

It was nerve-racking just getting back to the Golden Pistol, then sneaking in the back door and scurrying up the stairs.

But she made it.

And only when she had slammed and locked the door to her room, and leaned against it for a minute, did she start to tremble.

The shudders shook her delicate shoulders, and made her knees quiver beneath the gingham skirt, but gradually, with effort, she gained control of her emotions. Conquered the fear.

Slowly, unsteadily, she made her way to the bed and sank down upon it. Her fingers dipped into her skirt pocket. And drew out the gunslinger's wallet.

This was followed by his pocket watch, an ornate gold beauty dangling on a thick gold chain.

A shaky smile crossed her lips. And the last of the fear receded.

Josie tossed her loot on the bed and hugged her arms around herself. Nice work, she thought, resting her chin on her drawn up knees. Even though she'd left him the bills he'd tucked into his shirt pocket after the poker game, it was still a very good haul. Pop Watson would be proud.

Now all she had to do was stay alive. And find a way to ditch this town before she got shot, locked in jail, or strung up.

Jumping up from the bed, Josie grabbed her straw valise. She had little time to lose.

Chapter Three

Ethan Savage slept for no more than three hours that afternoon, despite having played poker throughout the preceding night. Then he had himself a bath, and a sandwich at the grease-and-smoke-filled cafe at the edge of town, and returned to the Golden Pistol in time to see the dancing girls perform and to find himself a bottle of whiskey and a new poker game.

He scarcely watched the girls. Once or twice he glanced at them, saw several of them meet his eyes and smile widely as they lifted their skirts and kicked their legs, flashing ankles and knees with abandon. Tempting, but he wasn't sure that even a loose woman would calm him tonight.

Maybe later he'd find out.

The whiskey at his elbow was good. He usually didn't drink much, though lately he'd turned to it more and more. It helped to soothe the restlessness that gripped him of late, a restlessness even the open splendor of the plains and canyons no longer seemed to ease. Even tonight, his mind couldn't concentrate on the game. He'd developed a sixth sense, an instinct, for when something momentous was about to happen to him—be it an ambush by enemies on a mountain pass, his horse going lame, a card opponent coming up with a straight flush.

Instinct. Ethan Savage was known to have it in spades.

And instinct told him tonight that something was going to shake up his dull little world.

Maybe tonight he'd get shot.

In all these years of riding, hunting, shooting, gambling, living the solitary life in a lawless land, he'd never been shot. But there was a first time for everything.

It would be a diversion, he told himself, almost smiling as he fanned out his cards.

Few people would consider his life dull. He roamed the West at will, hiring himself out as a professional gunfighter when he needed cash, now and then tracking down an outlaw to fill his pockets with enough bounty money to stake himself to the next poker game in the next town. All the towns were the same to him— Deadwood and Abilene, Tucson and Laramie, Fort Worth, Dodge. He'd passed through all the wildest places on the frontier in the past ten years, stayed awhile in some, lingered only a day in others, and it seemed to him that the frontier was dying fast. Getting civilized, fenced in, closed up.

Oh, there was still space enough, land enough, sky enough, but something told him that the wildest, grandest days were on the wane. The sun was setting on the West he'd made his own when he'd flung himself away from England all those years ago.

England. Why was he thinking of England now? He hadn't thought of his native land in months. Had almost succeeded in blocking it entirely from his thoughts, just as he'd blocked his accent from his voice, his memories from his brain.

He'd never set foot on British soil again. He was an American now.

"I'll raise you, mister," the old miner rasped with a smelly grin, throwing a pile of chips onto the table as one of the saloon girls refilled the glasses. The miner squinted through the cigar smoke. "What's it goin' to be?"

Before Ethan could reply, the doors to the saloon swung open and a neat little man whisked inside. He was small of stature, slightly built, and balding. He wore thin gold spectacles on a squashed little nose. He had a pleasant face, a round chin. He was handsomely garbed in a neat black suit and gray bowler, and his pebble-blue eyes scanned the smoky saloon with mathematical efficiency.

They paused upon Ethan.

Then the man started forward, crossing directly toward the poker table.

"My lord, a word with you," he said in a low, steady tone marked by a British accent.

That accent and the man's dandyish appearance, clearly out of place in this rough western saloon, told Ethan far more than he wanted to know.

"Damn it all to hell." He glared at the small man, the same glare that had unnerved many hardened gunmen who'd encountered it, and convinced a good number of them to back down before pushing him to a fight. But the Englishman remained outwardly calm, placid even.

"He sent you, didn't he?" Ethan threw a card, then glanced back up at the man. "After all these years? Whatever it is, I'm not interested."

"Sir, we must speak in private. The matter is of the greatest urgency."

"Git the hell out of here, fella," the miner exploded,

squinting fiercely at his cards. "Cain't you see we're tryin' to play poker?"

"Idiots who interrupt a game end up with an early funeral in these parts, mister," a cowboy in a plaid shirt warned as he gripped his cards between tense, callused fingers. "Git."

Ethan raised his brows at the little man, who was now dabbing with a handkerchief at beads of perspiration that had popped out along his temples.

"I'll await you at the bar, my lord."

"Go to hell."

He swung his gaze back from the Englishman to his cards, but the numbers blurred for a moment before his eyes. *Must be the whiskey,* he told himself, though he'd drunk only two glasses so far tonight.

Long practice enabled him to hide his emotions, to keep all he was feeling, or not feeling, concealed beneath a surly mask, but at the man's clipped words some of the color had drained from Ethan's swarthy cheeks, and his eyes glinted with a strange intentness.

Damn it all to hell, he thought, trying hard to concentrate.

But he lost the hand.

He moved a huge pile of chips in front of the cowboy and stood.

"Back in a minute. Play this one without me."

Ethan strode to the bar. The Englishman wasn't drinking. He was sitting there quietly, watching all that went on through the hazy smoke permeating the crowded, raucous saloon.

"My lord . . ."

"Don't call me that. I'm Ethan Savage. Clear?"

The other man coughed. "Is there somewhere we can speak privately, sir?"

Ethan glanced over at the poker table. He wasn't about to cash in his chips, leave the game, and take this damned nuisance in a bowler hat over to his hotel room for a chat. He wanted to get this over with as quickly as possible.

"Hey, you." He rounded on Stickley, the owner of the Golden Pistol, busily strutting around the premises, keeping an eye on all the saloon girls, the piano player, the roulette dealers.

"You got a room where my friend and I can have a private chat?"

He saw the instant calculation in the man's eyes and almost sneered. Ethan had been in town only a few days, but he'd already spent an exorbitant amount of money on liquor, had gambled extensively, and had kept the saloon packed with those who enjoyed watching him play. He was a cool gambler, with a hawk's eyes and a smooth deal, and Stickley was eager to oblige him.

"Upstairs, my friend. I have an office at the end of the hall. Last door on the right."

Nodding his thanks, Ethan turned and started toward the back stairs the saloon owner had indicated. He heard the Englishman following, but didn't bother to turn around to look.

Up a narrow flight of stairs they went, and down a thinly carpeted, poorly lit hall. As they approached one of the doors on the left, the one marked 202, it opened part way and a woman's voice floated clearly out into the hall.

"Jo, Stickley's mad as hell that you didn't dance tonight. He doesn't believe that you're sick. Says he's going to fire you in the morning. But I think he's really upset because he suspects what you did for Penny."

"Believe me, Rose, Stickley is the least of my problems."

Ethan halted at the sweet musical tones of the second woman's voice. It was her. That thief who'd tried to snatch his wallet today.

So. She was a dance hall girl.

He'd halted so abruptly outside the door that the Englishman very nearly plowed right into him but, at the last instant, managed to stop in time.

Ethan ignored him, and cocked his head to one side as he listened.

"What are you going to do, Jo?" the first woman asked, sounding nervous and upset.

"Get out of town on the morning train. And Rose, if anyone asks for me, anyone at all, don't tell them where I've gone. Please, just lie and say—"

"Don't worry about me, Jo. I'd never give you away. But where will you go, what will you do? I hate to think of you in trouble. Maybe me and the other girls can help—the way you helped Penny."

"The kind of trouble I'm in, no one can help."

Ethan stepped forward until he reached the doorway. Through the partial opening, he glanced into the room. And there was the girl, the thief with the incredible violet eyes. His mouth tightened as he took in her changed appearance. Though still wearing the gingham gown, she'd loosed her hair from its restrictive coil, and now it swirled down past her shoulders in a sensuous riot of rich mahogany curls. She was leaning over a valise, folding some item of clothing, and didn't see him. But the other woman did.

The dancing girl, still in her pink satin costume, gave a small gasp and pursed her lips. Quickly, she pushed the door shut.

Ethan continued down the hall. It was nothing to him

what became of that sneaky little thief. If she was in trouble, she no doubt deserved it. Probably had the law breathing down her neck.

Hell, it was no concern of his.

As he reached the end of the hall his thoughts jerked back to his own situation. Frowning, he entered Stickley's office and paced to the window as the Englishman quietly closed the door.

The room smelled of cigars. It was cramped and over-furnished, filled with a cluttered oak desk, a bureau, bottles of whiskey lining several shelves, a deeply worn ruby velvet chair and settee, and a patterned rug on the floor. The red-flocked walls were covered by elaborate gold-framed paintings—nudes, painted in bold and vibrant detail.

It was warm and stuffy inside, and Ethan resisted the urge to loosen his shirt collar as he swung back to face the Englishman.

"Out with it," he ordered curtly, his eyes sharp on the other man. "How the hell did you find me, and what in damnation does my father want with me after all these years?"

"If you please, sir, I had best start at the beginning. This is not going to be an easy interview and perhaps if you would care to sit down—"

"What's your name?"

"Latherby, sir. Lucas Latherby. I am a junior partner in the office of your father's solicitor, Mr. Edmund Grismore."

Grismore. He remembered Grismore—unpleasant, supercilious son of a bitch, the perfect lackey to work for his father. "Go on."

Ethan's hard gaze was pinned to Latherby's face as the smaller man gave a short nod and continued.

"I bring you, I fear, unfortunate tidings. Your father, the late Earl of Stonecliff, is dead."

Ethan's knuckles tightened on the back of the chair. His expression, however, remained unchanged.

When he accepted the news with stoic silence, Latherby cleared his throat and went on.

"It was ill health, I'm afraid, a steadily weakening condition which was worsened by his catching a chill and coming down with a fever. He suffered in the throes of it for a week, and then, alas, succumbed."

"So?"

Latherby's eyebrows shot up, then hastily down. He spoke again, more hurriedly. "So, I have been dispatched by Mr. Grismore to find you, sir—and may I say, it has been quite a feat to do so—to impart to you certain information which I believe you will find most interesting, and perhaps, not unwelcome."

Ethan walked to the shelf upon which Stickley had several gleaming crystal goblets set out beside a decanter of brandy. He splashed the dark liquor into a glass, then shot a questioning glance at Latherby, who shook his head in refusal.

"Tell me that you're almost finished and you're going to leave and let me return to my poker game—that's what I'd find welcome," Ethan rasped.

"No, sir, it is a bit more . . . complicated than that. According to your father's will, and assuming that certain conditions will be met, it is my duty to inform you that, well, that . . ." He swallowed, his gaze taking in the striking appearance of the man before him, his tall, hard-muscled form, the cold blue steel of the guns resting against his powerful thighs, the harsh line of his mouth, his very American way of tough direct speech.

"Out with it, you sniveling weasel!" Ethan commanded, and downed the brandy in one gulp.

"You are next in line to inherit your father's title and estates and his position as the Earl of Stonecliff," Latherby announced and bowed his head. "My lord," he added respectfully, and clasped his hands before him.

Thunderstruck, Ethan stared at him for several seconds, then gave a short bark of laughter. "The hell I am."

Chapter Four

"I'm no more in line to be the next Earl of Stonecliff than you are, Latherby." Ethan's sneer widened. "My esteemed brother, Hugh, has the honor of that particular headache. What the hell have you and Grismore been drinking, man? You're on a fool's errand. I am the *youngest* son of the late Earl of Stonecliff, and as my father and brother repeatedly told me over the years, before I left dear old England, it is as well that I am, for if Stonecliff were to fall into my disreputable hands, all of our ancestors would no doubt rise up in horror from their graves."

"Then I'm afraid there will be a bit of milling about in the family graveyard at Stonecliff Park, my lord, for you are indeed in line to become the next earl, to inherit all of your father's properties and lands. The grievous news is that your brother, Hugh, was killed some six months ago—thrown from his horse while hunting—a most regrettable incident. That makes you the only living son of the late earl. I regret the necessity of carrying to you two pieces of such sobering news."

Ethan felt a chill rock him. Hugh dead. And his father. He braced himself to reveal no outward reaction, but his legs felt shaky in a way they never had before, not when he'd faced down Billy Laredo in a gun duel, not when he'd been ambushed by a war party of Cheyenne in the desert with his horse lame and no water left in his canteen.

He turned away from Latherby, mechanically poured himself more brandy, and drank it without tasting a drop. Then he paced back to the window and stared down into the shadow-darkened street.

The crowds were gone. Night was falling like a gray shawl over the prairie and dusk softened the harsh outlines of Abilene. The men and women and children had gone home to their kitchens and parlors, chatting of the day's events, of the work to be done tomorrow, of the thousand little details of their lives and families.

And here he stood in a stranger's office above a saloon, discovering that the two people most closely related to him were both departed from this earth.

Good riddance.

He closed his eyes, knowing he should be ashamed of the thought, and in truth, he was. Half ashamed. There had never been any love lost between him and his father and brother. The Earl of Stonecliff had been a pillar of respectability in English society—he moved in the best circles, knew all the best people, attended all the best parties. And his heir—the thin, imperious, proper Hugh, who had so closely resembled the tall earl in his starchily elegant good looks, from his thin dark hair to his patrician nose and elegant hands—had always been his favorite.

In truth, Ethan had scarcely known his father or his brother, who was six years his senior. He'd spent the early part of his life with housekeepers and tutors and groomsmen, rambling around the country estate, Stonecliff Park, knowing almost complete freedom when his father and brother were at one of the other family homes or in London. And when they were ensconced at Stonecliff Park, with guests to be entertained, Ethan was always kept abovestairs, too young to mingle with company, and of no importance to anyone but his own good friend, Ham, the groom who'd taught him all he knew of horses, of riding, of the wondrous outdoors.

And when he was older . . .

Ethan grimaced and stopped the flood of memories. When he was older, old enough to no longer be hidden away in the country, the younger, unimportant son of a great man, matters between himself and the earl had gone from bad to worse.

Oh, yes, he ought to be sorry about his father, and about Hugh. But he wasn't.

And as for Stonecliff Park . . .

"I don't want it. You've wasted your time, Latherby. Nothing would tempt me to set foot on British soil again."

"But, my lord—"

"Call me Mr. Savage. I'm no English lord."

"But you will be, you must. You have only to marry and the title is yours."

"Marry!"

"Sir, I implore you. The lands and estates are in need of an heir. Think of the tenants, the servants, all those employed by your lordship. There are many to whom you are responsible, not the least of whom is yourself and your forebears."

"To hell with my forebears. And to hell with you. I don't want it—not an inch of it. Not a farthing, or a blade of grass on Stonecliff Park land, not a single lamp or rug or chair from that damned house—from any of the houses. And I damn well don't want to get married! Seems to me

I've got a cousin, name of Winthrop. He'd be glad enough of the place. Give it to him. You savvy, Latherby?"

And he stalked past the openmouthed solicitor without a backward glance and pounded down the stairs.

Ethan's mind churned with emotions he didn't want to feel, with thoughts he didn't want to consider. He hurled himself back into the main room of the saloon, nearly knocking down one of the saloon girls. He grabbed her in time, muttered an apology, and headed for the table.

A poker hand was just finishing up.

"Deal me in," he barked, and claimed his seat in his former chair.

Everyone at the table observed his dark face, the almost feverish glint in his eyes. They all sat up a little straighter, held their cards a little tighter, not knowing what had happened to so dangerously irk the tall stranger, but sensing, down to a man, that they'd best tread carefully with him from this point forward.

Ethan Savage was in a dangerous mood.

❈❈❈ ❈❈❈

Two hours later, he was losing heavily. And he was drunk. Drunker than he'd been in years, since he'd been a schoolboy at Eton who'd engaged in a drinking contest with five others and had won. In those days he'd never been able to refuse a contest, or a dare. It was only one of the things that had made his austere father and brother so despise him.

Since that night, he had imbibed sparingly. But now as he sat at the poker table in a haze of cigar smoke mixing with the saloon women's cheap perfume, while laughter and raucous talk rang out all around him, while the heat in the room made him perspire and itch to jump in a cool lake, he downed glass after glass of Stickley's whiskey and played hand after losing hand.

The father and brother who had ignored and deplored him his entire life were dead. Dead and buried. And buried with them, he told himself, were the ugly deeds they had perpetrated trying to keep him in line.

It was over now.

Yet the irony that the black sheep son, the one who had dared to befriend the lowly and the vulgar, the one who had been a disgrace because he'd refused to settle down and marry respectably and live the elegantly proper life they'd chosen for him, the one who'd sought out the wildest life imaginable in the American West, *he* was the one who had survived, the one who stood to inherit the vast and burdensome fortune of Stonecliff Park.

"Whiskey!" Ethan roared, and slammed the empty bottle on the table. The cards swayed in a dizzying blur before his eyes. The other men at the table were starting to rise.

"Game's over, Savage. That was the last hand, remember?" the cowboy reminded him with a grin. His words were slurred, his balance shaky. He was none too sober himself, though the miner's eyes were still bright as fool's gold. "You owe me, uh . . . one hunert and ten dollars." The cowboy belched, then grinned wider. "Ye-ep. Time to settle up and go home."

Home. Hell, Ethan thought with bitter self-mockery. He had no home. Never had. Just a saddle, a horse, a blanket, and the star-filled sky.

"One hundred and ten dollars, fair and square," he muttered, and dug into his shirt pocket. But the bills he'd stashed there earlier were gone—blearily he remembered he'd already spent them on his bath, his meal, whiskey, and poker chips for tonight's game. Grimacing, he reached into his vest pocket for his wallet.

Empty air met his groping fingers.

What the hell?

It wasn't there. Not in any of his pockets, not under the table. It was gone.

And the rest of the three-hundred-dollar pot he had won last night was gone too.

"That dirty, no-good lying little *bitch*!" he shouted to no one in particular, and all eyes in the saloon swung toward him. There was silence. The tall cowboy frowned through the blear of his own vision.

"You goin' to pay me or not?" he queried in a tremulous voice.

"No! Not until I get my hands on that thief." Ethan spun about and reeled toward the back stairs, dimly remembering where he had last seen the creature whose death, in his opinion, was now imminent. "Be right back."

"The hell you will," the cowboy bellowed, and caught him by the arm. "How do I know you won't—"

He never got any further. Ethan Savage's fist connected with the cowboy's chin in a punishing blow that sent the man skittering backward into the roulette table. Three men leapt aside just in time.

"What the hell do you think you're doing, mister?" the largest of them shouted, glaring from beneath ferocious red brows.

Stickley started forward, but it was too late. Ethan, veering toward the stairs once more, was intercepted by the cowboy, who had staggered up from the floor. The cowboy launched himself in a flying leap at the gunslinger Ethan spun on reflex and delivered another punch.

Then, for good measure, he hit the man next to the cowboy as well, who had stepped forward and tried to seize his arm.

This stocky, mustachioed man was none other than Sheriff Mills.

He went crashing into a group of townsmen playing faro.

As if a stick of dynamite had been ignited, the saloon exploded in a whirl of flying fists, upended chairs, shattering glass, thuds, grunts, and shouts. Sheriff Mills shouted for order and fired his revolver into the air. Someone hurled a chair at someone who ducked, and the chair smashed the long, gilded mirror behind the bar. The piano player ran for cover, the bartender began snatching glasses off the bar, the saloon girls dashed for the stairs. Two other men, locked in furious struggle, crashed right through the Golden Pistol's front windows and out into the hot, dark street.

"Enough! Enough!" Mills boomed, but his voice was drowned out by the thunder of fists and boots and the incessant tinkling of glass.

When it was over, nearly half an hour later, the Golden Pistol was in shambles. Downstairs, at least. The saloon women, who had retreated upstairs, were watching from the railing, shaking their heads in dismay.

"Men. Why do they have to fight all the time?" Rose's lips curled in disgust.

"I think that tall stranger is hurt," Josie muttered, watching with glum fascination as Sheriff Mills managed to snap handcuffs on the man she had robbed this afternoon. He was unconscious now, she saw, her stomach clenching. Blood ran down his handsome face from a cut above his temple.

"I want to press charges against this man, Sheriff. I

want him locked up until he's agreed to pay for all the damages incurred here tonight." Stickley fairly jumped from one foot to the other as the sheriff and his deputy, who had come running from the cafe when he'd heard the sounds of the fray, carried the big gunslinger toward the broken saloon doors.

"He's going straight to jail right now," Mills grunted, paying no heed to the blood on the stranger's face or his ashen color. "Damned bastard. Lucky if I don't throw away the key."

The doors creaked weakly shut behind them, and no one noticed the small balding man in the tidy black suit who quietly emerged from behind the bar, dusted himself off, and slipped out after them.

Josie scurried back to her room, much disturbed. She was trying hard not to feel sorry about the stranger, but without much success. She'd heard someone say that the fight had started when he couldn't pay up what he'd lost tonight at cards.

Horrible qualms of guilt assailed her. But the stranger could take care of himself, she thought as she locked herself in her room once more and threw a final few belongings in her valise. Judging from the way he'd used his fists, he was more than capable of taking care of himself—it had taken someone hitting him over the head with a bottle from behind to finally bring him down.

But she found herself hoping he wasn't seriously hurt.

Don't worry about him, worry about yourself, she scolded, steeling herself against emotions that tended to run away from her. There had been no sign of Snake or any member of his gang in the Golden Pistol tonight, and she drew some small comfort from the fact that they were probably holed up in Maizey's Brothel two streets over.

It was a place more to their liking, she thought darkly, suppressing a shudder.

I'll never have to see them again, she told herself as she unbuttoned her gingham. She already had the train schedule—now all she had to do was purchase her ticket as soon as the office opened in the morning, and get on board the train.

Josie folded the gingham gown—the best gown she owned, the one she'd worn for her wedding to Snake—and tucked it into the valise atop her dancing girl costume, a chemise, and a white cotton nightgown. Then she pulled on jeans and a flannel shirt, and a big oversize buckskin vest. When she left this room at first light, she'd have her hair tucked under a hat and a cigar between her lips, and she'd do her damnedest to look like a boy. In case she ran into Snake, she had to make sure he wouldn't recognize his runaway wife.

The last items she tucked into the sturdy straw valise were the most important ones—the letter fragment and the dainty little silk handbag that belonged to a girl she'd never met. And the small woolen pouch containing the two treasures that gave Josephine Cooper Barker the shivers whenever she drew them out, looked at them, touched them.

There was a possibility that she really might discover who she was this time. She had clues now—solid ones. The ring belonging to that poor young Englishwoman who'd been unlucky enough to have been held up by Snake Barker and his gang exactly matched the brooch that had been pinned to her swaddling clothes.

If they were from the same set . . . if they were family jewels . . .

Perhaps this Alicia Denby was a relative, or whoever had given her the ring was a relative.

She'd never forget that night in the hideout cabin when she'd first seen the ring. The moment Snake had dumped all the loot from the stagecoach holdup onto the wooden table that hot, windless night, she'd gone still as a statue. She'd stared transfixed past the pile of greenbacks and coins, the pocket watches and fobs, the lady's handbag and garnet earrings and bracelet and the ivory comb and the scrap of paper lying atop a crushed lace handkerchief. She'd reached out trembling fingers to lift the exquisite pearl-and-opal ring, cradling it in her palm.

It was lovely. Four small creamy pearls nestled around a shimmering opal, set within heavy gleaming gold. Her hand had tingled as she'd held it, for the ring seemed to pulse with heat and warmth.

"Like that one, eh?" Snake had chuckled, and snatched it from her. "Well, don't go gettin' attached to it, Jo. I'm going to sell it. It's probably worth damn near as much as all the cash we took off those folks today. You should have seen that pretty little English gal it belonged to—she stripped off her earrings and bracelet without so much as a whimper, but begged me to let her keep this. As if I'd let something so purty and so downright valuable slip through my fingers because of a few little tears."

"Maybe it was special to her." Josie had moistened her lips and fixed him with a wary stare. "You didn't hurt her, did you, Snake?"

Behind her, Spooner and Noah had burst into guffaws. "No need to come to that," Noah had told her, twirling the reddish brown ends of his mustache. "Soon as Deck stuck his gun in that old geezer's ribs and threatened to shoot, that gal couldn't hand the ring over fast enough."

Deck, Snake's cousin, tall and wiry with hair nearly as fair as Snake's, had snickered. "I wished you'd'a let me bring her along, too. Hell, you got yourself a fine-lookin' woman, Snake. The rest of us ain't got nothin'."

"You'd have brung her along, and that old geezer grandpop of hers would've had the law hunt us down like dogs." Snake had snatched up the gold pieces on the table and begun fingering them greedily, then had tossed one to Deck, Noah, and Spooner in turn. "With these, boys, you can buy yourselves a fancy woman when we go to town. Have a little fun."

"What . . . did she look like?" Josie had asked, trying to sound casual, her gaze still fixed on the ring Snake had set down among the coins.

"Who?" Sifting through the rest of the loot, Snake pursed his mouth in concentration as he judged each item's value.

"The English girl."

He'd shrugged, already ripping bills out of a handsome leather wallet. "Like she'd break if ya squeezed her. Hair yellow as a daffodil. Pale and skinny. Hey, why so many questions?"

He'd reached out one lanky, corded arm and smacked her on the bottom. "Go fix supper. I've got a hankerin' for fried chicken and peach pie. Hurry it up, me and the boys are near starved."

Now, in her room above the Golden Pistol, Josie reached for the folded scrap of paper and reread the letter that had been in Alicia Denby's handbag, the letter Josie had read in secret later that night.

Dear Miss Denby,
We regret to inform you that our records regarding

*the matter you inquired about are sadly incomplete.
We are unable to discover any information about the
individual you are interested in, but you may wish to
make further inquiries at the Margaret Mapleson
Foundling Home in Charlotte, North Carolina. Due to
severe overcrowding, many of the orphaned children
left in our care were sent there in the months following
the close of the War.*

The rest of the letter had been torn away. But reading
it, Josie had felt a chill. Miss Denby had been looking for
an orphan, an orphan born during the war. And Miss
Denby possessed a ring that appeared remarkably similar
to Josie's own precious brooch. The brooch that no one
knew about, not Snake, not Pop Watson, not Rose or
Penny from the saloon, no one.

What if she discovered she *was* related in some way to
this Miss Denby? Of course, Miss Denby was blond, and
she had brown hair, but that didn't mean she couldn't be
some sort of relation, a cousin, perhaps, or possibly . . .

Possibly even a sister.

A sister.

No. Josie shook her head, blocking this line of thought.
It was silly to get her hopes up. When she was a child and
had been taken into her first series of homes, she'd
always gotten her hopes up, always thought optimisti-
cally that she would find a home and a family, not just a
farm to work on, and supper to serve, and other people's
socks and hems to darn and animals to feed. But a *home.*
Hugs and warm words, a pat on the shoulder, shared sor-
rows and joys. It hadn't happened.

Pop Watson was the closest she'd come—and he'd
been a former snake oil salesman, carnival barker, and

pickpocket who'd married the hard-faced Montana widow who'd written to the Children's Society Orphanage seeking a boy to help her run her small ranch at the foot of the Beartooth Mountains.

Emmie Lou Dunner had been none too pleased when she'd had to settle for fourteen-year-old, small-for-her-age Josie when all the boys were taken. But things had gotten better for Josie at the Scarred Tree Ranch after Pop had come to live there two years later. Unlike long-nosed Emmie Lou, Pop treated her as if she were a member of the family. He told her jokes, complimented her cooking, even helped her with the endless chores Miz Dunner demanded of her each day in exchange for room and board. When Miz Dunner went out alone on occasion to visit a neighbor or buy supplies in town, Pop taught Josie how to pick pockets and how to cheat at cards. Pop Watson had loved her in his rough, rapscallion way, Josie was sure of it.

But after Miz Dunner died that winter, Pop had let the ranch go. He'd started spending nights in town drinking and gambling, not stumbling home until dawn.

When he'd met up with Snake Barker while playing poker at a hole-in-the-wall saloon on the edge of town, it hadn't taken much persuasion for him to join the younger man's outlaw gang. Then everything had changed. Over the next two or three years, he'd go off for months at a time, leaving Josie to fend for herself at the lonely, failing ranch.

She managed as best she could, and when Pop came home, he always had money. Josie didn't like knowing how he'd come by it, but she couldn't change Pop. He'd take the wagon to town and fill it to the brim with groceries that would last her for months. He'd bring her home licorice sticks and hair ribbons, just as he had when she was fourteen. And he told her stories about how he was saving his money and one day he'd buy Josie the most beautiful pink dress she ever did see.

He never bought her that dress. But he brought Snake Barker home for supper one night, let him and the boys lay low at the ranch, and it was then that Snake took one look at her and decided he wanted Josie Cooper to be his wife.

And when she balked at the advances of the swaggering young outlaw leader, despite his scruffy blond good looks and the crude compliments he paid her, Snake made it clear that Pop Watson was older now and expendable, that he couldn't ride as hard or shoot as straight as he had only a year or two ago, and if Jo refused to marry Snake, Pop was going to die.

But, Josie thought with a shudder, that was all behind her now. Snake was behind her now. She had escaped him, fleeing with the stolen loot and Miss Denby's ring, and the letter, and now, as she stared down at the pouch and ran a finger over the folded scrap of paper, she closed her eyes and turned her thoughts to the future.

England, she whispered to herself. *I've searched so long, so hard. But now, at last, maybe I'll find out who I am. Maybe I'll find the answers—once I get to England.*

Chapter Five

Ethan sprawled on the jail cot with closed eyes and a pounding head. Blinding red lights pierced the darkness beneath his eyelids, and his throat felt as if he'd swallowed a bucket of sand. He doubted he could move if called upon to do so—he doubted he could even open his eyes.

He wanted to dive down into the depths of unconsciousness and stay there, dark and hidden and quiet. But the pain hammered between his temples, his stomach fought the urge to heave, and he gave a low moan of disgust at his inability to pass out again.

"You awake, Savage?"

He ignored the rough voice snapping at him. Who the hell was it? Who the hell cared?

"Savage! Wake up, you damned son of a gun. Someone here wants to talk to you—though I'm damned if I know why."

When he heard the next voice, memory flooded back, unwelcome as a vulture.

"My lord, this seems an appropriate time to continue our discussion," Lucas Latherby said in his dry, distinct way.

"Go to hell," Ethan managed to rasp out, then groaned at the effort of speaking.

"Very well. If you truly wish me to leave you in this cell, I shall. But according to Sheriff Mills here, and Mr. Stickley, who owns the saloon you destroyed tonight, you will be here for a very long time. Unless, of course, you avail yourself of my aid."

Ethan ignored him. He was concentrating on opening his eyes. His eyelids felt as if they'd been scratched by shards of glass. He felt something warm and sticky on his face and brought his hand up slowly. Blood. His own blood.

Who the hell cares?

But the next moment, he became more fully aware of his surroundings and his stomach lurched at the sight of the cell bars.

"Let me outta here."

"Hmph. When hell freezes over," the sheriff growled.

With an effort, Ethan sat up, suppressing a groan of pain and dizziness. Sheriff Mills scowled at him from outside the bars, his thumbs hooked in his pockets. Owlishly, Lucas Latherby peered through his spectacles, studying Ethan with intent absorption.

Mills looked vexed beyond words. Latherby wore an expression of sympathy, and implacable patience.

"Hell, Mills, I'll pay Stickley for the damages. Open the damned cell door."

"You don't got one red cent to your name, Savage. That's what started all this, remember? You lost at cards to Jake Coombs and then tried to leave without paying. You're lucky that cowboy didn't shoot you down for trying to welch on your debt."

"Wasn't trying to welch. Was trying to find . . . her . . ."

"Who, my lord?" Latherby asked when his voice trailed off.

"The girl. The one who took my wallet earlier. I got it back, she must've stolen it again." A sudden thought made him feel gingerly at his shirt and blood-spattered vest, his fingers skimming lightly over bruised ribs. "Damn. That little bitch got my pocket watch, too." Fury sent him surging to his feet. For a moment, the world swayed perilously, and he gripped at the bars for support. Dimly he realized he was still drunk. The effects of all the liquor he'd imbibed would probably be with him well into the next day.

When the dizziness ebbed, he glowered at Latherby.

"Find her! She's got my money and my pocket watch! Go, man, start searching for her—"

"I'm not in a position to do that, sir. I am employed to represent the interests of the Earl of Stonecliff. Based on our last conversation, you are not that person—nor have you any interest in becoming him."

"Damn your weaselly face, Latherby. You, Mills! Go find that girl. She was medium height, slenderly built—skinny as a chicken if that helps, with brown hair, curly hair—hell, I don't remember the color of her eyes but—"

"Savage, you're loco if you think I'm going to hunt up some mystery woman in the middle of the night. Now listen here. You're the one who tore up Stickley's place, and you're the one who's going to rot in jail for it. Now, my missus is waitin' for me at home, and I'm leaving the deputy here in charge."

He turned to Latherby. "You've got to leave. It's after midnight, and I'm locking up."

"Latherby! You bail me the hell out of here right now or I'll wring your scrawny neck."

"I'm afraid I can't do that, sir. I have only been granted authority to be of service to the Earl of Stonecliff. I can hardly use funds which, upon your refusal to accept the title, will be due to your cousin."

"Winthrop!" Ethan had a vision of his foppish, mincing cousin with the greedy pond-blue eyes. Oliver Winthrop was forever licking the boots of Hugh and his father, running to them with tales of Ethan's exploits. It had been Winthrop who'd first told them about Molly.

Ethan's fingers clenched around the bars and he shook them mightily. "That worm doesn't deserve to get his oily hands on Stonecliff!"

"If you refuse to accept the terms of your father's will, then he is next in the line of succession."

"I don't give a damn about the line of succession!" The bars rattled beneath his furious grip, but remained intact. Ethan's eyes blazed with rage and frustration such as he hadn't known in a long, long time. Sweat streamed down his brow and temples, sheening his bruised face. His head ached, he hurt like hell, he wanted out!

Ethan Savage hated being locked up. It made him sick to his stomach. And he was sick enough as it was, considering all the rotgut he'd consumed. As he glanced at the small, contemptuous eyes of Sheriff Mills and the mild, apologetic ones of the solicitor, and then at the four-foot cell in which he found himself confined, rage and desperation surged within him. They mounted as Latherby gave a slight shrug and turned, starting toward the door after the hunch-shouldered sheriff.

"Latherby!"

"I regret, sir, that I am not empowered to help you."

"Mills!"

"Sleep it off, you young jackass!"

Ethan felt the pounding in his head increase. These four walls . . . they were closing in. He needed out . . . he needed a drink. . . .

"Latherby—you slimy sniveling son of a bitch—I'll do it. I'll meet the damned terms of the will. Get back here or I swear when I get out of here I'll plug you so full of holes you'll—"

Instantly, Latherby spun about and hurried to the cell door. "I am delighted, sir, that you—"

"Yeah. Sure. Just settle the hell up with Mills and get me out of here."

"Sheriff . . ."

"Hold on, now. This ain't how we usually do things." The sheriff held a hand up, his tone testy. "For one thing, it's got to cost at least two hundred dollars or more to fix up the Golden Pistol, and there's a fine to pay for public drunkenness and disorderly conduct—and fighting, and destroying property."

Latherby steepled his hands. "Yes, Sheriff. The total will be quite a large sum. Kindly tell me what it is."

Before Ethan had time to do more than pace a dozen or so times around the confines of the bleak little cell, he heard the key scrape in the lock.

"Maybe I can go home now," Mills grumbled.

"Like hell. Sheriff, I just remembered something. That little witch who robbed me was at the Golden Pistol tonight. In one of the upstairs rooms—packing a suitcase! She must be leaving town. You have to get over to the Golden Pistol and place her under arrest. Right now, before she can get away."

"The only place I'm going right now, young feller, is straight home and into bed!"

"Like hell. Latherby!" Ethan stuck out his hand.

The solicitor instinctively understood what he wanted. He dug inside his pocket and then placed a crisp hundred-dollar greenback into Ethan's palm.

Ethan waved it under the sheriff's nose. "Mills, this'll be the easiest money you ever made. All you have to do is lock that woman up in this very same cell tonight and it's yours."

The sheriff snatched the bill from him. He studied it a moment, eyes blinking soberly, then he nodded. "Can't turn my back on doin' justice," he mumbled.

Ethan Savage's lips drew back in a sneer. He started toward the door, the sheriff and Latherby trotting after. Suddenly Ethan swung around. "Latherby, I forgot something."

"My lord?"

"Token of appreciation for all the aggravation you caused me tonight."

"Sir?"

Ethan's fist swung out and connected hard with the solicitor's jaw. The man went down with a thud.

Ethan rubbed his sore knuckles, a hard glitter in his bleary eyes. "Don't thank me, Latherby. It was nothing."

❈❈❈ ❈❈❈

Josie had just fallen asleep on top of the bed, already dressed in her denim pants and flannel shirt so she'd be ready to move when the sun came up. She was dreaming of herself in a lovely open field, wearing a lavender dress, and in her dream she was opening the worn cloth pouch containing her brooch and her ring—but when she tugged at the drawstring the pouch was empty, and when she glanced up, there stood Snake right before her.

He was smirking at her in a way that made her want to knock the grin off his face, but also made her back up a pace. Then she saw that he held both her brooch and the ring in his grimy, nailbitten hand, and suddenly he was bending over a broken stone well, dangling them over the yawning black gap.

"You crossed me, Jo. You can say *adios* to these. And you're going down into the well next. . . ."

Her heart was pounding so hard, she could scarcely breathe. Pounding, pounding. Then she opened her eyes and realized with a raspy intake of breath that the pounding was coming from the hall outside. Someone was banging on the door.

"This here is Sheriff Mills. Open up in the name of the law!"

Jolting upright in the other narrow bed, Rose gaped at Josie through the darkness. "The sheriff! What's he want with us, Jo?"

"Not us. *Me,*" Josie whispered. Trembling, she flung herself up from the bed and put a hand to her throat. Think, think hard. "That gunslinger must've sent him— Rose, don't go to the door yet. Stall him."

Rose nodded, her dirty blond hair straggling forward over her shoulders as she slid from the bed and reached for a wrapper. Josie was already tugging on her boots.

"Open the door or I'll break it down!"

"Hold your horses, Sheriff!" Rose called out shrilly. "Can't a body make herself decent?"

Josie grabbed up her valise and ran for the window. She stopped only long enough to hug Rose good-bye, then heard the sheriff bellow again, demanding that Rose open the door. On an icy rush of fear, she threw a leg over the sill. She scrambled onto the overhang and dropped her valise down into the alley. If she lowered herself over the edge, holding on with her hands and then dropping down, she might just make it without breaking an ankle. She could make a run for it.

Her grip slipped as she heard Sheriff Mills thunder into the room above her. Hands slippery with sweat, she couldn't hold on. She fell from the overhang, smothering a cry of panic as she dropped off into open air.

Suddenly, instead of hitting the ground, she felt herself caught up by powerful arms.

"Ohhhh!" Her lips parted in shock. A jolt slammed through her as she was scooped up, caught against a wide, muscled chest. She stared into the fierce dark countenance of the man whose pocket she'd picked twice this very afternoon.

"Ma'am," he said with dry mockery. "May I have this dance?" Then his face broke into a demonic grin that froze Josie's blood.

"Let me go!" Wildly, she began hitting him over the head with her fist.

The blows narrowly missed the still oozing wound on his temple, and at any moment Ethan expected to have blood trickling once more down his face.

"Why, you little bitch," he muttered, setting her on her feet so sharply, her teeth rattled. One strong arm imprisoned her waist, pulling her so tight against him that she could scarcely draw breath. He pinioned her hands, halting the rain of blows.

Josie gasped as she struggled to free herself. He was all hard muscle and strength. He smelled of liquor and male sweat and there was a reckless, dangerous glint in his eyes that frightened her more than her fall from the overhang, though she would rather have eaten bullets than admit it.

"Mills!" he shouted toward the open window. "Down here. Come and get her."

"No!" Jo gasped, wriggling frantically. Uselessly. "You can't let him lock me up. You'd be signing my death warrant—you don't understand—"

"*You* don't understand, lady," he interrupted with a heartless laugh. "You've caused me a hell of a lot of trouble. Now it's your turn to lie in a jail cell and stare at the bars."

"I know what trouble is, mister, believe me, I do—I'm no stranger to it. But there's a reason why I took your things."

"Savage, you got her? Good work. I'll be right down," the sheriff called, leaning out the window.

"Please!" Jo begged, staring up at the gunslinger with wide, beseeching eyes.

The moon shimmered over her white upturned face. It wasn't all that cold a night, but she was shivering in his arms. He was aware of how soft her body felt pressed against him, of her small, high breasts, the curve of her thighs. She felt helpless and sweet. Yet he knew she was anything but sweet.

Still, the appeal in her face went beyond words—it reached deep inside and clutched at his heart. Or would have, if Ethan had let it for one minute.

"You're going to pay, lady," he said harshly, putting a hand to her hair and forcing her head backward so that her white throat above the collar of the flannel shirt was exposed and vulnerable. "Now where's my money and my pocket watch?"

"In my valise. Over there. You can have them back."

"Damn straight I'll have them back."

"And whatever else you want. I'll do anything, I'll pay

you double what I took . . . but please don't let the sheriff lock me up. I'd be a sitting duck."

"For who? Who the hell is after you?"

She didn't answer, just licked her lips. Nice lips they were, too. Lush and generous, the color of rosebuds. *Another lawman's after her,* he decided. *Someone more intimidating than old Mills.* Her shivering grew worse after he asked her the question. Tears gathered in the corners of her eyes. Brilliant eyes, he realized now. Mesmerizing. They were a clear, wondrous violet, like the wild flowers that grew in the glade beyond the pond at Stonecliff Park.

"I'll do anything," the girl whispered again just as Sheriff Mills stomped out of the Golden Pistol's back door and approached them, his weary face tight with impatience.

Suddenly an idea penetrated Ethan's bitter, half-drunk haze. "Anything, eh?" he repeated, and then chuckled long and low.

Josie stared at him fearfully. That chuckle sounded almost demented. "Yes, anything," she heard herself vow, but the words seemed unwise the moment they'd left her lips.

"Fine. Then you'll marry me. Tonight."

Now she knew he was demented. Loco. She struggled again to get away as Sheriff Mills reached toward her and she heard the clang of handcuffs, saw the silver glitter of them in his grip.

But as the sheriff reached for her wrist, the stranger shoved her back and placed himself between her and Mills.

"Hold on a minute, Sheriff."

Josie's legs shook.

"Huh?" Mills grabbed at his hat as a gust of wind whipped through the darkened alley.

"The manacles can wait until I've had a chance to speak to . . . the lady."

"So now she's a lady. You called her a dirty thief. Savage, is this the woman who stole your money and your watch or not?"

Ethan surveyed her, from the tousled mass of chestnut curls to the scuffed boots on her dainty feet. He nodded, no expression showing itself on his swarthy face. "It's her. But I might change my mind about pressing charges."

He dragged Josie along with him through the alley, out of earshot of the sheriff.

"Wait there and I'll let you know," he commanded over his shoulder, and Josie realized he was still drunk enough not to know or care that he was making enough noise to wake half the town.

She glanced helplessly at her valise, still lying where she'd dropped it in the dirt, with the brooch and ring inside. She didn't like having it out of reach. She didn't like anything that was happening to her.

"You can't possibly want me to marry you," she insisted, drawing a deep breath, trying to steady her shaky nerves.

"You're wrong, lady. I do. Seems I need a wife. I need one bad."

"Why *me*?"

"You're as good as any. Better than most, I'd say, since you'll make my dear old father spin in his grave." He gave a hoarse laugh and raked a hand through his hair, looking suddenly weary and half beside himself with anger—or was it grief? Josie couldn't tell which.

And then, as she started to back away, deciding he was crazed, he gripped her arm again and jerked her close.

"Not so fast, angel. How about it? You come to England with me and be my sweet little bride—and I'll see you're well taken care of. You'll live the high life, with servants, pretty clothes, all the baubles you want. Isn't that what a woman like you dreams of? You won't have to steal, and you'll have all the spending money you could want. But . . ."

His voice harshened and so did his grip, pinching her flesh. "After six months, it's *adios*. You get the hell out. I'll settle a fair amount of money on you, enough to set you up so you won't have to rob anyone else for a good long time, and then we get a civilized divorce and you get the hell out of England, out of my life, and never come back."

"So very romantic." Josie bit her lip, trying to stall for time, trying to think. She guessed it was the liquor talking. Why would any sane or sober man want to marry the woman who'd robbed him?

"Romantic," he sneered. "Don't think so. Strictly business. Something tells me you're not the romantic type anyway. You like money? I've got some—and I'll pay you to be my wife for six months. Yes or no?"

He was swaying on his feet, and Josie instinctively found herself steadying him. "You don't even know what you're saying," she managed to gasp on a half-hysterical laugh. "Or what you're doing."

"The hell I don't. I need a wife, and you're the one I picked. I'll bring a damned two-bit low-class vulgar thief to England and introduce her to all the swells! Lord, that's rich!"

He gave a shout of laughter. "It's the only way I'll go

back. I swore I never would, swore I'd never marry, and now, if I have to—"

He broke off, and Josie realized he hadn't meant to reveal this much. "If you have to, you'll marry a low-class thief? To prove what? To who?" she asked desperately.

"That's none of your business. You either marry me tonight—right now—or I turn you in to the sheriff. You'll sleep in a cell. Hell, you'll rot there." He stared down into her eyes, his own blazing with contempt and triumph. "So, lady, take your pick. Me—or that cell."

Mills marched toward them, his face wrathful, before Josie could speak.

"Well?"

"Leave her be, Sheriff. This lady's going to do me the honor of becoming my wife." His laughter rang out again so harshly that goose bumps prickled Josie's flesh.

"I didn't say . . ." Then her protest died on her lips as he turned those ice-gray eyes on her once more.

"Then say." His tone was low and warning, cutting in its impatience. "One way or the other, you damned hussy. Answer right now."

He was crazy. But she had to say something before Mills snapped those manacles on her. "Yes. Yes, of course," Josie heard herself murmur. "I'm going to marry him."

Never mind that I already have a husband—one who's hunting me down like a rabbit at this very moment. Now I'll have two. Neither of them worth a damn.

The sheriff stared at each of them with utter fury and disgust. "Damned if I know what the hell is going on here, Savage—but I'm going home. Unless," he added sarcastically, glowering up at the taller man, "there's something else I can do for you tonight?"

"Matter of fact, there is." Ethan was already weaving his way down the alley, dragging Josie with him. He scooped up the valise on his way, but never slowed.

"Tell me where I can find a justice of the peace."

❈❈❈ ❈❈❈

The groom wore a sneer. The bride wore pants. The justice of the peace, half awake and with his boots, trousers, shirt, and waistcoat pulled on hastily over his nightshirt, mumbled his way through the vows, while his wife, the witness, at the last minute whisked a handful of faded daisies from a vase on the whatnot shelf and thrust them into Josie's hand as a makeshift bouquet.

Josie peered dazedly at the wilted flowers, then at the flabby jowls of James Ezekiel Collins, the justice of the peace. His words droned in her ear. She felt as if she were floating in some dim and disturbing dream. The little parlor felt very warm and close after the chill breeze of the night. There were doilies on every crowded surface, atop the piano and the tables. Fussy fringed pillows were mounded on the sofa, the heavily patterned wallpaper was barely discernible for all the silver- and gilt-framed watercolors displayed upon it, and the occasional tables, dresser, mantel, and whatnot held dried flower arrangements and little carved animals and collections of china plates.

She felt as if she were being smothered by all this furniture, all this warmth and closeness, even by the odor of the fried chicken and onions that Mrs. Collins had apparently cooked for dinner and that still lingered in every dark, crowded corner of the parlor. She couldn't breathe.

There was only one consolation. A judge's house was

the last place Snake would come looking for her—if he was looking at all. She was safe for the moment.

Golden lamplight reflected upon the hard planes of her new groom's face. His eyes were beginning to lose their overbright luster now, and the liquor was slackening his muscles, but there was still about him an air of dark, reckless energy even more intense than what she'd glimpsed this afternoon. Of course, he hadn't been drunk this afternoon. He hadn't had bruises on his face, or blood on his vest—and he hadn't been possessed by this driven fury. He'd been angry, true, but not like this. Nothing like this.

Josie was already plotting her getaway. He'd pass out soon, surely, and she could run off. Why should she keep her vows to a man who'd forced her into this marriage, no less than Snake had forced her into the other one?

At least she was legally married to Snake. This man didn't have a clue that the ceremony being conducted for his benefit was nothing but a useless farce.

The moment he falls asleep, I'll make a dash for it.

But suddenly Justice Collins's droning voice—asking her if she took this man to be her husband—was interrupted by a furious knocking at the door. As Josie's heart thundered in her chest, Mrs. Collins admitted a harried-looking little man with a swollen red bruise on his jaw.

"No one invited you," the bridegroom snarled.

"Trust me, my lord, you don't wish to go through with this."

"The hell I don't. You said I needed a wife. I'm gettin' me one." Ethan spun back toward the justice, his expression grim. "Go on, get it over with."

Poor Justice Collins threw a glance of horror and

dismay first at Josie, pale and disheveled in her flannel shirt and jeans, and then at the tall angry man beside her. Josie almost felt sorry for him, he looked so confused.

"You sure you want to go through with this, little lady?"

"I do."

"There. She said it, we're done." Ethan seized his bride by the arm and started toward the door.

"Sir, you haven't taken *your* vows yet!" the justice exclaimed.

Ethan froze. He turned back, scowling. "Haven't I?" He searched his memory. "Well, then, what the hell are you waiting for? Hurry up or I'll start shooting at your feet, you old windbag."

The wife gave a screech of terror, and Ethan threw her a cool glance. "Sorry, ma'am. Don't normally cuss in front of a lady."

Josie swore the smile he gave her would have melted coal. Mrs. Collins sank down in a chair as if her legs had been knocked out from under her.

"Do continue, James," she croaked out.

"My lord." The little Englishman could contain himself no longer. "You are making a grievous—"

In less than the blink of an eye, Ethan drew his Colt .45 and pointed it straight at the balding little man. "One more word out of you, Latherby, and it'll be your last. Savvy?"

Swallowing hard, the Englishman nodded.

Ethan holstered the gun and nodded to the justice, whose face was now sheened with sweat.

"Uh, do you sir, s-solemnly take this woman—what's your name again, miss?"

"Josie. Josephine Cooper."

"Josephine Cooper, to be your lawfully wedded wife, to have and to hold, in sickness and in health, for better or for worse, till death do you part?"

Ethan shrugged. "That's what I'm here for, isn't it?"

"Sir!"

"I sure as hell do," he muttered. "Satisfied, now? Okay, lady, let's go."

"The ring, sir! You didn't place the ring on her finger."

Ethan stared blearily down at the ring he wore on his own hand. The one memento he'd kept of his past. He'd never been sure why. It had once belonged to his grandfather, whom he dimly remembered as a kindly old gentleman with very sharp blue eyes who had once given Ethan a puppy. And when his grandfather had died, he'd left Ethan this ring, a heavy gold signet ring, emblazoned with a square, glittering emerald.

"The ring, sir . . . you must put the ring upon her finger."

"Not this ring," he said roughly, glowering into the pale, drawn face of the thief. He rounded on the Englishman.

"Latherby, you wearing a ring? Take it off."

The Englishman opened his mouth to speak, took one look at Ethan Savage's fierce features, and clamped his lips together. He slipped his own gold ring off his finger and handed it over.

Grimly, Ethan slid it onto the girl's much narrower finger.

"I now pronounce you man and wife. You may k-kiss the bride," the justice murmured doubtfully.

"I don't think . . ." Josie started to back away, bumped into a chair, began to tumble down with it, but Ethan's strong arm grasped her and yanked her upright, then jerked her hard against his chest.

"It's gotta be official," he muttered against her lips, half to himself, and then his mouth closed upon hers.

She shut her eyes, horrified, praying the kiss would be short and peremptory. Surely with all these people watching . . .

But the presence of others didn't seem to bother her new bridegroom. His mouth claimed hers with the same arrogant force he'd displayed ever since she'd dropped into his arms from the overhang less than an hour ago. It was a hard kiss, hungry and devouring and strangely enthralling. It tasted of anger and mockery and raw physical need. His imperative mouth captured and held hers for what seemed an eternity. An eternity in which Josie forgot to struggle or try to push him away.

The last man to kiss her had been Snake. Snake, with his handsome, leering face, his wheat-blond beard scratching the flesh of her neck, his greedy hands ripping her dress.

The terrifying memory made her stiffen instinctively. Her new husband, somehow sensing her resistance despite his inebriated state, lifted his head and stared mockingly into her widened eyes.

"That'll do for now." He no longer sounded drunk. He sounded tired, drained. And very grim.

He pushed her away. "Latherby."

"Sir." The Englishman stepped forward, his head tilted to one side as he awaited further instructions.

"Keep an eye on my precious bride. Don't let her out of your sight." His voice had thickened, and Josie saw with a glimmer of hope that his face now looked weary and ashen. His lack of sleep was taking its toll. Her opportunity was coming.

"Reckon I'd best . . . get some shut-eye."

"Shut-eye?" the solicitor repeated blankly, but even as he spoke, Ethan slid to the floor, his head thumping against the leg of the sofa.

Josie, who'd tried to catch him and missed, now stared down at his prone form in dazed horror. Blood streamed from the reopened cut on his temple.

"Hell and damnation!" Justice Collins cried in a harried tone. "Now what the hell are we going to do?"

"Don't disturb yourself," Latherby said quickly, even as Josie knelt down beside the fallen man. "I'll manage everything."

"But Mr. Savage is bleeding all over my wife's new rug."

"Dear me!" Mrs. Collins shrieked.

"Get me a towel," Josie ordered, not glancing up. Her fingers tore at the collar of Ethan's shirt, loosening it. Concern and rising fear had replaced her hope of only moments before. All thoughts of fleeing had temporarily vanished.

The gunslinger's skin was ashen beneath its normal bronze, his breathing very shallow. Blood poured from the gash.

"Hurry!" she breathed. "Hurry with that towel."

Then she saw that the others had not moved. They stood gaping in frozen confusion—even Latherby remained rooted to the spot.

"For God's sake, don't just stand there," Josie cried. "He's reopened his cut, and I must stanch the blood! Hurry! There's no time to lose—or do you want to watch him bleed to death all over Mrs. Collins's new rug?"

"No!" Latherby shook his head fearfully. "Good God, no!"

"Then do what I say." Josie reached up and tore a lace cloth from the occasional table, heedless of the knick-knacks that went tumbling. She rolled it up and pressed it firmly against the gunslinger's cut. "Get me a towel, and a basin of water, and then fetch a doctor. *Quickly.*"

Chapter Six

A profusion of summer flowers bloomed across the Missouri countryside as the great black train thundered along its mammoth swath of iron tracks. With sunlight dappling the windowpane beside her, Josie leaned back against the upholstered seat of the first-class train car and stared unseeingly straight ahead. One finger absently stroked the frayed cuff of her sleeve—she'd changed this morning back into her reliable gingham gown—but she was unaware of the gesture. Beside her was her valise, and within it, still, were her treasures, along with the scrap of letter that was more precious to her than gold.

But everything else was different. Her life, her future . . . so different than it had been yesterday this time. Yesterday her only thought had been to scrabble together enough money to purchase a second-class train ticket east, and eventually to try to raise enough for passage to England. And to try to stay two steps ahead of Snake while she did it. Today . . .

Today she was married to a stranger, traveling in a luxurious first-class railroad car to New York and then on to England. She shook her head a little, dazed by how quickly her circumstances had changed and how, last night, after that unorthodox marriage ceremony, the efficient little Mr. Latherby, true to his word, had indeed "managed everything" with wizard-like skill.

While Josie had stanched the blood of her unconscious bridegroom's wound, Mr. Latherby had at last sprung into action, summoning a doctor in the middle of the night, seeing Ethan Savage carried upstairs to Justice Collins's spare bedroom, ordering everyone about with a clipped authority that brooked no argument. He'd somehow managed to keep Josie in his sights at all times, as if worried she would slip away, which she'd been far too busy to do, and yet he had also arranged, through Mrs. Collins, for three first-class tickets to New York on the 8:15 a.m. train and had managed to bundle all three of them aboard without mishap.

Josie had felt only a kind of drained relief this morning as the train chugged out of the station. There had been no sign of Snake since that one glimpse in the alley yesterday, and he hadn't seen her at all—and now she was headed east, where he wouldn't possibly think to look for her.

She ought to be able to relax. But she was on edge, her nerves frayed by the strangeness of her circumstances, as well as by the lack of food and sleep, for she'd scarcely had the time or the inclination for either one. As she sat alone in the plush red seat of the first-class car, she thought of the man she'd married last night, and realized that the strongest effects of the liquor must be wearing off by now. In the cold light of day, just what must Ethan Savage think of the situation he'd plunged both of them into?

His words about his father and his reasons for marrying her made little sense. But Josie sensed that beneath the handsome gunslinger's anger and drunken sneering, there had been pain. Deeply hidden pain, but pain nonetheless.

Just who was this Ethan Savage? she wondered, tapping a finger absently against her chin. And why in the world had he insisted on marrying her?

Don't start worrying about him, she admonished herself, her fingers digging into the soft upholstery of the seat. *He's not one of the orphan children, or a stray cat or a dance hall girl being misused by her boss. He's well able to take care of himself without any help from you.*

One thing was certain. Judging by all this luxury and the way Mr. Latherby jumped to do his bidding, it was clear that her new husband—her supposed new husband, who was still in his Pullman convertible berth sleeping off the enormous quantity of alcohol he'd consumed yesterday—must have a great deal of money. Far more than she'd guessed when she tried to pick his pocket.

Well, it wasn't money she wanted—it never had been. Josie'd been without money all her life, and she knew that it couldn't buy her what she was after. She wanted only the chance to get to England and search for someone she'd never met, someone who might prove very important to her.

But she guessed that her needs, her wants, would not matter much to Ethan Savage. He was a man determined to see his way to his own ends, and damn whoever got in his way. Like Snake, she told herself, hardening herself against him. All men basically are like Snake, wanting, using, hurting—trampling over any who get in their way, threatening and punching and even killing when thwarted.

If she was any judge of looks and behavior, Ethan

Savage would be every bit a match for her other husband when it came to being ruthless. He was even taller and more muscular, and he wore his guns with a confident ease that suggested he'd be good at using them. She'd already seen him use his fists during the brawl at the Golden Pistol. He was good at that, too.

Her heart shivered. She already knew firsthand that Snake could throw a good punch.

Her jaw throbbed at the memory, and Josie forced her thoughts back to her present situation. It was true enough that Ethan Savage might be ruthless and tough at getting what he wanted, but right now, it seemed possible that what he wanted might also be good for her. If this little arrangement he'd made with her enabled her to get to England and possibly learn something about her family, it was a good bargain. And eventually, he'd promised her, she'd have her freedom. He obviously didn't want this to be a real marriage any more than she did.

He'd better not, she thought fiercely, twisting Latherby's gold ring round and round her finger. *Seems to me I'd best make clear right from the start, that this marriage is going to be in name only.*

Especially since it wasn't even legal. But there was no way Ethan Savage would ever find out about *that,* she told herself, fighting off a twinge of uneasiness. Not unless Snake showed up blabbing that she was married to *him*—and that wouldn't happen. At least she *prayed* it wouldn't happen, prayed that Snake would never track her to England. She nibbled at her lower lip, trying not to think of how Ethan Savage might react if he ever learned that the woman he'd married during that ridiculous ceremony wasn't truly his wife.

And thank heavens I'm not, she thought, a frown

creasing her brow. One unwanted husband who demanded wifely duties of her had been quite enough—enough to last her an entire lifetime, she thought, her flesh growing chilled at the thought.

Ethan Savage may have kissed her at the wedding ceremony, but Josie intended to make clear that that was the closest he would come to claiming his husbandly privileges.

A flush burned her cheeks as she remembered that kiss. She unfastened the top button of her gown as her throat contracted. Then another one. *Arrogant, drunken man,* she told herself, yet wondered that the kiss hadn't repulsed her as Snake's had. Probably because it had taken her by surprise, she told herself. It had swept her up before she'd realized what was happening.

Well, *that* won't happen again. She'd simply lay out a few crucial ground rules for Ethan Savage, and then chances were they would get along just fine until this sham of a marriage ended.

Go ahead, then. What are you waiting for? she asked herself as she sat up a little straighter in her seat. *You need to set things straight with him so there are no misunderstandings. And there's no time like the present.*

She rose with a determined set to her shoulders and plucked up her valise. She wasn't sure if Ethan was in his compartment or in the parlor car, and she had no idea where Mr. Latherby was, but she decided to try the parlor car first. And as she edged along the aisle she made another decision: If Ethan Savage wouldn't promise to keep his distance when it came to matters of the flesh, she'd leave. She'd flee this husband, just as she'd fled the other one. Once they arrived in the crowded jumble of

New York City, Josie reflected, her courage mounting, that shouldn't prove difficult at all.

When she reached the door leading to the maroon and gold parlor car she saw her husband at once. He was sprawled in a wing chair before a large table near the rear of the car. Somehow, even in his rough western clothes, with a bandage wrapped around his head, he looked right at home in the sumptuously appointed car with its gold damask curtains and deep chairs. Latherby stood beside him. Neither man was facing her as she entered the long, luxurious car, yet their voices carried to her clearly.

"So you see, my lord, this will never, ever do. I tried to tell you last night—the fine print in your father's will clearly states that the woman you marry must be a *lady of quality*."

Josie shrank back behind the draperies. Hot color flooded her cheeks as Latherby's words penetrated.

"That . . . that girl in there is hardly—begging your pardon—a lady, much less a lady of quality. She is not at all what your father had in mind—"

A brutal bark of laughter cut him off in midsentence. "Damn my father to hell. Serves him right. I married her, and that's that. Who's to know or care anything about her, Latherby? You?"

"Ah, no, sir. However, Mr. Grismore, senior partner in the firm, has been charged with overseeing the fulfillment of the terms of the will. He will no doubt call upon your lordship after your arrival in London, and when you inform him that you have wed he'll naturally have to make a determination. Your father entrusted him to see that his wishes were carried out."

So that explained it. Josie swallowed hard as she huddled behind the curtain. Ethan Savage was after an inheritance. He'd needed a wife for that—but a very different sort of wife than the one he'd chosen in a drunken frenzy.

Not an orphan, a thief, a girl who'd marry a man to keep herself from going to jail—no. He needed a lady, a woman who bathed in scented water, who wore satins and silks, one who dressed her hair in a different fashionable style each day. Someone with accomplishments, who could manage servants, do needlepoint, and play the piano, not to mention make cool, polite conversation with other elegant people at a dinner party without spilling soup in her lap or dropping her elegant silver fork. *Not me,* she thought, swallowing hard. *Not me at all.*

So it will be over as soon as we reach New York, she realized, her fingers tight on her valise. *He'll want an annulment. We'll go our separate ways.* She was surprised by the little rush of disappointment that welled up in her chest. Wild as this whole marriage business had been, it had served her purposes admirably, at least for the time being. And she'd felt needed, important, for a very little while. But now, of course, Ethan Savage would wish to be rid of her as quickly as possible.

That would mean getting to England on her own.

Well, fine, she told herself, setting her lips together and clinging to the side of the car with her free hand as the train rocked and clacked down the track. She'd managed everything on her own all her life, and she could manage this too. Darned if she couldn't. At least she was out of Abilene, she reminded herself, taking a deep breath. And with Snake none the wiser.

"I should strangle you and Grismore." Ethan Savage bit the words out with grim fury. Josie peeked around the curtain, her eyes widening uneasily as he rose to his feet. "Why didn't you tell me this before?"

"You wouldn't let me, sir!"

"Damn you to hell. That little two-bit hussy is wrong for this. She's all wrong. I can see it now—she'd pick Grismore's pocket and then where the hell would I be?"

He began pacing back and forth, his long legs moving swiftly up and down the aisle. Josie suddenly realized on a needle of panic that at any moment he'd probably send Latherby to fetch her so he could announce that their little farce had come to an end.

He couldn't catch her here, listening, or he'd call her an eavesdropper as well as a thief. She had to go, to sneak back out to the other car. Cautiously she eased toward the door.

But suddenly the train rocked around a bend with a heavy jolting motion, and before Josie could catch herself she'd lost her balance and sprawled forward on the floor. Her valise went flying. And she landed with a graceless thump square in the carpeted aisle.

"What the hell?"

Ethan spun around at the commotion. When he saw his bride draped across the floor, his mouth tightened.

Latherby exclaimed, "Dear heavens!" but Ethan was already striding past him. As Josie tried to scramble up, he hauled her to her feet none too gently.

"What are you doing here?"

"I'm fine, thank you, so don't bother yourself on my account," Jo muttered breathlessly. She tried to shake free of his arm, but when she couldn't, she lifted flashing eyes to his face. "Don't worry—I'm not hurt at all."

"You will be hurt if you don't answer my question. What are you doing in here?"

"I was coming to see you."

"Why? To eavesdrop?"

"Of course not!"

His fingers tightened painfully on her wrist. "You, my sneaky little bride, are a liar as well as a thief."

He said it with certainty, with disgust, with crude frankness that sent blood roaring into Josie's face. Fine, if he wanted to think the worst of her, let him. She didn't care.

"Let me go!"

"When I'm ready."

He dragged her back up the aisle to where Latherby was gaping in open-mouthed dismay. The little man looked so distressed, Josie thought he might pop a blood vessel.

"My lord, you see what I mean," he whispered.

"I see exactly what you mean." Ethan pushed Josie backward and she landed with a thud in one of the deep plush crimson chairs. "Don't say a word. Not one word."

He turned his back on her and on Latherby, and stalked to the window.

Josie rubbed her wrist. She was furious—and totally humiliated. At that moment, staring at Ethan Savage's powerful frame, she'd have liked to have dragged him by his dark curly hair out to the platform linking the train cars, and pushed him off, sending him rolling, rolling down a gully until he landed at the bottom—in a rattlesnake pit.

The image almost made her smile with satisfaction. Almost. Instead she gritted her teeth, and sealed her lips, and watched him scowl out the window, imagining all too well what he was thinking.

She could hardly blame him—or Latherby—for thinking so badly of her. But it hurt even so. No amount of explaining would ever convince Ethan Savage or his Mr. Latherby that she was not the cheap little thief they thought her to be. She'd only stolen to get away from Snake—and she would never, ever take a penny from anyone who looked as if they needed it themselves. But Ethan Savage wouldn't believe that. Or give her a chance to explain it.

So what? Josie asked herself, shifting deeper into the plush chair. It shouldn't matter. Why should you care what he thinks?

She shouldn't.

But she did.

If Ethan felt her eyes burning into the back of his skull, he gave no sign of it. His thoughts were in turmoil, his jaw clenched as he fought to curb the fury inside him.

Above all else, he hated feeling trapped, enclosed, controlled. And that's how he felt now, trapped by the terms of his father's will—controlled by a cruel ghostly figure no doubt laughing from the grave, reveling in his discomfiture.

Marriage. He'd sworn ten years ago before all of London society that he would never marry. And he'd meant it, that long-ago night when he'd run away. But now here he was, tied to a cheap lying pickpocket with a mouth shaped as voluptuously as a courtesan's, with uptilted, violet eyes that could hypnotize mortals and gods alike, and a heart no doubt as black as a coal mine.

She couldn't be more wrong for his purposes. And she was clumsy, too, apparently, he reflected with a frown. He could imagine the picture she'd present tumbling down the steps of the Opera House.

Damn, he didn't want to be married at all, and he sure as hell didn't want to be married to this bit of fluff and trouble.

Feeling sweat break out on his brow, Ethan fastened his gaze on the open prairie rolling past—thinking of the Rockies, the Mogollons, the Sierra Nevada, of all the wild, untamed land of purple canyons and pine-crested peaks and cactus-studded desert he'd left behind. He couldn't believe he was actually heading back to London, with its crowds, its snobs, its rigid conventions, with memories of a past he'd spent the past ten years escaping.

Maybe he should just fold right now. Throw in his chips and call it quits—call this whole thing off. Damn Stonecliff Park. And damn the money. He took a breath, feeling better already. He could let the little thief go—get off this train and head for ... where? Silver City? San Francisco? Denver? Wherever the hell he pleased.

As if reading his thoughts, Latherby crossed the aisle and coughed quietly. His voice was low, as if to keep the girl from hearing.

"I'm sure I can imagine what you're thinking, my lord. Last night you made a mistake. But there is still time to rectify it. You could take care of this, er, *situation*—leave the girl at the next stop, and find yourself another ... wife," he whispered, throwing a glance over his shoulder at the pale, brown-haired girl sitting stiff and upright in her chair. "Someone more appropriate."

"I could, could I?" A number of men had seen that deadly glint in Ethan Savage's eyes, but none of them had lived to tell about it. Latherby took one look, swallowed hard, and continued forthrightly.

"You c-could, indeed, sir. And if you hesitate," he rushed on, "I beg you to consider that your cousin, the esteemed Mr. Winthrop, is no doubt walking through Stonecliff Park at this very moment counting the rooms, all two hundred of them. And noting on a ledger each stick of furniture which will become his if you do not return and meet the terms of the will."

"He's welcome to it. And you know what, Latherby? You're damned impertinent."

Yet the solicitor's words stirred something inside him. It wasn't only that he didn't want Oliver to get his hands on Stonecliff Park—though that was part of it. Oliver Winthrop was a sniveling weasel who'd had a hand in what had happened to Molly, and the last thing Ethan wanted was to see him prosper. But it was more than that.

Stonecliff Park meant more than land and money and gardens, more than ancestral paintings and crests, and tapestries dating from the days of the Conqueror.

There were scores of people on the property—housemaids, footmen, grooms, gardeners, cooks, scullery maids, coachmen, and tenants—all of whose lives and incomes would be affected by his father's death. Of the old retainers he would remember from his childhood, some had been more like family to him than his own father and brother. And now they were depending on him.

Their lives, he knew, would be better entrusted to his own hands than to Oliver Winthrop's pale, limp-fish, greedy ones.

He'd never thought to have the responsibility of rank and property and title—as a younger son it had never been a fixture of his future. Now circumstances had brought the unwanted responsibility to rest squarely upon his shoulders.

And as tempted as he was, Ethan was beginning to realize he couldn't just forget about it and walk away.

He slammed his fist against the paneled wall of the

parlor car, startling the girl and Latherby. They both stared at him as if expecting him to throw something next.

Ethan stalked to the girl and stood over her. She instinctively shrank back in her chair, then forced herself to lean forward again, her chin hitching up, up, up to meet his eyes.

She had spunk, at least. He'd grant her that.

He took his time studying her, ignoring the hot blush that stole into her cheeks. Because he'd acted rashly last night—unusual for him—a great deal now depended on this common thief. This slender violet-eyed hussy with her wayward brown curls and stubborn chin, who had picked his pocket twice in one day, and had danced at the Golden Pistol, displaying her dainty ankles for all of Abilene to admire, was far from being a lady.

Yet, it wasn't all bad, he thought, his brain finally beginning to turn the matter over more coolly. The deal he'd struck could have been worse. Much worse.

With any other woman, he'd be stuck for life. Someone proper and honorable never would have agreed to a short-term marriage for the purposes of securing his inheritance. But this thief had. She knew the terms and had made the bargain. A short-term marriage, then good-bye. Forever.

That certainly suited his purposes. It would nicely circumvent his father's machinations, and leave him the inheritance without the encumbrance of marriage.

So it was one point in the girl's favor.

And studying his bride's fine-textured skin, the delicate bones of her face, those luminous eyes beneath fairy-winged brows, he could actually see possibilities. With the right clothes, a few lessons in speech and deportment . . .

If she was a thief and a dancing girl, maybe she could be an actress too.

A good enough actress to fool Grismore, and the rest of London, for a few short months, and then it would all be over.

But it was essential he keep her in line.

"I want to speak to my wife," he told Latherby, his gaze still riveted on the girl's face. He saw her eyes widen, her mouth part in surprise, before she clamped her soft lips together again. But the tip of her tongue emerged to circle them nervously.

"Latherby, leave us alone."

Chapter Seven

"Don't look so terrified." Ethan's mouth curled upward in a scornful imitation of a smile as the parlor door clanked shut on Latherby and they were finally alone. "I'm not going to shoot you."

The edge of mockery in his tone set Josie's teeth on edge. She had too much pride to let anyone think she was a coward. "I know that. And I'm not afraid of you, so don't convince yourself that I am."

"If you had a lick of sense you would be." He stepped back a pace, pushed the hat back on his head, and she could see his eyes. They gleamed so dangerously out from beneath his frowning black brows that Josie nearly froze in horror, but she forced herself to fold her hands together in her lap and to school her face into a calm expression.

"Hungry?" he asked, with a gesture indicating the silver platters set out on the table behind him.

She shook her head.

"Cup of coffee?"

"Why don't you just say what you have to say, Mr. Savage, and get it over with."

The black brows shot up. What might have been

amusement leapt into his eyes for a moment, then was quickly extinguished, replaced by cool appraisal.

"You don't resort much to feminine airs, do you, Miss—"

"It's Mrs." Her blue eyes flashed into his. "Mrs. Ethan Savage. Or did you forget."

"I wish the hell I could."

Misery descended on her. "This was all your idea, not mine." She sprang up from the chair, her hands clenched into fists. "And I know you're regretting marrying me, and I'm not so pleased with it myself, but if you think I'm just going to sit here and let you insult me and yell at me and try to bully me, well, you can think again." She spun around and started desperately up the aisle, but before she'd taken two steps, Ethan gripped her by the arm and whirled her back.

"Not so fast."

"Let me go!"

"I wasn't trying to insult you. Don't be so damned prickly. Though I must admit I wasn't exactly thinking clearly when I married a thief."

"I'm not a—" She broke off, and bit her lip. "All right, I admit I took your money." Because she was ashamed the words came out in a muffled choke, and she covered it by glaring at him.

He glowered back, his eyes looking darker now, almost black.

"Not only my money."

"Fine, so I stole your pocket watch."

"You'd have taken my pants if I'd have blinked."

She opened her mouth to protest, and he went on roughly, cutting her off. "Don't waste your breath. Just fork over what's mine."

Her blue gaze clashed with his ominously dark one. "I would," she murmured tightly, "if you'd let go of my arm."

He glanced down and realized how fiercely he was holding her. Quickly he dropped his hand.

Josie was aware of his gaze on her as she retrieved her valise with all the dignity she could muster and began rummaging through it. She felt the heat of that dark gaze through all the layers of her clothes. Digging beneath a clean chemise, the worn pouch containing her treasures, some other clothes, and a hairbrush, she at last came up with the handkerchief in which she'd wrapped Savage's heavy gold pocket watch and wallet. She handed them over in silence.

All the while Ethan's eyes nailed her. She sensed the tension rippling through him, sensed he wasn't anywhere near finished with her yet.

"Anything else you have to say to me?" she asked at last, hoping the tartness of her voice hid how ashamed she was. She couldn't blame the man for considering her a thief—that's what she was, wasn't it?

He folded the greenbacks away and slipped the pocket watch inside his vest pocket. His face was grim. This little hussy showed no remorse. There was something hidden beneath that edge in her voice, but he doubted it was shame—probably regret, regret that she'd been caught and forced to face her victim.

Victim? Right now she seemed more like his victim than the other way around. Clearly ill at ease, tense, and fatigued, his dainty little bride looked a bit the worse for wear. There were lavender shadows beneath her lovely uptilted eyes, and her skin was white as a lily. He guessed she probably hadn't slept more than an hour or two, or eaten anything since sometime yesterday.

But that's not my problem, he told himself. *She's nothing to me, nothing but someone to use for a while and then get rid of. She'll be well rewarded, and that's all that a woman like her cares about.*

"I've got plenty to say to you, lady," he answered her evenly, noting the way she lifted her chin as he spoke. "But let's start with two things. First off, Latherby says you nursed this cut of mine last night, that you stanched the blood. He tells me you showed quick thinking." His voice was flat. "For that, I owe you thanks."

Astonished, Josie could do no more than nod. An embarrassed flush crept once more into her cheeks. She felt the warmth of it, and cursed herself for never having learned to control her blushes. "I didn't do anything special. Just what anyone with half a brain would have done. Well, actually, I did learn something about nursing from the Beckers." Because she was nervous around him and his intent way of studying her made her uneasy, she kept babbling, unable to stop. "I lived with them for a time, you see, and I learned some things. Mrs. Becker's mother had nursed injured soldiers in the War Between the States, so even years later, whenever anyone in town couldn't get hold of the doctor they called on her and—"

"I don't give a damn about the Beckers," he interrupted, taking a step closer. His hands shot out and gripped her shoulders. "I think you're trying to change the subject."

"No, I—" She broke off, too flustered to explain. She did have a custom of talking too much, especially when she was nervous. It had irritated everyone she'd ever lived with, except Pop Watson.

"Go on," she said more quietly, fighting the urge to hang her head. "What was the other thing you had to say to me?"

Ethan scowled as her lashes swept down over her incredible eyes. Strange how innocent she looked, though he knew damned well she was far from innocent. But she *looked* guileless and sweet, pristine as a farmer's daughter, or someone who'd teach school—not like a thief. And she had a sweet, melodious way of talking that did something strange to a man's insides.

He whipped his mind back to the matter at hand with the expert self-control he'd developed over the years. *You're too experienced to fall for a con artist's wiles,* he told himself brutally. *Stick to the point. Do what you have to do right now. Scare the hell out of her.*

"Here's the other thing." He yanked her toward him swiftly, so swiftly, she gasped in fright. "Consider yourself warned that if you give me any trouble—a drop of trouble—when we get to England, I'll make your life such a living hell you'll wish you'd never been born. You'll end up in Newgate prison, and it's far worse, I promise you, than an Abilene jail cell."

Staring up into the terrifying harshness of his features, Josie had no doubt he meant what he said. Suddenly the parlor car didn't feel large enough for both of them. He towered over her, his arms snaked about her body, his chest hard as granite against her quivering breasts. She wanted to shrink back, to run from the coldness she saw in his eyes, and from the hot pleasure his nearness stirred inside her, a pleasure that frightened and baffled her. But instead, she did what she'd learned to do in the orphanage when she was cornered by a bully, what she did whenever she wanted to survive. She took a deep breath and thrust herself forward straight into the fight.

"And let me give you fair warning, Ethan Savage. If you give me any trouble, any trouble at all, I'll tell everyone in London exactly what you've done, that you married a woman you didn't even know just to get around the terms of some will. Just so you could get your paws on the money—"

He dragged her chin up, his long fingers clamped to her cheeks. "You know all the angles about money, don't you. What's your name again?"

"Josie," she bit out. She fought back tears of pain as his fingers dug painfully into her face. "Josephine. I told you during the wedding ceremony. Don't you remember, *darling*?"

He grinned. An unpleasant grin. "I only remember one thing about that ceremony—except for Latherby trying like hell to stop it. Know what that one thing is?"

She shook her head, as much as she could, when he was imprisoning her jaw.

"This."

Without warning, his arms tightened around her waist and his face lowered swiftly toward hers. Josie's heart leapt into her throat. He was going to kiss her again.

He smelled faintly of soap, and of whiskey and of man, and it was not unpleasant. But he was too strong, too near, holding her too tight. She felt overwhelmed, and suddenly she was reminded vividly and horrifyingly of Snake, of his crude strength and brutal hands and of how he had hurt her. She'd vowed that night she'd run away never to let any man hurt her like that again.

She heard him laugh as if from a long way away.

"Drunk as I was, I couldn't forget lips like yours, angel."

"Let me go."

His face dipped lower, his mouth only a breath away from her trembling lips. "No need to act shy with me. I happen to know you had a job dancing in front of a whole saloon full of men. Don't tell me you didn't sleep with the customers."

"How dare—"

His fingers locked on her wrist as she tried to slap him. "And now you're my sweet little wife, remember. You're legally mine. I can kiss you if I want, Josie. Touch you. Bed you."

Panic clawed through her. An image of Snake pushing her down on the floor, pinning her arms, yanking her skirt up, filled her mind. She kicked at Ethan's shin, and pushed against him with all her might. Ethan continued to hold her, without any noticeable difficulty, but his soft mocking laughter had changed to a frown.

"What in damnation is wrong with you?"

"You might have married me, but you don't own me! Nobody owns me! I never agreed to let you . . . to behave as if . . . our bargain never mentioned—"

"Marital relations?" he suggested helpfully, burying his fingers in the sensuous cloud of her hair.

"Yes! No! I mean *no* to marital relations! If you touch me, this marriage is over."

She was shaking from head to toe. There was a panicked wildness in her eyes that Ethan had seen before in hunted animals and that made him release her abruptly.

"You have something against marital relations?" he asked sardonically, but as he studied her pale face, the quivering lower lip, he wondered what in hell she was so afraid of. Could it be that his delectable little bride was a virgin?

Impossible.

"This marriage is a sham. I agreed to it only to stay out of jail, so if you try to take advantage of me, I'll have no choice but to leave. Do you hear me? I'll run away, our deal will be over, and you'll be left to explain the disappearance of your wife. I don't think you want that."

His eyes narrowed. "It *would* be damned inconvenient and you know it."

"Fine. Then we understand each other."

He didn't understand anything about her. A beautiful thief and liar who'd marry a man to stay out of jail, who wore provocative costumes and showed her ankles to a roomful of leering men, but wouldn't let him touch her. A virgin? A prude? Not likely. Or was she just particular, and he didn't measure up?

Ethan nearly chuckled. He'd never had any complaints before. Women tended to be downright fond of him, despite his disinterest in fancy wooing. He guessed it was something other than that. She looked shaken still, as if she were clinging to her self-control with every drop of willpower she possessed.

"Have it your way, lady." Reluctantly he released those springy chestnut curls, undraped his arm from her waist, and took a step back. His eyes lingered briefly, with faint regret, at those temptingly full lips. "It's just fine with me. I'm not all that interested."

"Good!"

"Latherby's arranged separate compartments on this train, and I'll have him get the same on the ship. At Stonecliff Park, there's enough rooms for twenty people to live without ever having to see each other. But you and

I will see each other. For a few months, we'll put on quite a show."

"That's just fine with me. As long as it's only in public. You agree to that?"

"With pleasure, ma'am." He spoke with an exaggerated drawl, and his smile was full of mockery. "I'll survive somehow without the benefit of your affections."

"And I without yours. Then our business is finished. Except for some details. When will this . . . marriage be officially over?"

"Six months. Then you leave and never—and I mean never—show your face to me again."

"With pleasure." Josie mimicked his cavalier attitude. Six months. During that time she could begin her search—discreetly, of course. At the end of it, she'd know if it truly led her to her past or only in circles once again.

She'd just have to take what came at that point.

"Don't you want to know how much money I'm going to settle on you when this is over?" he asked.

Startled, she glanced up from her reverie. "It doesn't matter. Whatever it is, it's more than I have now."

He looked surprised, and his glance sharpened on her. Josie took a deep breath. "If that's all, I'd like to rest awhile in my compartment."

"That isn't all."

She waited, bracing herself for she knew not what. It occurred to her that for the next six months she was going to be very much in this man's power. Except for that one condition she had set forth, he would control how she spent her time, where she went, how she dressed, what she could do and could not do—in fact, he would control most everything about her life—until this ridiculous charade of a marriage was ended.

And just who was he? What kind of a man had she thrown in with?

She had no clear notion. There was something compelling about him, a rugged, singular strength, a damn-it-all-to-hell arrogance, a seething anger, but beyond that . . .

She knew there was more. She'd glimpsed it in his eyes when he'd spoken of his father turning over in his grave. And she sensed there was far more driving him to this bargain than mere financial gain.

If there was one thing she'd learned growing up in too many places to count, it was that, for good or bad, people were usually much more than they seemed.

"I've already warned you about giving me trouble when we get to England. And I want to be sure you know what kind of trouble I mean."

"Then why don't you tell me?"

"If you steal so much as a button from anyone we meet—if you pick one pocket, pull one trick—"

"I won't."

Ethan stretched out a hand and caught her chin. His eyes locked upon hers with ruthless warning. "You're damn right you won't," he told her quietly. "And remember that if you break your end of the bargain, I'll have no compunctions about breaking mine."

He released her abruptly as Latherby reentered the car, leaving Josie to wonder if he was referring to revoking the money he'd promised to give her at the end of their "marriage"—or to his promise not to force her to perform her wifely duties. She was left to guess, for the solicitor came forward then, glancing worriedly from one to the other, and giving a little cough.

"Latherby, you're about to become a very busy man."

"My lord?"

"We won't be depositing the lovely Josie at the next stop after all. She will be accompanying us to England— as befits my wife. It occurs to me that she'll need some instruction."

"My lord!" Latherby's jaw dropped. "You can't mean—"

"The hell I can't. Are you refusing your aid?" Ethan raked him with a steely gaze that had the solicitor gulping.

"No, certainly not, but . . . there will be much to do, my lord, if we're going to embark on this mad scheme. There will scarcely be time—I think we must begin some lessons at once. If this woman is to pass as a lady of quality and win the approval of someone as austere as Mr. Grismore, we have our work cut out for us."

"You mean *you* have your work cut out for you," Ethan snapped back. "You've already buried me up to my chin in legal papers and financial documents I need to read and sign. As of now, my wife is your responsibility."

"My responsibility?" The solicitor blanched. "But what do I know about teaching someone how to be a lady?"

"A hell of a lot more than I do." Ethan Savage returned to the table and sank wearily into his chair, scowling at the pile of papers before him.

"She's all yours," he told Latherby, with a certain cold pleasure. His gaze raked the girl with her simple rumpled gown and her tumble of unruly hair and her blazing, defiant face.

"Take this little gypsy and turn her into a countess."

"A countess?" It came out as a croak. Blankly, Josie stared at him.

His eyes flickered with a glint of harsh amusement.

She felt horror rise within her. A strange light-headedness swept over her—no doubt because she'd gone so long without a bite of food.

But oh, heavens, for a moment there she'd thought Ethan Savage had said she must be transformed into a countess.

"Yes." Latherby turned to her when Ethan didn't answer, only continuing to stare at her with that maddeningly calm expression. "Come along, miss . . . I mean, ma'am, I mean . . . my lady. We have much to do. And much to learn. You were married last night to the Earl of Stonecliff. Which makes you, for the foreseeable future, and may heaven help England—his Countess."

Josie's knees buckled. She grabbed at a chair for support, missed, and as the train pitched once more around a curve, she tumbled headlong. Flying, she landed smack across Ethan Savage's lap.

"As I said, Latherby," Ethan said coolly as he held an armful of soft, mussed woman who for the moment was too frozen with shock to move. "Better get down to business. You've got your work cut out for you."

Chapter Eight

"We're nearly there. Are you ready, Josephine?" Mr. Latherby's voice sharpened as he studied Josie by the light of the carriage lamps. "Look alert now. This is to be your first real test."

Even as he spoke the carriage turned wide, clattering down a tree-flanked road shrouded in fog.

Ready? she thought, controlling the panicked urge to push open the carriage door and bolt into the dark night. *I'll never be ready for this.*

But there was to be no bolting. Ethan Savage rode beside the coach on a magnificent white horse, which glimmered in the mist like Pegasus. *He'd probably lasso me and simply drag me up the drive to the house if I tried to flee,* she reflected bleakly.

But then her practical mind recalled that Ethan Savage had no lasso. He no longer even wore a gun belt and holster or the two deadly Colts. Sometime during the course of their journey, he had shed those staples of the American West. He had altered subtly, even his voice losing some of its western inflection. He now wore an English black-and-gray-checked sack coat over gray corduroy trousers. With his gleaming riding boots, top hat, and gloves, he looked every inch the English gentleman, while she . . .

Well, she thought, staring down at the new scarlet merino cloak Mr. Latherby had purchased for her in New York, and the snug lavender kid gloves and boots—she looked, on the outside at least, like an elegantly proper lady.

"My lady? You must remember to answer when someone speaks to you. It is rude merely to stare into space."

"Sorry, Mr. Latherby . . . er, I beg your pardon," she amended quickly, lifting distressed eyes to him. "Damn it, I'll never pass inspection, not even by the servants."

"Calm yourself, do calm yourself," Latherby urged. Nervously he snatched his spectacles off his nose, frantically polished them with the sleeve of his coat, and then shoved them back in place. "I beg you to remember what is at stake. His lordship could not only lose everything, he could lose face, irrevocably, if this debacle is discovered."

"You care about him, don't you, Latherby?" Josie asked suddenly, as she observed the beads of sweat forming on the solicitor's high brow. Latherby didn't normally get himself so worked up, she'd noticed during the time she spent with him on the Atlantic crossing.

"Of course. He is my client. I'm responsible—"

"It's more than that. You like him."

"I do."

"Even though he's rude to you, he is arrogant, insufferable, and orders you around."

"Here we are."

Panic squeezed Josie's heart and she forgot all about Latherby as she turned stricken eyes to the window and gazed out at the long gravel drive. The horses were flying along it far too quickly. When she saw the house looming up out of the fog, her throat constricted.

This was to be her new home. Temporarily. But, of course, temporary was the only kind of home she'd ever known.

It was a great house, huge beyond words, beyond anything her imagination could conjure. She had an impression of vast 'spaciousness, of lofty white stone that gleamed like pearl in the night, of graceful columns and arched windows, of tall, ghostly trees and damp rolling lawns. Through the swirls of mist she glimpsed the outline of gardens, of bordered flower beds, shrubs, statuary, and thought she could make out the shadows of the vast luxuriant park Mr. Latherby had described to her while they were at sea. Leaning forward on her seat, she thought she saw in the distance the silver-blue glimmer of a lake.

She had only a glimpse of everything, an impression, but she saw enough to know that it was finer, grander, more awe-inspiring than anything she could have dreamed of—like something out of a storybook.

Before she could collect her wits, the carriage door was flung open by her husband, and Ethan swung her down without ceremony. She had no sooner recovered from the sensation of his warm, strong hands clamped around her waist than he gripped her arm, as if afraid she really would bolt, and he was half dragging her toward the battalion of servants who had streamed out of the great white house upon hearing the sounds of their arrival.

The Sussex country air smelled of rich damp earth and grass and roses as Ethan propelled her toward the line of servants. For one brief moment Josie lifted her face to the mist and let it soak into her upturned cheeks, hoping it would revive her. She felt faint. Despite the fringed cloak that enveloped her in such luxurious warmth, she felt as cold as the icy churning sea she'd crossed to reach this destination.

Ethan Savage greeted his obviously atwitter staff with a curt nod, his handsome face a dark mask locked in frozen civility. He proceeded to present his wife with a swift series of introductions. Josie nodded inanely at Perkins, the butler, who studied her with somber, knowing eyes that seemed able to pierce her soul and see at once that she was as phony as the thin smile he bestowed on her. Dry-mouthed, she moved on, murmuring "how do you do" to Mrs. Fielding, the housekeeper, who beamed at her with real warmth. Despite her nervousness, Josie found herself beaming back.

But then disaster struck. Lulled into a false sense of security at having gotten past the first two members of the staff, Josie unthinkingly began to return the curtsy of Agnes, the cook, sinking into a curtsy of her own before she heard the collective gasp of those watching and Ethan seized her elbow with a fierce pinch.

She jerked upright, the enormity of her error striking her. A gasp of horror escaped her lips, and her pale skin turned red as a strawberry. As her eyes met those of the astonished cook, Josie saw reflected the same stupefaction now mirrored in the gazes of the rest of the assembled staff.

"I—I—" she stammered, fumbling for a way to explain, but Ethan, tight-lipped, merely yanked her ruthlessly forward, and she realized too late that explaining herself to a servant was every bit as improper as curtsying to one.

"My wife, Lady Stonecliff," Ethan muttered grimly to a bow-kneed little man with eyes that were no more than mud-colored slits. "Ostley, our groundskeeper."

"How do you—"

But before she could even finish murmuring the words, he hauled her forward yet again to nod dimly at a pair of grooms. Her spirits sank down to her kneecaps as she realized he didn't even want her to risk saying anything to these people, that she had already teetered out on shaky ground, and all he wanted was to get this over with as quickly as possible.

There was scarcely time after that to nod, much less smile or try to speak as Ethan drew her along past an assortment of staring footmen, housemaids, scullery maids, and gardeners who bowed or curtsied respectfully, and whose names and faces were immediately after an indistinct blur. As they finally reached the end of the line, Josie heaved a sigh of relief. Ethan nearly dragged her up the stone steps and through the handsome carved portals of Stonecliff Park.

Then she was inside a magnificent towering hall nearly as large as the entire main room of the Golden Pistol Saloon. A dazzling crystal chandelier, marble floor, and lovely, intricately carved furnishings surrounded her with timeless beauty.

"Mrs. Fielding, kindly see to my wife."

Ethan threw Josie the briefest, most disinterested glance before shrugging out of his coat and handing it and his hat to a waiting footman.

"Yes, my lord." The housekeeper's face beneath her white lace cap was wreathed in smiles. "Allow me to show you to your rooms, my lady."

Feeling almost numb, Josie allowed Mrs. Fielding to

lead her toward the wide central staircase. Ethan was already disappearing into one of the drawing rooms, followed by Mr. Latherby.

Josie concentrated on reviving her composure as she was bustled upstairs, through a stately portrait gallery, and along a series of elegant gaslit corridors where an occasional potted palm, gilt chair, or mahogany table adorned with a vase of flowers broke the pleasant monotony of gray-painted walls and rose and gray carpet.

At last Mrs. Fielding ushered her into an enormous bedchamber and sitting room furnished in pale yellows and creamy whites. Everything was so lovely, Josie could only stare in wonder. Though it was summer, a cozy welcoming fire in the marble hearth filled the room with lovely radiant warmth against the chill of the fog-laced night.

"You'll want a tray sent up, my lady, with some tea and biscuits and perhaps some soup after your journey," Mrs. Fielding said kindly. "Ah, it's dreadful to have to be traveling the roads on a night such as this." She tsked regretfully and moved a chair closer to the fire. "Especially with some of the dark doings that have been going on of late. I'm sure you've heard of Pirate Pete and his gang of cutthroats. Nasty scoundrels whose grandfathers were buccaneers, they say—they fancy themselves as pirates who do their plundering on land. They've been crawling out of the slums of London where they belong to rob decent city folks in their homes—and now some say they've even ventured into the countryside, if you can believe that. *I* wouldn't want to be out and about on a night like this, with the likes of them roaming about."

She caught herself up quickly as she saw the surprise

on Josie's face. "Oh, I beg your pardon, my lady. Don't you pay any heed to my rattling on."

"The roads are not safe?" Josie asked, surprised because she had thought that compared to life on the western frontier with its outlaw gangs, Indian raids, gunmen, and wild, lawless towns, England would be tame and peaceful and quiet.

"Oh, yes, quite safe," Mrs. Fielding assured her instantly. "And especially here in Sussex. We've never had a bit of trouble. Ah, here's Devon now, to take your cloak. My goodness." She chuckled as she helped Josie slip out of the garment and then handed it to the slender, pink-cheeked housemaid who looked to be no more than sixteen. "His lordship did not even give us a chance to take it from you in the hall, but never mind that. Here, come sit before the fire, you're quite chilled, and I'll go fetch that soup. If there's ever anything you need, only tug this bellpull here, my lady. In the meantime, Devon is to wait upon you and I'll bring your tray up myself directly."

Josie stood with her hands leaden at her sides, her feet seemingly planted into the floor. Both Mrs. Fielding and Devon were watching her expectantly.

Say something. They expect you to say something.

"Th-thank you, Mrs. Fielding. I hope it's no trouble."

"Trouble?" The housekeeper beamed at her. "Of course it's no trouble. Not a bit of it."

If the woman thought it strange that the earl's bride seemed stiff as a board and her shoulders were trembling beneath the fine blue-gray faille traveling dress with its black lace trim, she gave no sign of it. Josie smiled gratefully and allowed herself to be led to the comfortable chair by the fire. Sinking down upon the soft cushions, she couldn't help but think that the less she said to Mrs. Fielding or anyone until she was more sure of herself, the better.

Actually, though Josie did not know it, the housekeeper was already forming a favorable opinion of her. Mrs. Fielding had a sympathetic heart, and she had already concluded it must feel strange for a lady to come to her husband's home for the first time. Especially when that lady was no doubt fatigued and half frozen. *And,* the housekeeper thought regretfully as she threw her drained-looking mistress one last glance and headed toward the door, *my own foolish talk of Pirate Pete and his men probably frightened the poor fragile thing to death.*

"You just rest a bit and let the fire warm you, my lady. I won't be but a twinkling." She went out, thinking how good it was to have a master and mistress here at Stonecliff Park once again, and imagining the happy day when children would once more race through the nursery wing and play hide-and-seek in the gardens.

For perhaps the next hour Mrs. Fielding and Devon fluttered around Josie, serving her, seeing to her every wish—or what they perceived as her every wish. Her real wish was to be alone. To have a chance to take in what was happening to her, around her.

This house, for one thing. Ensconced in surroundings far more luxurious even than Mr. Latherby had prepared her to expect, more than anything she could possibly have imagined, she felt swallowed up. The enormous four-poster bed had pale yellow silk hangings and masses of deep, gold-fringed pillows. The dressing table with its white lace antimacassar was made of carved ivory, the mullioned windows were wide and high and draped in

white and yellow floral silk. There was a silk sofa in the
sitting room, and deep comfortable chairs and seascapes
on the walls and vases of roses, bowls full of floating
lilies.

And then there were the servants.

A short time ago Josie had been scrubbing pots and
pans in the grimy kitchen of the Golden Pistol. She'd
fried eggs, boiled coffee, made soup and steak and bread
for an endless succession of strangers—a servant herself.
And before that, she'd once worked as a chambermaid in
a seedy Kansas hotel, changing soiled bed linens,
sweeping floors, dusting old, scarred furniture in musty
little rooms.

Now she was to be waited on. Pampered in this lovely
bedchamber, helped into a lilac silk wrapper, her hair
brushed till it shone. The shock of it worked its way
strangely through her stunned system.

She was being readied for her husband, Josie realized
belatedly, as her tired and stunned mind clicked onto the
careful ministrations of Mrs. Fielding and Devon. It was
the newly returned master's first night at Stonecliff Park
with his bride.

"That will be all, Mrs. Fielding," she said abruptly,
jumping up from the chair before the dressing table and
twisting her hands together. The heady scent of roses
from the vase on the dressing table filled the room,
sweetly at odds with the sudden unease in her stomach.
"It's late. I'm sure you and Devon are ready to get some
shut-eye . . . I mean to retire," she added, remembering
Latherby's careful coaching in Things to Say to Servants.

Devon smiled and bobbed a curtsy. Mrs. Fielding
smoothed one last chair cushion on her way to the door.

The housekeeper thought she knew just what was

unsettling the new lady of the house. She guessed that the lovely young countess was anxious for the Earl to come to her, to draw her into his arms and lead her either to his own massive bedchamber, which adjoined the sitting room, or else to the bed in her ladyship's own room. It was growing late—well past time for the Earl to officially welcome his bride to her new home.

Mrs. Fielding, always a romantic, though she herself had been a widow for the past nine years, blew out a gusty sigh as she closed the bedchamber door behind her and the maid.

Yes, it was easy to see that the Earl and his Countess were perfectly made for one another. Their love must be quite sublime. The young man they had last seen so many years ago had grown even more handsome over the years, with a keen, almost dangerous edge to him that somehow only added vastly to his appeal, to her way of thinking.

And his bride . . . Well, the Countess was so beautiful with her gleaming hair and those dainty features and mesmerizingly brilliant eyes.

Mrs. Fielding experienced a tiny quiver in her throat as she reflected upon how lovely a moment that would be for both of them when Lord Stonecliff came upstairs to claim his bride.

❈❈❈ ❈❈❈

The bride was quivering too. But not from heady anticipation. Alarm quivered through her bones and jangled her nerves.

Would Ethan Savage dare come here tonight? Now that they were here in his ancestral home, safe in the world he knew and that was totally unfamiliar to her, a world where he was master and everyone here would scamper to do as he bade, would he honor his end of their agreement and leave her be?

She'd scarcely seen him in New York, or on the voyage across the Atlantic. True to his word, he'd had Mr. Latherby arrange for separate staterooms, and they hadn't even dined together, for he'd ordered most of her meals sent in to her stateroom—hiding her from society, she guessed, for as long as he was able. When she'd ventured out on deck, she'd been accompanied most everywhere by Mr. Latherby, who used every opportunity to teach and lecture her about the do's and don'ts of proper etiquette.

Don't stare at people, Josephine. It's rude. Vulgar.

Don't hunch your shoulders, Josephine. Stand up straight. Countesses don't stoop.

Don't use a spoon for your peas, Josephine. Break your roll into pieces, Josephine. No, no, never dip it in the beef gravy! And don't even think of licking your fingers!

Cover your mouth when you yawn, Josephine. Better yet, don't yawn at all.

Stop fidgeting, Josephine. Ladies appear composed at all times. And countesses are never ruffled.

Well, she'd be more than ruffled if Ethan Savage walked in that door right now. Somehow, just the sight of him ruffled her. And his touch. That moment when his hands had circled her waist and he'd swung her down from the carriage with such effortless ease.

Ruffled was hardly the word for it, Josie thought, and felt her stomach tighten.

Why did he have to affect her in any way whatsoever? It had been this way from the first moment he'd flicked those icy gray eyes over her. Something had started to burn inside her. And the flame hadn't gone out. In fact, it had grown stronger since that afternoon in the parlor car when he'd come so dangerously close to kissing her again.

She'd actually prowled the ship sometimes, hoping to catch a glimpse of him. But, of course, she didn't see him much. Because he didn't want to see her—he avoided her. He loathed her.

Which meant she was probably safe tonight, and every night. Ethan Savage was a complicated man, a man with secrets and much on his mind. He had made it very clear right from the start that he wasn't interested in being bothered with her, that she was someone useful to him— useful for a while—but beyond that he would not give a second thought, or a second look, to the lying thief he'd been forced to ally himself with.

He'd clearly made her Mr. Latherby's responsibility.

She ought to be thankful.

Josie went to the wash basin and splashed cold water on her face. She was patting her skin dry with a thick, fluffy towel when she heard a step in the hall. The towel fell to the carpet. Her hands flew to her throat.

But the steps went clear past without wavering, and then, though she ran to the hall door and pressed her ear against it, there was silence. If it was Ethan Savage, he had gone to bed.

Without disturbing her.

As a curious disappointment rushed through her, she bit her lip and wondered with a flash of panic what was going to become of her.

She had left everything behind, everything. Not that there was much to leave. The answers to her questions might well lie in England, and so she had come here—

but not at all the way she had planned when she'd grabbed Snake's saddlebag containing the stolen loot and the letter and jewels he'd taken from Miss Alicia Denby, and run off.

She'd come as the wife of the Earl of Stonecliff, a countess, and who ever could have planned on that?

It will all work out, Josie told herself, as she had so many times before in her life when she was frightened of the future, uncertain how she would find her next meal, where she would sleep, how she would fare in yet another stranger's home.

She paced across the elegant room in her bare feet, her wrapper whisking about her narrow ankles. Curling up on the window seat of that firelit bedchamber, she stared unseeingly out at the dense darkness of the estate's grounds, with the mist just beginning to lift and clear, and reviewed in her mind every word of the letter that had been in Alicia Denby's handbag. Starting tomorrow, she would question each person she met, ask if they knew of a young woman named Alicia Denby—

"You're not figuring out a way to make off with the silver, are you, bride?"

Josie's heart nearly exploded with fright, and she bolted to her feet. She'd never heard a thing. Not a footstep, not the turning of the doorknob. Yet there stood Ethan Savage, dark and powerful as always, though his face looked a bit tired and drawn beneath those frowning ebony brows.

He came toward her slowly, and she held her ground with effort, but he paused at the edge of the Persian rug, his hands deep in his pockets, his tie and collar loosened.

"That's not it?" he mused, studying her enigmatically.

"Then what has you so deep in thought that a bear could have roared in here and you'd never have noticed? Regretting your decision to keep our marriage in name only?" A slow grin almost touched his eyes. "If that's what you want," he said casually, "I could probably be persuaded to oblige."

Chapter Nine

"Don't you dare try anything of the sort." Josie answered quickly, lest he come any closer. She wiggled her cold toes against the carpet. "I should tell you, if you lay your hands on me—or even *try* to so much as kiss me, I'll scream." She took a deep breath and met his gaze with a flash of blue fire. "What will your servants think of their precious earl then?"

"It wouldn't matter to them in the least. Plenty of servants have seen and heard plenty of black deeds done within such elegant walls," he sneered. He cast himself down into a wing chair and grinned wickedly over at her. "But I'm not planning to lay hands on you again. For any reason. Unless you return to stealing. So, Josie, if not thievery and vice, or a passionate evening with me, what were you contemplating just now? You looked a thousand miles away."

She didn't understand why he was here, if not to threaten and bully her—or to push his claims as a bridegroom. She shrugged and turned away from him, pacing to her dressing table, where she could watch him in the mirror. She paused before the vase of roses and brushed a finger across the fragrant petals.

"I don't recall that sharing my private thoughts was part of our bargain. I'll keep them to myself, thank you."

He laughed. A harsh sound. Yet there was something beneath it, something wild, edged in pain. She turned quickly. He was raking a hand through his hair, a hand that was perfectly steady, yet she saw that in his eyes was a desperate ferocity on the verge of exploding.

"What is it?" she asked quickly, forgetting everything but the anguish pulsing beneath his careless facade. She crossed to him without thinking, and knelt by the chair, instinctively touching his hand, which rested upon the carved arm.

"What's wrong?"

His eyes fixed on her, hard and silvery as polished stones. "You don't really give a damn, do you?"

"Yes. I do. Why shouldn't I?"

"Why *should* you is more to the point." His lip curled derisively. But as she continued to stare at him, moved by something she didn't understand, by a sense of haunted pain that had entered the room with him and clung to him beneath the rakish facade, Ethan Savage's features tightened. "You want to know what's wrong, Josie? Being here, back here in this house. That's what's wrong."

"But why? It's your home."

"Home." He threw back his head and laughed bitterly. "It's never been a home."

He was coldly, furiously sober, she saw, with a breath of relief. His eyes glittered, but not with the effects of liquor. They glittered with sorrow, with hatred, with feelings so intense and bitter, they must be tearing him in two.

"They're depending on me. Every person you've met tonight is depending on me. All those servants, and the tenants besides. And that means they're depending on you. You'd better not let them down."

"I won't. I promise you, I'll do my best."

"If not for them, for the burden of all this." He threw a quick, bitter glance around the glowing, lovely room, a glance that seemed to encompass far more than just its regal confines. "I'd never willingly set foot on this damned British soil again. Much less at Stonecliff Park. My ancestral home." He gave another bitter laugh, and reaching out, cupped her small chin in his hand. She flinched, but his fingers didn't hurt this time. They cradled.

"It was never a home, Josie. I loved this place when I was a boy, it was all I had, but it was never a home. Not the way you'd want a home to be. Not like yours probably was."

She said nothing, merely stared at him, watching the scowl tighten his beautiful, sensual mouth, the way his gray eyes seemed to glint like frosted starlight as the firelight flickered over that hard-planed face. "Tell me about your home. Did your mother darn socks by the fire on some farm? Your father carry you about on his shoulders? Your brothers and sisters race you to school in the mornings?" There was mockery in his voice, and perhaps a tinge of envy.

"No." She spoke quietly. He still held her chin, and his fingers burned gently into her skin. How strange to be kneeling beside his chair like this, him touching her, not harshly, but softly. Listening to her. Yet that coiled tension was still rippling through him. "I never had a home either. Not anyplace . . . permanent."

"Parents. Brothers and sisters."

"No."

He frowned. He let go of her and straightened in his chair. "So where the hell did you grow up?"

"Nowhere. Well, everywhere. I'm an orphan," she explained, sitting back. His black hair had tumbled over one eye and she resisted the urge to brush it back. She kept her hands clasped in her lap. "I was adopted by various people. It never worked out for very long. Until I was older and I lived on a ranch in Montana. *That* was sort of a home. But Pop Watson . . ."

Her voice trailed off. How could she explain Pop Watson to a man like him? *Pop Watson was the one who taught me to pick pockets,* she would say, and he would remember all over again why he couldn't trust her. And besides, Pop Watson had been shot during a getaway two days after she'd married Snake. She didn't want to discuss that either . . . didn't want to remember any of that awful time after she met and married Snake.

"It's not very interesting," she finished lamely.

She was hiding something from him. Maybe the truth, Ethan reflected, his gaze hardening. Maybe this whole orphan story was a scam, something to win his sympathy, make him less careful around her. He steeled himself against the interest that had begun to tug somewhere inside him. He switched it off, the way he would extinguish a lamp when dawn's light flooded into a room. She had a lot to learn about him, if he thought she could get to him that easily.

Ethan's gaze shifted from her dainty, deceptively vulnerable face to the lilac wrapper. It had draped open as she knelt upon the floor. The creamy swell of her breasts rose modestly above a silky matching lilac gown. He was amazed by how intrigued he was by the sight. He'd seen women much more generously endowed, and he'd seen them stark naked. But he was fascinated by the glimpse of her slender, femininely curved body, and was disappointed when she, noticing the direction of his gaze, hastily yanked the wrapper tight and stumbled to her feet.

If he were a gentleman, he'd have helped her rise. But he was no gentleman, and he suddenly didn't feel it would be wise to touch her in any way, and he let her struggle up by herself. Then he rose, towering over her.

"I've kept you long enough. Get some shut-eye. Some sleep," he amended, with a brusque laugh. "I'd best get used to talking like an Englishman again since I'm stuck here. We're both stuck here," he told her, shooting her a warning look. "You'll need to be on your toes tomorrow and every day after. Latherby will continue to teach you, but we'll probably go to town in a few days. I have business to see to once I've tended to a few things here, and we'll have to see Grismore. And you'll have to meet people."

"I know."

"Scared?"

She shook her head quickly, then knew that the quick color in her cheeks betrayed her. "A little," she admitted, tossing back her hair.

"You ought to be. There's some civilized aristocrats on this side of the ocean who would think nothing of gobbling you up alive. You'll have to be on guard all the time. And don't expect me to charge in and rescue you if you get into hot water."

"I wouldn't expect that." Yet he saw her gulp, before she straightened her shoulders. "I'll pull this off without a hitch," she assured him, her tone very definite, and against his will, something in him responded to the courage that must have taken, to the way she just stood with her head up and her hands still, though he sensed his words had struck fear in her, indeed saw it in the way her lips trembled after she finished speaking. But even as sympathy flashed through him, he doused it.

She's a thief. A scam artist. You never know when she's acting, when she's got a plan spinning beneath that gorgeous exterior. She's already picked your pocket twice. Because of her you landed in jail, and needed Latherby to get you out. She deserves neither sympathy nor admiration. Treat her like you would a rattler.

"You'd better pull it off," he told her curtly, and swung away from her with an easy motion. But not before she saw the coldness in his eyes. He stalked to the door that led to his own quarters and left her alone without another word.

Josie couldn't sleep for quite some time.

The sheets were heavenly soft, the bed more comfortable than any she'd ever known. A light breeze sighed at the windows. And shadows danced upon the high-crowned ceiling of the airy room. But it was well past midnight when she was finally able to tame the restlessness inside her, and drift off. And then she dreamed.

She dreamed that Ethan Savage came into her room. Quietly. He came through the sitting room, from his own adjoining chamber. He wore a burgundy dressing gown, partially open to reveal a broad expanse of dark chest. He approached through the deep, silent darkness and stood over her bed.

In her dream she struggled onto her elbows, watching him, too stunned to scream, too overcome by the dark beauty of him to do anything but stare openmouthed, her heart leaping into her throat. And then she saw the rock-hard glint of his eyes as starlight beamed in the windows, saw the thick, curly black hairs on his chest, the slight mocking lift of his eyebrows, and she knew suddenly that this was no dream. He was here, looming over her bed, advancing upon her with a sudden breathtaking swiftness.

"Don't scream, damn you," he said irritably, clamping a hand over her mouth so that she could not possibly scream, could not even whisper. He climbed into bed with her, his hand still over her mouth. The bed sagged beneath the weight of him, and a strange fear and even stranger excitement charged through her.

"It's not what you think, bride," he said roughly, and to her amazement, released her. He threw himself down then, his head hitting the big fluffy pillow beside her. He was no longer even looking at her. He was staring at the ceiling, as she had done for so long before she'd managed to find sleep.

"This is a necessary evil," he muttered softly.

What did that mean? Was he going back on his word? Had he intended to come in and rape her while she slept?

She jumped up as if she'd been stung by a hornet, and flew out of bed. She stood just out of his reach, gaping down at him in fear. "You are plain loco," she whispered, not knowing whether to run fleeing down the hall, screaming to wake the dead—or to hit him over the head with a candlestick or the rose vase before he could seize her again. "I won't have this. I won't! Get out of my room!"

"Not until I've done what I came to do."

"We had a bargain."

He sat up, turned, punched the pillow he'd just been lying on, and tugged the tucked-in blankets out from beneath the bed. "We still do," he told Josie as she stood there in her nightgown, barefoot, shivering, her hair spilling like liquid bronze down her back.

"I only came here to mess up your damned bed. So that in the morning, when the maid comes in to clean the room, she'll think we spent the night as a proper husband and wife should have spent the night." He grinned wickedly at the girl staring at him in amazement. "Together," he added in a sardonic tone.

"Oh." It seemed a stupid, pitiful thing to say. She realized, now that the fog of fear and confusion had lifted, that he was right, of course. It would look quite strange to a servant if in the morning the master and his new bride had both been seen to have slept alone in their separate beds, if those beds were neat and tidy, the covers on the opposite side of the bed undisturbed, no articles of clothing strewn about, no sign of one or the other in any room but their own.

"Well, all right," she said cautiously, still eyeing him with suspicion, "but why didn't you think of this earlier?"

"Because I thought of it now. Wait a minute." He rose from the bed with catlike grace and crossed to the chair where she had neatly draped the lilac wrapper. He tossed it in a heap on the floor.

"And a pillow," he muttered. Lifting one from the bed, he sent it, too, sailing to the floor.

"That's enough." Josie wrapped her arms around herself, feeling quite breathless from the cold. She was about to yank up one of the blankets to cover herself when Ethan Savage turned to her and something about his intent stare kept her rooted to the spot. His gaze was ruthless, all-seeing. There was a considering hunger in it, a hunger that made her all too intensely aware of her own scantily clad body. She gave a tiny gasp, and quick heat raced through her. And with it came a stab of fear.

She felt the sheer silken nightgown clinging to her body almost like a second skin. The cold air caressed her bare arms, shivered across her breasts, rousing her nipples to frozen peaks. Danger hung in the air, a danger she could sense as a mouse senses a hawk about to swoop, a danger that left her throat dry and her knees weak, yet she commanded herself to act, to do something before it was too late.

But even as she moved, grabbing up the blanket to wrap it around her, Ethan moved faster, and tore it from her hands.

"One more thing. The pièce de résistance." He reached up and fisted the front of her nightgown, his fingers crumpling the smooth satin ribbons into twisted shreds. As Josie gasped in shock, he ripped the gown apart.

She screamed, and the sound rang through the room louder than a gong. And—she was sure—echoed up and down all the corridors of the house.

She and Ethan gaped at each other. Then he gripped her arms and stared into her shock-darkened eyes, overcome with incredulous fury.

"What the hell did you do that for?"

"What the hell did *you* do *that* for?" she countered furiously.

His breath was warm on her face, his mouth taut. "I figured a ripped gown would be the most convincing evidence of all. What the hell did you think I was doing?"

"Let me go."

"So you can scream again? No way, sweetheart."

"I won't scream, but . . . don't look at me. Don't look at me, damn you." The gown was falling down around her bare arms and her breasts spilled impudently out of the torn fabric. Ethan told himself it was only pure male interest that made him want to look, but deep inside he knew it was more than that.

The sight of her, chestnut hair rioting about her shoulders, skin smooth and pale as ice and bared to his view, eyes more vivid than wild violets, burned into him, branded him. She was stunning. Warm and female and furious . . . and sexy as hell.

Don't look.

He wanted to do a hell of a lot more than look. He wanted to scoop her close and feel those lovely firm breasts pressed against him, to rip the rest of the nightgown away so he could explore them with his hands, rub the nipples between his fingers, scrape them ever so lightly between the edges of his teeth. He wanted the silk of her hair to glide against his skin, the feel of her lips to make him forget how much it hurt to be back in this house.

He wanted to bury himself in her. To watch those violet eyes darken and go wide, wider, to hear her breath rasp in her throat with a woman's desire.

But it was clear she wanted none of these things, or if she did, she was a damned good actress. She ripped the blanket from him, flung it around her like a regal cape, and whispered angrily, "Get out."

"Someone might come to investigate that scream. If they do, I'd better be here."

"Oh no you don't. Get—"

"Quiet!"

He seized her, blanket and all, and held her still, listening. There were no footsteps. Only silence. A deep black, echoing silence that boomed in her ears louder than a tree crashing to earth.

"Luck must be with us," Ethan mused.

She wondered if he had any idea how hard he was holding her, how intoxicating it felt to be pinioned so hard and so close against his fierce strength.

"If anyone heard you scream, they must think it's from the throes of passion," he continued, his breath rustling her hair. He shifted his grip slightly, nestling her more comfortably against him. "Unless Latherby heard," he went on softly. He sounded almost amused now. "His room is just around the corner. He's probably concluded that I've murdered you."

"I'm going to murder *you* if you come into my room like this again," Josie managed to whisper weakly. Still locked against him, still weak in the knees, she struggled for control of her own body and emotions.

Ethan Savage gave a low laugh.

How intimate and treacherously pleasurable this felt, cuddled in the blanket, held against him so tight, she could scarcely breathe. His chin and jaw were shadowed with dark stubble that only enhanced his rough, vivid handsomeness. His chest felt rock hard and oddly comforting. But it was the unguarded expression in his eyes that pierced the armor of her fear and distrust. He looked, for the moment, almost like a small boy trying to get away with a wild adventure, loving the danger of it, laughing at the possibility of getting caught. And at that moment she saw the boy he must have been once—wild, full of energy, full of mischief, and at the same time, all alone in this great house, except for the servants.

The energy was still there, pumping through him, fierce and exciting, and so was the mischief—and she saw, studying the granite lines of his impossibly hand-some face, so was the loneliness. It was etched in those unfathomable eyes, carved in the harsh lines of a mouth that seemed to have forgotten the ease of open laughter.

"What are you staring at?" he asked suddenly, scowling down at her, and once again a lock of his hair, which had tumbled across his eyes, tempted her. She clenched her hands around the blanket that concealed her nakedness, refusing the impulse to brush the dark lock back and let it slide through her fingers.

"I was thinking that it's been a long time and no one's come to check on me." Josie felt both hot and cold, shaky and strong. Something had happened just now, when she'd watched Ethan. She was no longer frightened, no longer alarmed by the warm, strong nearness of him.

"I think," she said softly, as some new emotion trembled uncertainly inside her, "that we're safe."

"Safe?" He released her so suddenly, she nearly dropped the blanket, then scrunched it tight again. He deliberately took two steps back. "We won't be safe until you've passed inspection by Grismore and all of London society. There's a long way to go yet, sweetheart."

"Don't worry." Why did she suddenly want to reassure him, to ease the lines of tension around his eyes? "I can pull this off."

How coolly he looked at her. A muscle jumped in his jaw. "One lie, a dozen, a hundred, it's all easy for you, right?" he asked sarcastically.

She shook her head, wishing he didn't always think the worst of her. "I didn't say it would be easy."

He grunted something and strode to the door. "There may be visitors tomorrow." He paused and glanced at her over his shoulder. "The news will get around fast that we're here. You'd better get some sleep if you want to be on your toes when the neighbors show up to inspect the new Countess of Stonecliff."

"I *was* sleeping," she reminded him softly. "Before you woke me."

"Then go back to sleep. I won't be returning. Your virtue is entirely safe." He said it dryly, with veiled contempt, and the door closed behind him before Josie could think of anything to reply.

Still clutching the blanket to her, she slipped back into the bed. And lay there between cool sheets, trembling. But not from cold, and not from fear.

From a nameless emotion that tugged at her insides until she felt raw and broken, that stirred her with a yearning so sweet, it was unbearably painful.

No, it can't be, she whispered to herself, over and over again. *It can't be that I'm beginning to care for him. Not for Ethan Savage.*

But her heart whispered back that she was.

"I'm doomed," Josie said to herself, tossing and turning in the bed. Tears welled in her eyes. "Doomed to misery, having such thoughts, such feelings for a man who hates me. Next thing, I'll be falling hopelessly in love with him!"

The thought had her bolting upright in alarm.

"No," she told herself, staring wide-eyed into the cool rose-scented darkness. "No. It won't come to that. Never."

But she couldn't be sure—the way she felt right now, she couldn't be sure of anything.

Her luck hadn't changed. It would never change.

It just kept getting worse.

Chapter Ten

Morning dawned rosily at Stonecliff Park. Sunshine flooded the dining room and glistened on the immaculately polished silver platters, the sideboard, the frames of the paintings. It glowed on the chestnut curls of the new countess as she sat alone at the long table, slowly chewing her bread and butter, and taking absent sips from her china coffee cup.

She felt wretched. The poor night's sleep had left puffs beneath her eyes, and her brain felt as if it had been buried in gritty desert sand. Simple Josie Cooper Barker felt like an imposter in the elegant teal silk morning gown Devon had laid out for her. Before, she'd owned one gown—one simple gingham gown. Now her closet was filled with scads of gowns—morning gowns, walking gowns, tea gowns, traveling gowns, evening gowns. They were made of lace, of silk, of velvet, of muslin and satin and tulle.

In the chest of drawers were piles of gloves, fans, handkerchiefs, stockings, petticoats. All purchased by Mr. Latherby in New York. All belonging to this phantom countess, this creature married to the Earl of Stonecliff.

And somehow, *somehow,* she had to convince everyone she was to meet in the coming days and weeks and months that she *was* that creature, that lady, that elegant, well-bred, and proper bride.

And no longer only for her own sake. Something had changed last night. Perhaps everything had changed. Now she thought not only of herself, of her goals and needs, of the bargain she must keep.

She thought of Ethan Savage. Of the duty he felt toward this house and those who inhabited it, a duty toward his heritage that seemed to go deep even though there was no love lost between him and the father who had left all of this to him.

She didn't know the reasons, the whys or whos, she only knew that it was important to him—important enough to bring him back to England despite his misgivings, to compel him to take his place in this house and in London society, though from what she'd observed he would much rather be in a saloon in Abilene up to his elbows in smoke and whiskey and cards.

"This is dreadful, Lady Stonecliff, just dreadful." Mr. Latherby blew into the library in a feverish rush, his spectacles sliding down his nose in his agitation. "Callers. Already. And we haven't had a moment to *review*. And I saw his lordship ride out not a quarter of an hour ago. He'll be gone for some time and we—you— must deal with them all alone!"

He finished just as Perkins appeared in the doorway.

"My lady, Mr. Oliver Winthrop has called to pay his respects."

"Who?" Josie wrinkled her nose. The name sounded familiar. "Who the hell . . ." she mused, then gasped as

Lucas Latherby gave her elbow a vicious pinch. "I mean, how delightful. Send him . . . show him in."

Apoplectic rolling of the eyes from Mr. Latherby had her amending quickly, "To the morning room," remembering at the last moment that this is where the lady of the house customarily received her early visitors.

"Well, I'm sorry," she told Latherby crossly, the moment the butler had departed. "But he took me by surprise, and as you said, there was no time to review——" She broke off, suddenly recalling where she had heard the name before. Winthrop was the awful relative who would inherit Stonecliff Park if Ethan Savage did not meet the terms of the will. She disliked him already.

"Come on, guess we can't keep him waiting," she muttered, and started toward the door, but Latherby let out a smothered oath.

"No, no, no! Josephine—Lady Stonecliff—how many times must I tell you it's unladylike to career across a room like . . . like some kind of racehorse headed to the finish line."

Josie stopped short, cursing her own carelessness. He was right. *Slow down, Jo. Think before you speak, move with grace, keep your fingers from fidgeting, don't shuffle your feet, don't laugh too loud, don't plop into a chair, don't stare at people, cover your mouth when you yawn.*

Reciting this litany mentally, she forced herself to walk with careful dignity through the hall. Only then did she remember that she didn't know which of the numerous doors led to the morning room. Panic surged through her, faltering her steps, but even as she half turned to confess her ignorance to Mr. Latherby, she saw Perkins, waiting patiently to open the door for her.

"Thank you, Perkins," she murmured.

"You're welcome, my lady."

So far, so good. Her heart pounding, she passed into the morning room, and there, in a wide sunlit parlor fronting the gardens, she found a rotund little man with a high forehead, smooth baby-pink cheeks, and little milky blue eyes that for some reason made Josie think of a pig.

He had been pacing back and forth before the mantel. But he froze when she entered the room, and she saw his hands tighten on his ebony-handled walking stick. He wore jaunty striped trousers and a black-braided sack coat. His dark brown hair was parted down the middle and flattened on top. It shone with a thick layer of Macassar oil.

"Good morning," Josie said politely, not at all liking the way his little pig's eyes bulged out as they fastened on her. "You are my husband's cousin, I believe. I am . . ." She paused, suddenly realizing she didn't know quite how to introduce herself. I am Lady Josephine? Countess Josephine? Call me Josie? Lady Savage? All Latherby had told her about rank and nobility and titles flew out of her head, and she repeated blankly, "I am . . ." then gulped and said, "very happy to make your acquaintance."

"Lady Stonecliff, a pleasure." His gaze swept over her, head to toe, missing nothing. He didn't look as if it were a pleasure though. He looked pained.

Was she so improper then? Could he see that she didn't belong here just by the way she stood, by something indefinably common in her bearing, in her features? She saw shock, and a twinge of anger as he twisted his small pursed mouth into an artificial smile.

"We are cousins, my lady. Do call me Oliver. And may I call you—"

"Josephine."

Mr. Latherby coughed, and she added quickly, "Do you know Mr. Latherby? My husband's solicitor." She was proud of herself for recalling the word. "Won't you sit down, Mr.—*Cousin* Oliver," she corrected smoothly, and indicated the sofa behind him.

"Don't mind if I do." That simpering, false smile again. His eyes slid to Latherby, back to Josie again, studying her curiously, then darted back to Latherby once more—pointedly curious as to why her husband's solicitor was chaperoning the Countess in her morning room when he must have work of his own to do.

And Josie saw Latherby looking torn between excusing himself, which she guessed would be the natural thing to do, or staying to keep an eye on her and step in if she started to do or say something totally unladylike.

"It's perfectly all right, Mr. Latherby. I know Lord Stonecliff asked you to keep me company until he returned, but now that Cousin Oliver is here, I won't . . . shan't be lonely at all." She bestowed on him what she considered her most dignified smile, despite the unease prickling through her.

And as she had given him no choice, Mr. Latherby left them—but not before shooting Josie one quick warning look while Oliver Winthrop was engaged in settling himself more comfortably upon the sofa.

Winthrop refused her offer of refreshment. "No, no, dear lady, I came merely to confirm for myself that the rumor I heard this morning was true. Never did I think to see my esteemed cousin Ethan again. Not in England, at least. No indeed, not after the manner in which he took his leave."

"Oh?" Josie scarcely knew what to say and hoped the simple word would do. She was fascinated by what

Oliver Winthrop had just said, and even more so by the way he had said it. Though polite, his words barely hid a snide dislike of Ethan, and that made her dislike *him* even more intensely than she had at first sight. But she kept her expression neutral and waited for him to continue. She herself had wondered why Ethan had left England to begin with, why he had traveled to America, why he was so angry about coming back.

If she played her cards right, perhaps she'd find out.

"Well, yes, it was *quite* a scandal you know. A dreadful scandal. It's doubtful anyone in proper society will accept him back now." Winthrop nodded with smug assurance. His eyes blinked slowly at Josie and his lips pursed, and she knew what he was deliberately leaving unspoken.

Nor will they accept you.

"I'm sure you're wrong," she said more sharply than was polite, but at that moment she didn't care.

"Oh, don't be so sure. Between the girl, and the scene he caused, and the bloodshed—"

"Girl?" Josie heard herself repeating in a thin voice, one that made Oliver Winthrop lean toward her, lips curling.

"My dear cousin, don't think I'm trying to discourage you or to cause you any pain. No, my intentions are only to warn you that, well, your husband has a vile temper. And a taste for unacceptable women. At least he did," he amended with a dry, mocking laugh, and again his eyes inspected her. "My dear, if you think to conquer London society, you are doomed for disappointment. Though I personally find Americans to be quite interesting and amusing, many of my fellows don't share my sentiments. And Ethan is no favorite due to the way he humiliated his father and brother, and took up with that low-class little tart—"

"If you say her name, Oliver, you will never live to see the streets of London again," a low, deceptively soft voice warned from the doorway, and Josie jumped as she turned her head to see Ethan standing just inside the room.

"Darling," she cried, frightened by the cold, dark expression on his face. Oh, dear, he was going to kill Oliver Winthrop right this very minute, shoot him dead on this beautiful rug and spatter blood all over those lovely blue curtains, and that would not be a very good beginning to his tenure as the Earl of Stonecliff.

Then she saw that he wasn't wearing his guns—and recalled with relief that he had shed the garb and gear of the gunfighter. This morning he wore the riding breeches and jacket of an Englishman. But standing there, tall, glowering, his booted feet planted apart, his hands clenched in fists, and a savage light in his eyes, he appeared not a speck less dangerous than if he held both Colt pistols drawn and loaded, pointed straight at Oliver Winthrop.

Winthrop seemed to agree. He sank back against the cushions of the sofa, all the pink color draining from his face. He gaped at Ethan as if the devil himself had materialized in a puff of black smoke.

"C-cousin!" he croaked out with a pathetic attempt at joviality. "I was just—"

"Shut up, Winthrop. Not another word. Get out and don't speak again."

"But—but—"

Ethan came forward with his strong easy stride, and with one hand he lifted Winthrop from his chair.

"I suppose I'll be forced to run into you at clubs and balls and card parties," he said in a calm, pleasant tone belied by the deadly glint in his eyes. "But I'll be damned if I'll entertain you here. Don't call again. Here or in London. Is that clear? You've met my wife, you've seen that I'm back, and you know now that you'll never get your muddy little paws on Stonecliff Park, so there's nothing more to be said between us."

"Really, Ethan . . . there is no reason to bear such a grudge . . ."

Ethan dropped Winthrop back on his feet. Then he hit him, his fist slamming into the other man's face with a whooshing, pummeling force that sent Winthrop toppling backward over the sofa.

"Ethan!" Josie darted forward as her husband rubbed his knuckles. "You'll hurt your hand! Goodness, you didn't have to hit him that hard."

"What about me?" Winthrop gasped in horror, grasping weakly at the back of the sofa as he attempted to rise. "I'm blinded. Blinded! I won't be able to see for a week. Good Lord, man, you're as mad as ever. Violence. *Violence*. All because I paid a call."

Ethan strode around the sofa and hauled him up on his feet. Winthrop cowered, trying feebly to break free, but Ethan only tightened his grip and marched him to the door. As Perkins came running and yanked the front door wide, Ethan tossed the sniveling man out into the sunshine.

"He's not to be admitted again," Ethan told Perkins as the butler shut the door on the sounds of Winthrop's outraged howls.

"Yes, sir. Begging your pardon, sir."

Ethan stalked back into the drawing room.

"Why were you entertaining that son of a bitch?"

His ferocity shook her. Josie went very still. "Because he came to call. I thought it was the ladylike thing to do. Perhaps you should give me a list of people I can and cannot see," she added, suddenly angry that he was angry with her, when she'd only been trying to do what she was supposed to do—pose as his proper, dutiful wife.

"Perhaps I should. Latherby!" The solicitor's footsteps tapped through the hall as Ethan paced back and forth to the mantel.

"My wife has just been engaging in idle gossip about me with a member of my family. Obviously, her education is lacking."

Latherby shot Josie a glance that made her want to sink through the floor. "Yes, my lord," he said humbly. "I'm sorry, my lord."

"It wasn't like that," Josie protested, scurrying after Ethan as he paced to the window. "It wasn't like that at all."

She stopped short as he spun about suddenly to confront her.

"Wasn't it?" There was a contemptuous curl to his lip as he raked her up and down. "You obviously still have much to learn about being a proper English wife. Latherby, if you can't do better than this, you'll sorely regret it. Work with the girl, night and day if you must, but whip her into shape before I take a crop to both of you."

He started toward the door, sparing Josie not even a glance, but paused on the threshold to growl over his shoulder, "I almost forgot. Tonight I'm forced to take her to a damned dinner party, so do what you can before then. I ran into Lady Tattersall while I was out riding and she wouldn't take no for an answer."

He shifted his gaze, leveling a thunderous frown at Josie. "Be ready to depart at seven. And God help me," he muttered under his breath as he turned and left the room.

Ethan walked straight out the door, veered down the sloping lane to his left, and cut through the gardens. He needed to be outdoors, breathing in fresh air, clearing his head, calming his temper. He walked quickly, his long legs eating up the ground beneath him, though he scarcely realized where he walked. The sight of Oliver Winthrop had inflamed him as if all of it had happened yesterday. Good Lord, where was his famous cool control, the legendary deadly calm of Ethan Savage, hired gun?

Seeing Winthrop, the first time since that night all those years ago, had lit a fire in his blood.

And it had brought Molly's image searing into his brain again, as if she had never left. And maybe, he thought, stomping through green fields, jumping a brook, heading toward a belt of trees, maybe she never had.

He almost heard her silvery little voice, almost smelled the fresh rose-and-vanilla scent of her. "Ethan, do come in. I've missed you ever so much! Ethan, you shouldn't have. These flowers must be ever so expensive. You don't have to bring me something every time you call, you know!"

Sweet, innocent, unspoiled Molly. His heart tore in two, remembering. Remembering what they'd meant to each other, and how she had trusted him, and what had happened to her for daring to love an earl's son.

And Ethan sank down on a fallen log in the wood, and buried his head in his hands. The pain was sharper since his return to England, and he was quite certain that nothing would ever take it away.

Presently, glancing up, he noticed a cottage several

hundred yards ahead, nearly hidden by a rise in the ground and a copse of ancient trees. The stocky figure chopping wood outside struck him as oddly familiar. He rose slowly from the log, staring.

It couldn't be. Couldn't . . . it was.

He started forward at a run.

"They told me you were retired. No longer living at Stonecliff Park," he said as he slowed to a halt before the wide-shouldered, gray-haired man who set down the ax at the sight of him.

"I am. And I don't."

"But you're here . . . so close. . . ."

"You want me to leave, lad?" The scraggly gray brows drew together in a questioning glance that pierced Ethan to the bone with its familiarity.

"No. *No.*" Ethan stared at the man who had been more like a father to him than his own father ever had, the man who had taught him to ride, to shoot, to mend his puppy's cut paw, the man who had let a small boy trail after him when he went about his work day after day after day, and he swallowed past the lump in his throat as he started forward, arms outstretched.

"Ham." The name burned in his gut, squeezed like an anvil at his heart. He reached the old groom, and with a rough sigh, clasped the bewhiskered old groom in his arms. "Ham, you old gaffer, I'd given up on ever seeing you again."

∗∗∗ ∗∗∗

"So you never did find it, did you, lad? I'd hoped you would."

"Find what?" Ethan peered up from the tin cup of

steaming tea Ham had set before him, a baffled expression on his face.

"Happiness. Peace. A kind woman to love and to love you back." Ham rubbed his whiskers thoughtfully and watched Ethan, studying the changes in the boy he'd known, who'd now become such an imposing figure of a man. "Yours was always a restless spirit, lad. And when you went to America I hoped you'd find the balm there you needed to soothe it."

"I found myself there. That was enough."

Ham's shrewd brown eyes, flecked with olive in the sunlight that streamed into the cottage, never wavered from Ethan's face. "But you've still got that restlessness inside you. You're still . . ." He trailed off. He'd been about to say unhappy.

"I'm resigned to my fate."

"Without hope?"

"Hope of what?" Ethan studied him, amused. "Peace? I haven't exactly led a peaceful life. But I've found some moments of it. Sleeping under the stars in the Arizona desert, or beneath the Mogollon Rim. Riding through the Rockies. Wandering through country so beautiful, it hurts to look at it, with no strings on me, no one to tie me down or pull me back."

"Some strings are good."

"You want strings?" Ethan's short laugh filled the tiny spaces of the scrubbed and tidy cottage. "I've got plenty now."

"Aye, all this rich and beautiful land, the title you inherited from your father. The houses, all of 'em. The responsibilities of wealth most only dream of. And a wife."

"That's right, a wife." Ethan drained the tea and set the

cup down with a rattle on the table, remembering how wildly lovely Josie had looked last night, the impossible brilliance of her eyes, the rich glory of hair spilling across her bare shoulders.

He scowled at the tin cup, suddenly wishing it was filled with brandy to help soothe and dull the memory.

"I heard about her already." Ham picked up his pipe and tobacco, and shifted his weight in his chair, noticing that the dull flush that had entered Ethan's cheeks at mention of his wife was the same brick-red hue as the rag rug beneath the young earl's feet. He suppressed a smile and spoke with deliberate casualness. "Word spreads fast, it does. They say she's a lovely thing. That's why I was a mite surprised—"

He broke off.

"Surprised about what?" Through narrow eyes, Ethan watched the groom tamp down tobacco as if nothing else mattered.

"To see you still so restless. I thought if you were married . . . unless, lad, you didn't marry for love."

Ethan gave a harsh bark of laughter. He raked a hand through his hair, then stood up and began to pace. "Still as keen as ever, aren't you, Ham? Well, you're right. I didn't marry for love. I married because of my father's will—because I was drunk, because I acted in haste, and anger, and spite. I married a damned thief—and now I've got to pass her off as a lady."

He sighed as Ham stared at him incredulously.

"No!" the groom exclaimed.

"Yes." Ethan's lips twisted with cynical amusement. "Reckon I'd better explain."

When he was done, the old groom whistled slowly

through his teeth. "So, there's no feeling at all for this lass? You're going to send her away in six months?"

"Sooner, if she fails at any point along the way and brings the whole scheme crashing down." Ethan was surprised by the clenching of his gut as he thought of this possibility. He recalled how Josie had knelt beside him last night when he'd been so wound up about being back—of what she'd said about her past. That she'd never had a home either.

Could it be true? Was the sweetness and concern he'd seen in her eyes real, or was it all part of her act? And today, she'd actually worried about his hand when he'd struck Winthrop—any other woman would have gone weak in the knees over witnessing that sort of violence, or would have tried to tend to the fallen man, offering apologies and excuses—but not her.

Something about that made him think of Molly, though why, he didn't understand. Those two were completely dissimilar, in looks as well as in nature. Molly had been small, exquisite, and dark, her hair black and sweeping down her back like a midnight waterfall. Her skin had been very white, her cheeks pink and round in a beautiful Irish face that was lush with sweetness. And she had been innocent, shy, sheltered from the ways of the world, unsuspecting of the casual cruelty that had been visited upon her. Josie Cooper, on the other hand . . .

His jaw tightened at the thought of her. She was stunning too—with her luscious cloud of curls, the seductive uptilted shape of her eyes, their astonishing violet color. She was taller than Molly, not so round, more slender, yet every bit as alluring, with a coltish sensuality that heated his blood despite all his efforts to remind himself that she was a common pickpocket and liar, the last person he could afford to get involved with—especially now.

And he told Ham exactly that as the groom watched him through the smoke that rose from his pipe.

"Seems to me you're already mighty involved with her, lad."

"Not for long."

"What'll become of the lass when she leaves?"

"That's her problem. She'll have money. She can do as she pleases. So long as she doesn't trouble me."

Ethan stood, his chair scraping across the rug. "Reckon I'd best get back, Ham. But what about you? Are you comfortable here? Happy? Why don't you come and live back at the house? There's a dozen empty rooms in the east wing. You could take your pick."

"This is my pick." Ham clapped a gnarled hand on Ethan's shoulder as together they walked to the door. "If I've got leave to fish in your duck pond, to pick berries in those woods, to do a bit of hunting without being arrested for poaching"—he grinned at the quick sharp look Ethan threw him—"then I'm fine and dandy."

"You damned old curmudgeon," Ethan growled, struggling to conceal the emotion that welled up in him as they walked out of the cottage into the blazing golden afternoon. He turned to stare long and steadily at the old groom with whom he'd wandered this rolling, fragrant green land on so many other days just like this one.

"Anything you need, Ham. Anything at all. It's yours."

"I have what I need."

"Next week, when I get back from town, I'll come chop firewood for you."

With a small choking sound, Ham yanked his pipe out from between his lips and shook his head at the younger man. "No, Ethan, my lad," he said firmly. "You won't. That wouldn't be fitting. Not fitting at all. You're the earl now, not a boy out on a lark."

"Think you can stop me, old man?" The look Ethan shot him was full of playful challenge. "I've chopped plenty of wood in the past ten years and not once for anyone I gave a damn about. I can sure as hell chop wood for you."

And clapping the old groom on the back, he turned and sauntered back the way he'd come, feeling far more cheerful.

Ham watched him go, torn between gladness at having him back, and concern that the boy he'd taken under his wing so many years ago had never yet found the happiness that had been denied him in childhood.

But he'd seen something in Ethan's eyes when he mentioned his wife. Something that gave him hope, despite the lad's harsh words. Something definite enough to make Ham decide that one of these days—and the sooner the better—he'd like to meet the new Countess of Stonecliff and judge for himself.

Chapter Eleven

※

You can do this. Of course you can do this. All you have to do is walk down those stairs and pretend you're acting in a play. You're not you—you're someone else. A countess. A lady. A wife.

"Is something wrong, my lady? Are you not pleased with how I arranged your hair?" Devon asked anxiously, and Josie realized that she'd been scowling at herself in the mirror.

She shook her head, for a moment unable to speak. Then she managed to say in what she hoped was a dignified tone, "It's lovely, Devon. I don't believe it's ever looked as pretty as it does tonight."

The girl beamed at her. She dropped a curtsy and began moving about the room, tidying the bed, picking up stray items of discarded clothing.

Josie studied her own reflection in the mirror. A sensation of stunned unreality surged through her. The gown of deep rose moiré with its silk overskirt trimmed with black silk roses was without a doubt the most elegant, sophisticated, and gorgeous dress she had ever seen. And it made her look like someone else, she decided on a gulp of nervousness. Like someone she didn't recognize.

Her upswept hair, gleaming with a coppery sheen in the hissing yellow gaslight, was adorned with a small cluster of silk roses as well. Only a few carefully chosen wisps floated out from that elegant topknot to skim softly about her cheeks.

Her gaze moved lower. Goodness, how slender and—yes—voluptuous she looked in that low-cut bodice and tight skirt with the small bustle and the elaborate lace-edged train. Even her shoes were exquisite—rose satin slippers adorned with pearl rosettes and tiny glimmering jewels.

If only her cheeks weren't so pale. If only she could catch her breath. Tonight would be her first major test, and if she failed, it would all be over.

Ethan Savage would send her away. He'd probably put her on the next steamship for America himself—and she had never even had a chance to try to find Miss Denby.

The thought that she wouldn't see Ethan Savage ever again was not lost on her—it made her spirits sink to her toes—but she pushed this prospect from her mind.

She wouldn't fail. She would succeed.

But first she had to find the courage to leave this room.

She saw Devon casting anxious glances at her beneath her lashes as she gathered up the gown Josie had worn this afternoon to be sponged and pressed. The girl was wondering why she didn't go down. It was growing late.

"Don't wait up for me, Devon," she said, rising from the chair with her knees quivering. "We may be quite late."

"Yes, my lady."

And then she gathered up her jeweled evening bag, her gloves, and her embroidered chiffon fan, and swept from the room, mindful to take small, careful steps in the tight-fitting gown, her head held high as Mr. Latherby had instructed. As she descended the staircase she heard footsteps far below and saw Ethan stride to the bottom of the stairs. He put a hand on the banister and scowled up at her.

She wondered if he had scowled at that other girl the same way. The one Cousin Oliver had told her about. No, Josie decided, on a wave of glumness, he had probably smiled at her. And laughed with her. And complimented her. Whoever she was. It sounded as if he had defied his father because he cared for her, so she must have mattered to him—mattered a great deal.

She wished she knew the story of that girl. She had to believe that knowing would somehow help her understand Ethan Savage. And perhaps reach him. Because she knew that beneath his restlessness, his arrogance and harshness, there was not only anger, but a deep, long-buried pain.

Josie wanted . . . what? To ease it somehow. Perhaps even to heal it, to soothe away the trouble knotting in his soul.

But she realized as he stared up the staircase at her with such remote coolness that she had a better chance of sprouting wings and flying than of ever getting the chance to try.

How devastatingly handsome he looked in his black evening coat and vest, his high-collared, snowy linen shirt looking even whiter against the bronze of his skin, his raven hair gleaming in the light of the chandelier. Somehow the elegance of his attire, its very correctness, made him look all the more rugged and dangerously handsome. His expression didn't change as she descended toward him. Well, perhaps a bit. His eyes grew even frostier. Josie fought back rushing disappointment.

What had she expected, that he would gape at her openmouthed and spew out a babble of compliments he couldn't contain?

She told herself she'd best forget about dazzling Ethan Savage, and concentrate instead on not falling down the stairs.

Ethan, meanwhile, had all he could do not to grit his teeth. Damn, the vision coming toward him was enough to make any man drool. The little thief he'd dragged into the garbage-strewn Abilene alley looked as if she'd been born in a palace. Her hair shone like copper in the chandelier light, her fine-boned face held the delicate beauty of some long-ago storybook princess, and the eyes gazing down into his with eager brilliance shook him to his soul.

And mixed in tantalizingly with all this heart-stopping loveliness was the unconsciously sensual sway of her hips as she took her dainty steps, the slender curves accentuated by the tight sweep of her gown. It didn't help that he remembered all too well the feel of her atop his lap. He battled a fierce urge to vault up the stairs, scoop her into his arms, and savor the softness of her pressed against him once more.

Lunacy, to be sure. The last thing he could afford to do with his untrustworthy new wife was display any sign of affection or weakness. Then his goose would be cooked for sure.

But what grist for the mill it would provide the servants, Ethan thought, suppressing a devilish grin. His sense of humor could readily appreciate the gossip that would fly belowstairs if he were to dash up the steps and sweep his wife into his arms before one and all. He was almost tempted to do it—not only to experience the delights of Josie Cooper Savage pressed up against him, but to see the expression of shock on the faces of the servants gathered in the hall.

John, the footman, stood at attention, ready to open the door for them when they departed. Rupert, another footman, and Perkins had been passing through the hall, but now each had come to a complete halt and all three servants were staring up as if transfixed at sight of the delicate, exquisite woman descending the staircase.

Ethan was sorely tempted. But sanity won, and he stayed where he was, concentrating on maintaining his equanimity. It helped to remember just who that woman coming toward him really was: not a princess, not an angel, not even a lady, just a thief and dance hall girl who'd steal him blind if he gave her half a chance.

But if she was going to continue to look this fetching every time he encountered her, he'd need to find himself a mistress in London pretty damn quick just to keep himself distracted.

Josie's stomach fluttered more and more nervously as she neared the bottom of the staircase. When she saw that the butler and two footmen had paused in the hall to watch her progress, her breath locked in her throat. The way they were staring at her, she wondered frantically if the silk buttons of her bodice had come undone, or the ribbons of her shoes had come untied. She offered the servants a hesitant smile, then couldn't resist glancing down at her shoes, just to make sure.

"Don't look down!" a voice hissed angrily from a doorway below. Latherby's voice. Her glance flew toward him uncertainly, and her hand faltered on the banister. The sudden movement sent her teetering over the step, and the next thing she knew her fan went flying and she was pitching forward, a scream bubbling in her throat.

Then she was caught in a powerful pair of arms that were beginning to feel treacherously familiar. Ethan clutched her fast against his chest.

"You clumsy girl, this will never do," the solicitor groaned, rushing forward, then suddenly froze as Ethan's gaze swerved to him, and Latherby saw that the Earl's eyes were like gray ice. Too late the solicitor became aware of the presence of the servants, of the horrified shock with which they were staring at him.

He had just insulted the Countess of Stonecliff, his employer's precious bride.

"I . . . I beg pardon." He shoved his spectacles up onto his nose with fingers that visibly trembled. He stared from Ethan to the servants and back to Ethan again with deepening red color splotching across his face as Perkins dashed forward and scooped up the fallen fan, presenting it to the Countess with a bow.

"My dear Countess, I, uh . . ." Latherby seemed to be choking out the words. "Forgive me, I was, er, only concerned that you not hurt yourself."

"It's quite all right," Josie managed to say with a weak smile. She bestowed a stronger one on Perkins as she accepted the fan in trembling fingers. "Don't give it another thought."

Ethan set her down and turned toward Latherby. "Your services are no longer required in this house."

"What? My lord . . . I beg you . . ."

"You are to leave at once." Ethan flicked a glance at Rupert, the taller of the two footmen. "Bring another carriage to the door for Mr. Latherby. My wife and I will be leaving for Lady Tattersall's directly—tell Charles to walk the horses while he waits. I need a few words with Mr. Latherby before he departs."

Taking Josie's arm, Ethan took her into the library. Latherby followed, head bowed, well aware of the three servants' stunned and disapproving gazes that bored into his retreating back.

No sooner did he close the library door than the solicitor began to speak. "My lord, I didn't notice them standing in the hall. I didn't think."

"That's right, you didn't think. There's no way you can stay here now, after insulting my 'Countess.' And *you*." Ethan turned to Josie. Glowering, he studied her, his gaze raking her from head to toe. "You were doing just fine until you let yourself get sidetracked. You even had me fooled—almost. It's that dress, I reckon. Makes you look downright respectable."

Respectable? Was that the best he could do? He made it sound as if she resembled a wrinkled, cherub-cheeked preacher's wife!

Beautiful, was what she longed to hear. Or *elegant.* Maybe *ravishing.* It didn't matter that *respectable* was what she was aiming for.

"You're too kind." Violet sparks began to flash in the depths of her eyes. She arched her brows, regal as a duchess. "I'm overwhelmed by such flattery."

Ethan fought back a grin. Wasn't that just like a woman to take a compliment the wrong way? Those adorable lips were actually pouting.

"Josephine," Mr. Latherby cut in desperately. "Stop fiddling with your fan. I've told you time and time again that ladies don't—"

"Latherby, that's enough!" Ethan glowered at him, all of his amusement vanishing. "Damn it, man, you don't let up. Are you always this tough on her?"

"This tough on her? Whatever do you mean, my lord? I'm only doing what you told me to do. You explicitly instructed me—"

"You tell me," Ethan commanded, swinging his attention impatiently to Josie. "Does he treat you like this all the time?"

Surprised, she weighed how to answer. Poor Mr. Latherby was terribly critical, but he was only doing his best to fulfill the job Ethan had given him. He was even now staring at her beseechingly, as if begging her not to crush him any further in the eyes of his employer.

"I guess I make a lot of mistakes," she said carefully, not meeting either man's eyes.

She felt Ethan's gaze resting on her speculatively, and twitched a nervous hand across her skirt.

"The *lady*"—was it her imagination, or did he emphasize the word—"is trying to protect you, Latherby. Which is a hell of a lot more than you deserve." He paced to the window, then swung back, frowning at the solicitor. "So listen to me. You've got to clear out. The servants here will know something's not right if I let someone who spoke so insultingly to my wife stay under my roof—and in my employ. So from now on you'll work for me from London."

"But—but—she's not ready. I can't be responsible—"

"I'll be responsible." Ethan cut him off. "Go to London, tell Grismore my wife and I will receive him in town next week. And get my town house ready for our arrival. We'll be coming up tomorrow."

"Yes, my lord."

"Does my father—*did* my father keep a separate staff for the Stonecliff House?"

"Oh, yes. Stonecliff House is completely staffed. But your lordship, who's going to help this girl—er, Lady Stonecliff?" Latherby put in anxiously.

Josie had been wondering the same thing.

"Let me worry about that." Ethan waved a hand at Latherby. "Get going. Josie and I have to get along to Lady Tattersall's dinner party before the other guests drop dead of starvation waiting for us."

Lucas Latherby bowed his head. "I'm sorry," he uttered in a resigned tone. "I was only trying to help. Josephine," he said, shaking his head as Josie regarded him expectantly, "don't ever look down at your feet while you're walking down the stairs."

"I know that," she grated out.

"Then why did you do it?"

"I just forgot . . . because Ethan and Perkins and Rupert and that other footman were all staring at me and I thought my shoes were untied or something else was wrong—"

"They were staring at you, no doubt for an entirely different reason!" Latherby snapped. "Now, I thought you were a sensible girl at least, if not a true lady, but if you're going to act like a witless goose, it'll never serve. See that you do everything Lord Stonecliff tells you to do. And *observe* the ladies you'll meet tonight—they will be your best teachers. Behave exactly as they do. And don't say damn or hell or—"

"Latherby, shut up!" Ethan interrupted, staring back and forth between the two of them in amazement. "You can't stuff a lifetime's worth of knowledge into her head in the space of a minute, and you're just going to confuse her."

"I'm not confused," Josie snapped, gripping her fan more tightly because her palms were beginning to sweat. "I'm nervous. Let's just go. And get it over with."

Ethan jerked a thumb toward the door. "You heard the lady."

"That's the problem, my lord," Latherby fretted as he moved reluctantly to the library door. "She's not yet a lady, and I don't know if she'll ever be one."

"From now on, that's my problem," Ethan growled. "I'll see you in town."

When the door finally closed behind the solicitor, Josie began to pace around and around the walnut-paneled room, suddenly overcome by an urge to delay the ordeal of the party.

"This won't work," Ethan remarked suddenly.

"What?" She stopped short, staring at him. "I mean . . . I beg your pardon," she added in frustration.

"This won't work," he repeated. "The way you look . . ."

Her heart sank. So it was obvious even with the dress, the fan, the gloves, the fancy shoes, the upswept hair, that she was only an orphan who'd done odd jobs all her life and struggled to get by, not a fine lady. If he could tell, so could everyone else.

"Give me a chance," she exclaimed. "I'll change my dress . . . something fancier, I'll stand straighter, I'll—"

"It's not you." He snagged her wrist as she tried to rush past him toward the door. He held her still. "It's this."

With his finger he traced an invisible arc across her throat.

Not understanding, Josie lifted wide, questioning eyes to his.

"And this," he added, lightly pinching the bottom of her ear as he tried not to drown in the ocean blueness of those magnificent eyes. "And this."

Holding up her hand, he clamped hold of her wrist. "No jewels. Lady Tattersall and the other women at that dinner party tonight will know instantly that something's dead wrong with this marriage if you're not wearing diamonds or rubies or emeralds in all the right places."

Jewels. Of course. She thought of the portraits she had seen in the gallery upstairs, of all the ladies in their fine dresses and even finer jewels. Her thoughts jumped to the brooch and ring, but she could scarcely whip them out and wear them—Ethan Savage would accuse her of stealing them!

"Well, goodness, I left every single one of my diamonds back home," she murmured. "And I believe my rubies must have fallen overboard into the Atlantic, and as for the sapphires—"

"You've made your point." He released her wrist and started toward the door, half smiling. "Don't wander off. I won't be long."

Josie threw her gloves, fan, and bag down on the desk and began to pace. Trying to blot out everything else, she frantically reviewed all that Latherby had told her up until now. If she made some terrible mistake, she knew, it would all be over. She'd be shipped back to America—and Snake. And she'd never have a chance to find Miss Alicia Denby.

And she'd never see Ethan Savage again. Never have a prayer of making him think of her as anything other than a worthless thief.

"What in hell were you thinking about just now?"

His voice made her jump. How long had he been gone?

She'd been spinning wool; she hadn't even heard him open the door when he returned.

"Nothing," she lied.

He advanced on her slowly. The guilty flush of color flooding her cheeks was not lost on him. Suspicion hardened inside him. He'd better be on guard. The devil only knew what she was up to.

"Maybe you were figuring the odds of making off with these—wondering if you could get clear away without my finding you."

He held up a necklace—a heavy strand of rubies set in ornate gold so incredibly beautiful, it made her gasp.

"No." Josie could only stare. "Oh, no," she breathed. "I wouldn't—"

Red fire flashed bewitchingly before her eyes. Heavens, they were gorgeous. And there were glittering earrings to match. And a ruby-and-gold bracelet that looked to be part of the same set. She couldn't possibly wear these.

"They were my mother's." His tone was cool, impersonal. She wondered at his total lack of emotion when speaking of his family, as if he had sealed away every human feeling, every intimate connection many, many years ago. "They're worth a fortune—but I wouldn't recommend trying to steal them," he warned softly. "It wouldn't be healthy."

"I would never do that."

"Not if you know what's good for you," he agreed.

Anger quivered through her then. And with it came injured pride. He thought she had no scruples at all, that she was as devoid of feeling as he was. Challenging him, she lifted her chin and met his gaze directly.

"If you're so worried why let me wear them? Why show them to me at all?"

"Do I look worried?" he asked with a mocking hint of a smile. But there was steel beneath it. "Come on, Josie. They're yours for tonight, and when needed in London. Put them on fast—we're late."

But because he was so near, and watching her so intently, her fingers fumbled clumsily with the necklace's clasp, and in the end he had to help her with it. As she stood with her back to him, their bodies were so close, she could almost feel the power-edged heat of him burning through her gown. Josie prayed for her heart to stop its mad pounding, for the feelings inside her to stay locked tight deep within her chest. She held her breath, aware of everything, of the heat and weight of the rubies at her throat, of his strong hands working carefully at the delicate clasp, of his breath warm and steady on her neck. She resisted the urge to spin around, rise up on tip-toe, and taste his kiss again, to give herself up to those warm, slow lips. But she wanted to. Heaven help her, she wanted to.

"Done. Let's see."

A wave of shakiness swept through her as he turned her to face him.

Josie met his gaze shyly. She felt her breath coming in quick, ragged bursts. She wondered if he would notice her quickened breathing, the rapid rise and fall of her breasts.

Of course he would! He was a man, wasn't he? All men noticed such things.

Delicate pink color like the mist of dawn tinged her cheeks as he studied her in silence.

There was a darkened intensity in his eyes. She

searched them, but was frustrated to find that beneath the shock of silky black hair, those gray eyes were as unreadable as always. No recognizable flicker of emotion betrayed what he was thinking—about her, about the jewels, about anything.

Then, with a light finger he touched the rubies glittering at her ears, then the necklace at her throat.

"You'll do."

But his voice held a note she hadn't heard before. Josie stared at him, trying to see beneath the cool crystal gray of his eyes, but he turned away swiftly and handed her the gloves, bag, and fan she'd left on his desk.

"Come on—before Lady Tattersall decides to box my ears," he said darkly, and Josie, who couldn't imagine anyone daring to do any such thing to him, allowed him to escort her to the door.

In the carriage, with the horses clattering beneath a delicate half-moon, she lapsed into silence. The heat of the necklace pulsed at her throat. She didn't know that in the light of the carriage lamps, her skin gleamed richly white against the rubies' dark fire, or that Ethan was having difficulty keeping himself from glancing at the swell of her breasts above the low-cut rose moiré gown. She knew only that he was sitting silently across from her, his expression completely unfathomable as the horses drew them nearer and nearer to the ordeal ahead.

"Perhaps you should tell me something about Lady Tattersall and the other guests I'm to meet," she ventured at last as her nervousness mounted.

"Lady Tattersall is my godmother. She's a dizzy, good-hearted old bird—a peacock, more like it," he added with a curl of the lip. "As I recall, she always loved parties and the whirl of London's social season more than life itself, but she's never had an ounce of spite in her as far as I could tell. You don't have to be frightened of her."

"I'm not frightened." Josie clasped her hands tightly in her lap. "I don't frighten easily."

"Damn straight." Ethan shifted in his seat, edging nearer to her. "You didn't frighten the first time I caught you stealing my money," he said softly. "In fact, you had the cold hard nerve to go ahead and steal it again—and to take my pocket watch. Not many men would have dared to cross me like that—especially when they'd been warned."

"I was desperate. I had to get out of town."

He remembered the terror in her face when she'd seen someone pass in the street while he held her captive in the alley. An echo of it glowed in her eyes even now. He saw her swallow hard in the thin moonlight beaming in the carriage window and wondered just who or what had triggered such intense fear.

"They can't get you now," he said roughly, wondering why he was bothering to reassure her. "But just for the record, who was after you? The law?"

"No. Just . . . a man."

His eyes narrowed.

"A man I knew," she finished tautly.

What had that man done to her to instill such fear? Or maybe more to the point, what was he going to do if he caught her? For a moment Ethan felt a black surge of fury at the hombre who had filled her with such terror, and his muscles tightened as if he were about to do battle, but he immediately relaxed them, angry at his own reaction.

It meant nothing to him what had befallen her before

they'd met. Nothing. And it would mean nothing to him what happened to her after she'd finished this little job.

And probably, he added darkly, annoyed by his own ready sympathy, she deserved whatever the unknown man had had in store for her.

"Did you pick his pocket, too?" he asked, his face very hard in the moonlight.

Josie's finger tightened in her lap, the knuckles whitening. "No. But . . ." What could she say? *I did steal from him?* Hardly.

She thought of the beating Snake had given her, how she'd felt the life draining from her as he mercilessly struck her again and again, threw her against the wall, kicked her in the ribs as she lay broken and moaning on the floor. She thought of how she'd fled, battered and terrified, taking the loot-filled saddlebags and Miss Alicia Denby's stolen belongings with her.

"It's a long story," she said coolly, fighting to keep her expression calm, to not let him see anything of what she was feeling. She leaned back in her seat, ending the conversation by looking out the window deliberately.

Secrets. She was full of secrets.

The last thing he needed was to get involved with her and her schemes. It was burdensome enough being back in England, taking up the reins of his father's empire, and facing down the memories of Molly and the fate she'd met at his father's hands. He didn't need to worry about a deceptively angelic piece of fluff whose shady past was very much her own problem.

"I almost forgot to tell you," Ethan said as the carriage pulled up before a graceful stone-and-stucco mansion nearly as impressive as Stonecliff Park. "In addition to my godmother's friend Colonel Hamring, and some stupid young debutante and her chaperon, my cousin will be dining here too. Since he's in the country, sponging off the few friends he has, he's wangled himself an invitation. He's always had a way with hostesses, and Lady Tattersall has known him since he was a boy."

"You're not going to hit him again, are you?"

"Who knows?" Ethan shrugged. "Depends on how much the evening needs to be livened up."

A giggle burst from her at this, but she quickly smothered it with a gloved hand as he led her up the walk. But not before she heard Ethan Savage's short answering chuckle.

It occurred to her that if they'd met under different circumstances, they might have been friends. If he'd watched her dance one night, and had offered to buy her a drink afterward. If she'd entered into that poker game he'd been playing, and won a few hands. She'd certainly have been drawn to his darkly handsome looks, to the cool way he handled himself. She might even have wondered what it would be like to let him take her to his room . . . and make love to her.

That thought shocked her. She'd been a virgin until she and Snake were married, and based on the things he'd done to her, she wished she could have remained one forever. Knowing what she did, she ought to run like hell at the very notion of going to bed with a man. Because if what Snake had done to her was what it meant to make love, Josie knew she'd rather go to war. At least then she'd be armed with a weapon with which to protect herself.

Based on what she'd learned about what went on between married men and women, she knew that if Ethan

Savage ever decided to try to break their agreement, she would flee England faster than a bird on the wing.

She would *never* be any man's victim again. But remembering the powerful effect of his kiss, the way his arms felt around her, she felt a piercing curiosity that kept growing stronger. Something deep and secret inside her yearned to find out more, to find out if with another man, with Ethan Savage and the feelings she had for him, things might be . . . different.

But she pushed these thoughts away as Ethan raised the knocker. It wasn't going to happen. She wouldn't let it happen. After her experience with Snake, she'd be a fool ever to get within spitting distance of Ethan Savage or any other man ever again.

When no one answered the loud rapping, Ethan frowned and tried again.

"Strange. Every light in the place is on and none of the servants are coming to the door."

Josie leaned over to try to get a peek through the windows, but the drapes were drawn, and she couldn't discern any shape or shadow through the heavy fabric.

"I don't understand. If they're expecting us . . ."

"Old Whitley must be going deaf as a doornail." Ethan turned the knob. The door swung open on a wide, elegant hall adorned with handsome French wallpaper, but whose dark marble floor was marred by a servant's sprawled form.

The liveried man lay facedown, unmoving. Blood trickled from a gash at the back of his head and dripped into a small puddle on the floor.

"Oh, my, God, Ethan . . ." But even as Josie started toward the man in alarm, she felt herself grasped from behind and hauled brutally backward. An arm encircled her throat, and she saw the glint of a knife. Her unseen assailant pressed the glittering tip up toward her cheek. At the same time she was engulfed by a stench of garlic, gin, and unwashed flesh.

"Don't ye move now, neither o' you. The lady won't be so pretty if I have to use this on her, me lord. So don't you try nothin'."

And then she turned her head ever so slightly and saw Ethan, frozen beside her, his features locked in a stone-cold mask of utter calm. But she could also see the big black pistol stuck against the back of his head—though not the man who held that pistol.

Or the one brandishing the knife an inch from her own face.

"I said *don't move!*" the man behind her roared, and tightened his arm around her throat. The knife angled closer.

Josie gasped, but managed to remain motionless.

"If you hurt my wife, all of England won't save you from me," Ethan said with deadly calm, and for an instant the blade hovered.

Then it eased away, an inch. Two. She heard a rough laugh. "Don't want to hurt her, me lord, but we will if you make any trouble. Now get in there with the rest of 'em. We don't 'ave all night."

And the front door of Lady Tattersall's house slammed shut behind them.

Chapter Twelve

Fear tumbled through Josie as she was shoved into the large drawing room that veered off the hall. Someone pushed her so forcefully, she literally catapulted into the knot of people huddled in front of the sofa, and Josie felt herself caught and steadied by a tiny red-haired woman in a high-necked green gown.

"There, dear, you're all right. Don't be f-frightened," the woman whispered bravely, her fingers clinging to Josie's arm, whether for Josie's benefit or her own was a matter of opinion. Her small lips were trembling, and her velvety brown eyes were very wide, but her doll-like face held a rigid calm as she tried to smile reassuringly.

Behind her, Josie heard rough laughter.

"All right, ladies and gennelmen. Time to hand over yer pretties." A stout man of average height addressed the group in a gravelly tone. She realized that he was the one who had grabbed her, for he held a knife in his heavy gloved hands. He wore dark, patched clothes in poor condition and a black cloth face mask that covered all of his features save for fierce, slitted black eyes. "Tiny's goin' ter make the rounds now and all ye'll 'ave to do is drop all your baubles in this 'ere sack," he growled. "And be quick about it. Wouldn't want your fine supper ter get cold, now would we?"

He gave another guffaw of laughter. Then the tallest, broadest, fattest giant Josie had ever seen lumbered forward with a gunnysack clenched in his bear-sized paw.

It was then that the fog of shock evaporated and everything clicked into place. The men who'd accosted them were none other than Pirate Pete and his cohorts, the very same thieves Mrs. Fielding had spoken of the other night.

Thieves. Josie could scarcely believe it. More of her own special brand of bad luck. She'd escaped Snake Barker and his brutal gang of outlaws only to end up robbed at knifepoint by England's most notorious bandits.

Instinctively, her hands flew to the ruby necklace at her throat, the one that had belonged to Ethan's mother. A tiny sound of dismay escaped her, and she peered quickly over at Ethan, who had been herded with the other men near the far end of the sofa.

But Ethan wasn't looking her way. He was studying Pirate Pete and the third man, the tall, slim, muscular one brandishing the pistol. He, too, wore a black face mask like Pirate Pete and the giant, Tiny.

Oh, please don't let Ethan get himself killed, she prayed instantly. The expression on his face frightened her. Josie had only known Ethan Savage for a short time, but she knew him well enough to be convinced that he wouldn't stand idly by and allow himself to be robbed— not without putting up one hell of a fight.

But how could he fight? He was unarmed. And these men had knives and guns.

Yet one look at his set, cold face told her that Ethan would not let such minor inconveniences stop him.

Tall and lean in his dark evening clothes and white tie,

he stood a little apart from the other men. Far from looking the least bit cowed by the outlaws, he looked faintly bored. But Josie saw the tension in his shoulders, the tautness of his long fingers as he gripped the back of a chair.

And she knew that he would try something, anything, rather than let these thieves make off with his jewels and money without a fight. Panic sparked through her.

He would get himself killed.

Beside Ethan, Oliver Winthrop trembled like a rabbit who'd stumbled into a fox den. He kept rubbing his hands together in a nervous gesture that failed to keep the uneasy twitch from his neck. Beside him was a stocky older gentleman with an imposing mustache and the stern face of a walrus. He was scowling from beneath heavy black brows at the giant who had halted before the ladies and was now holding out the open gunnysack.

"Oh dear, oh dear. Why me?" The buxom woman in the elaborate dress and glittering jewels wailed. Her red face was puffed with fear. Josie guessed that she was Lady Tattersall, for the word "peacock" never could have applied to the tiny auburn-haired woman in her rather old-fashioned plain green dress, and the only other lady present was a rail-thin black-haired beauty with extraordinary lily-white skin and perfect features who was much too young to be Ethan's godmother.

"There are surely scores of dinner parties going on all over the county tonight—why on earth did Pirate Pete have to choose *mine*?" she uttered miserably.

" 'Urry up with it, my lady, or I'll see you 'ave somethin' else ter weep about," Tiny grunted. Josie felt a surge of sympathy for her as she fumbled in terror with the clasp of her diamond necklace.

"Come on! We don't 'ave all night."

Behind the mask, his eyes were opaque and empty, like blank wooden coins. The massive girth and size of him dwarfed all three women, and instilled such terror in Lady Tattersall that her fingers trembled all the more.

"Here, let me help her," Josie said, stepping forward. The small auburn-haired woman gave a small gasp as Josie slipped past Tiny and put a steadying hand on Lady Tattersall's wrist.

"Let me do it," she said quietly.

"Oh, thank you . . . Lady Stonecliff. We haven't been properly introduced, but since you came in with dear Ethan, or actually were pushed in with dear Ethan, I have assumed—"

"Quit yer squawkin'!" Pirate Pete stuck his knife in his belt, strode forward, and without warning, grabbed Lady Tattersall by the throat. He ripped the necklace from her as Josie's fingers fortunately finished unlocking the clasp. "And them rings and earrings, too," he barked.

"And you're next, me li'l pretty," he told Josie, his gaze skimming over the rubies at her ears and throat, then lingering a tad longer over the enticing whiteness of bosom showing above the bodice of her gown.

"Maybe ye'd like ter come with us when we've finished 'ere," he invited with a wide, crooked-tooth grin. "You're a good mite prettier than all these 'ere baubles."

"No, thank you," Josie replied with prim dignity, biting back the urge to tell him that she'd sooner tangle with a barrelful of skunks. She'd already had the dubious pleasure of being an unwilling companion to a band of outlaws, and had no intention of ever doing it again. But it seemed wise not to antagonize Pirate Pete at this moment.

There had already been violence enough in this house tonight. She was still worried about the butler in the hall, and wondered if anyone lay injured elsewhere, needing help.

The sooner the outlaws finished their business and left, the quicker they could take stock of the situation and see what could be done.

So she held her breath until Lady Tattersall had dropped all of her jewels into the gunnysack, then Josie slowly removed the intricate gold-and-ruby earrings.

She hesitated for a moment, glancing at Ethan before dropping them into the bag. He gave her a sharp nod. She let them fall with a soft thud.

"Now the necklace, and that shiny bracelet and yer gold ring. Then you, Blackie, you're next," Pirate Pete told the ebony-haired girl, who looked revolted at having been addressed by such a low personage.

Josie held the necklace a moment too long, loath to drop it in the sack, and Tiny grabbed it from her. "Ye can always 'ave yer rich lord buy you another one," he rasped.

She turned anxious eyes to Ethan as first the necklace and then the bracelet clanked into the bag. The only change in his cool expression was a slightly more pronounced whiteness around his mouth. She knew that if the third man did not have his pistol leveled at the ready, Ethan might have done something very foolish.

Josie forced herself to remain calm as she watched the outlaws relieve the black-haired girl of her jewels, and then move on to the little red-haired woman who was trying so hard not to appear frightened, though her blue-veined hands were trembling. She had little jewelry, only a simple cameo necklace and tiny jet earrings, which she tugged from her ears slowly and then dropped into the sack.

"Not worth nearly as much as the rest of it, but we'll take 'em all the same," Pirate Pete sneered, and suddenly gave the frail-looking woman a shove that sent her sprawling down upon the sofa.

"Miss Perry! Oh, dear God help us!" Lady Tattersall moaned in dismay.

"Don't you dare touch that lady again!" the walrus-faced man shouted.

Pirate Pete ignored them both. "You certain that's all you 'ave?" he demanded of the woman.

Terrified, she nodded, her lips trembling.

"Well, then, it's the gennelmen's turn." He spun away from her in disgust. "Lucian, give over that popper," he ordered the third man, who handed him the pistol. Brandishing it, Pirate Pete surveyed the group of finely dressed men.

Josie prayed again that Ethan would do nothing foolish. *This isn't Abilene and you're not wearing your guns,* she admonished him silently, but she had small hope that such facts would deter him. He looked grim as death, and more than ready to avenge the shaken Miss Perry.

Oliver Winthrop, on the other hand, showed no desire to put up a fight. His valuables went into the bag without his uttering a peep, nor did he even meet the eyes of any of the outlaws as they watched his quick, nervous movements with jeering amusement.

The walrus-faced man was next. Josie could see his chest swell with indignation as he was forced to hand over a heavy gold pocket watch, money, a signet ring, and a jeweled stickpin. He glared at both Pirate Pete and

Tiny, and the helpless rage he obviously felt vibrated through the room. Yet wisely, he refrained from speaking aloud his contempt for the outlaws, and they moved along to plant themselves before Ethan.

"Fork over the lot o' it, yer lorship." Pirate Pete leveled the black pistol at Ethan's heart. "And be quick about it. We still 'ave to get the lady of the 'ouse to show us where her other lovelies are 'idden."

"What?" Lady Tattersall gasped. "Haven't you taken enough? Oh, I shall faint! I cannot bear it. . . ."

Tiny snarled at her outburst, and Pirate Pete rounded on her, his black eyes glinting. "Stop yer screechin', ye old bag o' oats, or Lucian will cut yer tongue out, he will."

At this, Lady Tattersall shrieked, and Lucian yanked a knife from his pocket, a wicked-looking weapon with a long, glittering blade, and stalked toward her.

"Calm yourself, ma'am," Ethan ordered sharply. He turned an icy sneer on the outlaw leader. "Don't you think you've bullied enough women for one night? I've a better proposition for you."

Pirate Pete eyed him suspiciously. But Ethan saw with satisfaction that Lucian had halted his advance on Lady Tattersall, and even Tiny had stopped fingering through the bag of goodies to fix him with a hard blank stare.

"Leave the women alone, and let's finish this business away from this place. If you dare," Ethan suggested with a taunting edge to his voice, "come to my house. Stonecliff Park. It's close by, and contains just as many valuables, perhaps even more. I'll turn them over to you without shrieking, I can promise you that."

"Now why would the likes 'o ye be willin' ter do

that?" Pirate Pete demanded, his finger playing along the trigger of the gun.

"What do you care," Ethan countered with silken calm, "so long as you get your booty?"

It was at this moment that the older gentlemen could contain himself no longer. With an oath he threw himself forward at Pirate Pete and grabbed for the pistol.

Pirate Pete jerked the gun away as the other man tried to wrest it from him. It went off, and the walrus-faced man clutched his arm in rage, all four ladies screamed, and then everything happened at once.

Ethan reached into his boot with lightning speed, drew out a hideaway gun, and fired at Pirate Pete. Tiny threw himself at the outlaw leader at the same time, knocking him out of the way and taking the bullet meant for him. It barely slowed his huge form, though it tore through his massive shoulder. Lucian raised his knife and leapt toward Ethan.

And Josie snatched a candlestick from the table beside her and swung it at Tiny's head.

In the hissing blaze of the gaslamps illuminating that exquisite and very crowded drawing room, pandemonium ensued. Of one mind, Lady Tattersall, Oliver Winthrop, and the black-haired girl scattered toward the French doors off the dining room, while the auburn-haired lady knelt instantly beside the walrus-faced man, handkerchief in hand, and tried in vain to stanch the blood spurting from his arm.

Ethan's hideaway gun went flying as Pirate Pete fell against him, and the next thing Ethan knew, he had his hands full dodging Lucian's viciously thrusting knife. He managed to move in following one quick thrust, and to grab the outlaw's sinewy arm. With a twist, he had the knife. He stabbed brutally, expertly, just once—straight into his attacker's chest.

But at the same moment, he saw Josie strike Tiny with the candlestick.

The giant never even blinked. But he thrust an elbow back at the girl, and sent her spinning to the floor.

Then he turned on her, those blank eyes suddenly lit with unholy rage.

Ethan yanked the knife from Lucian's chest and shoved the man away from him. He lunged toward Tiny, but before he could reach him, he was tackled by Pirate Pete.

"I'll teach ye to try an' pull yer tricks on me!" the outlaw leader roared as he and Ethan went down flailing together on the floral carpet. They rolled sideways into Lady Tattersall's gold-rimmed marble table. It overturned with a crash. Pirate Pete came out on top and raised the pistol to fire down into Ethan's face, but Ethan grabbed his wrist and twisted. A mighty struggle for the gun began.

And in the meantime, Tiny bore down upon Josie, still sprawled, winded, on the floor.

When she looked up to see that huge form advancing on her, she froze. By the time she regained her wits and tried to roll aside, he was upon her. He picked her up as if she were a rag doll, held her with her feet dangling off the ground, and shook her.

Then he set her down with a thump that rattled her teeth, drew back his hand, and struck her full across the face.

Josie staggered back upon the sofa. Blinding pain enveloped her, the way it had the night Snake had beaten her senseless, aching through her bones, her cheeks, her skull. But she wasn't senseless, not yet. Her ears ringing, she pretended that she was. Her heart pounded like an anvil as she felt Tiny's paws seize her, turning her so he could better inspect the damage he'd inflicted.

Standing over her, he spoke gruffly, almost playfully.

"Wake up, you, so's I can give you more what-for."

She half opened her eyes, trying to look dazed. The slow, vicious smile that spread across his massive face filled her with tingling fear. He edged closer, sausage fingers flexing, reaching for her throat. . . .

Josie drew her leg in swiftly, then kicked out as hard as she could. As if she were doing a fierce movement in a wild dance at the Golden Pistol, she kicked him square in the nose with all her strength.

He gave a howl of pain and clutched his face as blood spurted from both nostrils. Before he could try to grab her again, Josie flung herself sideways and off the sofa, darting away.

Tiny started after her. But Miss Perry glanced up from her ministrations of the fallen man and stuck out her foot. Tiny tripped.

But it only slowed him, and did not fell him. He cuffed Miss Perry as he stumbled past, and caught Josie just as she reached the French doors. He seized her arm and twisted it.

"First I'm goin' ter break your arm and then that leg that you kicked me with," he grunted. "And then, me fine lady, I'll bloody *your* nose."

Josie bit back a scream of pain as her arm nearly snapped. She opened her mouth, closed it, felt her knees go slack. He was twisting her arm slowly, smiling all the while, enjoying her pain and her terror.

She never saw Ethan come up behind Tiny. She didn't know that he had managed to wrench the gun away from Pirate Pete, but that in the struggle it had gone clattering across the room, nor did she know that he had landed a blow that left Pirate Pete dazed and dizzy flat on his back on Lady Tattersall's bloodstained carpet.

She only knew that something hit Tiny with savage ferocity from behind, and that the wounded and bleeding giant groaned and released his hold on her arm. Josie sank to the floor, clutching her bruised arm—and saw that, like a huge grizzly bear, Tiny had flung himself about to confront whoever had slammed into him.

And that someone was Ethan Savage.

For a moment, the drawing room blurred and swam before her eyes. As large and strong as Ethan was, Tiny loomed over him. The giant outlaw had been shot through the shoulder and his nose was bleeding, perhaps broken, but he still glared malevolently and stood squarely, menacingly, on two feet.

There was blood on Ethan's face too. His shirt and jacket were ripped, and his dark hair hung in his eyes. But he, too, was steady. And icy calm. He grinned at the other man, a taunting, sneering grin.

"Come and get it, Cyclops. Or do you only fight women?"

"You're askin' fer it, yer lor'ship," Tiny vowed, his eyes glistening with anticipation.

"See how I'm trembling?" Ethan's laugh was colder than mountain snow. "They should have named you Ugly, not Tiny. Ugly, I'm going to bury you."

Tiny didn't know what Cyclops meant, but he knew Ugly. And the contemptuous tone and expression of the other man infuriated him into an even greater state of fury. With a howl he lunged at Ethan, his right fist already swinging.

Josie watched in horror, her heart in her throat.

But Ethan ducked the blow with smooth agility. Off balance from the force of his swing, Tiny tilted forward just as Ethan smashed his fist up into Tiny's chin. The punishing blow resounded like a shot through the drawing room.

Tiny went down on one knee. He blinked in surprise. Ethan slammed another blow down upon the giant's back. And another. This time, soundlessly, the outlaw toppled to the floor.

But Josie saw, just beyond Ethan, that Pirate Pete had crawled to his knees. He shook his head as if clearing his senses. Then he clambered to his feet with surprising alacrity, made a grab for the gunnysack on the floor, and started at a lumbering run toward the hall.

"Behind you—he's got the jewels," she cried, and tried to rise, but Ethan had already wheeled around. He dived after the outlaw leader and managed to snag the gunnysack, but Pirate Pete slipped free of his grasp and bolted from the room.

Josie struggled to stand. Miss Perry needed help nursing the walrus-faced man, Ethan was coming back toward her now, looking worried, and she knew there were better things to do than cry like a baby and dwell upon her own hurts. But dizziness washed over her as she staggered to her feet, and then Ethan stepped over Tiny to scoop her up in his arms and her senses floated for a moment as he carried her to the sofa.

"How badly are you hurt?" he asked as he gently lowered her onto the cushions.

"Not . . . too bad." She bit back a wince. The fury darkening his face shocked her. He looked as if he could kill someone at that moment with his bare hands.

"I'm fine," she murmured faintly. "My arm is sore, but it's not important."

"I'll see both those bastards hanged." Ethan touched her face, brushed a gentle finger across her smooth, fine-boned cheeks that were ashen with pain. The sight of that twisted giant hurting her had filled him with a blood-rage he hadn't felt since he'd gotten news of Molly's death. He hadn't thought anything could affect him like that again.

"Hold on, Josie, while I tie that son of a bitch up—"

There was a crash.

As Josie and Ethan glanced around, they saw Tiny running across Lady Tattersall's darkened garden, leaving in his wake shards of broken glass from the French doors.

"The hell you will . . ." Ethan shot after him, but just as he reached the French doors a soft, desperate voice halted him in his tracks.

"My lord, wait!" Miss Perry quavered as she glanced helplessly up from the side of the fallen man. "I think you'd best fetch a doctor quickly. It seems to me Colonel Hamring is going to die!"

Chapter Thirteen

The next hour was a whirlwind of frantic activity. A number of servants were found trussed or struck unconscious in the stables or the kitchens or the cellar, and one footman was sent for the doctor, another for the village constables.

A blanket was thrown over Lucian's corpse. And Lady Tattersall, Oliver Winthrop, and the black-haired girl—whose name, Josie discovered, was Miss Rosamund Crenshaw—all returned, babbling on and on about their terror, the humiliations they'd endured, the horrible ordeal they'd survived.

Ethan, in the meantime, took over the care of Colonel Hamring and as Josie watched worriedly from the sofa, proved himself to be quite competent at cleansing and stanching the wound, then wrapping it tightly in towels that the housekeeper, once freed from her bonds, brought him at a run.

Each time Josie tried to rise from the sofa to help him or Lady Tattersall or Miss Crenshaw, who had collapsed in a wing chair moaning that she felt faint, Miss Clara Perry drifted to her side and gently pushed her back upon the turquoise damask cushions.

"No, no, my dear—you heard what your husband ordered. You mustn't move until the doctor has seen you and gives you permission to get up."

"But I'm fine."

"Don't listen to her." Ethan spoke over his shoulder as he wound the bandage tight around the Colonel's wound. "She stays put or I'll hog-tie her to that sofa myself."

Miss Perry's velvet-brown eyes grew round. Josie could understand why. There was no mistaking the ruthlessness of Ethan's tone, and the woman didn't know him well enough yet to realize that he was not nearly as imposing a tyrant as he made himself out to be. At least not to Josie.

"But Ethan, you know I have nursing skills," she argued from the sofa, horrified by the weakness of her own voice. She tried again, attempting to sound stronger. "If you'll only let me take a look at the Colonel—"

"No!" Even Josie bit her lips at the dark, quelling glance he threw at her, unmistakable with warning. "Don't move."

So she'd stayed where she was, and Miss Perry had dabbed a cool cloth upon her head, and tenderly examined the bruises on Josie's arms, giving a whimper of distress when she saw them already purpling in the lamplight—and to tell the truth, Josie had been glad to lie still. Her heart was finally beginning to slow down to a normal beat, and the trembling of her body was not as intense as before. But her arm still hurt, the pain throbbing outward in two directions—down the bones leading to her wrist, and up through her shoulder.

But she didn't complain. She tried to smile up at Clara Perry, who was watching her anxiously. Josie whispered, "I've married a very stubborn man."

"Oh, yes, my dear, perhaps," Miss Perry whispered back. "But such a very *handsome* one." Miss Perry then blushed clear up to her hairline.

To try to distract herself from her own pain and the terrifying memory of that moment when it had seemed Tiny would actually rip off her arm, Josie studied the small-boned woman who was now turning the cloth over and laying it gently once more upon her brow.

Miss Clara Perry appeared to be nearing fifty years old. There were tiny spider veins in her delicate hands, and small lines crinkling at the corners of her eyes. She had a sweet wren's face, and soft red hair that curled pleasingly around a countenance that was pure kindness, though her cheeks did appear to be somewhat pinched into perpetual anxiety. Her manners were quiet and humble, as were her clothes. Not for her were the handsome richness of Lady Tattersall's trained, beaded dinner gown, or Miss Crenshaw's elegant peach-and-cream lace. She was Miss Crenshaw's chaperon, Josie remembered, yet even as she pondered this, the black-haired girl intruded into her reverie.

"Cousin Clara! Cousin! Is it possible you can attend to *me* for a moment? Mama sent you up here to join me in Lady Tattersall's company with the hope that you would take care of me, yet here I sit, nearly swooning, and you have yet to bring me any smelling salts!"

"Oh, forgive me, Rosamund dear, but Lady Stonecliff has been dreadfully hurt by that horrid monster and—"

"And we are all most grateful to her," Lady Tattersall interrupted, tottering over on the arm of her footman and peering down at Josie through wide, moist blue eyes. "My dear, how calm you were throughout that dreadful ordeal. Offering to help me when I'm sure that scoundrel would have choked the life out of me only to get that necklace from around my throat. And then actually striking that other man—well, my godson has certainly chosen himself a great and courageous lady!"

Josie felt surprise at the gushing compliments of her hostess. "Th-thank you. But I only did what anyone else would have done," she replied diffidently. Lady Tattersall shook her head.

"No, no, no! The rest of us were quite in a tizzy. Couldn't think or scarcely speak at all!"

As Josie remembered how Lady Tattersall had carried on lamenting her misfortune and annoying the outlaws all the while, she had to hide a smile. "I'm only sorry poor Colonel Hamring is so badly hurt." Anxiously, she peered over as the Colonel let forth a moan.

Ethan adjusted a pillow beneath the Colonel's head, then stood. "He'll live if the damned doctor gets here soon. Ah, here they are," he muttered with relief as the doctor and three sweating, breathless constables rushed in ahead of Lady Tattersall's footmen.

After that, events swirled together in Josie's head. The doctor, upon completing his ministrations to the injured man, pronounced that Colonel Hamring would survive, and ordered that he be carried up to one of the guest bedrooms, where he could be made more comfortable and where he could rest. The lower floor of Lady Tattersall's house became a beehive of frantic activity as the constables took over, carrying Lucian's body outside, searching the grounds, and questioning everyone. Then the gunnysack containing all the jewels was opened and all the stolen property returned to the rightful owners.

With painstaking care, the constables wrote down all that had happened. After conferring among themselves, they spoke solemnly about this being the second incident of Pirate Pete and his cohorts' moving from London to rob people in their homes in the country—the first such robbery in Sussex.

"At least this time they didn't get away with the booty," Sergeant Webb muttered, with a nod of acknowledgment to Ethan. "And the scoundrels lost one of their own."

"I am offering a reward, Sergeant, for the capture of Pirate Pete and the man known as Tiny." Ethan glanced at each of the police officers in turn, his eyes very hard, leaving no doubt of his resolve. "Ten thousand pounds to anyone who provides information leading to their arrest. Let's see if that smokes out someone who knows where these curs skulk and hide."

"An excellent idea, my lord. Most of them in the rookery are likely scared to death of Pirate Pete—he's killed four men already, so far as we know—but for a sum like that, someone's sure to give over a bit of information. But, sir, I suggest you take care. Once word gets out, Pirate Pete won't take kindly to having a price on his head. Things might get tight for him, if you know what I mean. And also . . ."

Sergeant Webb paused, choosing his words. "Pirate Pete has a reputation as a man who won't take any slight lightly. He's bound to be nettled with you for killing one of his men, and foiling him tonight. You may want to take extra care for yourself, and your lady, if you know what I mean."

"I know exactly what you mean." Ethan's gaze shifted to rest upon Josie, motionless and pale on the sofa. "I'll take care of what's mine," he said grimly.

Josie gave her head a shake as he advanced toward her.

She knew what he was planning even before he reached out his arms.

"I'm able to walk," she protested. "It's my arm that is hurt. My feet are in good working order, Ethan."

"Yes, my lord, that's exactly right. You ought to take good care of the sweet dear," Miss Perry cried approvingly as the Earl of Stonecliff swept up his bride as if she weighed no more than a kitten.

"Cousin Clara!" Miss Crenshaw snapped. The sight of the handsome earl carrying that chestnut-haired girl in his arms as if she were some fragile treasure that might break filled her with unreasonable jealousy. She was in her second Season and no one in or out of London had yet looked at her with the kind of intensity she had seen sizzling in the Earl of Stonecliff's eyes when he gazed at his bride.

"I have a headache, Clara," she sniffed piteously. "I require rest, a glass of ratafia, a cool cloth—I need you to attend to me, if you can spare yourself from fawning over Lady Stonecliff. . . ."

The black-haired girl's voice faded disconsolately away as the young countess was carried across the drawing room.

"There, there." Comfortingly, Lady Tattersall patted Rosamund Crenshaw's arm. "We'll all feel much more the thing tomorrow, I daresay. Though I shan't sleep a wink all night."

"Nor I," Oliver Winthrop declared. He mopped his brow with an already sopping handkerchief. "Sergeant, I require your men to see me back to my inn. The Green Duck. And a guard must be posted outside all through the night."

Josie didn't hear the police sergeant's reply for Ethan

bore her into the hall without so much as a backward glance or a good night. Lady Tattersall's belated farewell echoed through the hall after them, but he didn't slow his steps or respond in any way.

"How rude of you," she murmured as he carried her effortlessly down the dark, tree-lined drive toward the carriage.

"Seems I'm rusty on all the little niceties," he growled, his arms tightening around her as he glanced down at her wan face. The moonlight revealed the weariness and pain behind her eyes, though she tried to hide it with a weak smile. But she couldn't hide her beauty, shining out like a luminous moonbeam, even after what she'd been through. And she couldn't hide her strength either. Ethan was remembering how steady she'd been through the entire ordeal, how she'd tried to help Lady Tattersall, how she'd swung that candlestick at Tiny when she thought *he* was in danger.

And it had cost her dearly.

Somewhere inside of him, he vowed that Tiny would one day pay, and pay in spades, for what he'd done to her.

"What is it? You look so fierce," Josie whispered as they neared the carriage and the footman threw open the door.

"It's nothing. It needn't concern you."

Nestled against the implacable solidity of his chest, Josie marveled at how safe and comforted she felt. Pampered. A unique feeling. No one had ever paid much attention to her hurts or her feelings. She was sure that it was only for show, however—that for the sake of their charade, Ethan was determined to demonstrate to everyone how solicitous he was of his "wife."

That was why, when they were settled in the carriage,

and quite alone, she was surprised to find him still watching her intently, a worried frown between his brows.

"You don't have to fuss over me anymore, Ethan. No one is watching."

"I'm not fussing over you."

"What do you call it then?"

"Taking care of you." His tone was curt. "You had a bad time of it tonight. And you handled it admirably."

Josie lifted her shoulders in a shrug. "It's not the first time I've been around brutes and thieves," she explained.

She was so matter-of-fact that anger twisted through him. Anger at the rough times she had known, of experiences that must have branded her for better or worse, where possibly—if it was true that she was an orphan— no one had been there to look out for her, to give a damn if she was hurt or afraid or alone.

With a flash of shame he remembered how roughly he'd treated her that first day in the alley, and again on the train.

"We were all so worried about Colonel Hamring that no one thought to ask *you*." Josie's luminous violet eyes were turned upon him with such vibrant concern that for a moment Ethan lost himself in them. "Are you all right?" she asked, searching his face. "Are you hurt?"

"I've been hurt worse."

"What you did tonight—I've never seen anything so brave. You fought all three of them, with no one to help you."

"You helped me."

She smiled ruefully, shook her head. "I tried, but—"

"You helped. It took courage to go after Tiny that way. And look what it got you," he added, suddenly reaching for her arm. Gently he lifted it, pulled back the sleeve of her gown, and in the lamplight studied the bruises marring her pale flesh.

The icy fury coiled tighter inside him. Suddenly a vision of Molly flashed into his brain. He remembered Molly's pain, Molly's suffering. Molly's death. All because of him.

He cursed under his breath and released her, throwing himself back in his seat. "If you want out of our deal, just say so," he said in a short, hard voice that held an undercurrent of tension so powerful, it vibrated through the air. "I won't hold you to it under the circumstances."

"What circumstances?"

"There's a cutthroat gang that might come after me, according to the constable. You didn't bargain on that when we set up this marriage arrangement. I'll put you on a ship for America tomorrow if you want to cut your losses and run."

"Where I come from, a deal is a deal."

"Not if I say you can break it."

She shook her head, and several wispy curls that had escaped their pins during the fray tumbled into her eyes. She pushed them back. "I'm not interested in breaking it," she told Ethan in a low tone, wondering why he looked so grim, why he was suddenly willing to forfeit everything when before it had seemed so important.

He was silent, staring at her. "So. You must enjoy living the high life. Willing to take risks to keep the fancy roof over your head, all these pretty dresses . . . it's only for six months, sweetheart," he reminded her coldly now, for part of him hoped she would decide to run for it, to bolt back to America. He didn't want her blood on his conscience, too. He was suddenly beginning to feel that he was very bad luck for beautiful women.

"I have my reasons," she said in a quiet tone, and there was a flush of pride in her cheeks now, one that enhanced the brilliance of her eyes, and made her look all the more stunning as she sat in his carriage, her back very straight against the ruby velvet squabs.

"So you're staying the course."

"That's right."

"And you're not afraid."

I'm more afraid of returning to America—of having Snake find me. Of never locating Alicia Denby, of discovering who I am. And of never seeing you again.

But aloud she said the other truth that was rolling around in her head. "I don't believe you'd let anything awful happen to me."

Silence filled the carriage. Outside, the darkness was thick and close, but for the faint sheen of moonlight silvering the treetops and hedges that lined the road. She saw Ethan's brows draw together, sensed the tension ricocheting through him. For a moment he looked thunderstruck, then he gained control of himself and bit out with a savagery that quickened her heartbeat, "How can you trust me so much when I don't trust you worth a damn?"

When she just stared at him, he leaned forward and cupped her chin imperatively. "Answer me." The words seemed torn from him.

They brought forth an answering torrent from her.

"I saw you back there. You fought all of them. You weren't even afraid. You protected me. No one's ever done that." She rushed on, the words tumbling out. "And another thing. You speak your mind—not many people do, at least, not many I've known. So often they'd come to the orphanage and say they wanted to adopt a child— to raise and care for one—but when they brought me home with them, all they really wanted was someone to do chores and ease the burden on their farms or in their stores. You've set out what you expect me to do, and you've been plain about it from the start."

His eyes glinted at this, and she hurried on, trying to finish before she became too embarrassed and lost her nerve. "And there's more. I sense something in you . . . I can't explain it, but I don't think you'd let anything happen to me. You're not that kind of man."

"You have no idea what kind of man I am." It was a snarl, ripped from his throat. Where before he had seemed restrained, almost approachable, now she saw fury.

"Why are you so angry?" Josie took a breath, alarmed by the rigid tautness of that lean face, by the granite flash of his eyes.

"Because I trust you? Because maybe I—"

"What?"

"Like you . . . a little."

"You're a fool." He leaned back in his seat and laughed at her, a cold, hard, infuriating laugh that hurt more than if he'd struck her across the face. "I've done nothing to make you like me or trust me. And as for me, there are few people I like, and fewer even that I trust. And you're not among them, my fine little thief. But I'm responsible for you, so I'll see you come to no harm while you're . . . what? Married to me? In my employ? Which term best describes our little arrangement?"

"No words can do justice to it," Josie cried, stung. She was shaking now, fighting back tears. The tentative emotions of trust and warmth had vanished, and anger was seeping in. Anger with herself as much as with him, for having dared let down her guard for a moment. She'd mistaken his playacting concern for the real thing, she'd actually told him that she liked him, she'd tried to be a friend to him and he was turning it on her, making her feel a fool.

You are a fool, a frantic voice sneered inside of her head. *To feel about him as you do. He hates you. You're nothing but the worst kind of stupid, senseless fool.*

Tears burned. She turned her face away and stared blindly out of the carriage window. Suddenly her arm hurt again, but not nearly as much as her heart. She longed for Stonecliff House, for the solitude of her room, her bed, to be free of his presence, free to weep in privacy, to soak her pillow with tears, and pour out all the agony of her heart.

The carriage ride home seemed endless. When the horses halted at last in the sweeping drive, Josie flung herself at the carriage door before the footman could even jump down to open it. She leapt out into the fresh night air, and clutching her skirt, started at a run up the walk, but Ethan was there beside her in a flash, his hand heavy on her shoulder, spinning her around.

"Spooked you, have I? Now you see why it doesn't pay to think of me as a friend."

"If you mean that you've driven me away from that idiotic notion—yes, you have. Now I'm tired. My arm hurts, and if you'd *kindly* let me go, I want my bed."

He wanted her bed too. With her in it.

The realization came as a shock. An unwelcome one that pierced him with terrifying reality.

And somehow he couldn't let her go. His fingers circled her uninjured wrist, and the other arm snaked about her waist. He was oblivious of the footman discreetly driving the carriage off to the stables, oblivious of the scent of late roses and freshly cut grass that wafted in the darkness. Oblivious of everything but her.

A war was raging inside Ethan at that moment. Lord help him, she was incredible, standing beneath the moon in the shadow of Stonecliff Park, the wind whipping her hair around her face, her delicate jaw taut with anger, and pure feminine fire flashing from her amethyst eyes. He ought to let her go, he ought to bolt across the gardens and meadows of Stonecliff and dive into that pond, let the chill water crash through his heated body and banish the desire raging in his loins.

He had called her a fool. But he was the fool. Because he wanted her.

Wanted a beautiful thief who couldn't be trusted. A woman who held his future within her dainty hands, who could ruin him or blackmail him if she chose, if he let her have even a small bit of power over him. A woman who might face danger now because of him.

She's not Molly, an inner voice shouted.

She's nothing like Molly.

But for the first time since Molly died, he wanted one woman, one particular woman with a need that burned through his bones, that seared his soul, that ripped through him more agonizingly than a thousand arrows.

There were a dozen reasons to stay as clear of her as possible, to feel nothing, to think of her as only a pawn in this game he played with his dead father's tyrannical will.

A dozen reasons to subdue the emotions she evoked in him despite all his resolutions and his resolve.

And only one reason to keep her here within his arms,

to draw her closer, as he was doing now, to lower his lips toward hers.

"No!" she murmured in a ragged tone, and tried to pull away.

"Yes." Ethan yanked her back. "I need . . . to . . ." For once in his life, he was at a loss for words. Confusion filled him, a most undesirable emotion, and because of it he latched on to the one reason he could justify to himself, the one reason he could give her for why he was hanging on to her for dear life.

"I'll prove to you that I can't be trusted. That you should be as wary of me as you would be of Tiny, or of that man you were running from in Abilene. You should run from me too. I'm worse than all of them."

"That I believe," she cried, panicking because what she saw in his eyes was raw and wild and dark, and it reminded her of Snake.

"You're about to believe more."

She trembled all over at the ruthlessness in his tone, at the dangerous nearness of him as his face loomed over hers.

"Consider this a warning of what will happen if you try to get near me, try to manipulate me."

"I wasn't . . . I was being honest, trying to be your friend."

"Big mistake." He wanted to scare her, he told himself as he clamped her against him. To keep her from reaching out to him again, from touching him, not literally with her fingers, but with that haunting trust in her eyes, be it real or phony.

He had to drive her away.

So he pulled her close, closer, until her breasts were crushed against his chest, and her slender body trembled like a windblown flower in his grasp, and then he lowered his mouth to hers and kissed her.

He wanted it to be a hard kiss, a frightening kiss, one that would make her fear that he'd betray their initial agreement, that if she didn't keep her distance and watch her step, he wouldn't think twice about breaking his pledge.

It started out that way, and he heard her whimper as his lips captured hers, and dominated them with a harsh power that was meant to terrify her. But as she tried fearfully to wrench away, something in the pitiful effort smote him. And something in those silken, vibrant lips affected him in a completely unexpected way, turning his anger to a different kind of heat, jolting and equally powerful, but tempered with a gentleness that stunned him as the kiss evolved into one of inexplicable tenderness.

Instantly, the fearful tension drained from her stiffened body. He felt the quiver slide all through her. And most startling of all, her warm, sweet mouth parted, gasped, and clung to his.

"Ethan, oh, Ethan," she whispered in wonder, and he was rocked by the effect her soft voice had on him.

This wasn't working out the way he'd planned.

"Unless you like playing with dynamite, sweetheart, don't try to be anything to me but what you were hired to be—a phony wife." He tried to sound sneering and cold, but his hands were circling her waist, tracing the provocative outline of her hips, even as he breathed in the sunshine-and-honey scent of her.

"We have a bargain," Josie heard herself saying as she tried frantically to summon the shreds of reason. But her senses were swimming. The solid muscular feel of his torso and long, hard thighs pressed against her, heated her blood. He smelled of soap and sweat, and in the moonlight his bronzed skin and glinting eyes looked so fiercely male, it took her breath away. And when he'd kissed her—he'd been trying to be cruel, she knew, for she'd read his mood and sensed the anger in him, but he hadn't hurt her, hadn't inflicted pain the way Snake had. There was no meanness in him. His mouth had devoured, tormented, and commanded hers, but she'd never been afraid.

And she'd never felt so alive.

"Sure we do. A bargain. Right." Mockery edged his tone. His hand twisted in her hair, forcing her head back. And his thumb traced the fragile line of her cheek in a taunting caress.

Once again, fear crept back. Josie stared at him, wide-eyed, as the last wisps of pleasure ebbed.

"You promised."

"Sure, sweetheart. That I'd keep my distance so long as you did your part. But your part doesn't include trying to draw me into your web."

"I'm not—"

"Under your spell."

"I'm not!" Trembling, Josie tried to wrench free, but he held her easily. The power in him frightened her. Her eyes blazed up into his as sanity and anger and trepidation flooded back. She despised him. What he aroused in her was so contradictory, so confusing, she felt as if she were being torn asunder. And she didn't care for it one bit.

Part of her was being drawn into *his* web, under *his* spell. He had awakened wants and needs and glorious sensations she'd never imagined. And the other part of her, the cool, sensible part, was furious. She felt trapped, vulnerable, for she had begun to let herself care, begun to dream that he might care for her as well, if only a little—and it wasn't true. He cared only for his plan, for their arrangement, for keeping her in line and under his control.

"Let me go."

"Had enough? You'd think a con woman and thief would be made of sterner stuff."

"I've had more than enough! Being manhandled by Tiny was plenty for one evening, I don't need to be manhandled by you as well. You're hurting my arm."

Hell and damnation. He'd forgotten about her arm. In chagrin Ethan released her with an abruptness that left her stumbling. He took a step backward, breathing hard, deliberately putting space between them.

"Go," he muttered between clenched teeth. His eyes were narrowed on her shaken face, his whole body tense with the rigid control it took not to touch her.

"For God's sake, *go!*"

The shouted command sent her running, her skirts gathered in one hand. He watched her flee up the walk, push open the heavy door, and disappear inside.

And slowly, struggling for reason and control, for understanding of his own dark feelings and behavior, for *sanity,* Ethan followed.

※⚡⚡⚡※

Josie tossed her bag, fan, and gloves onto a chair and rushed to the bureau where she had hidden her precious pouch beneath layers of silk gloves, shawls, and handkerchiefs. She dumped the contents into her hands, and clutched the brooch and the ring tight, as if drawing strength and sustenance from their glowing forms.

To hell with Ethan Savage! She had a purpose in being here far more important than this sham she had agreed to for his sake. And the sooner she was able to leave Stonecliff Park and this horrible mockery of a marriage behind and commence her search, the better!

Trembling, she forced her thoughts along a sensible path. Her brooch and Miss Denby's ring were part and parcel of the same set, she was certain of it. What if they were family jewels? Her family's jewels? That was far more important than winning a smile, a kind word, a damned insulting *kiss* from Ethan Savage!

She had to find Alicia Denby.

And she would. She would think about how best to do that, and forget about Ethan Savage, his conflicts with his father, and the mysterious past with the woman Oliver Winthrop had referred to—the very mention of which had driven Ethan to violence.

She no longer cared!

Pacing like a lioness about her room, she drove his dark, intensely masculine image from her mind, banished the gentleness with which he'd carried her to the carriage, the passion with which he'd kissed her outside only a short while ago—drowning each memory and feeling in rising waves of cleansing anger.

Seizing the jewels and stuffing them back into the pouch, she replaced them in the bottom of the drawer and somehow managed to undress and fling herself into bed without allowing herself to reflect another moment upon the wild events of this night.

Each time a thought of Ethan Savage—of his words, his arousing touches or deep, wicked kisses—intruded into her mind, she flung it away.

She would make a fool of herself no more. And she'd steer clear of him all right. If that's what he wanted, that's exactly what'd he get.

She tensed when she heard him enter the adjoining bed-chamber, but his footsteps came nowhere near her door.

And at last Josie drifted off to sleep, but it was a fitful, unhappy sleep, from which she awoke often. And when she did sleep she dreamed uneasy dreams—blurred, unnerving visions of Snake and Tiny and Pirate Pete creeping through her mind.

At one point she screamed, and bolted up, hugging herself in the darkened room, shivering in the cool rose-scented night air that floated through the open window. The silence hummed around her.

And as her heartbeat slowed and the blood stopped pounding through her head, she realized that she probably hadn't screamed aloud at all. It was all a dream. Only a dream.

She'd been dreaming that Snake found her. He'd trapped her here in this very room, he'd demanded the stolen loot she'd run off with, and the jewels from the stagecoach robbery. And he'd jeered at her that she was going to pay for leaving him—and even more for stealing from him.

The merciless smile on his face had frozen her blood. And then, in her dream, he'd clenched his fists and his eyes had glittered with that vicious light she knew so well and he'd come at her . . .

Go back to sleep, she whispered to herself in the dark, as goose bumps prickled her flesh. *Snake is far away in America. He has no idea where you are.*

It was only a dream.

❈❈❈❈ ❈❈❈❈

Sedalia, Missouri

Penny Callahan beamed across the table at Rose MacEwen as the two former dance hall girls chatted over lemonade in the gingham-curtained dining room of Grover's Hotel.

"I'm so glad you left the Golden Pistol, too, Rose. It's good you got away from Judd Stickley and that whole life. You'll like it here in Sedalia, I just know you will."

"I'll like it better if I meet a handsome young farmer like you did," Rose retorted, laughing. For the first time in years, her heart was filled with hope and happiness. It had only taken a letter from Penny telling her of her good fortune in having met and become engaged to Ben Winters to convince her to try her luck in a new place, starting a new life.

"It seems like Sedalia's a real nice town," Rose added, glancing out the window at the women bustling along the boardwalk with children in tow, at the sunny street crowded with wagons and horses and buggys.

"It is. Oh, it is, Rose. And you'll meet Ben tonight. He's bringing a neighbor along to have supper with us—this man's a farmer like Ben. He has the nicest smile. And he wants to meet my pretty young friend from Kansas."

"Thanks, Penny." Rose shrugged, not wanting to appear too excited. But it would be wonderful to meet a man who only knew her as Rose's friend, and not as a dance hall girl. Who knew what might happen?

"Don't thank me. Thank Josie Cooper. If it hadn't been for her, I'd still be trapped back at the Golden Pistol taking orders from Judd."

The fair-haired man at the table behind that of the two women set his fork down on his plate of boiled mutton and went still as a stump.

"I know." Her pixie face solemn, Rose leaned toward Penny. "I never met anyone like Jo before. She was always willing to go out on a limb for me, or for any one of us."

"She gave me the last of her money so I could take the stage out of town and leave Judd before he knew what I was doing. If she hadn't talked me into it and pushed the money on me, I never would have met my Ben, and Judd would still be . . . still be . . ."

Penny flushed at the memories of how she'd let Judd Stickley into her bed anytime he chose because she'd been too scared of losing her job to refuse him.

"And if you hadn't gotten away, Penny, I never would have thought of leaving the Golden Pistol either," Rose mused. She traced a finger around the rim of her glass. "But I sure hope Jo's okay."

The man at the table behind them waved away a waitress who tried to remove his nearly empty plate. His slate-blue eyes shone as he shifted forward in his chair, listening.

"When I heard she married that handsome gunman in Judge Collins's study that night and hightailed it out of town with him, I nearly fainted," Rose continued. She took another sip of lemonade. "The judge's wife told Mrs. Lorrimer at Mason's General Store that they were headed for New York City—and then *London, England*." She shook her head in amazement. "Seems that gunfighter is some sort of English lord. The Earl of someplace."

"Imagine our Jo married to an earl—that makes her

almost a princess or something," Penny exclaimed, her hazel eyes dancing.

"I just hope she's happy. He was sure a handsome cuss, but Jo was trying to run away from him last I heard." Slowly, Rose lifted worried eyes to Penny's face.

"Want to know what I think? If Jo didn't want to be with that hombre, she'd find some way to get away from him." Penny nodded, aware that she wanted to believe that the friend who had helped her escape Judd Stickley was now as happy as she herself was. "She told me once about her husband—she was scared to death of him. Not that she would admit it—Jo's not like that, you know. But I could tell by the look in her eyes when she talked about him."

"I know. She told me she didn't ever want another husband—and now, poor kid, she's got herself one."

"But maybe she's loco in love with him. He could be rich. And you said he was handsome, didn't you, Rose?"

"Terrible handsome." Rose nodded emphatically.

"Then let's drink to Josie," Penny said, grinning. She lifted her glass of lemonade. "Let's hope her new life is as wonderful as mine . . . and as yours is going to be, Rose."

The women clinked glasses and giggled.

Behind them, the fair-haired man with the stubbly blond beard shoved back his chair and strode from the dining room.

He found Spooner, Deck, and Noah in the corner saloon and pulled himself up a chair. "Boys." He grinned at the three of them. "I just had me a spell of powerful good luck. Seems I know where my bitch wife made off to."

"Does that mean we're going after her?" Deck tossed his cigar butt on the floor and ground it with his shabby-booted heel. "We're gonna get back all that loot and them jewels we took off that English lady?"

"Damn straight we are. We head out today." Snake grinned at his cousin and reached for the bottle of whiskey in the center of the table.

"Well, all right!" Noah whooped. "Won't little Josie be surprised?"

"Sure she will. And soon as I catch up with her, I'm gonna skin my little honey alive for thinking she could jest up and leave me like that. Yes, sir, I surely will."

Snake's ice-blue eyes lit with anticipation as he tilted the bottle back and drank. His rough-hewn handsome face glowed. Nobody crossed Snake Barker and got away with it. Especially not some uppity woman. And when he'd finished teaching his stupid slut of a wife a lesson for stealing from him and running off behind his back, why, that skinny little Josephine Cooper Barker would sure wish he'd just gone and killed her.

But Snake knew mere killing was too good for her.

"Uh, Snake?" Spooner broke into his reverie, his tone uneasy. "What about the big payroll coming through on the stage next week? We got the job all planned."

"So?"

"So maybe we should just forget about Josie, leastways for a while, and stick to business. There's gonna be a pile of money on that stage—"

"I don't give a red-hot damn about that stage!" His face red with fury, Snake surged up from his chair, grabbing Spooner by the collar and yanking him forward across the table.

As several men in the saloon turned to stare at him, he froze, glaring at Spooner, then plopped back down and took a deep breath.

"I want my wife back, boys," he rasped in a lowered tone, but one that left no doubt of his determination. "You hear? I want her—and everything she took from me. And I'm gonna get her. So boys, you and me are going on a little trip."

"Where, Snake?" Deck asked eagerly, licking his thin lips with anticipation.

Snake gulped the last of the whiskey and wiped his mouth on his sleeve before he answered. The words danced from his tongue.

"England, boys. We're goin' to take us a boat to London, England."

Chapter Fourteen

Josie tossed and turned all the rest of the night and awoke groggily to the song of birds in the garden. Her arm hurt the moment she sat up, and with the pain came a rush of memory.

"No, no, no," she groaned, plopping back down among the pillows. It wasn't only the nightmare of the robbery that made her close her eyes tight, but the memory of that scene with Ethan. She still smarted at the sting of his treatment of her. She wouldn't ever let her guard down with him again, ever even consider reaching out to him as a friend—or anything else.

She ought to stay clear of him. She *wanted* to stay clear of him. Yet she found herself jumping out of bed immediately after entertaining this thought, and wondering if she would see him downstairs at breakfast.

With this in mind, she hurried through her toilette, selected a pretty floral muslin gown, and brushed her hair until it shone. It fell in gleaming waves, loose and luxurious, then she tamed it into a quick chignon before leaving her room to make her way through the long hall that led to the stairs. She wasn't trying to impress Ethan

Savage, she told herself, squaring her shoulders as her hand closed on the banister. Or even hoping to see him.

No, she just wanted to look her part, and that meant not going about this exquisite house like a ragamuffin. She had to look nice in order to play her role—the servants would certainly raise their brows if she came down in her old gingham, with her hair tangled like a mop. So she told herself as she entered the dining room, her heart beating a bit faster as she anticipated seeing Ethan at the head of the long table.

But he wasn't there. The dining room was empty, save for the dazzling bouquet of fresh-cut summer roses nestled in a crystal vase at the center of the table and the silver coffeepot and china cups set out on the sideboard.

"Oh, my lady—such a surprise." Mrs. Fielding had been bustling toward the back hallway when she saw her new mistress from the corner of her eye. She hurried into the dining room after Josie, her arms full of fresh linen. "Never did I expect you would be awake and about so early—nor that you'd come down for your breakfast. His lordship gave specific orders that you were not to be disturbed for any reason, and that Devon should bring you a tray in bed. And indeed, my lady, after all that has happened—"

"You know about the robbery? Ethan told you?"

"Oh, yes, my lady." The housekeeper clicked her tongue in dismay. "How horrid for you, and for everyone in that house. I won't sleep a wink tonight thinking on it! His lordship went out a short time ago to see how Colonel Hamring fares this morning. Dear me, what a sweet boy he is—Lord Stonecliff, I mean." She blushed and shifted the linen in her arms. "I beg your pardon, but I can't help feeling pride at what a fine man our young master has turned out to be. Seems like only yesterday he was a wee child, and now he's a grown man—and such a strong, handsome man at that."

Yes, and a cynical, irritating one as well. Josie slanted a glance at the housekeeper as she poured herself coffee at the sideboard. "It's difficult for me to imagine my husband as a *sweet boy,* Mrs. Fielding. But since you knew him in those days, I'll take your word for it."

"Oh, yes, indeed, my lady. He was ever one to be asking questions, mind you, and loved to tag about with the gamekeepers and the gardeners and the grooms, especially Ham, I recall—but never was there a kinder, more thoughtful child. . . . Well, now, listen to me running on." She shook her head and smiled apologetically as her mistress took a thoughtful sip of coffee. "It's good to have him back, that's all I'm meaning to say. After that last to-do he had with the old earl, I never thought to see Master Ethan on our good English soil again. But one never knows how things are going to turn out now, does one?"

"No, I suppose not." Josie took a breath, hesitating. She desperately wanted to ask Mrs. Fielding about the rift that had occurred between Ethan and his father, but she knew it wasn't the "ladylike" thing to do. Mr. Latherby would have scolded her like a squawking old crow, and Ethan . . .

Ethan would be mad as hell if he caught her questioning the servants about him behind his back. Still, she was just angry enough with him to go ahead and do it.

She opened her mouth to ask the question, changed her mind, and instead took a gulp of coffee, cursing her own scruples. Before she could make up her mind whether or not to proceed, she was rescued from her dilemma by Mrs. Fielding. The housekeeper recalled herself to her own position, and to her duty toward the mistress of the house.

"Begging your pardon, my lady, for talking your ear off. If you'd like, I'll see to your breakfast."

"Don't bother, Mrs. Fielding, there's no need to go to all that trouble. I'll just mosey on down—I mean, go into the kitchen and scramble myself an egg. . . ."

Her voice trailed off. The housekeeper looked as horrified as if she'd suggested going down to the stables and munching on straw and manure.

"My lady, it's no trouble, none at all," Mrs. Fielding assured her in faint tones. "If you'll only care to have a seat here in the dining room you'll be quite comfortable, and I won't be but a minute."

She vanished before Josie could protest. Josie stared after her, realizing she'd made a serious mistake. With a sigh, she set down her cup and went to the window, gazing out at the lovely peaceful lawns and yew-rimmed gardens dappled by sunlight.

The trouble was, she wasn't accustomed to being *useless*. She could probably whip up a breakfast every bit as tantalizing as Cook's, and in less time. But she was expected to steer clear of the kitchen and allow herself to be waited upon.

It shouldn't be so hard, she thought with a wry shrug. It's what many people dream of. But she wasn't used to being idle, to not having a purpose each day, work to do, something to accomplish.

You do have something to accomplish, she reminded herself as she slipped into a chair. You have to see your arrangement with Ethan the Terrible through to the end, send some money off to Mrs. Guntherson at the orphanage for the children—and find Alicia Denby.

A thought occurred to her as the dining room doors swung open and Mrs. Fielding breezed in, followed by John and Rupert bearing trays with silver-covered platters.

"Mrs. Fielding," Josie said as the footmen busied themselves setting out an enormous breakfast on the sideboard, "I wonder if you happen to know of an acquaintance of mine—I met her when she was in America recently. Her name is Miss Denby. Miss Alicia Denby."

She held her breath as the housekeeper tilted her head to one side, considering. "No, my lady. I don't believe so. Lord Stonecliff and Mr. Hugh never did entertain much in this house—except for a hunting party now and again. So we didn't have many dinners or card parties or such. I'm sorry, my lady."

"That's all right. If Ethan still intends to go to London today, I imagine I'll meet some people—make the acquaintance of some who might know Miss Denby."

"Aye, my lady, that you might. His lordship has already informed us that he plans to set out early this afternoon."

Beaming, the housekeeper surveyed the spread upon the sideboard with approval, then took her leave.

Alone once more in the sunlit dining room, Josie shook off a twinge of disappointment. What had she expected, that she would find Miss Denby on the first try?

It would take more luck than she'd ever known to track the girl down. But what she lacked in luck, Josie knew, she made up for in sheer grit and persistence. Now that she had actually taken the first step in trying to find Miss Denby, even while she was still "married" to Ethan Savage, she felt better. She would make it a point to become at least polite acquaintances with several fashionable people in London and continue asking until she found someone who knew of her. That way, when this farce of a marriage ended—if not before—she'd be ready to move forward.

The idea that she might at last be near to tracking down Miss Denby, and to learning something definite about her own parentage and how she came to have the brooch, sent what little appetite Josie had sailing out the window.

She nibbled at bread and jam, tasted a forkful of eggs, and sipped half a cup of coffee. Her eyes shone with dreams of the future. But when she shook herself, and glanced at the sideboard, she returned to the present with a jolt. Her breakfast was done—and a mountain of food still remained.

Josie's eyes narrowed. She thought of how the children in Mrs. Guntherson's care would squeal with joy over the repast that had been offered her. And what of the poor people right here in England? According to what Mr. Latherby had told her, there were teeming slums in London filled with men, women, and children living in squalor, most of whom would no doubt sell their souls for such a meal.

She pushed back her chair and went in search of Mrs. Fielding.

"I scarcely touched my breakfast," she said crisply, as the housekeeper, who had been showing one of the housemaids in the small withdrawing room the correct way to polish the lamps, turned away from the task to give her mistress her full attention.

"And I wish what is left of the meal to be distributed among those who are needy here in the area. There are needy people here in the country, aren't there?"

"Well, yes, my lady." The housekeeper looked doubtful. "Many. But—"

"Is there any reason why it can't be done?"

"No, my lady, of course not. But the late earl never—"

"The late earl is dead. And I am mistress of this house now." Josie smiled pleasantly, but her tone was firm. She ignored the freckled maid who gaped at her in stupefaction. "I would like Rupert or Charles or one of the grooms to distribute the food to those who need it. And also, Mrs. Fielding—"

"Yes, my lady?" the housekeeper quavered as Josie broke off, thinking.

"Is there an orphanage in the area?"

"Not here in Sussex, my lady. I believe there is one in Kent County. It is more than an hour's drive from here."

"I'll want to visit it when I return from London—to bring some food and blankets and clothing for the children. Will you help me to collect what I need? I would imagine there are probably piles of old but useful things packed away in attics or spare rooms all about this house."

"Yes, my lady. Of course there are. I'll be happy to assist you." There was a newly respectful expression in Mrs. Fielding's eyes now. Josie smiled.

"Thank you. We'll do that as soon as I return. I wish I had some idea how long we're going to be in London."

But before she had time to ponder this further, Perkins appeared in the doorway.

"Lady Tattersall to see you, my lady."

And Josie had to set aside her newfound project, and concentrate on remembering her lessons as she walked slowly and sedately to the drawing room to receive her guest.

Lady Tattersall looked none the worse for wear this morning. Her saffron gown was as elegant as ever, and every curl on her head was immaculately arranged beneath a small, feathered hat where silk grapes were clustered together in a tight band of gold satin.

"Dear Ethan came by a short time ago to see Colonel Hamring and I just had to repay his kindness and see how *you* were faring, Lady Stonecliff." At Josie's invitation she seated herself on the pale green sofa and clasped her fan between her gloved hands in a dramatic fashion. "Ah, my dear, do you mind if I call you Josephine?"

"Please do, ma'am," Josephine managed to utter before Lady Tattersall raced on.

"Well, Josephine, I am mortified, absolutely mortified, that such horrid, unspeakable violence took place in my home and befell my guests. Can you ever forgive me?"

"There is nothing to forg—"

"When I think how close we all came to losing our lives . . . well, it doesn't bear thinking about, now does it? Thank God for Ethan—so amazing the way he subdued those cutthroats, was it not? And, of course, Colonel Hamring behaved with great bravery. And you, my dear! You were positively heroic!"

"Oh, no, not really."

"Yes, yes. I must say, when I heard that dear Ethan had married a young woman from America, I wondered what kind of a person she might be, because the last girl he took up with was totally unacceptable—though what happened to her was a tragedy, just a tragedy, you know, and—"

"I've heard something about this girl," Josie broke in, but got no further before Lady Tattersall clapped a hand to her own mouth, and then rushed on, her words tumbling like a waterfall.

"Oh. Dear me. I never should have brought it up."

"Now that you have, Lady Tattersall, may I ask you a question?"

"Of course." But there was a shrill wariness to her voice. No doubt she was ready to bite off her tongue for having allowed it to wander so carelessly to this topic. Here was her godson's new young wife, and she had babbled to the girl about a woman from his past.

"Who was this girl my husband once . . . loved?" Odd, but the last word stuck in Josie's throat. Lady Tattersall regarded her knowingly.

"It doesn't matter, my dear. He loves you now—can there be any doubt? Look how ferociously he defended you last night."

"Oh, I'm in *no* doubt of my husband's feelings for me." Josie summoned a smile. "But you see, Mr. Winthrop mentioned her, too. And Ethan has told me some of the story," she lied, steadily watching Lady Tattersall's face. "I didn't want to press him for details because it seemed quite painful."

That much at least was true. The painful part. He'd knocked Winthrop across the room and inflicted a good deal of pain on him. She held her breath, waiting to see if Lady Tattersall would fill in the story. If she refused again, Josie would have no choice but to let the matter drop. She could push only so far. But to her relief, Lady Tattersall must have been eager to discuss it beneath her show of reluctance, for she needed no more urging than this before she fluttered her fan and began to speak in a low, rushing voice like that of a gurgling stream.

"Her name was Molly Flanagan. She was a shopgirl.

Poor as a mouse. Lived with an aunt and an uncle who toiled in one of the factories. I believe poor Ethan met her when he went into Madame Fanchon's, a very exclusive milliner's shop, to purchase a hat for . . . for . . ."

"Yes?" Josie wasn't about to let Lady Tattersall back away from the tale now. "For who?"

"For his mistress," the older woman burst out, then fanned herself frantically. "But all it took was one glance at this Molly—she was lovely, I heard—and Ethan forgot about . . . that other woman whom he had no intention of marrying, of course, and began actually *courting* this girl, this nobody."

Lady Tattersall shook her head sadly, then stared at Josie in alarm.

"I hope I haven't lessened your respect for your husband by telling you this," she said in dawning horror. "Any man is susceptible to a pretty face, even a common one, and I'm sure Ethan simply lost his head—"

"You haven't changed my feelings toward him in the least," Josie interrupted impatiently. "But what happened to Molly? Did they become betrothed?"

"No. Yes. Well, I'm not certain. You see, that's when all the trouble began, when it became known." She sighed. "Molly Flanagan was scarcely someone the old earl would ever have countenanced as a wife for his son, even his younger son, as Ethan was. He forbade Ethan ever to see the chit again."

"And then?"

"And then, oh, it's quite dreadful, my dear."

A knock sounded on the drawing room door and Lady Tattersall clamped her lips together as the butler entered. "My lady, Miss Perry and Miss Crenshaw have come to call."

Josie could have screamed at the interruption. Just as she was about to find out what happened to Molly! It took all of her self-control to keep from grinding her teeth in frustration.

But both Lady Tattersall and Perkins were watching her, waiting for the correct response. She had no choice but to give it. "Show them in, Perkins," she managed with a most ladylike little nod.

Though Josie was glad to have the chance to see Miss Perry again, she didn't feel nearly as warmly toward Rosamund Crenshaw. During the next half an hour she forced herself to listen politely to the black-haired girl's shrill recounting of the previous night's events, to her exclamations of how terrified and shaken she'd been, of how thankful she was that her jewels had been restored to her, and of her admiration for Lord Stonecliff's heroism.

"Lady Stonecliff showed herself to be equally brave," Miss Perry pointed out with her gentle smile. At this Miss Crenshaw's beautiful pale face seemed to grow cold as marble, and she raised her brows at her chaperon.

"Brave? Perhaps." Miss Crenshaw gave a shrug, then turned to Josie with a slight smile. "Forgive me, Lady Stonecliff, I don't wish to appear rude, but I think your actions were foolhardy. For a lady to actually swing a candlestick at a man . . ."

She shuddered. "You invited attack upon yourself by behaving as a common hooligan. And you suffered for it. One should remember that violence is hardly appropriate behavior for a lady, no matter the circumstances."

"My dear, she was trying to aid her husband!" Miss Perry exclaimed, and Lady Tattersall echoed this, but Miss Crenshaw's fair skin flushed an unbecoming mottled red.

"I fail to understand! You have all the sympathy in the world for *her* and none for me." She turned wrathful olive-green eyes on Miss Perry. "May I remind you, Cousin Clara, that it is my mama who gives you a home and the bread that you eat and the clothes that you wear. Not Lady Stonecliff. And last night, while I was terrified and hiding out-of-doors all alone, you were concerned only with helping Colonel Hamring and tending to Lady Stonecliff. You gave me no thought—no thought whatsoever."

"That's not true, dearest," Miss Perry protested. Though her voice was calm, Josie saw the pallor of her cheeks, the frightened dismay that entered her eyes.

"I believe it is."

"But no—I was most terribly concerned for you, for all of us, only Lady Stonecliff was injured and—"

"I wish to go home. To London. Now, today." Miss Crenshaw swept suddenly to her feet. "I believe Mama will have something to say to you about your conduct during this holiday, *dearest*."

Observing the black-haired girl's rising indignation, and Miss Perry's distress, Lady Tattersall hastened to intervene. "Now, Rosamund, my love, you're still distraught over all that happened last night and who can wonder at it? But, please, don't make any rash decisions while you're so upset—why don't you come to tea this afternoon and we can have a nice quiet chat? It is the country air that will settle your nerves in a day or so, not the frantic pace of London."

"I've decided. I'm going home!" the girl announced, and nodded curtly toward her hostess.

"Good day, Lady Stonecliff."

She started toward the door, obviously expecting Miss Perry to follow meekly, which she did.

But Josie moved more quickly, dodging into Miss Perry's path and waylaying her.

Josie had begun to realize during this interchange that Clara Perry, like herself, must be alone in the world. A poor relation, who lived with the Crenshaw family and was made to feel like a burden and a servant as she endured the "kindness" of their generosity. Josie had lived in many places where she'd been made to feel unwanted and unworthy, and fury rose in her like a swift summer storm as she saw Miss Perry's eyes brim with tears.

She put a detaining hand on the auburn-haired woman's arm. "I want you to know that my husband and I will be driving up to London today as well. You're welcome to visit us—I believe the house is in Mayfair."

She looked to Lady Tattersall for confirmation. Ethan's godmother nodded.

"And if you would care to stay, for as long a visit as you want—er, wish—you would be most welcome."

Miss Crenshaw whirled and glowered at her. Josie ignored it. Miss Perry squeezed her hand gratefully, but only said in her quiet way, "You're very kind, but I believe the Crenshaws have need of me." She looked uncertainly toward Rosamund, who just stared at her without any softening of expression.

"They are my family, you know." Miss Perry took a shaky breath. "But I'm certain Miss Crenshaw and her mama and I will look forward to calling on you, Lady Stonecliff."

"Hah." Miss Crenshaw gave a most unladylike snort.

Josie turned toward her. But Rosamund immediately swept toward the door once again.

"Miss Crenshaw!"

The cool imperative of her tone forced the other woman to stop and turn. Josie came forward and smiled tightly.

"Miss Perry is welcome to visit me in Mayfair at any time, but if your mama is anything like you, I hope she'll stay away. As for you," she continued in a low pleasant tone, "don't bother to pay me a call in London or anywhere else unless you can keep that spoiled, sneering expression from your face and behave with civility. I'm sure you didn't learn your manners—or lack of them— from Miss Perry."

For a moment there was a shocked, white-hot silence. The very air in the sunny green drawing room seemed to quiver. Then Josie heard Lady Tattersall's strangled gasp.

I guess I've done something awful, she thought, and knew she ought to be sorry. But she wasn't. She decided to finish the business with a flourish. "You may go now," she said in the same dismissive tone Latherby had taught her to use with the servants.

Miss Crenshaw blanched. Miss Perry turned ashen. And from the sofa, Lady Tattersall gave a gasping, choking cough.

Miss Crenshaw didn't answer. At least not in words. But the icy fury in her eyes spoke volumes as she drew herself up very straight and marched from the room.

The sizzling tension left with her, but an atmosphere of stunned horror remained. Miss Perry threw Josie an anguished glance before scurrying after her charge. And before Josie could think of a way to apologize for her behavior, Lady Tattersall, too, rose to her feet, nearly dropping her fan in her haste.

"I must be going, my dear. So sorry . . . will see you in London no doubt . . . going to town at the end of the week . . . good day to you."

She was gone before Josie could even nod. Josie sank dazedly down upon the sofa.

What have I done? Dear heaven, what have I done?

The answer was all too obvious. She'd ruined everything. *Everything.* Losing her temper, speaking to Miss Crenshaw that way, shocking everyone . . .

Miss Crenshaw would no doubt rush back to London and tell everyone that the Earl of Stonecliff's bride was an ill-mannered witch, not a lady at all. And when Lady Tattersall arrived, she would have to confirm it.

Pressing her hands to her cheeks, Josie remembered what Winthrop had hinted at yesterday. That Ethan would have difficulty being accepted and received in society—because of what had happened in the past. And now his "wife," the one who was supposed to convince all of London, and in particular Mr. Grismore, that she was a lady, and help pave the way for his return, had demonstrated clearly that she was not a lady, but a shrew.

But Miss Crenshaw deserved it, she thought in despair.

Yet she knew that didn't change what she'd done. Everything was spoiled. Mr. Latherby had made it clear that a lady never displayed her temper or spoke rudely under any circumstances. And Miss Crenshaw's rudeness would not matter—*she* wasn't the one with something to prove.

Josie jumped up to stare sightlessly around the pretty, airy room. *Mr. Grismore will hear of it,* she realized, and felt sick to her stomach. *He'll decide that you're not what Ethan's father would consider a lady, and Ethan will lose Stonecliff Park and all his money and everything that ought to be his.*

She cried out in frustration, unable to bear the scenario unraveling before her mind's eye.

With a choked cry she raced across the drawing room, threw open the French doors, and rushed out into the gardens.

She needed to run, to flee the oppressive thoughts circling through her brain. Golden sun beat down upon her shoulders and her heavy brown curls as she bolted past the hedges and rose gardens, the neat formal borders and gushing fountains, and gained the stretch of flowing emerald lawn.

Her heart pounding, she kept on. She flew past chestnut trees and orchards, past stands of silver birch and pines, across a meadow that sloped toward the pond, where water lilies floated. At last her breath began to burst through her lungs in painful gasps, catching in her throat. Her steps slowed and she struggled to ease the aching in her sides.

She found herself in a fragrant green clearing that might have been an enchanted spot from a storybook, and slowed to a walk. But though she longed to throw herself down upon the grass and weep, she couldn't seem to stop moving. Driven, though more slowly now, she came out suddenly through a grove of trees and saw a stream glinting blue and silver in the sun, and a man fishing from the velvet bank that curved alongside it.

In surprise, she stopped dead and stared at him.

He lifted a hand. "Morning, my lady."

"Good morning."

She studied him as she approached. He wore old

clothes, somewhat baggy and shabby in appearance, but his face with its gray whiskers was scrubbed clean. It was a ruddy, pleasant face, and there was a friendly twinkle in his brown eyes that reminded her a bit of Pop Watson and the way he would wink at her when Miz Dunner was being especially grumpy and particular about chores.

"So you're the Countess," the man said, and she realized that despite his smiles and twinkles, he was appraising her as carefully as she was appraising him.

"For the time being." Immediately Josie wished she could stuff the words back into her mouth. "I mean—oh, damn it—I mean—my gracious, I'm not myself today. You must forgive me, Mister . . ."

"You can just call me Ham, my lady. And there's no need to apologize. Knowing Ethan as I do, I've seen how the lad can addle anyone's brains, even a fine and sensible lady like yourself."

"You know Ethan?"

"Aye, as well as I know this land all the way from the park and the lane to the bracken at its farthest boundary. I once was the earl's head groom, back in the days when your Ethan was a boy."

"I see." Josie settled down upon a fallen log and pushed her hair out of her eyes. The chignon had come loose during her wild run, and half the pins must have scattered across the lawns and gardens. She plucked the few remaining ones from the coil and let it all spill down, knowing she must look a scraggly sight, but too hot, tired, and curious about Ham to care. "You don't work at Stonecliff Park anymore?"

"No, my lady. I've a small farm on the outskirts, not far from here. Took it over from one of the old earl's tenants with wages I saved up over the years. You see, I quit my position at Stonecliff Park the night young Ethan left London. I left too and found me a job on the London docks. Didn't fancy working for the earl anymore after that night."

"What in the world happened that night?" Josie cried, gazing at him with mingled frustration and fascination. She felt the hot color filling her cheeks. How pathetic to be questioning a former servant this way, but she had to know. Everyone else in England seemed to know!

"Have you asked the boy?"

"You mean Ethan? No, I can't."

"And why is that?"

"Because he won't answer me. At least, I don't think he will. And besides, I don't want to hurt him," she said slowly, knowing that this was the true reason. "Whatever happened between him and his father—and his brother, too—was painful to him. Deeply painful. And I'm afraid that bringing it all up again will only hurt him, remind him. . . ."

"Ah, so you care about him, lass."

Though softly spoken, the words were a statement, not a question. Ham's eyes were fixed upon her with rapt attention.

"Don't tell him that or he'll bite your head off," she muttered, and again was immediately horrified by her own careless honesty.

"I mean, of course I do. He's my husband and—"

"It's all right, lass." The groom chuckled. "I know all about the circumstances. Ethan told me himself. I know why he married you, and why you married him."

She went very still. "He told you—about Abilene?" she asked with a jolt of shock.

Calmly, he nodded.

So he knew. Knew she was a thief, a dance hall girl, a nobody. Josie plucked a handful of grass and crushed the blades between her fingers.

"Who are you?" she asked again. "Not your name, but who? Who are you for him to trust you so much? It seems to me that he trusts few people, and confides in even fewer."

"Aye, that's Ethan." A small grin twisted Ham's mouth and he nodded approvingly at her, though there was a hint of sadness in his eyes. "I've known him since he was a wee lad. Abandoned him they did, that father of his, and his own brother, Master Hugh. Paid him almost no heed at all—too busy they were, to bother with a child. He took to following me about, and you might say, my lady, that we became like family. I was most likely the closest thing to family he's ever known."

She heard pity and sorrow in his tone. And remembered what he'd said: he'd left Stonecliff Park the night Ethan had quarreled with his father and fled London.

"You care for him, too, Ham?" There was hope in her tone. "I'm glad. So glad." Josie scrambled to her feet, tossing down the fistful of crushed grass. "I'm glad that back then—and now—he has someone around him who cares."

"And what about you, my lady? He has you now, doesn't he? And you care."

"Yes, I care," she said tremblingly. "But . . ."

She hesitated, then surged on. The man knew the situation, after all. There was no reason to hold back. "I've done something terrible. Something awful. I've ruined our plan. You know about the plan?"

He nodded, and set his fishing pole down upon the bank. "Aye, that I do."

"Well, it's going to fail now. I've done something . . . said something—" She broke off, despair rushing through her again, filling her with a hopeless sorrow that blocked the words.

Ham stared at the willowy beauty whose glorious violet eyes shimmered with tears. "Tell me, lass," he urged gently.

And then from behind her came a voice that scraped through the clearing like rock across glass.

"Tell me, too, angel." Ethan glowered from beneath a tree, his mouth curled mockingly. Despite the sunlight slanting through the clearing, touching her with its golden warmth, Josie was chilled by the icy silver of his eyes.

Before she could move, he strode forward, tall and handsome in his riding clothes, his gait long and smooth and quick as a cougar's.

"What has my contrary little bride done now?"

Chapter Fifteen

H am broke the long, thin silence. "Aha. Seems to me I'd best be going."

He picked up the fishing pole and sent Ethan a glance from between furrowed brows.

"Now, lad, whatever trouble there is—"

"I will deal with it." Ethan's cold gaze stayed on Josie's face.

"Well . . . easy, lad. I taught you that oftentimes wild things need gentling, remember that?" When Ethan didn't answer, the groom moved off with a quick, bracing nod at Josie. His footsteps rustled in the grass and faded away when he disappeared beyond a thicket of bracken.

Wild thing. That's exactly what she looked like, Ethan thought, tension twisting through him as he studied the beauty facing him. Gold glimmered in her hair as it streamed in a frenzied cascade around her shoulders, and he longed to touch it, to bury his face in it. She looked half angel, half hellion standing there, slender as a reed, with her eyes glowing defiantly at him. Their color would put the finest sapphires to shame, but it wasn't only their brilliance that drew him—it was the depths of emotion that shone within. Much as she tried to hide it, they mirrored her thoughts—thoughts that were troubled right now. Troubled and guilty—and worried.

She looked very nearly as distressed as she had back in that Abilene alley, when he'd taken pity on her and let her go. When she'd thanked him by picking his pocket for the second time in a day, he reminded himself.

Don't be fooled by her again. It was far too easy to be taken in by such large, anxious eyes and trembling lips.

" 'Fess up. What's happened?"

"You won't like it."

She forced herself to stand perfectly still as he studied her on that lovely green bank with the stream gurgling at her back.

A part of her wished she could lie to him and escape his anger with a clever, believable story—she'd learned to do that while growing up, and though it went against her forthright nature, it had been partly responsible for her survival. Yet even as the temptation flitted through her mind, she knew it would only delay things. Ethan would find out the truth of her blunders soon enough.

Though he didn't touch her, she felt trapped. They were alone but for the drenching sunshine, the twitter of birds. Stonecliff Park, the house, stables, servants, were a long way off, and here there were only ancient trees, quiet, the sweep of land and wild flowers. And Ethan Savage, handsome as sin.

"If it's that bad, you'd better get it over with."

"You'll be angry." Her eyes flashed. "I know I shouldn't have done it, but she had it coming. Only now all of London will know that I'm far from being a perfect, mushmouthed, prim and proper lady."

"You're stalling, my love."

He said the words lightly, coolly, but the sound of them on his lips brought heat flooding to her cheeks. *He's mocking you. My love. It's a turn of phrase,* she told herself and she tilted her head up to meet his eyes. Keen and hawklike, they regarded her from beneath those dark slanting brows, seeming to pierce right through her. Some unseen force grabbed her by the throat and squeezed tight, making breathing difficult. Why did this always happen when he was near?

Tell him and be done with it! "I insulted Rosamund Crenshaw."

To her surprise, his face relaxed and he looked amused. "That's all? I reckon she deserved it."

Josie nearly smiled. He only reverted to his western style of talking when he was alone with her. Somehow it made her feel closer to him. He had become very much the Englishman of late—dark, dashing, aristocratic. Except, of course, when he'd thrashed Oliver Winthrop— and Lucian and Pirate Pete and Tiny. Those were the gunfighter's fists in action.

She found herself grinning up at him.

"As a matter of fact, she did. If you'd only seen how badly she treated Miss Perry. Ordering her about, threatening to tell her mama that Miss Perry had paid more attention to Colonel Hamring and to me than she had to *her,* flinging it in Miss Perry's face that the only reason she had a home, and clothes on her back, and food was because of her mama's generosity." The words were tripping over themselves. "I know what it's like to be beholden to other people—to have them rub your face in the fact that without them you'd be nothing and to make you feel as if—" She suddenly fell silent, turning away.

Ethan put a hand on her shoulder and swung her back. "Is that what they told you when you were taken in, Josie? That you were nothing?"

"Some of them tried." She kept her tone light. "But it didn't bother me," she added quickly, a bit too breezily. "I just did what I had to do to stay out of trouble and then if it got too bad, I'd run away."

"And do what?"

"What difference does it make?" She tried to shrug away, but he gripped both her shoulders and held her still. "What's important is what happened today with Miss Crenshaw."

"No. Tell me what you did after you ran away."

She swallowed. His fingers were digging into her shoulders. His gaze was digging into her soul. She struggled to keep him out. "I found various jobs, in between ending up at another orphanage. Usually cooking. I'm good at cooking," she said, her chin angling up. "You ought to taste my corn bread. That's what I did in Abilene, you know. I only filled in at the dance hall when someone was sick—most of the time I worked in the kitchen and . . ."

"And you picked pockets."

"Only when I really needed money to get by. I'm not proud of it!" she cried defiantly, trying to twist away from him, but failing. "I only stole from people who looked like they could afford to spare some money—like you. You'd just won the big poker game and I'd given my last dime to a girl who needed to get away from Judd Stickley, but I needed to get out of town, too, and fast."

"I know. That man who was after you. My question is why?"

She gritted her teeth. His hands were heavy on her

shoulders, wearing away at her will, grinding down her resistance. "What makes you so interested suddenly?" she demanded, glaring at him from beneath a sweep of tawny lashes.

His eyes bored into hers. He couldn't tell her that he'd been interested, been curious for a while now, but had been fighting it—unsuccessfully. Now he needed to know.

"Just answer the question."

Behind her the wind sighed through the trees. Josie was gazing into Ethan's eyes, searching his lean, dark face. She was unsure what she searched for. Beneath the rugged masculine features, the cynicism and cool veneer, she glimpsed something more. Something keen and demanding. Something intense that belied the outward calm.

She felt something pulling her to tell him. His will. Strong, dominant, but ... gentle. It was the sudden gentleness in the fingers that clasped her shoulders that was her undoing.

"That man who was after me—he was an outlaw. His name is Snake Barker." The words, held in for so long, just poured out and kept coming. "He and his gang— they'd have killed me if they caught me. They'd been hunting me for weeks." Just saying Snake's name had triggered a spasm of fear in her stomach, but it faded as she continued to stare into Ethan's eyes.

They were even darker, more intense than before. They burned into her, hot as ice.

"Why?"

"I stole from him. It was loot—money and things he'd stolen from others. I did it to get away and ..."

She hesitated.

"Go on."

It came out in a rush. "And for revenge. Snake beat me one night, he beat me senseless. He finally passed out from all the liquor he'd drunk, and I woke up on the floor." The horror of it returned, flashing through her with a wave of nausea, of sick, shaking fear that shuddered through her whispered words. It rocked her so deeply, she didn't even feel the lash of tension that coiled like a whip through Ethan's body, didn't even see the cold, deadly fury clamp over his features.

"I felt like every bone in my body was broken—but lucky for me, they weren't. I crawled past him, to the door, then I managed to get up. Everything hurt. I ran . . . I took the saddlebags filled with loot, a horse. . . ."

The lovely grassy streambank faded, the blue dazzle of the English sky, the grandeur of the great house that rose beyond the trees. She was back in that hideout cabin again, the stench of liquor and Snake's sweat and her own blood filling her nostrils. And the pain blurring her eyes.

"I rode as far as I could . . . stayed a short time only in each town . . . knew he was coming after me, there'd be no stopping him the next time. He'd kill me. He wouldn't stop until I was dead. I crossed him, you see, when I took what was his—I crossed him bad . . . but I'm not sorry I did, I needed to get back at him for what he'd done. And I needed money, and I needed that—"

She broke off in horror, coming to her senses just in time. She'd been about to say "needed that ring that belonged to Miss Denby. . . ."

What spell had Ethan Savage cast on her? She'd told him too much and what was worse, he'd brought her to tears. Hot, stinging tears had welled up in her eyes, and it took all of her strength to blink them back.

"Let me go," she gasped raggedly. To her mortification, two tears slipped out and trickled down her cheeks. "I want to go back to the house."

"Not yet."

"Yes! Let me go!"

Instead, his hands slid roughly around her waist and he pulled her against him. His strength surrounded her. An electric heat sparked between their bodies. Josie gasped at the force of it, her head flying up, her eyes wide on the unfathomable gray gaze staring back at her.

His arms tightened. She felt the length of him, long and lean and hard, pressed against her. But instead of her shrinking from him in fear, some primitive instinct took over. Want and need had her melting against him. How strong he was. How solid, his body like sculpted iron. It felt good to be held by him like this—why did it have to feel so good?

Her hands splayed across his chest, delicate fingers trembling over the hard muscles. Her head was still thrown back as she stared at him half in trepidation, half in anticipation, trying to read beneath the cynical exterior, to see beneath the dangerous glint in his eyes.

She couldn't read what she saw in his face, couldn't fully understand why his arms tightened so restrictively around her and held her fast, as if he were afraid she would vanish like mist if he didn't hang on tight enough.

"So that's why you agreed to marry me that night—why you were so desperate to get out of Abilene pronto—to come to England." The words rasped out of him. He wiped a tear from her cheek, so gently, it made her tremble. "So that this outlaw couldn't find you?"

Was he angry? His eyes glittered, his jaw was

clenched. But Josie thought she heard understanding in his tone.

"Yes, because of that and . . ." There was more, there was Miss Denby, the search she needed to commence, the strange fascination she'd had with him right from the first, but before she could say anymore, Ethan's hands, those strong, capable hands, slid to her hair. They smoothed through the velvet skeins, caressing, stroking, and she felt her senses dwindling fast.

"Did you know, even then, Josie, that I'd never let him touch you? Never let him hurt you?"

His voice was low, growling, dangerous.

Wildly, she shook her head. What was he saying?

"If you'd told me that day in the alley, I'd have protected you."

"I'd picked your pocket, Ethan." A half-crazed laugh bubbled in her throat. "You were ready to murder me yourself."

"Not quite," he muttered grimly, then had to suppress a groan as she turned those deep violet eyes upon him with questioning innocence and he felt himself drowning in their spell.

He battled for control. Best to get her away from him, fast. To step back, take time to think. Without the sunshine-and-flower scent of her filling his nostrils, without the soft handful of her lush curves playing havoc with his blood.

"What that man did, Josie, that Snake Barker . . ." He drew a breath, tried to drop his hands from her, but only stroked his fingers deeper in the cloud of her hair. He had a mind, one day, to sail back to America and hunt down Snake Barker like the animal he was. That would give him infinite pleasure, to kill the bastard and leave him for the vultures. "No man has a right to do that to a woman."

"Try telling that to Snake. Ethan . . ."

"What?"

"I can't belive that you care." She swallowed hard. "That you . . . Last night you said you don't even like me, remember. Or trust me."

"I like you a hell of a lot more than I care to admit," he grated, the words torn out of him, and as her delectable mouth dropped open in surprise, he suddenly hauled her even closer and lowered his lips to hers.

He hadn't meant to kiss her. Hell, he hadn't meant to touch her, or to hold her like this, every inch of their bodies touching, with her pretty breasts crushed against his chest, her hips molded to him. But once he'd started, he couldn't seem to stop.

Just like he couldn't stop kissing her.

He heard her moan deep in her throat, but it wasn't an unhappy moan, nor was the way she slid her arms around his neck an indication that she wanted to be set loose. Which was damn well good because after the first taste of those lips, Ethan had no intention of setting her loose.

He deepened the kiss as her mouth parted and shaped itself to his. Heat seared, then the sweep of his tongue found hers, and he felt her quiver all through her body. She tasted sweeter than warm summer honey. More intoxicating than the most potent, delicious wine. He wanted to drink her in, swallow her up, devour her in one long, delicious never-ending gulp.

Ethan had thought his blood couldn't grow hotter than it was, but suddenly, as her tongue touched his, and tentatively flickered between his lips, the fiery heat and knife-edged need in him intensified by several hundred degrees.

His hands stroked down her hips and cupped her

bottom with a need that was fast building to a raging obsession.

Josie felt herself spinning through waves of pleasure, pleasure so deep and fiery and joyful, it burned out everything else. Reason, sanity, dignity—gone, gone, gone.

Her fingers curled in the thick silk of Ethan's hair. Her mouth covered his with giving surrender. Heat swept through her body, sultry flames that incinerated every rational thought and left only the hunger of need, the hot raging of desire.

As she clutched him to her, she felt his tension and his strength and his incredible, powerful need answering her, demanding her.

Wondrously, she responded, her body unable to fight the primitive response. It began deep inside the lonely feminine reaches of her soul and burst forth like an avalanche.

"Josie, do you know how long I've been wanting to do this . . . ?"

"When you kissed me at our wedding, I never wanted you to let me go."

"I never should have." His mouth pressed against her throat.

"You had to . . . you p-passed out." Her laughter tickled against his mouth. He kissed her bruisingly.

"Shows you what a damned fool I was . . . and still am."

Laughter trembled through her, then turned to a pleasured gasp as his hands found her breasts.

Oh, in the name of heaven, what was he doing to her?

Taking her to heaven, she thought, and then all thought dissolved in a bathing cascade of delight.

Ethan's thumbs brushed the hard peak of her nipples,

sending shock waves of pleasure. She closed her eyes, letting sensation flutter lightly at first, then deepen until she clutched him in desperation.

His mouth burned ruthless kisses down her throat, then claimed lower territory, nipping and teasing through her gown even as his hands circled and stroked, driving her wild.

When he backed her against the trunk of a tree, and proceeded to run his fingers along the buttons of her gown, Josie felt her knees wobble.

She'd never felt anything remotely like this before— Snake had taken her, hurriedly, greedily, slamming against her, even his kisses hurtful and wet and disgusting. Never, never, had he touched her with this rough magic that brought a different kind of pain, a desperate ache so intense, so simultaneously bitter and sweet, it made her yearn and shiver and cling like ivy to stone.

Ethan's kisses scorched, but the pain was pleasurable, like strong, hot wine warmed by the sun that burned clear through to the soul.

And then suddenly, as they sank to the grass, their bodies locked and entwined while Ethan lowered her upon the velvety streambank, a sound reached them from just over the rise. It was a soft sound, but distinct, and so oddly intrusive, they both heard it and froze.

"What the hell?" Ethan's head flew up. He frowned, the instincts that had always alerted him to danger, and that had kept him alive in the untamed West for so many years, asserting themselves in a rush. He dropped Josie into the softness of the grass and sprang to his feet.

The sun shimmered in her eyes, and reality came crashing back. Josie found herself with her gown unbuttoned, her hair wild, her lips bruised and hot from the force of his kisses. She was lying on the grass, heat flowing through her body in palpable waves. And Ethan was standing over her, very still, listening, his face dark and dangerous.

But Josie was less concerned about the sound they'd heard—a strange sound, rather like a hiccup, or a sneeze—than she was about the situation in which she found herself now that the madness of passion had fled. Good Lord, what had she been doing? What had she been *thinking*?

That was the problem, she decided dazedly. She sat up, a trembling hand fluttering to her throat. She hadn't been thinking at all.

Ethan moved slowly, in a smooth, catlike prowl, toward the rise that cut up from the landscape just ahead of the clearing. But at the sound of Josie lurching to her feet behind him, he turned his head to look at her. He halted.

She knew from the intent expression on his face that he was listening for another sound, but she was too upset to care.

"You broke your promise!" she burst out in a strangled whisper.

For a moment he seemed torn between investigating the sound and coming back to her. But when she whirled away from him to begin fastening the buttons of her gown, and he heard the sob break from her throat, he started toward her.

He caught her as she was trying to run back toward the house.

"You're not going anywhere yet. What promise did I break?"

"About us . . . our . . . marital relations. We had a b-bargain."

"Seems to me I wasn't the only one breaking it. Or am I wrong, sweetheart?"

There was laughter in his eyes. And tenderness. But because he was right, and she knew herself to be equally to blame, Josie's anger mounted. She thrust his hand from her arm.

"Don't touch me. Don't ever touch me again."

"Josie . . ."

"I mean it. Everything was easy before. We had an agreement, a business arrangement, and we both knew what was involved. Now you're changing the rules. I won't have it. I won't!"

Ethan's eyes narrowed on the blazing whiteness of her face. "You weren't so all-fired-up about the rules a few minutes ago, Josie."

"That's not fair!" Shame and rage vibrated through her voice. "You promised me! I only wanted to play my part and then g-go—just as we agreed. You're treating me like . . . like a harlot. . . ."

"No," he said sharply. There was an odd, challenging light in his eyes. "Like a wife. My wife. That's what you are, Josie."

But she wasn't. She was Snake's wife.

She broke free of his grasp and started back toward the house. Part of her wanted him to stop her, to kiss her again until her senses whirled, and nothing mattered but the sweetness she felt in his arms. And part of her wanted to race as far from him as she could get, a safe distance, whatever that might be, where she wouldn't be subject to the power he had over her.

But he didn't stop her. She didn't even know if he

watched her. She ran on, her skirts clenched in her fists, her feet flying over the meadow. And she didn't stop until she had sped in a blur past Mrs. Fielding and Perkins and reached the solitude of her own room.

By then two truths were hammering through her, both so huge and frightening, she collapsed onto the bed, unable to stand.

The first truth was that she had left everyplace that had ever been home to her, every person who could have been called family. She was destined to run, to leave, to wander. And she would leave this place too: Stonecliff Park, London, England—whatever "home" she might know during this marriage with Ethan Savage.

That was one truth, but it was the other, larger one that brought tears springing to her eyes and caused her chest to ache with unspeakable pain.

The other truth was that she had fallen inescapably in love with Ethan Savage. And if she didn't find a way to fall out of love with him, this time when she left, she would leave a chunk of her heart behind.

A chunk? Her whole heart.

He may as well cut it out with a Bowie knife and set it on his mantel. It would be his.

Josie knew she'd die from the pain of leaving him. Unless she could stop what had already begun. Unless she could stop herself from loving this black-haired man whose hypnotic lips and riveting gaze and powerful arms aroused her as no other man's ever had, whose voice could be cutting, or unexpectedly gentle, who made her want to tell him everything and know everything of him, who made her ache and smile and cry and think about him night and day, when there were a hundred other things she ought to be thinking about. . . .

Stop loving him.

But how?

They were going to London today, to continue this charade—if they could bluff it past Miss Crenshaw's whispers. They would be together in the city, even more than they had been here.

The sob broke from her then, a long, low, agonized cry muffled behind shaking hands.

How was she to stop the very beating of her heart?

⊗⊗⊗ ⊗⊗⊗

Ethan Savage did not go straight back to Stonecliff Park when Josie fled. He turned instead and went immediately in search of Ham Tyger.

The former groom was buttering bread for a sandwich. A wedge of ham sat on the kitchen table as he held the knife and glanced up at Ethan in the doorway.

"I'm leaving for London this afternoon, Ham."

"So I've heard. Will you have a bite of lunch with me before you go, lad?"

Ethan shook his head. "That's not why I'm here. There's something I need you to do."

"Aye, lad. Just ask it."

Ethan came forward and leaned both hands upon the back of the chair. "Listen then. Here's what you must do."

⊗⊗⊗ ⊗⊗⊗

He waited until all sounds, all footsteps, had faded away. Until silence claimed the clearing near the stream. Then, when only the chatter of the birds and the harried scrabbling of a squirrel remained, he sat up from within the curve of the rise and drew a deep breath.

He'd gotten drunk last night, after all he'd gone through, and slept it off for the most part at the inn. But then, of all the damnable things, he'd awakened early with a raging headache and a restlessness that no amount of strolling around the courtyard of the inn could relieve.

He'd rented a horse from the landlord and ridden out, thinking the air would do him good. Naturally he'd come here, to Stonecliff Park.

Not to the house, of course. Ethan mustn't see him or he'd hit him again. But he'd needed to ride the glorious meadows and pastures, view the fishpond, the fine trees, the salutary stream, which should have been his . . . his!

He'd known it all along. The bitch was no more a lady than he was! What had she said: she'd been a dance hall girl? And a cook! And a thief!

Oliver Winthrop wanted to laugh out loud. But Ethan might still be nearby, so he clapped his flabby fingers over his mouth and silently thanked his lucky stars that his horse had thrown him, that he'd ended up sleeping off the last effects of the liquor here beneath this bloody rise, just out of sight of the stream.

That had been a bad moment though, when he'd sneezed. Fortunately, his luck held and Ethan had been too distracted by the girl's charms and her tears to investigate properly.

But then my big handsome cousin has always been a fool for the cheap little tart, hasn't he? Winthrop smirked to himself as he reached for his bowler nestled in the grass.

Ah, now he had ammunition. Now he had a way of getting what was rightfully his—of snatching it right back from his lying, cheating cousin. He'd make Ethan pay for hitting him, for trying to steal Stonecliff Park from him under false pretenses.

And that little hussy would pay for helping.

Dusting off his trousers, and setting his bowler on his head, Winthrop stood unsteadily and glanced around to get his bearings. Then, picking his way as quickly and quietly as he could, he headed back toward the Green Duck Inn.

He wanted to get the afternoon train to London. That would put him in the city this very afternoon. There were matters of great importance to see to—and not a moment to lose.

Chapter Sixteen

London.

It was a city of striking contrasts. By day there was a panorama of fashionable shops, elegant homes, grand carriages, and fashionable parks. By night the glimmer of moonlight and fog and hissing gaslight across damp cobbled streets, the gaiety of dinner parties, and card parties, and balls, of opera at Covent Garden, and Gilbert and Sullivan at the Savoy.

On one side of town, beggars and drunkards and prostitutes prowled the streets of the rookery. On the other, often only a few blocks away, ladies in velvet cloaks and silks and taffetas chatted and flirted with gentlemen in swallowtail coats, walking sticks, and silk top hats.

London was a great city, a monstrous city, a mysterious city, where the grand homes of those in society, the pleasant streets and footmen and gardens, stood in stark contrast to the smoke and factories and gin houses that choked the slums of the poor.

Josie saw much of it—the gaily magnificent part of it—on Ethan's arm during the week.

And everywhere she went, with everyone she spoke to, she asked about a young woman named Alicia Denby.

All to no avail. Lady Cornish, who invited her to walk in Hyde Park, had never met any such person. Miss Peabody and Mr. Himple, whom she met at the Savoy Theatre one night, looked puzzled and assured her that if the young lady lived among fashionable people in London, they would surely have known of her. And the very old, very intimidating dowager Lady MacCormick, whom she screwed up her courage to ask while shopping in Regent Street, only stared at her from beneath haughty silver brows and sniffed that she had never heard of such a young lady, and therefore this Miss Denby person must not be a young female whom the Countess should care to know.

Ethan had happened to stroll by the window at that moment and spotted her, and she had quickly changed the subject before he came through the door. The last thing she wanted was for him to discover she was searching for an English girl named Alicia Denby—she didn't know how he would react to the idea of her searching for a possible relative, and she had no desire to find out. This was *her* secret, *her* dream, Josie told herself. It had nothing whatsoever to do with Ethan Savage or his plan to attain his inheritance.

An inheritance that began to appear overwhelmingly impressive. Not only was there the country estate, with all its accompanying gardens and grounds, the carriages, horses, furnishings, and retinue of servants, but Ethan's house in Mayfair proved every bit as lovely in its own way as Stonecliff Park. It boasted three drawing rooms, a music room, a ballroom, a dining room where twenty guests could be comfortably seated, and eight bedrooms, including a suite much like the one she and Ethan shared in the country—separate rooms linked by a sitting room, and a private door between.

He hadn't tried to avail himself of that door, not once the entire week they'd been in London. He hadn't tried to kiss her again. He'd been like a stranger during all of these days, speaking to her only when it was necessary, leaving her side as soon as he saw that she was able to manage the company in which she found herself. And spending considerable time at his club, coming home when she was already in bed, and though she was wide-awake, she never heard his step come anywhere near her door.

They hadn't spoken anything but trivial niceties to each other in all this time.

Which was just as well, she told herself as the footman handed her down from the carriage in front of Stonecliff House. If she was to have a prayer of keeping this arrangement with Ethan on a proper businesslike footing, and of saving her heart from being broken when the six months was up and Ethan sent her packing, she would need to keep as much distance as possible between them.

His attitude toward her had altered dramatically, Josie reflected as she mounted the steps, a package tucked under one arm—the new silk gloves she'd just purchased to wear to Lady Cartwright's dinner party tonight folded snugly inside. Ethan treated her with chilly politeness when they were alone—and with heart-stopping warmth and attentiveness when they were out in society. It was all Josie could do when she looked into his frankly admiring gaze or danced with his arm tight around her waist, to remember that it was all a game, a pretense. All for the purpose of inheriting his title and lands, and

Stonecliff Park, which would no more be a part of her life in a few months than Ethan would.

She was about to enter the town house when a flash of movement caught her eye, and she turned to see Miss Perry hastening across the street toward her. There was a bright smile on her face, and she gave a little cheerful wave as she quickened her step, but so intent was she on reaching Josie that she failed to notice the carriage suddenly swerving down the street, bearing down right upon her.

"Miss Perry, look out!" Josie screamed, and in a flash dived off the steps. Startled, Clara Perry froze on the spot, which put her exactly in the path of the horses. She turned her head and shrieked in horror as she saw what was about to befall her.

Josie leapt at her and pushed her from beneath the beasts' plunging hooves at the last moment. Amid the sounds of the horses' terrified whinnying and the curses of the frightened driver, they tumbled to the ground.

A moment later Ethan's white-faced footman reached them. Sweat poured down his face as he helped Josie to her feet.

"My lady, are you hurt?"

"N-no, John. I'm fine." Breathless, Josie knelt beside the auburn-haired woman. "Miss Perry, are you all right?"

"My goodness, Lady Stonecliff." Miss Perry's gown was torn at the hem and there was soot on her face, but she gained her feet steadily enough with the aid of Josie and the footman. "Why, you saved my life!"

"Oh, no, Miss Perry. Of course I didn't. I only—"

"Don't argue, Josie." Ethan's voice, coming from behind her, made her spin around in shock. Did the man *always* have to sneak up on her this way?

"Miss Perry is absolutely right. You did save her life—
and nearly lost your own!"

He was pale. She'd never seen him look so shaken.
With rough strength he grasped her arm.

"I saw everything. Happened to be glancing out my
window—" He broke off abruptly, glaring down at her
through fierce gray eyes that might have been made of
smoldering coal. "And that was the most idiotic—and
most courageous—thing I ever saw."

"It wasn't courageous. I didn't even think . . . it all
happened so fast."

"You might have been killed, you little fool!"

"But I wasn't. And neither was Miss Perry," she
pointed out a bit smugly.

He gave her a long, incredulous look, then his fingers
tightened on her arm as the footman stooped to retrieve
the fallen package. "I believe some refreshment is in
order, ladies," he grated out. "To celebrate your narrow
escape." With a grim nod to the still trembling Miss
Perry, Ethan led Josie firmly toward the house.

"You're angry . . . but I had no choice!" Josie turned to
him swiftly as they preceded the others into the hall. "I
had to do something. . . ."

"I'm not angry. But if you'd been hurt . . ." He drew in
his breath. "I'd be a hell of a lot more than that," he muttered, almost inaudibly.

Her eyes widened at this: for a moment it sounded like
an open admission that he cared about her—but then she
realized how stupid it was to think that—and she understood exactly what he meant. Of course he'd be upset if
she was hurt—or killed. It would hamper his precious
charade.

"I'm fine," she whispered, her whole body taut as Miss

Perry reached the hall. "Don't worry—your plan hasn't been endangered."

Ethan wheeled on her so abruptly, she took a step backward, but he said nothing, though there was a hard, bitter tension in his face that she didn't understand. They were both conscious of Miss Perry coming to a halt behind them.

"Oh, dear, I've come at an inopportune time—I'm so sorry. Perhaps I should return another afternoon."

"No." The smile Josie flashed was brilliant as she spun away from Ethan to take the woman's arm. "I'm so very glad to see you—and without Miss Crenshaw," she added shamelessly. "Come into the withdrawing room and have some tea."

Ethan did not join them for tea, and a short while later Josie heard him go out. She tried to forget that fierce expression in his eyes right after the accident, tried not to wonder what it meant, and concentrated on centering her attention upon Miss Perry, who needed a bit of drawing out before she admitted, even obliquely, that things were quite bad with the Crenshaws.

"Don't think I am not grateful to them, for I am, my lady," she said earnestly, and took a quick, nervous sip of tea. "But it is . . . not always comfortable for me there—I daresay it is of my own doing," she added hastily, and blushed, before rushing on to say, "How can I be so ungrateful? My relations are kindness itself. If not for them, I don't know what would become of me—"

"You'd be a good deal happier," Josie cut in promptly, then gave her a sheepish smile. "I know it's unladylike of me to say that—and it must reinforce what Miss Crenshaw has already been saying about me ever since that day."

"No one heeds her, my lady." Miss Perry patted her hand and smiled. "Everyone I have encountered since returning to London—everyone who has met you, that is—is full of your praises. Most have concluded that Rosamund is simply jealous because you have married a handsome and titled man, while she is still . . . well, you know . . ."

"Yes, I know. She is still shopping for a husband—and heaven help the one she selects." Josie grinned. Sometimes she could no more control her forthright tongue than she could stop breathing, and Miss Perry, though outwardly shocked, seemed beneath it all to be amused by her statements. Not for the first time, she began to suspect that beneath that very shy, pleasant exterior was a woman with a genuine sense of humor and a truly kind soul.

"Well, once again, I'm forgetting to be a lady." She sighed and set her teacup down. "Forgive me, but sometimes it's difficult to remember."

"Oh, no." Miss Perry set her cup on the small marble-topped table and studied Josie quietly. "In my opinion, you are always a very great lady."

Josie gaped at her. Then she burst out laughing.

"It's true, Lady Stonecliff. Oh, I know. These days, those who are most fashionable preach and prattle on about ladylike ways—and that is all well and good, but I remember some very great ladies who were never afraid to speak their minds, or to act upon their convictions. And you remind me of them—the ladies I looked up to when I was young, those of the finest birth, who often gave the most lavish parties, who *led* society and didn't merely follow it. No, when it comes to heart and sensitivity and courage and wit, my dear, you are every inch a lady."

When she'd finished this impassioned speech, Miss Perry looked quite as stunned as Josie did upon hearing it.

"My lady, f-forgive me. I never meant to speak so freely," she stammered.

But Josie was touched. She'd rarely heard praise or kind words in her life, and that they came from someone as sweetly respectable as Miss Perry, overwhelmed her. She moved nearer to Miss Perry on the sofa and touched her hand.

"Thank you. I'm very grateful for that . . . and very thankful to have you as my friend."

Glancing down then, she noticed the simple gold-and-pearl ring Clara Perry wore, and it occurred to her to wonder suddenly why Miss Perry had never married. Of course, even she knew better than to broach this most sensitive subject, but the other woman, noting her glance, and with a quick one at the loose gold band on Josie's finger, spoke in response to her unasked question.

"No, my lady," she said softly. "I never married. I was betrothed once, though—when I was a very young, very foolish woman." Her voice broke a little, but she recovered it before Josie could think of anything to say.

"His family made him break it off, you see."

"Oh, no!"

"It happens that way sometimes." There was no bitterness in her tone, or in her gentle eyes, only a trace of sadness. "It was all hushed up. They felt I wasn't good enough for him—he was a viscount, and my father only a country squire, and they wished a better connection, someone with a substantial fortune."

As Josie made a sound of protest, Miss Perry shook her head. "No, no, it was all for the best. If he had loved me, you know, no amount of pressure could have forced him to break it off. And if he did not . . . then I am better off not being married to him . . . for I loved him too much to settle for anything less than that."

Only the ticking of the mantel clock broke the cool silence of the room. "Yes, I feel the same way. Without love, marriage would be . . . torture," Josie said softly.

"I always thought so."

"And . . . there was never anyone else?"

Miss Perry's shoulders lifted in a tiny shrug. She gave a wan smile. "No one offered. I suppose it was partly my own fault—I withdrew from society after that. I was young and foolish—and by the time I was ready to show my face again, everyone considered me to be upon the shelf."

"What happened to the young man?" Angry at the unknown viscount, Josie watched Miss Perry's face closely as she replied.

"Oh, he married an heiress and now there are three grown sons. Our paths crossed a few times over the years and I must say, the whispers were not too unbearable. We spoke civilly to one another—rather like strangers."

"How awful."

Miss Perry nodded, then seemed to brace herself, her shoulders straightening. "He died six years ago of some inflammation or other. So it is all in the past now. I have long since come to believe that it was simply not in my destiny to be married—to have my own home and family."

She sounded so calm, so without bitterness, that Josie couldn't help but gaze at her admiringly. She knew why she had liked Miss Perry so much, right from the first moment they met. Miss Perry not only had a generous heart, she was a survivor. She didn't complain, she bore what she had to, and survived.

"I enjoy hearing about the past," she said slowly, her mind shifting to another subject, and wondering how to broach it. "I would like to ask you . . . I hope you won't think I'm prying, but . . ."

"Go ahead, my dear."

"Do you know anything about my husband's past? I gather it's common knowledge—except to me. He loved a girl named Molly once. Lady Tattersall told me a little about her, but we were interrupted before I learned what happened to her—or why Ethan quarreled with the old earl and left London."

"Now that," Miss Perry remarked softly, "was a tragic story."

"You know it then." Eagerly, Josie searched her face. "You know what became of Molly."

"I know what most people know—what was guessed at, hinted at." Miss Perry regarded her soberly. "That the shopgirl loved by the Earl of Stonecliff's younger son died when she was run down by a carriage after leaving work one night—run down much as I almost was this afternoon, my lady. Only, according to rumor and gossip—that occasion was no accident, but deliberate."

For a moment Josie could only stare at her. Then she found her voice, though it came out in a hoarse gasp. "Murder?"

"It could never be proved, of course." Though there was no one else in the room and they couldn't possibly be overheard, Miss Perry dropped her voice to little more than a whisper. "But everyone knew that the earl objected to his son's involvement with the poor child, and the night Ethan Savage left England, he—"

She broke off, pursing her lips together in an agony of hesitation.

"Please tell me all of it," Josie pleaded, her mind spinning with thoughts of Ethan, a younger, more vulnerable Ethan, in love ... battling the will and wishes of his father.

"On that last night, Ethan burst into the ballroom of Lady Tattersall's house—she was sponsoring the coming-out party of her niece—and before one and all, he ..." She took a deep breath. "He accused his cousin Oliver Winthrop of carrying tales to his father, and he accused the old earl, his own father—and his brother, Hugh—of hiring scoundrels to murder that poor girl, to run her down and leave her dead in the street. And he threw Hugh across the room, quite shattering a good number of furnishings and valuables, and he told his father, before everyone who was assembled, that with Molly dead, he would never marry, he would leave London and never return ... that if he ever saw his father or his brother again, he would ..." Her voice dropped even lower, quivering. "He would tear them limb from limb."

"My God."

Josie stared down at her hands. Her heart was twisting inside her, twisting painfully like a rag being wrung out to dry. "He must have loved her so very much ... so much ... with all his heart."

"He gave up everything because of what happened to her. London spoke of little else for months—though in whispers only, of course." Miss Perry seemed to have forgotten all about the young countess as her memory drifted back to the gossip and rumors that had swirled through salons and theatres and dining rooms.

"I remember that the earl declared himself well rid of so wildly scandalous a son, and everyone agreed with him—but from that moment on, though I only watched from the corners, you know, and never spoke once to the earl in my life, or to Ethan Savage until his return—I secretly admired that wild, handsome boy for loving with his whole heart. One can't help but admire it. Oh, dear," she murmured suddenly, dismayed by the stricken expression on Lady Stonecliff's face, and realizing in dismay how she had been carrying on most tactlessly about the Earl's first love to his brand-new bride.

"But that was all in the past, you know—a *very* long time ago. He obviously loves you now with the same depth and intensity, Lady Stonecliff, or he never would have subjected himself to returning to England, to taking over the responsibilities left to him. A man like Ethan Savage wouldn't have married for any reason other than love." She smiled warmly and with encouragement, her words emphatic. "You are a very lucky woman, my dear. As I'm sure you well know."

"Yes," Josie murmured, pasting what she hoped was a tranquil smile on her face even as her heart was breaking. "I'm lucky indeed."

She cast frantically about in her mind for another subject. She didn't trust herself to speak another word about Molly, or that night when Ethan had made clear to everyone just how much she'd meant to him.

Fortunately, at that moment, she remembered something else she hadn't yet had the chance to ask Miss Perry.

"There's a young lady who traveled in America recently," she said, using the same words she'd voiced nearly a dozen times in the past week when broaching the subject at parties, the theatre, or while riding in Rotten Row. "And I would dearly like to find her again. Her name is Miss Alicia Denby." She held her breath and watched Miss Perry's face. "Do you know her?"

To her disappointment, the other woman shook her head. Just as all the others she'd asked had done. "No, I'm afraid not. But then I don't know nearly as many people, my lady, as Rosamund, or Lady Tattersall. Indeed, Lady Tattersall knows everyone! Have you asked her?"

"Not yet." Trying to hide her disappointment, Josie explained. "She just arrived in London, and I haven't seen her yet—not since that afternoon at Stonecliff Park. But I'll ask her tonight at the Cartwright ball."

"If anyone knows Miss Denby, it will be Lady Tattersall," Miss Perry assured her, and rose to take her leave.

"You'll be attending the ball tonight, Miss Perry?"

Within Miss Perry's doll-like face, her rich brown eyes sparkled. "Oh, yes, the Crenshaws are all going, and I've been kindly included in their party. I understand that Colonel Hamring will be there, too. His first outing since his injury." Miss Perry blushed. "He has been kind enough to call on me, to thank me for caring for him that night."

"Has he?" Josie studied her intently, noting the high color rushing into her dainty cheeks.

"Well, that seems only right," she pointed out. "Your concern and care for him that terrible night was admirable."

"No, no, it was the Colonel's actions that were admirable. He risked his life. I never saw anything as brave as what he and your dear husband did that night."

"And he is a fine-looking man, too," Josie added,

nearly chuckling with delight as Miss Perry's eyes seemed to glisten.

"Yes, quite handsome," she admitted, and the pink color in her cheeks deepened.

"I must be going," she said suddenly, and reached for her handbag. Her usually steady fingers were trembling a bit as she clutched it. "I've just realized I have no idea what I'm going to wear this evening."

"Whatever you choose, I'm sure Colonel Hamring will find it most becoming." Josie didn't know what devil made her say that, but Miss Perry, though she turned red as an apple, only sighed.

"I daresay he'll scarcely notice. I seem to recall in the past he has occupied himself in the gaming rooms, playing cards with the gentlemen, and rarely dancing. He probably won't even realize I'm there. And he certainly wouldn't bother himself over me if he did. Not that I would wish him to," she added hastily.

"Of course not." But *we'll just see about that* is what Josie was actually thinking as she watched Miss Perry go down the steps and turn up the street with a wave.

As she went upstairs and along the corridor to her own bedroom, Josie tried to concentrate on the possibility of a romance between Miss Perry and Colonel Hamring, and what she could do to further it. It was a much more pleasant topic than the other one she kept having to block from her mind: Ethan's overwhelming love for Molly. His pain at her death, and during the years following it. The ache he must feel for her, which no doubt was stronger now that he had come home to England where they'd met and loved.

Why *had* he come home?

It wasn't for the money. Josie knew that as well as she

knew how to lace her shoes. She'd seen Ethan's torment that night he'd heard from Latherby about his father's will, when he'd gotten himself roaring drunk and forced her to marry him. He hadn't been a happy man—ecstatic over an inheritance. He'd been tortured, driven, enraged.

What had he said that first night in her bedroom at Stonecliff Park? *They're depending on me. Every person you met tonight is depending on me. All those servants, and the tenants besides. . . . If not . . . I'd never willingly set foot on this damned British soil again."*

Something about this sense of duty, this owning up to his obligations, touched her more deeply even than his courage against Pirate Pete and Tiny. The only other person she'd ever deeply cared for was Pop Watson, and Pop, for all his good qualities, had never owned up to much responsibility. But Ethan hadn't tried to escape his. Despite the cost to himself, despite the fact that he'd vowed before all of London society never to return, when duty had summoned him, he'd answered. He'd returned to face one and all. That took a rare courage.

I've never had a real home, Josie thought as she closed the door of her dusky-pink and cream room. *I've never had an attachment to a place, a spot where I mattered, where I couldn't just up and leave, and no one would much notice or care if I never came back.*

A place where I belonged.

But Ethan did. He belonged here in England. He belonged at Stonecliff Park. Deep down, whether he knew it or not, he was rooted to this lovely green land, rooted to Stonecliff Park, to all those attached to it and who were dependent on him.

Rooted in a way she could never be to anything—or, she thought on a small sob of despair—to anyone.

Don't get attached, she warned herself as she paced to the window and stared down past the gate into the quiet, tree-shaded street. *To Ethan or to Stonecliff Park, or to this beautiful, comfortable house. They're not yours, they were never yours. It's only for a few months.*

Loneliness engulfed her then in quick, drowning waves. And with it came a quiet grief. As the sun dipped lower in the sky and the shadows lengthened and began to fall, she stood at the window and shook with silent sobs.

Chapter Seventeen

"My congratulations, Josephine—er, my lady." Lucas Latherby pushed his spectacles up on his nose as Ethan stood aside so that she could join them in the library.

"You have done it. You look precisely, without a doubt, like a lady. The transformation is ... awe-inspiring. Your hair—why, every strand is perfectly in place. Your carriage, excellent. Even the demure expression upon your face—"

"Enough, Latherby," Ethan interrupted irritably as Josie came forward and he closed the library door. "She's been dissected by you quite enough for a lifetime."

He studied her, though, as she accepted the goblet of brandy he offered her and took a dainty sip. Lord, she was an incredible sight. A vision in a glimmering beaded evening gown of midnight blue, her skin glowing like rich pale cream against it. Her eyes glowed nearly the same shade as the dramatic hues of the gown. And around her throat were the Marsdale pearls, passed down through his mother's family for generations.

She had not yet drawn on her gloves, and he found himself staring at the gold ring on her finger. Latherby's ring, he remembered now, and suddenly felt uncomfortable. As if it were months ago and not merely weeks, he found himself remembering how adverse he'd been to slipping his grandfather's ring onto her finger the night of their wedding. Now he felt a twinge of resentment about her wearing as a wedding band a ring that belonged to Latherby.

He was toying with the idea of having her take it off and put on the emerald ring here and now. The thought gave him pleasure. He didn't know why. But then he noticed that there were pale lavender shadows beneath her lovely eyes. Her fine-boned face looked pinched and tense, despite the smile she bestowed on Latherby over her brandy goblet, and Ethan forgot everything else.

"What's wrong?" he demanded, studying her with penetrating hawk's eyes as she turned her carefully neutral gaze upon him.

"Why should anything be wrong?"

He didn't know. He only knew that the easy smile wasn't in her eyes. The lilt had vanished from her voice. What in hell had happened to take all the sparkle out of her?

"Did you hurt yourself this afternoon when you threw yourself in the way of that damned carriage?" He stalked toward her and gripped her wrist so she couldn't turn away. His eyes inspected her, searching for a bruise, but all of her white exposed skin, from her throat down to the lush expanse of bosom displayed by the low-cut gown, was sumptuous perfection.

"No, of course not, I'm tired, Ethan. That's all."

He didn't believe it for a moment, but he wasn't about to call her a liar in front of Latherby. Beneath his thumb, he felt her pulse throbbing, and still watching her eyes, he began to stroke her wrist with his thumb, very gently holding it, brushing his thumb back and forth lightly across her delicate skin.

"Latherby came by to tell me that Grismore is most eager to make your acquaintance and settle the terms of the will."

"Oh." Josie felt electricity jolt through her as Ethan's thumb flicked back and forth across her wrist. The gaslight globes in the library hissed softly as she fought to think clearly, to keep her emotions under tight control.

Her pulse raced faster. The knowledge of his deep and indelible love for Molly rested heavily upon her shoulders. If she didn't want to make a complete fool of herself, she must keep her feelings for him hidden deep inside her soul.

"So," she asked as steadily as she could beneath that steely gaze, and with her wrist captured by his hand, "when is the inspection to be held?"

That surprised a grin from him. "Inspection? You make it sound like you're a horse I'm planning to buy."

"No—more like the horse you've already bought." The words were out before she realized just how inelegant they sounded. She threw a mortified glance at Latherby, bracing herself for a reproof.

But that gentleman had been observing with acute shrewdness the way the Earl of Stonecliff was gazing at his dance hall bride. Was that . . . *could* there be tenderness in the Earl's eyes?

Where was the coldness? The anger, the sarcasm?

He saw warmth, amusement, interest. And admiration.

His thoughts spun, but he had the wit to hold his tongue as he turned to the Countess.

"The interview will be held next Tuesday, if that is convenient for you and his lordship, my lady."

"My lady? Come now, Mr. Latherby, since when have we been on such formal terms?" A more natural laugh sprang to Josie's lips, and a pretty spark entered her eyes. "It's only me—your same old clumsy Josie."

"You are quite transformed, my lady. I am nearly speechless!"

"You?" Now Josie did laugh, a delightful musical sound that warmed Ethan's heart inexplicably and seemed to mellow and soften all the austere masculine shadows of the room.

"Latherby also came by to tell me that he believes the police have several new leads concerning Pirate Pete and his cohorts. They last robbed a house in Belgravia, and there are rumors that they've been seen at some of the public houses near the gasworks. Other witnesses have placed them at an inn as far away as Tunbridge Wells. The landlord's being questioned. But at any rate, the police are hunting them with a vengeance, and they ought to be in custody soon. So you don't have to worry."

She took another sip of brandy and shook her head. "I'm not worried. Do I *look* worried?"

She did, but not about that, Ethan guessed. Yet he was relieved to hear the lighter note in her voice and hoped it meant her troubles were lifting. Whatever they might be.

"If anything," Josie continued, arching an eyebrow, "I'm worried that we'll be late for the party and insult Lady Cartwright." She smiled then, that wonderful smile, and Ethan felt aching tension ripple through him. He had an enchanting view of lush, slightly parted lips.

"Did you know that she works tirelessly on behalf of the new foundling home? We had a conversation about it at the races just the other day. I offered to help her," she added, half challengingly, as if wondering how he would react to this announcement.

"Suit yourself." Ethan knew that whatever Josie and Lady Cartwright and the other ladies of London who were so inclined might do to aid the poor orphaned children of the rookeries could hardly make a dent in their troubles, but every bit would help. He'd already made arrangements for some of his newly inherited wealth to go toward bettering some of the conditions of the slums—squalid, brutal conditions that bred criminals like Pirate Pete, Lucian, and Tiny, and many others not so bold or vicious, but equally as desperate. The difference between the rich and middle classes, and those of the poorer working classes, was staggering and pathetic. In his years as a gunfighter, there'd been many times when he'd tried to use his gun to help and protect those who were too weak to protect themselves—now he had the means to help those who were weak and vulnerable in a different sort of way.

It didn't surprise him that Josie was interested in helping too. Mrs. Fielding had mentioned to him before he left Sussex that the new lady of the house was seeking ways to aid the poor of the district. And considering her own background, it made sense. But not everyone would take action as she was doing, Ethan reflected. Some would simply exult in their own good fortune and the luxuries that had fallen into their laps—and not give a damn about anyone else.

"We'd better be going." As she set down the goblet, he took her arm. "I'm sure you don't want to miss one moment of Miss Crenshaw's scintillating company," he added wickedly.

As Latherby watched Ethan Savage hand his delicately

beautiful wife up into the carriage, the astounding thought that had entered his head earlier returned, even stronger than before.

Ethan Savage was falling in love with that chit—or more likely, had already fallen. And fallen hard.

What in heaven must the old earl be thinking now, providing he could think from his grave? His plan for manipulation and revenge was possibly bringing his wayward son *happiness*—not the misery and entrapment he'd planned.

But, Latherby pondered as the carriage clattered away into the misty night, how long would it continue so?

Especially in light of a certain visit he himself had been paid only this afternoon by Mr. Oliver Winthrop.

A most interesting and highly profitable visit.

Latherby grimaced, remembering with a heavy heart the way Ethan had looked at his wife tonight in the library.

He squared his shoulders, put his bowler on his head, and set off into the darkness.

Chapter Eighteen

"I don't care a fig for what Rosamund Crenshaw says—it is my belief that Lady Stonecliff is a breath of fresh air."

Lady Cartwright held court at the center of a small group of ladies near the refreshment table. Behind her in the brilliantly lit silver ballroom, fragrant with cut flowers and perfume, men and women in all their bejeweled finery drank champagne, chatted, strolled, and danced.

"In the short time I've known her, I've not once found her lacking in courtesy—and there is something so sweet about her. Perhaps it's the American touch, which I happen to find appealing. She has even offered her help at the foundling home. I like her—I like her very much."

Lady Cartwright was pleased to see Lady Tattersall nodding agreement with her. "Oh, yes, she's a dear girl." Lady Tattersall turned slightly so that she could catch sight of Lady Stonecliff as she was whirled across the dance floor in her husband's arms. With approval she noted how closely Ethan was holding her, how adorably Josephine tilted her head up to gaze into his eyes. They appeared oblivious of everyone and everything else.

"She is exactly the sort of wife my godson needs—vibrant, you know, not the least bit insipid. Ethan would be bored to tears with someone strictly conventional."

"Well, I have heard some rumors about her background in America," sniffed the third matron present, the pale, broad-shouldered Duchess of Melling. Her beetle eyes narrowed on the waltzing couple, who appeared, at least from this distance, to be very much in love. Which in itself, she concluded, was a vulgar display and wholly inappropriate. What person of quality married for love?

"And if there is any truth to them—"

"Of course there isn't," a new voice piped in. "And it is unbecoming to accept as truth that which is only idle gossip."

In surprise, all three women turned simultaneously to find Miss Clara Perry regarding them with a martial light in her eyes.

As they parted to admit her to the circle, Lady Cartwright, Lady Tattersall, and the Duchess all had to suppress gasps of astonishment. The mousy Miss Perry never spoke up so forthrightly—particularly to a group of ladies she only happened to be passing by and had overheard.

There was something else unusual about her tonight. In place of her usual plain gray or russet gown of somewhat old-fashioned style, she was wearing a fashionable ensemble of water-green taffeta, embellished by a black silk sash and buttons and a narrow paneled skirt complete with a quite elegant lace train.

"Forgive my intrusion, your grace," she continued, peeping up at the Duchess with nowhere near her usual shyness. "But I have found it wise not to believe hearsay. From my own knowledge of her, I can say that Lady

Stonecliff is everything admirable. And aside from that, if she has won the heart of the Earl of Stonecliff, who are we, or even my own dear cousin, Miss Crenshaw, to argue?"

Lady Tattersall beamed. "Quite."

"I wholly agree, Miss Perry." Lady Cartwright smiled warmly at the woman she'd never really spoken to before, someone she'd only noticed at the fringes of the fashionable crowd. "Well said, my dear."

"Hah!" The Duchess flushed, her skin taking on the shade of rotten grapes. She was not going to be bested by some insipid poor relation of the Crenshaws! "Don't be so sure of Lord Stonecliff's taste when it comes to females," she snorted. "Or have you forgotten that he once bestowed his deepest affections upon a shopgirl?"

Miss Perry opened her mouth to reply to this, but before she could utter a word, Lady Tattersall fired the parting shot. "You really ought to pay a bit more attention, my dear—and make use of your eyes, your ears, and your wits as well as your tongue. Anyone with any degree of sense can perceive that Lady Stonecliff is certainly not a shopgirl!"

And with this, she tucked Miss Perry's arm in hers and swept off with her. Lady Cartwright, smiling, quickly excused herself from the Duchess of Melling's company, leaving that fuming lady to stare balefully at the handsome young couple still waltzing dreamily across the marble floor.

But things weren't going quite as smoothly between the Earl and Countess as they appeared.

The evening was taking its toll on Ethan. Hell, the whole week was taking its toll. Every moment he spent with her, playing the smitten husband, filled him with a seething frustration. Because after only a few minutes in her company, he always found himself wishing they could cast off the pretenses and just be themselves. Wishing he could say things, think things, *do* things proper English peers didn't say and think and do.

"You dance well," he told Josie as they whirled past velvet curtained alcoves and potted palms. But what he really wanted to tell her was: *You feel like an angel in my arms. I'd like to show you heaven in my bed.*

She answered in the same polite tone he had used. "I've had a lot of practice."

Practice? She meant at the Golden Pistol. Dancing with cowboys, miners, townsmen—old drunks and overgrown boys and every kind of scoundrel from gambler to gunman. The image of her dancing with them, flirting with them, possibly *sleeping* with them, set his teeth on edge.

"Ahuh. I'll just bet you did."

His mocking tone and narrowed eyes brought a flush to her cheeks. Her chin flew up at a defiant angle.

"That offends you? I don't see why it should."

"It doesn't. I don't give a damn what you did before, or what you'll do after." Beneath her perfectly poised expression, Ethan thought he saw her flinch.

Good, he thought, his lip curling as he steeled himself away from sympathy. *She wants a strictly businesslike relationship—wants me out of her bed, even with a marriage license that gives me permission to go there—then, fine. That's what she's got.*

But how many had gone there before him? It was none of his business. And didn't matter a damn. She'd made it clear she didn't want him in her bed—and far be it from him to go where he wasn't wanted. But now he could only remember with disbelief how lightly and casually he'd made that promise on the train, and assured her he'd have no trouble keeping it.

What had he told her? *Have it your way, lady. It's just fine with me. I'm not all that interested.*

Somehow or other, he'd gotten to the point where he was a hell of a lot more than interested. On the verge of loco was more like it.

When she'd almost been run down by that carriage, bringing back hideous memories of what had befallen Molly, he'd had to fight to keep from snatching her into his arms and crushing her against him with relief.

"Ethan, the music's stopped. The dance has ended. *Ethan . . .*"

Her quiet, urgent voice recalled him to the present with an unpleasant jolt. He looked down at the heart-stoppingly beautiful woman in his arms and knew he'd better get off this dance floor and away from her pronto. He had to keep up the pretense, and at the same time, keep her at a distance. But this dancing business was pushing things. Holding her in his arms during this damned waltz had made his loins ache and his mind fill with urges he'd never experienced toward anyone he'd done "business" with before.

He'd be damned if he'd dance with her again.

"Let's go." He half dragged her toward the refreshment table with its snowy cloth and fountains of champagne.

"Think I'll join the gentlemen at billiards." He was no longer in the mood for pretenses. He sketched the briefest of bows and without a backward glance left her with Miss Perry.

Josie watched him go with torn emotions. Beneath her outward calm, her hands were clammy. She didn't know how to act with him, what to do or say. Since that day by the river, when they had both apparently realized how important it was for them to keep their distance, and abide by the rules of their agreement, he had treated her with cool formality when they were alone, and with charming attention when they were in public.

And it was best that way, she knew. But it was also awkward. Not to mention difficult. Always having to guard her tongue, and her heart. Always having to pretend that it meant nothing to her when he touched her, or looked at her, or spoke to her in public in that warm, interested way of his. Because none of it was real, she reminded herself. And if she forgot that for more than a moment, she was nothing but a fool.

The sensation of dancing in his arms, of being held close and tight, and whisked across the floor as if she weighed no more than a button, had been intoxicating. If only it were real—the light in his eyes as they danced, the intense way he held her, looked at her, listened to her.

That day on the banks of the river, it had all seemed real enough. And there was no one about but the two of them. But he had only said what he had because of the passion of the moment, she told herself.

All men said things in passion they didn't mean, made promises, led a girl on. She'd heard and seen enough in the Golden Pistol to know how men used women when they wanted to get them into their beds. And Snake . . . Snake had made promises at first when she'd wed him— about giving up the outlaw life, about making her happy, about finding them a place they could call home.

Each promise had been empty as a valley creekbed in summer. And worse, Snake had hurt her. She'd never known anything could hurt so bad as what had happened when he'd tossed her down on the bed on their wedding night and torn off all her clothes and thrown himself down upon her. . . .

Ethan just wants to do that, too, she reminded herself. *He wanted to do it on the streambank and that's why he told you all those things. Things he thought you wanted to hear. It was a trick, a ploy, to get you to break the agreement. There was nothing more behind it. He doesn't care about you. No one's ever cared about you— except Pop, a little, and Mrs. Guntherson at the orphanage. Why should you think a man like Ethan Savage would care about you?*

"What is it, my dear? What's wrong?" Poor Miss Perry was staring at her in dismay. "You look positively pale. Are you ill?"

"No . . . I . . ." Josie hastily recalled herself to the present. She wondered for how long Miss Perry had been speaking to her and she hadn't heard a word. "I was only . . . feeling sad that I haven't seen Colonel Hamring all evening," she said quickly, blurting out the first excuse that came to mind. "And I wanted to inquire about his recovery."

"I haven't seen him yet myself." Though her voice shook a little over the words, Miss Perry's sweet face almost hid her disappointment. But Josie knew it must be intense.

Only look at how lovely Miss Perry was tonight— Josie had never seen her in such a becoming gown.

"I see you chose what to wear—it is beautiful," she said with a smile.

"Oh, well, I had been saving this gown for a special occasion . . . not that this occasion is special, for why should it be? But . . . the urge to wear it suddenly came over me. . . ." Her voice trailed off. "Silly, I suppose. Most silly."

"Will you walk with me?" Josie took her arm, leaving Miss Perry little choice. She had scanned the crowded ballroom swiftly and could see no sign of the Colonel. Perhaps he was gambling in one of the other rooms, or playing billiards. Perhaps if they strolled around a bit they would spot him.

But to Miss Perry she only said, "It is so stuffy in here. I need a breath of air."

They paced through the garden, chatting companionably, then returned to the house and leisurely crossed the hall. "I've heard that Lady Cartwright's music room is exceptionally beautiful—"

Josie broke off as she suddenly spotted Colonel Hamring emerge from a room down the corridor, where she had earlier seen men playing cards.

"Colonel Hamring, do come help me. Miss Perry is feeling faint," she called softly, and with satisfaction saw his head jerk up.

"What's this?" He reached them in several quick strides. "Miss Perry, are you ill?"

"No, I'm fine—" She nearly squealed as Josie pinched her arm. "Faint, yes, feeling a bit faint," she amended, casting the girl beside her a frantic glance.

"Here, ma'am, take my arm."

"Colonel, please help me get her into the music room." Josie allowed an expression of great concern to settle over her features. "Some air will do you good, my dear. Yes, that's right, do lean upon the Colonel. He won't let you fall. We'll be there in a moment."

She watched from beneath her lashes as Colonel

Hamring—who appeared recovered from his injury—
attended to Miss Perry with kindness and concern.

"Oh, no, I'm feeling much better," the lady protested
when he insisted upon bringing her a glass of water.

"Now what sort of a gentlemen would I be not to take
every care of you—especially when you nursed me so
bravely after that recent altercation, ma'am?" He patted
her small hand with his much larger one, and hurried off
with brisk strides.

"What are you doing, Lady Stonecliff? How could you
lie to him that way?" Miss Perry stared at her in dazed
shock.

"It was easy." Josie clapped a hand over her mouth to
suppress a giggle. "And it's for a good cause. Now when
he comes back . . . hush, here he comes."

And she moved away from the edge of the sofa as
Colonel Hamring reappeared with a goblet of water.

"I'm sure she only needs a few moments of rest and
quiet," Josie murmured. "There was a gentleman who
waltzed with her a bit too roughly, I'm afraid, and it
made her quite dizzy," she added, and was pleased when
Colonel Hamring scowled.

"What? No excuse for that," he exclaimed, tugging on
his mustache.

"No, indeed. Colonel, I'm sure *you* would know the
proper way to waltz with a lady as delicate as Miss
Perry."

"Eh? Certainly. Certainly. Well, I haven't waltzed
much in my life, never went in much for dancing, but I
would certainly try."

"Excellent. I'm sure she wouldn't refuse you, but you
will wait to dance with her until she's had a moment to
recover, won't you?"

"Of course, of course."

"There's no need," Miss Perry protested, but Colonel Hamring shook his head, looking more than ever like a gruff old walrus.

"Nothing would give me greater pleasure, madame, than to waltz with you and show you how a gentleman properly treats a lady," he said. "But not until I'm certain you've recovered."

"You're too kind." Miss Perry threw a desperate glance in Josie's direction as she saw the Countess edging toward the door.

"Ah, where are you going, Lady Stonecliff?"

"To find my husband. He must be searching for me by now. I'll return as soon as I've set his mind at ease."

And she slipped out of the music room, leaving Miss Perry and the Colonel alone.

Josie was very well pleased with herself. She had no intention of finding Ethan however, for the strain of holding her feelings in check and playacting an all too painful role was wearing on her. Besides, if he was busy playing billiards with the other men, he wouldn't be missing her in the least—and would probably be annoyed at the interruption.

She slipped among the other guests ambling through the house, many of them couples strolling arm in arm. A flutter of loneliness stole through her.

She shook off the sensation, drawing on her common sense. This was no time to be mooning over a man who could only hurt her. This was a perfect time to find Lady Tattersall and question her about Miss Denby.

She smiled and nodded politely to those she passed, but made her way purposefully through the various lovely rooms and passageways until she at last spotted Lady Tattersall.

Ethan's godmother was emerging from the sitting room into a wide hallway set with gilt chairs and small marble-topped tables. The carpet beneath was a rich floral, and there were several gold-framed paintings on the walls. She was speaking to Lady Cartwright—they appeared deep in conversation, but when they saw Josie they paused and smiled, beckoning her to join them.

She came forward into the hall, but before she could say a word, her gaze was drawn to the lustrous painting hanging just above Lady Cartwright's head. There two fair, elegantly clad young women were seated upon a sofa, while another stood just behind and to the left of them, holding a small bouquet.

Something about the woman who was standing drew her attention. She stared at the heart-shaped, angelic face, the uptilted eyes as blue as violets, the full, smiling lips. And then her gaze moved to the soft sky-blue crepe gown and fell upon the delicately glinting brooch.

Shock jolted through her. *The brooch*.

Her brooch!

With her throat closing, Josie stepped closer, then craned her neck, staring at the pearl-and-opal brooch in the portrait.

"Who . . . is this?" she heard herself ask in a voice that was thick and raspy and totally unlike her own.

"My dear, are you well?" Lady Tattersall stared at her in concern. "You look as if you'd seen a ghost!"

"Yes, I'm quite well, but . . . who is this? Lady Cartwright, please tell me."

"Well, that is a portrait of me, dear. There, sitting on the sofa beside my sister, Georgina. I'm in the peach gown and she is in white. And the girl standing beside us in blue was our cousin, Charlotte. Heavens, Lady Stonecliff—do sit down. You look positively faint!"

"No, I'm not going to faint. I'm not. I'm fine."

Trembling and white, Josie struggled to take in the meaning of Lady Cartwright's words. Instead of sitting down, she continued to stare at the painting, at the face of Charlotte, at the brooch glittering upon her breast.

"Your *cousin*?"

"Why, yes. Our mothers were sisters. We were very close growing up, but . . . my dear, why are you so curious?"

"Lady Cartwright, do you know of a young woman by the name of Miss Alicia Denby?"

There was silence as Lady Cartwright stared at her, stared at the young countess with the pale face and the intense, almost pleading eyes.

"Why, yes," she said slowly, and beside her, Lady Tattersall gave a slight, surprised nod of recognition as well.

"Why, yes, I do. She's Charlotte's daughter—and therefore my cousin. But she rarely goes out in society. How, my dear, did you come to know of her?"

Josie felt the room start to spin. "Lady Cartwright," she gasped, pressing both hands to her suddenly light head. "I think I *should* sit down after all."

"Stonecliff can't seem to lose tonight," young Lord Willowton grumbled as he and his companion, the Marquis of Cavenleigh, eldest son of the Duke of Melling, stalked out into the garden for a breath of air. They'd both drunk more than enough for one night, and they'd both lost heavily at cards and billiards to the Earl of Stonecliff.

"Well, if you had a wife who looked like that one, you'd be flying pretty high too." Lord Cavenleigh scowled.

"Don't want a wife. Don't want to be married," Lord Willowton mused, sinking down upon a marble bench and sighing heavily. "But wouldn't mind finding the Countess of Stonecliff in my bed. Wouldn't mind at all."

"From what I hear, my friend, it could well come to pass. The beauteous countess might not be quite the lady her fine clothes and elegant face would have you think. I heard a rumor, a tantalizing rumor . . . quite scandalous really."

"Really? Do tell all."

"Spent some time at my club today and the word going around is that she used to work in a dance hall in America. In the West, you know, on that wild frontier." He began to snigger as his friend's eyes widened. "It appears she's nothing but a cheap little hussy Stonecliff picked up on his travels."

"No!"

"Oh, indeed." He laughed uproariously. "So you might well be able to lure her to your bed, Freddy—only don't let Stonecliff catch you. What I heard is that she's as common as—"

He never finished the sentence.

Ethan Savage grabbed him up by the scruff of the neck, spun him around, and glared like the devil incarnate into Cavenleigh's pale green eyes.

"Stonecliff . . . er . . . I didn't mean . . . believe you've misunderstood . . ."

"Let me make sure you don't misunderstand this," Ethan snarled, and slammed his fist into Cavenleigh's jaw.

The young lord went down with a muffled groan.

Ethan seized him, hauled him up, and hit him again, this time in the midsection. Lord Cavenleigh landed in the flower bed.

Lord Willowton backed away in terror.

"Not so fast." Ethan stepped over Cavenleigh's moaning form and grasped Willowton by his pristine silk lapels.

"If you or your friend say one more word about my wife—to anyone, ever, anytime—I'll beat you both to such bloody pulps, your own mothers won't recognize you." His tone was soft, silky smooth, but laced with unmistakable, very lethal danger. Willowton quailed beneath the murderous gleam emanating from deep within the other man's eyes.

"I won't . . . I wasn't . . . but I won't . . . I was only admiring—"

Ethan punched him in the chin, and watched as Willowton sank to his knees, blood spurting from his soft, weak mouth.

"Don't," Ethan advised in a voice thick with fury. "Don't you or your pompous little friend even dare to look at her."

Chapter Nineteen

It was no use.

No matter how hard Josie tried, she couldn't sleep. She tossed and turned in the soft wide bed, twisted and punched her pillows, kicked off and yanked at the blankets.

She was wide-awake.

Outside, a mist-white moon rode the midnight sky. Wind fluttered the pale curtains at her window and brought with it the perfume of roses from the small, gated garden.

Long hours stretched until dawn. But she couldn't stay in bed one minute longer.

Feet bare, she padded into the hall, her hair loose and flowing. She wore only her white silk nightgown—no need for a wrapper since no one would be up and about at this hour. Any sane person would be sound asleep.

Perhaps a dish of tea would help. Dish of tea? Josie grinned ruefully at herself. She was beginning to think like an Englishwoman.

With a candle held aloft she made her way through the darkness and slipped into the kitchen. There she lit a lamp and put a kettle on to boil. She whisked toward the cupboard in search of cups, then nearly screamed as she saw Ethan in the doorway.

His tall form filled the narrow opening. He was watching her, an unreadable expression in his eyes, a brandy goblet held carelessly in one hand.

Her fingers flew to her mouth to smother the scream. "Are you trying to scare me to death?" she managed to croak when she could find her voice again.

He didn't answer. He simply looked at her.

Josie felt her heart begin to hammer. There was something about him tonight—something sleek and perilous. The aura of danger clung to him as it had that first day in Abilene.

He still wore his evening clothes. But his tie was loose, his shirt unbuttoned at the collar, open to reveal an expanse of dark muscled chest. His eyes glittered.

"You've been drinking," she murmured, half to herself.

"Not enough, sweetheart. Not nearly enough."

He wasn't drunk. She could see that as he swaggered into the kitchen and came toward her. Beneath their glitter, his eyes were keen and cold. There was tension in him, coiling through the powerful muscles of his wide-shouldered frame, hardening the set of his jaw.

"Would you like tea?"

"Not a chance."

"Coffee?"

"Nope."

"Eggs and ham and buttered toast and some jellied tarts?" She was only half joking. "I'm a cook, remember. I could whip up any of those things before you could say—"

"I'm not looking for sustenance." He drained the brandy in one burning gulp and set the goblet on the table with a sharp ping. He advanced a step, closing the distance between them to a mere two feet, watching her eyes go wide and a pulse jump in her throat. "At least, not that kind of sustenance."

Josie could only gaze at him in helpless awe. This tall man with his piercing eyes and black aura of danger—what was he thinking? Feeling? Wanting?

The same as all men want, she told herself in a desperate surge of fury. *To use you. To take his pleasure, satisfy it, and then move on. He's going to divorce you in a matter of months. And send you away, forever.*

That thought shot some fight back into her weakening senses. She gripped the table hard, and pressed her lips together, as if somehow signaling him to keep away, keep out.

Ethan saw it, and it made him want to seize her and show her that she couldn't chase him away or shut him out so easily. It was only with consummate willpower that he kept his feet rooted to the floor, his arms clenched taut at his sides.

A violent restlessness had possessed him this entire night, growing more intense as the hours passed. The strain of watching her charm everyone at the party tonight, of knowing she was his but wasn't his, had been bad enough. But then after hearing those cowards Cavenleigh and Willowton discussing her as if she were a common tart—something had twisted like barbed wire inside him.

He knew those were just the start of the rumors. It would get uglier.

Even punching those pompous bastards hadn't eased the mounting tension inside him. He hadn't been able to stop thinking of her the entire night, even when he was gambling, even when he'd talked of everything under the sun to dozens of people he didn't give a damn about, eaten a tasteless dinner everyone else had raved over, even when he'd allowed himself only one waltz with her the entire evening.

And when he'd heard her light step on the stairs, glimpsed her nightgown-clad form from his study, watched her glide along the hall and into the kitchen, he'd felt as if someone had bashed *him* in the stomach.

There'd been no choice but to follow.

So now here he was, less than two feet from this tantalizing creature he'd wed in a judge's study in Abilene, and he was locked in a bloody inner struggle for self-control that threatened to rage outward.

To keep from reaching for her, he raked his fingers through his hair. It was damned near impossible to rein in red-hot hunger and primitive urges when she looked lovelier than the most succulent peach, fresher than a rosy strawberry glistening with dew. He wanted to drown in those violet eyes of hers. Eyes that seemed to singe his soul. He wanted to bury his fingers in the soft, lush riot of her hair. Taste and stroke every inch of silken skin, the small, beautiful mounds of her breasts, every curve from her shoulder to the arch of her delicate little foot.

But he remembered how she'd run from him at the stream. Accused him of changing the rules. And from then on, she'd pulled back from him in every way. The whole damn week in London he'd felt the difference, felt her distance as if it were a block of ice lodged in his throat. That's how she wanted it, he reminded himself grimly. And he'd be damned if he'd give her another chance to spit in his face, accuse him of breaking their bargain, and push him away yet again.

If it was cold and businesslike that she wanted, that's what she'd get.

"Why aren't you in bed?" he demanded, then swiftly amended it. "I mean, asleep. It's the damned middle of the night."

"I know that. I could ask you the same question."

His mouth twisted. Her gumption was as much a part of her as the sweep of her cheekbone, and the voluptuous shape of her lips. He tried hard to be irritated by it, but it only inspired an amused warmth.

Unthinkingly, his gaze dipped lower, from those stubbornly set lips to the pale neckline of her gown and the twin mounds of her breasts clearly and saucily outlined beneath the whisper of silk.

And it was at that very moment that Josie herself suddenly remembered what she was wearing—and what she was *not* wearing.

She let out a squeak. Her arms flew to her chest, crossed there, clung to the wispy fabric of her nightgown. Ruby color rushed like fire into her cheeks.

She half turned her body away from him and started toward the door with as much dignity as a hasty exit could afford. "I couldn't sleep. But I'm tired now. Think I'll go to bed. . . ."

He snagged her arm as she tried to scoot past him. "What's your hurry?" he asked inanely, knowing full well why she wanted to get the hell out of there. But he didn't want her to leave. Not just yet.

"It's late. I'm tired. And I'm not properly dressed."

Let her go. Just let her go. But he couldn't release her arm.

"You're dressed just fine."

"No, Ethan, I'm not. Please let me by."

"What are you afraid of, sweetheart?"

"Certainly not you! But it isn't right . . . I'm in my nightgown—it isn't proper."

"Neither is pickpocketing." He tried desperately to lessen the intensity of desire swamping him by attempting a joke. "But that didn't stop you."

She went still as death. Ethan could have kicked himself. What kind of idiotic thing had that been to say? He'd been rambling, trying to delay her going upstairs and leaving him.

"Sorry, I didn't mean that the way it sounded."

"Yes, you did." Pain shimmered in her eyes. Her voice was a whisper. "You can't ever forget that, can you? Or else you won't. You still think of me as a—"

"No, I don't. I swear." Roughly he pulled her against him. "That's the trouble, I've stopped thinking of you that way."

"You just proved . . ."

"Proof? You're looking for proof of how I feel? I can give you that easily enough."

"Let me go."

"Not until I've shown you how I feel."

"I know all about the way you—"

Before she could finish the sentence his lips closed over hers, rendering her incapable of thought, much less speech. The kiss was deep and violent. Her throat shivered and her knees turned to soup.

"I could kiss you and kiss you and keep kissing you from now until the end of time," Ethan groaned, and his hand wound through her hair, gripping it tight. The other held her against him, so that the whole length of her body burned against his. "I want you more than I've ever wanted anyone, anything. . . ."

Josie was trembling all over from the power of that kiss. Her lips felt bruised. Her skin was hot. She was clinging to Ethan even as she knew she should be pushing him away.

She had no defenses left. If he didn't stop looking at her this way, touching her, kissing her . . . she was lost. Lost . . .

There was only one thing that might stop him, stop both of them before they made a horrible mistake.

As he lowered his mouth toward hers again, she gasped out a single word.

"Molly."

It was Ethan's turn to go motionless as a post. With one hand still entwined in her hair, and her body bent slightly back, he halted while leaning over her, his lips a breath away from hers.

"What did you say?"

"Molly!" Tears sprang to her eyes. "You wanted Molly more than anything. You loved her more than you could ever love . . . anyone," she finished lamely, feeling her heart slice in two as she saw the rage in his eyes.

"Who told you about Molly?"

"What difference does it make?" She pushed him away, frantically, and this time he was so stunned at hearing her fling the other woman's name at him at such a time that he let himself be shoved back.

"She's here, between us. You loved her, you grieve for her still. She is in your heart."

"So what the hell does that have to do with you?" he demanded. His bronzed skin had turned to ash.

She wanted to cry out to him: *She's where I want to be. In your heart. And there's no space for me. . . .*

But the shreds of pride kept those words locked inside.

"I won't be used." How thin and hard her voice sounded, squeezing out those pathetic words. "Used . . . like a harlot. Like someone who doesn't matter. Used only because you can't have her, but you want a woman's body in your bed, someone who can be tossed aside when you're done . . . conveniently forgotten . . ."

"Is that what you think?" He clenched his fists. Fury lashed through him. "Damn you, Josie, is that what you really think?"

He swung away from her and slammed his fist down on the table. The resounding thud echoed through the kitchen, making her jump, fear gleaming in her eyes.

His rage only mounted, a biting, wicked black rage that ripped through his chest, his gut. Every muscle bulged and quivered. "Get out of my sight while you can. Before I do something I'll regret. Do you hear me? Get out!"

She hadn't meant to stir such a reaction. "Ethan, it's just that . . . someday I want more." Her voice was quavering. "I want . . . to be loved by someone, the way you loved Molly. It may never happen but—"

He pushed her across the room with controlled force that cost him dearly. "Get out!"

The air of the kitchen vibrated with the depth of his fury. She saw the heat ignited in his eyes, the tension coursing through his tall frame, and fear at last penetrated even her pain and confusion. She fled past him with a stifled sob, dodging up the stairs.

Sweat burst out on Ethan's brow. My God, that's what she thought of him. That he still loved Molly, that he only wanted to take her to his bed—what? Once, twice, or for the duration of this ridiculous marriage, and then— what had she said—*toss her aside? Conveniently forget?*

He drove his fist down on the table again, heedless of

the servants he might wake. To hell with them. To hell with her. To hell with everything.

And then something exploded inside him. Fury, hot and wild and flailing.

If that's all she thought of him, if that's how she saw him, maybe he should just prove her right. Prove how callous and ruthless and single-minded he could be. Prove how little he cared, that he was nothing but a selfish bastard. . . .

He flung himself from the kitchen and into the hall. She had just reached the top step, and turning, saw him standing below.

Something in his eyes must have warned her. Her lips parted, fear filled her face. Even as he lunged for the steps, she was running.

Chapter Twenty

Josie bolted into her room, every nerve alive with panic. As she heard Ethan pounding up the steps after her, she slammed the door and locked it, then darted to the other door, the sitting room door that connected their bedrooms.

Her fingers shook as she twisted the lock. She backed away, hands to her throat, her heart slamming in her chest as she gazed fearfully back and forth between both doors.

Suddenly there was a crash. The sitting room door shattered inward, the wood splintering, flying across the carpet.

Ethan stood framed in the shattered opening.

A cry of terror lodged in her throat. She'd never seen him look like that. His eyes were narrowed and cold as daggers as he stepped over what was left of the door and stalked toward her.

She fled toward the other door, the one leading to the corridor, seeking escape, but Ethan lunged after, pinning her with his body against the door.

"You're not going anywhere, Josie. Did you really think a lock could keep me out if I want in?"

"No, Ethan! Let me go! What are you planning to do?"

He gave a harsh laugh. "You know what I'm planning to do, sweetheart." His breath rasped in her ear. His voice rang with a deadly purpose that sent broken shivers through her heart. "It's not like you to ask idiotic questions."

He spun her around in his arms, locked her hands above her head, and held her imprisoned between him and the door. Her breath came in ragged, terrified gasps, and her eyes shone with a panic that only increased his anger.

"Ethan, you promised . . ."

"I promised to love, honor, and cherish, and so far I haven't done that, sweetheart. So let's start with love."

"This isn't love—"

His mouth claimed hers. The kiss was savage. "Are you sure?" he grated, lifting his head for only a moment to stare into her eyes. Then his lips descended again. His tongue forced itself into her mouth, searching, plundering, driven on by the low moan in her throat.

Josie fought like mad. But she couldn't budge him, stop him, free herself of him. She twisted and squirmed, but all the while her own body and senses were betraying her. She felt as if she were melting—no, igniting, was more like it. A flame caught hold within her, fanned out, flickering ever stronger.

"Ethan . . . no, please. Don't . . . do this." The plea was mixed with a sob wrenched from the depths of her battered heart.

She felt him stiffen at the sound of that sob. His lips froze just above hers. They were heartbeat to heartbeat, their bodies rigidly pressed together, and she could feel the huge, hard ridge of his manhood against her nightdress, feel every taut muscle up and down the length of his frame.

Another sob, one of mingled fear and craving, spilled out of her, and he raised his head and stared down into her tormented face.

"Are you so sure this isn't love, Josie?" he asked hoarsely. Suddenly his eyes glittered with a fierce, agonized longing that slashed at the remnants of her heart. "Then maybe I'm not doing it right."

And to her astonishment, he released her hands, letting them drop numbly to her sides. She was too stunned to move. She could only stare at him, her breath coming fast and hard in her chest.

Then his hands touched her lightly. They caressed her shoulders, her arms, then slid to just beneath the swell of her breasts. Staring into her eyes, Ethan ran his hands slowly down the trembling length of her until they spanned her waist.

Her lips were quivering. With a slight, tentative smile, Ethan sought her mouth again, this time brushing them with the gentlest of kisses, and then another, and another, each one hotter and sweeter and deeper than the one before.

Wonder swept over her like sun-warmed honey. She was melting, melting against him, into him, into herself. His violence hadn't hurt her. It had frightened her, but not hurt her. But this sweetness, these tender kisses, were killing her.

"I'd never hurt you, Josie," she heard him mutter against her hair, and then her arms went around him, clasping his neck, holding him every bit as tightly as she wanted him to hold her.

"I love you, Josie, don't you know that by now? Or don't you think I'm capable of it?"

There was bitterness and self-mockery and pain in his voice, and reflected in his eyes.

Josie cupped his face in her hands, her fingers trembling. "But you can't." Her voice cracked. "No one's ever loved me. Not *really* loved me. You can't possibly."

"I not only can, you little fool, I do . . . I do. . . ." He gave a hoarse laugh as he gripped one of her hands and pressed it to his lips. A thrill of fire raced down Josie's spine.

"Sounds like I'm saying marriage vows again. Maybe, just maybe I am, Josie, for the very first time."

And then as he read the wonder and doubt and, yes, disbelief in her eyes, anger swept through him again, warring with his efforts at patience.

"Molly's ghost isn't between us, Josie. Only your fears are, your doubts."

"You loved *her*."

"Yes, once, a long time ago. And she died." Now it was his turn to cradle her face in his hands. It didn't matter how she'd learned about Molly—maybe it was for the best that everything be clear between them. Her bones felt so fragile beneath his fingers. Her eyes were huge violet pools watching him with an unwavering intensity that ripped through his chest.

He struggled for words even as his heartbeat accelerated, even as the beauty and fragility of her soul and her spirit touched him. "We were young . . . she was lovely, sweet . . . and she was taken from me, by my own father and my brother, with help from Winthrop, because she wasn't deemed good enough. Good enough! They weren't fit to kiss her hand. And they killed her, and I could never forgive them for that. But . . . it was young love, Josie, new love, and I'll never know if it was meant to last. It was years ago, and she's gone." His eyes darkened with both sadness and acceptance. "She's *been* gone. I've moved on. I never thought I'd love anyone else like that again—and I don't."

She drew in her breath, and his hands clamped down on her shoulders, gripping hard. His eyes blazed into hers. "I love you differently from the way I loved her. *I'm* different now than I was then . . . I love differently, feel differently. And, my sweet, foolish, beautiful little love—believe it or not, I'm prepared to spend this entire night making you believe it. Hell, the rest of my life making you believe it. I love you for *you,* because of *you*—because I can't think of anything or anyone but you! You're in my heart, Josie, you're in my head, and you're in my blood."

He gave her no time to doubt, to question. He dragged her to him and his mouth covered hers. The heat from him flamed into her. Her whole body quivered with it. His mouth burned down her throat like hot silk. And his hands . . . Josie shuddered and trembled at the fierce exploration of those strong, demanding hands.

"Ethan, I want to believe you," she gasped, her arms around him as the sensations washed over her in wave after delicious wave.

"Then believe." His tongue caressed her lips. Her mouth parted, senses swimming.

"Don't . . . lie to me. . . ."

"Is this a lie?" Their lips met, clung, burned.

"Is this a lie?" He traced the outline of her breasts beneath the nightgown, cupped them gently but firmly, kneading them with his hands. When her eyelashes fluttered with delight and her head tilted back as she gave a quivering gasp, he grinned and slid one hand down her hip to cup her bottom.

"Is the way I'm looking at you a lie? Josie, can't you see the answer? Look at me, sweetheart. Look into my eyes. My damned love for you is eating me alive."

She couldn't think anymore, but she could see. She saw the urgency and tenderness gazing back at her, and something else, something darker, more exciting. Need glinted at her, and a desire so ferocious, it had to hurt. She recognized the pain of aloneness in him—perhaps she'd recognized it all along, from the first time he'd kissed her in Judge Collins's study.

Incredibly, she recognized something else too. Love. Love shook Ethan Savage's tall, massive frame, it glittered darkly in his eyes, it pumped through his heart. She felt the jolt, the electricity and the sparks. She threw herself against him.

"I love you too, Ethan! I need you. I need you to hold me, to kiss me. . . ."

"Glad to oblige," he rasped, and then he was kissing her, and undressing her in the dark of the bedroom, sliding the filmy fabric up across her hips and breasts, above her head, then in one motion tossing the nightgown to the floor.

The long, heavy ringlets of Josie's hair cascaded forward across her cheeks. They fell about her shoulders, wild and dark, trailed over her breasts, caressed the pale smooth skin that gleamed in the moonlight tiptoeing in through the windows.

If Ethan was hard before, he was now a rock. His eyes drank in the sight of her lovely pearly breasts with their delicate rose tips, her narrow waist, smooth flat stomach, the lush curve of her hips. Her legs were long and silky, her shoulders sensuously rounded. She was magnificent— dazzlingly feminine, intoxicatingly sweet. And shy. Her cheeks glowed with a blush that would rival dawn.

"You're so beautiful," he managed to croak out as her smile wavered and then grew steadier and she slipped forward sleek as velvet into his arms.

Beautiful? He called me beautiful. And he was gazing at her and touching her as if she were beautiful. Josie's hands skimmed over the breadth of his shoulders, exploring the hard bulge of muscle beneath his fancy white shirt. She continued along the corded muscles of his arms, her head tilted back all the while to savor his deep drowning kisses.

A feverish trembling whisked over her. She wanted to touch him, to see him, all of him. Previously unknown needs and longings tangled through her as she wrapped herself against him, almost too weak with desire to stand.

"Ethan, it's your turn—to take off your clothes," she heard herself whispering, and felt her face flame.

He grinned at her and caught her beneath the knees, scooping her up into his arms.

"So it is," he chuckled, nibbling at the corners of her lips as he carried her toward the bed. "Fair's fair, I always say."

She laughed softly, her arms wound around his neck. "I never heard you say any such thing."

Ethan lowered her onto the bed with infinite gentleness. Her mouth was sweet and soft and giving—and clung to his with such ardor, he thought he'd explode before he could strip off his own clothes.

Slow, he'd go slow. That's what he planned. Slow kisses, slow touches. But the desire lashed at him, and Josie's hands working at the buttons of his shirt, trailing across his chest, drove him to an aching frenzy.

Sweat shone on his naked chest and torso. His clothes landed on the floor in a heap, and then only the two of them were in the darkened room, the two of them and the moonlight and the scent of passion heavy in the air.

He leaned over her and kissed each of her breasts. Leisurely, his tongue curled around first one nipple— caressing, tormenting, teasing it into a taut rose peak— before grazing its way across her flesh to savor the other.

He was driving her mad, utterly mad. Josie arched her back, writhing with delight. Pleasure floated through her with such wild sweetness, she began to ache. Ethan's hair was thick and soft beneath her hands. He smelled of brandy and sweat and cigars, and as her fingers swept across his powerful shoulders and along the muscles of his bronzed back, she felt herself giving up everything to him, pride, dignity, embarrassment, hesitation . . . all dissolving beneath the onslaught of his hands and the warmth of his wicked mouth.

Without thinking, Josie's legs snaked around his, pulling the long, heavy length of him down full upon her, but when she suddenly felt the huge, solid hardness of him against her thighs, panic struck, slicing cold as ice.

"No, Ethan, no, don't!" She froze for a moment, then began to push and writhe, trying to scramble out from under him.

Ethan rolled off her and stared, his breath coming hard. There was fear in her eyes. *No,* he realized with shock. *Terror. And misery. Why?*

"Don't . . . do this to me, sweetheart. You can't want to stop now. What is it, what's wrong?"

She didn't know what to say, how to explain. With all of her heart, she wanted to press her body up against his, to be held tight and close, to be kissed by him until the world rocked and swayed and disappeared and there was only this room, this time, this man—a swirl of heat and sweetness and pleasure.

But there wouldn't be pleasure if she let him do all he wanted to do. There would be pain. Terrible pain.

"It's going to hurt. I'm afraid, I don't want . . ."

He smiled in relief, and reached out to take her hand, pulling it up to his lips. He nibbled a finger, then brushed a kiss across her palm. "It's true that it sometimes hurts the first time, Josie, but . . ."

It hadn't sunk in to him until just now that this would be her first time. He drew in a hard breath as anticipation sharpened. "I'll be gentle, sweetheart. And very careful of you. I'd never do anything to hurt you on purpose, I'll go easily until—"

"No, it always hurts!" She yanked her hand away, her eyes flashing with dismay. There was a sob in her voice. "Don't lie to me!"

"I'm not lying."

"You are—it will hurt. It always does for the woman. I love you, Ethan, and I'll try to let you do it if that's what you want, but . . ."

Ethan could only stare in amazement at the torment in her beautiful face. "What do you mean, it always hurts for the woman?" he demanded, his voice more harsh than he intended. "Who the hell told you this nonsense?"

"No one told me, I know."

He watched as she struggled to sit up. Her hair spilled forward over her breasts in dark rippling waves, and her lower lip was trembling, no longer with passion but with anger and fear.

Something went still and cold and dark inside Ethan. His mouth whitened and thinned to a grim, hard line. "How do you know, Josie? Tell me."

Chapter Twenty-one

His voice was quiet, but the unmistakable note of command in it had her lifting her head to meet his eyes. Anger gleamed in them. *Oh, God, what had she said? He would guess now, he would know.*

It was too late for secrets. When he grasped her arm and ordered her once more to tell him, she did.

"Snake." It came out in a rush. "Whenever Snake did that . . . did *this* with me, it hurt, it hurt something awful. Almost as bad as when he beat me that night. He—"

"You went to bed with that outlaw?" Stupefaction left him numb. Then it quickly gave way to a leap of realization. Shock stabbed through him like a steel-edged bayonet. Ethan stared at her with rigidly clamped jaw.

"He *raped* you?"

The murderous fury blazing in Ethan's eyes terrified her almost as much as the prospect of having him thrust himself into her had.

"It wasn't that exactly—not the way you think. He forced me, yes. I hated him, but . . . we were married."

Josie felt her heart pounding so fast, she thought she would pass out. "Ethan," she pleaded brokenly. "I . . ."

"Let me get this straight. You married an outlaw who beat you and forced you to—"

"He forced me to marry him." Shame flooded through her, hot and scalding. "I didn't want to, but he would've killed Pop Watson if I didn't—and Pop was the closest I ever had to a father! Ethan, don't be angry with me. It was only for two weeks. Then I ran away. Pop was dead and . . . I never loved Snake, I've only loved you. I'll try. I'll try to let you do it to me and to like it. I will."

"Josie!"

She never wept openly before anyone, hadn't for as long as she could remember. Only in private—hot secret tears, secret sobs. Now, though, tears burned her eyes, spilled out. Her shoulders shook with pain-racked weeping.

"Please don't stop loving me because I married a man like him!" she gasped.

This time as he gathered her close he could feel her entire body quaking—not with desire, he realized, but with anguish that she might be rejected, thrust away yet again as she had been over and over in her life. His arms enfolded her, holding her against him as if he would never let her go.

"Shh, sweetheart. Shhh."

She clung to him and sobbed, her face buried in his chest.

"Cry it out then if you have to," he told her grimly. Female tears usually left him unmoved, but these burned into him like scalding bullets. "It's behind you now. It's all behind you."

He thought of the life she'd known, the loneliness, the thankless work, the scraping to get by and stay alive without a home, without family to love or shelter her—

and at last he thought of the desperation she must have known finding herself at the mercy of a brute like Snake Barker.

A dam of pity and love burst inside him, burst so fast and furious and icy cold, it rushed over him like a Rocky Mountain falls.

"I'm going to go back there one day soon, Josie, and hunt that animal down and send him straight to hell." His voice was a harsh cracked whisper against her hair. A vow. "But before I let him die I'm going to—"

He broke off, deciding it was better she didn't know what he was going to do to Snake Barker before he finally allowed him to die. A woman shouldn't have to think about such things.

"No, Ethan, don't go near him!" Alarm chased away the last of the receding sobs, and she lifted a pale, tear-streaked face to his and threw her arms around his neck.

"You don't know Snake—you don't know what he's capable of. I don't want you near him, anywhere near him!"

He was both touched and amused by her concern for him. He had a mean reputation in the West and too many notches on his guns to count. And he'd taken on enough vicious men to understand how they thought, enabling him to predict their actions ahead of time, which gave him a keen advantage. But he didn't want to upset Josie now by promises of revenge, especially if she was going to worry about him.

It had been a long time since someone had worried about him.

His hands curved around her nape and gently massaged the tense muscles of her neck. "I'm not going anywhere yet. Not till we've settled one or two more things."

"What things?"

"Your marriage to this hombre. It was legal?"

She bit her lip and nodded. "Justice of the peace. Just like ours." She took a breath. "I wore that gingham dress, the same one I had on when I picked your pocket."

The misery in her eyes almost made him cut short the questions, but there was more he had to know. "And did you end it legal?" he asked carefully.

She shook her head.

Ethan's breath whistled out sharply. "So, damn it, you're not even my wife."

"But Ethan, we can still—" She stopped and reached out, touching his face. "I feel like your wife. Lord knows, I never felt like anything but a cook and a pack mule and a whore to Snake Barker."

She dropped her hands and swallowed back another sob, covering it with a gasp and a sniffle. Then she pushed back her hair, suddenly aware that she was buck naked and so was he and they were half sitting, half lying on the bed, their bodies curled together, brushing. . . .

"Josie, what Snake did to you—it wasn't making love. You didn't want him. It was rape." The coldness in his eyes now came from a place deep inside himself, a place she couldn't go. "And in the very near future," he said softly, "I'm going to kill him for it."

As she started to protest, he placed a gentle hand across her lips and smiled very tenderly but with great firmness down into her eyes.

"No need to discuss that right now. It can wait. Right now I've got some real good news for you."

She moved his hand away, clasping it tight in hers. "What news, Ethan? I could use some good news right about now."

"What you and Snake did together in your marriage bed is nothing at all like what you and I are going to do on this bed."

As he spoke he eased her down across the wide, fluffy bed, smoothing her hair out on the lace-edged pillow and gazing down at her with a calm certainty that nearly burst Josie's heart in two with wanting him.

"We'll do whatever you want," she agreed instantly. "The kissing part was just wonderful, and the touching, and I can learn to like the other. . . ."

He started to grin, then stopped himself, and cupped her chin in his hand. "Do you trust me, Josie?"

"If I didn't, do you think I'd have let you take my clothes off and come this close to me after what I went through with Snake?" she demanded softly, breathily, and then her eyes met his and she spoke with fervent conviction.

"Yes, Ethan, I trust you."

He drew a hand lovingly through her curls. "Then believe me when I say I won't hurt you—I'd never knowingly hurt you."

This time as his mouth descended on hers, she met his kiss with eagerness, leaning forward, lips parted and soft. She pulled him down atop her and stroked her hands through his hair.

"I believe you," she whispered against his mouth.

Then her lips moved against his. Her breath warmed his mouth, her tongue met his in a teasing, delectable dance. With moonlight streaming over their coiled bodies, she slid her hands across his shoulders, down his splendid back, inviting him nearer, drawing him to her with magic, yearning touches.

The complete trust in her eyes, in her yielding body as it melted against his, was like a jackhammer through his gut.

"Josie, I'm going to love every inch of you until you know the truth about what should be between a man and a woman." His mouth scorched a reckless path of kisses down her throat. He found the trembling pulse in the hollow of her neck, and brushed his lips against it, feeling it stir and flutter.

He vowed to find the strength to go slowly, to cool his own rampaging want of her enough so that when he claimed her, she would know nothing of pain, only ecstasy.

"I'm going to make you forget everything and everyone," he promised, and could have sworn he heard her whimper with pleasure.

His hands were thumbing her nipples, doing wondrous things to her breasts, while all the while his eyes gleamed knowingly down at her and his lips dipped down her flesh to nibble with tantalizing kisses and gentle bites.

"Please . . . do," she managed to gasp before he caught her mouth again and she had no breath left with which to speak, no space in which to doubt.

And then the kisses deepened. And he began to stroke her belly, her thighs, the soft, dark bed of her womanhood, his hand steady and slow and deliciously arousing. Josie was lost. Deliciously, intoxicatingly lost.

She made a mewing sound, low and soft and female, deep in her throat, and saw him smile.

His hands kneaded, caressed. He was awakening sensations that made Josie blink and gasp with wonder. Moaning, she lifted her hips, shifted, and felt her breath stop as his fingers slid inside her. Soft, velvet fire licked through her.

She clung to him, inhaling the scent and warmth and strength of him as his mouth trailed lower, exploring uncharted paths.

Sensation after sensation swam through her. She shuddered beneath the onslaught of his hands, his lips, his teeth, and heard herself begging him, though she knew not for what.

Certainly not to stop.

The marvel of it enveloped her as he slowly, relentlessly aroused every inch of her vibrating body. What *was* he doing to her? In the name of heaven . . .

Heaven. That was it, Josie thought, with the last shreds of reason fleeing her spinning mind. *He'd abducted her to heaven.*

When he took her hand and moved it lower, so that she touched the hardness of his shaft, she felt her fingers tremble. But there was no fear in her, only longing, a ragged longing as she stroked him and explored.

Ethan knew when she was ready, and he knew when she had reached the point of nearly unbearable pleasure. His own heated need had been doused in patience, but now it was flaring like a torch. He wanted her so badly, he ached in places he'd never ached before. Her damp, flushed skin and glazed eyes beckoned him, her luscious body, slick and welcoming, was about to discover the difference between a clumsy brute who used an unwilling woman for his own pleasure, and a man who knew how to drive a woman he loved to the edge of distraction, to the very brink of out-of-control desire, and then tip them both over the cliff into a plunging delirium.

"Ethan, oh, Ethan." Her mouth was muffled against his shoulder as he shifted his weight, levering himself with his arms.

"Scared, Josie? Don't be, sweetheart. I won't hurt you."

"Scared . . . ummm . . ." she gasped, wrapped in fire. "I'm scared you'll stop. And scared where this . . . is headed . . ."

"It's time you found out where it's headed. Where we're both headed," he whispered, his eyes glinting down at her with fierce love. He lowered himself to the willing, arching warmth of her and felt her trembling welcome as he slid inside.

He felt her every quiver, absorbed every moan into his pores. Her eyes were shining with need, bluer than any ocean. Her skin was damp and fragrant like an awakening flower, and as he plunged in deeper, and plunged again, taking all of her, becoming one with her, their hearts began to race in unison.

And they began to soar. Faster and faster, higher and higher, crashing through space and time and the boundaries of joy. With her arms enfolding him, clinging to him, and their lips seared together, they flew through sweet chaos, past aching, explosive need, beyond what either had known of desire.

Josie felt her senses reeling. It was like plummeting down a tunnel. Nothing at all like before.

This was sheer raw pleasure, soaring rapture . . . this was love, love, love. . . .

Then she could think of nothing as sensation after sensation caught her up in a delicious whirlwind. Her legs wrapped around him, gripping him with frantic urgency, her hips arced and writhed. The earth rocked and the world fell away, and she and Ethan spun into midnight blackness and dizzying blinding light and heaven was a glimmer at the end of the tunnel and she was flying toward it, crying and thrusting and rejoicing.

They slammed into that glimmer and exploded. To-gether—breathless and shuddering and holding to each other for dear life—they embraced the wonder of the moment. Their separate selves joined and clung and then in unison shattered—shattered into a glorious shower of sharp, bright, and radiantly falling stars.

❧❧❧ ❧❧❧

Josie awoke to a seashell-pink dawn floating through the last shadows of night. Creamy light stole through the window of her room and across the pale carpet. It touched the bed, bathing her and Ethan in a delicate morning glow as they lay peacefully entwined.

Her head rested against Ethan's broad chest. Their legs were tangled, and the bedclothes were scattered wildly on the floor.

Josie had never felt so comfortable.

Beside her, Ethan's skin felt smooth and warm. She remembered all that they had known together here throughout the night, remembered every joyful moment, and she could no more keep from smiling than she could stop herself from drawing breath.

She let out a sigh of pure contentment, thinking Ethan asleep. But his leg immediately draped over hers when she let out that sigh, as if to keep her there, close, and she knew instinctively he, too, was awake.

"Ethan?"

"I've been thinking." He spoke quietly, his breath ruffling her hair. "You've kept a lot of loneliness locked inside you, Josie. A hell of a lot of pain. With everything you've known and had to go through, I don't know how you've kept such an open heart."

"You have one too." She pushed herself up on an elbow and smiled at him. "I knew all along that you were just trying to appear tough and mean and ornery on the outside, but that deep inside you were a little itty-bitty pussycat—oh!"

She gave a stifled shriek as he tugged her over and down atop him, wrapping his sinewy legs about her so she couldn't escape.

"Maybe more like a tiger," she gasped laughingly as he placed one hand behind her head and pressed her face down toward his. He savaged her mouth with a long, devouring kiss that left her mouth bruised and aching for more.

When he let her breathe again, she leaned both palms on his shoulders and nipped softly with her teeth at his dark-stubbled jaw.

"Imagine—what if I hadn't picked your pocket that day?" she mused. "We would never have met."

"Want to bet? It was fate, destiny, sweetheart—and you can't escape your destiny." He toyed with a long, luscious strand of her hair. Early sun was gilding the chestnut waves to a fire-tinged bronze.

"Funny thing is, I knew that day in Abilene that something was up. Felt it in the saloon right before Latherby walked in and told me about Hugh and my father. Didn't know exactly what was about to happen, but knew it was something big."

He grinned as he wound the strand of hair round and

round his finger. "Truth is, I thought I was going to get shot."

"Shot!"

"Yep. Never was shot before. Strange that in all those years I never caught a bullet. I'd been stabbed twice, and knocked out cold more than once, dragged by a horse, chased by a bear . . . but never shot. Was damned sure it would be that night."

His eyes gleamed at her, twin gray flames in the handsomest face she'd ever seen. "But I reckon what had happened was," he continued slowly, "I *was* shot—that afternoon in the alley. Shot not by a gun, but by an arrow."

She raised her eyebrows, mystified.

"An arrow belonging to a pesky critter who goes by the handle of Cupid."

She grinned. The smile swept across her entrancing face and lit her eyes with a light so incandescent, it put the dawn to shame.

"Me too," she whispered, and reaching up, began to trace the firm lines of his jaw with her fingertip.

"It's strange but you sound as if you're still that other man—Ethan Savage, the gunfighter," she whispered.

"I am."

She nodded, and gazed down into his eyes with instinctive understanding. "A part of you is still tied to the West, to America. And missing it," she added, sympathy spilling through her heart.

"Those were good days, a good life." His face took on a faraway expression. "Riding through mountains high enough to skim the stars, camping out in canyons so beautiful they'd break your heart, sleeping under a full moon with the coyotes howling in the distance. Or just watching the eagles circle through that great big sky, or some wild horses coming down to drink at a stream. But since I've come back—"

He stopped, then sat up, sliding her over next to him, one arm stroking across her satiny shoulder.

"Never thought I'd say this, or feel this, but England has a hold on me too. It's different this time. Feels different. Maybe that's because you're here."

A flush of pleasure swept through her, turning her skin aglow.

"Josie, tell me something," he said suddenly. "Do you like it here?"

"I'm learning to like it. More than I ever thought I would. Especially Stonecliff Park. Something about it . . . the peace, the beauty. I feel . . ." She shook her head, wondering. "At home. Strange, but I feel more at home here, and happier, than any place I've ever lived before . . . even with Pop."

"Could that be . . . dare I hope . . ." His eyes gleamed into hers as he stroked her breasts and watched the violet depths of her eyes sparkle and darken. "Could that have anything to do with the company you've been keeping?"

"You mean Miss Perry? Oh, yes, she's *so* pleasant and kind. And Lady Tattersall—I am certainly fond of her . . . Ethan!" she shrieked as he threw her down among the pillows, climbed atop her, and began to tickle her ribs.

"Ethan, stop!" she gasped, and his hands stilled, but the dangerous glint still blazed in his eyes, and his mouth was grinning wide with deviltry.

"Well?"

"Yes—yes. It has something to do with you—I sup-pose!" She laughed, and then gave a shudder of pleasure as he lowered himself full upon her and began to nuzzle the delicate shell of her ear.

"It has . . . a great deal to do with you," Josie breathed.

And in the pearly light of morning found herself in the delightful position of being sweetly, relentlessly, helplessly ravished all over again.

Chapter Twenty-two

A molten sun sailed through the summer blue sky as Josie's footman helped her alight from the carriage in Belgrave Square. No breeze disturbed the heavy green leaves of the trees. The street was quiet, elegant. Trees shaded the walk, and there were lovely rhododendrons clustered behind the fence that boundaried the garden.

She stared up at the imposing house before her, her heart lurching into her throat.

During the drive to the address Lady Cartwright had given her last night, Josie had gone through myriad emotions: excitement, trepidation, hope, and fear of disappointment being the most prominent. But now as she gazed upward at the handsome house with its elegant portico and large bay windows, it was hope that made her hands tremble.

Perhaps my luck is finally changing. I found Ethan and he loves me. He loves me! And perhaps now I'll find out who I am and where I came from.

"Should I wait, my lady?"

"Yes, walk the horses, Rupert. I don't expect to be long."

In truth, she didn't know what to expect. What if no

one was at home? she wondered nervously as she went up the steps. What if they refused to see her. What if . . . what if . . . what if . . .

The door was opened by an immensely tall footman.

"Yes, ma'am?" he asked, deferentially, taking in her fashionable gown of Prussian blue silk with its smart lace train, and her pink hat and parasol.

She presented the small gilt calling card Ethan had ordered made up for her. "I should like to see Miss Denby," she said with all the quiet dignity she could summon through the waves of nervousness that washed over her.

She held her breath, half expecting to be told that no one by that name lived there, that Miss Denby did not even exist, even though Lady Cartwright herself had known her!

"Kindly wait in the morning room, my lady. I will inform Miss Denby that you are here."

She paced and paced about the morning room, her heart beating uncomfortably fast. In her little silk handbag was the pouch with her brooch and her treasure—or more properly, Miss Denby's treasure. If nothing else, she could now return it.

But how in the world would she explain how she came to possess what the stagecoach robbers had taken from Miss Denby?

Josie bit her lip and strode to the polished marble fireplace, then paced to the window, staring out at the clipped yews and rhododendrons without really seeing them. The lovely blue and green room receded and she was alone with the overwhelming enormity of this step she had taken. What if Miss Denby was as hateful and superior as Miss Crenshaw, and drilled her with questions, the answers to which could be humiliating for her—and for Ethan.

Oh, why hadn't she waited until she could discuss this with Ethan and could consider his advice? Why had she been so hasty, after having searched and waited all this time?

Ethan had been called away on business early this morning—he was interested in becoming involved in Parliament and had been invited to a meeting with several influential lords. Josie had been soaking in the bathtub when he came to find her. She'd scarcely had time to do more than sputter a surprised good-bye and give him a soul-tingling kiss before he'd strode out, whistling, and she was alone, with no opportunity to tell him about the jewels she'd been keeping hidden, her hopes about Miss Denby, or her intention to find and question her today.

When you come home this afternoon and find him, you'll both sit down to tea, side by side upon the sofa. And you'll hand him one of Mrs. Chupp's delicious savories and you'll tell him then, you'll tell him everything. And maybe you'll even have some answers. Maybe you'll even know who you are.

Not that it would matter to Ethan. The wonderful thing was that he loved her for who she was—herself. She couldn't see that changing, no matter what she learned today.

But this did matter to her—the prospect of finally *knowing*. It mattered a great deal.

The sound of the door opening had her whirling around, eager and afraid all at once.

She went very still when she saw the girl hesitating on the threshold.

The girl was perhaps two or three years older than she, and taller by several inches. Like a pale flower stalk, Josie thought. She looked delicate and shy. Clad in a simple olive-green tea gown, she had a narrow figure, and gold curls lighter than sunshine. Her eyes were of a soft porcelain blue set within a pretty, sensitive-looking face.

Those blue eyes were fixed upon Josie with something close to wonder.

She came into the morning room slowly and paused, her head tilted to one side as she studied her guest.

"Do I know y-you, Lady Stonecliff?" she asked softly, the glimmer of a shy smile on her lips.

"No, Miss Denby, we've never met." Josie hoped her own smile would put the other girl at ease. Miss Denby seemed timid as a mouse! Though her manner was friendly, it seemed as if she wasn't used to receiving company.

"Lady Cartwright is a friend of mine. She told me how to find you."

"How to find me?" Surprise rounded Miss Denby's long-lashed eyes. With a start, Josie noticed their shape—they were uptilted at the corners. "I'm s-sorry." She sounded flustered, and threw Josie a look of quiet dismay. "I don't mean to be rude, but I don't get much company. I don't go out into society very much—" She blushed richly. "Please won't you be seated," she said with a slight shake of her head, and indicated with a small, graceful gesture the yellow sofa opposite the window. "And t-tell me what I can do for you."

"My question might sound odd, but . . ." Josie took a

deep breath and plunged on. "Were you held up by outlaws some months ago on a stagecoach in America?"
she blurted out, suddenly too excited for slow, polite
explanations.

Miss Denby, who had just seated herself in a wing
chair, gripped the arms. "How did you know that?"

"Because . . . oh, damn it, I mean, drat it, I . . . I think I
have your jewels. Do these belong to you?"

And Josie unclasped her handbag, drew out the pouch
with shaking fingers, and dipped her hand inside. When
she pulled out the opal-and-pearl ring, the bracelet, and the
precious scrap of letter, the fair-haired girl gaped at them.

"Yes. Those are mine!" A smile of joy lit her face. She
stared in rapt amazement at the ring, unable to tear her
gaze from it. "Oh, but this is w-wonderful. How kind you
are to return them! How did this come about? Did the
sheriff catch those men and . . . no, no, that isn't it, is it?
It c-couldn't be. He would hardly have sent you—"

"I found them. I mean, the outlaws had them and I . . . I
stole them back for you." The irrepressible grin sparkled
across Josie's face. Her heart was suddenly full of a light,
fluttering hope. The words poured out in a torrent.

"When I saw a painting of your mother last night at
Lady Cartwright's home, I noticed the brooch she wore.
It's almost identical in design to this ring."

"Yes, they're from the same set."

Josie felt a rising excitement. "That's what I guessed.
I've been looking for you so that I could return the ring,
and I asked Lady Cartwright the name of the lady in the
painting. When she told me, she said your mother was
her cousin. And when I mentioned I was looking for a
Miss Denby she told me about you. . . ."

She drew breath, then her voice dropped lower with contained excitement.

"I have something else to show you, Miss Denby." She drew out the brooch. Now that the moment had come, she felt unexpectedly calm. Except for the seesawing of her stomach.

"This brooch. It looks the same as the one in the portrait. The one your mother was wearing. But . . . it's mine."

She halted at the stunned expression that had come over Miss Denby's face. The girl looked as if she'd been dunked in a vat of ice water.

"Miss Denby?" Josie jumped up, still clutching the brooch and her handbag. "Are you all right?"

"Y-you . . . you . . . Where d-did you get that brooch?"

"I'm an orphan. The woman who ran the orphanage where I spent my first years told me this brooch was pinned to my swaddling clothes on the day I was found."

Alicia Denby looked as if she would swoon. She was staring at Josie with wide, glazed eyes. She came to her feet, swaying a little.

"Dear God. It's you. You're her." She gazed in shock from Josie's face back to the brooch, and then gazed frantically back at her guest again, scrutinizing her with swift, desperate intensity.

Her entire body began to shake. Then she darted forward so suddenly, Josie stiffened. Alicia Denby clutched her arm with trembling fingers.

"Lady Stonecliff . . . you must be—unless this is some h-horrible mistake—you must be . . . you must . . ."

"Who?" Josie could barely speak. "Tell me please. I've been trying to find out my entire life!"

"Josephine!"

"Yes, that's my name." Now it was her turn to clutch Miss Denby's arm. "There was a note with the brooch. It said *Baby Josephine*."

Miss Denby stared wildly, searchingly into her eyes, her face taut with shock, joy, wonder.

"You are my sister!"

Chapter Twenty-three

A bird warbled in the garden. Its voice lilted through the beautiful, silent morning room. Josie found that for once in her life she couldn't speak a word. She could only stare with mute shock into Miss Denby's overjoyed face.

"How do you know?" she finally managed.

"I know. Believe me, L-Lady Stonecliff, I *know*. Why, look at your hair. It is the same shade, the same as Papa's. Our papa. I resemble Mama more, but you and I both have her eyes, these uptilted eyes. Don't you s-see?"

And then, before giving Josie a chance to reply, she clasped her hands together almost in supplication, as if fearful that this wonderful gift might be only a dream that would vanish in a moment.

"Oh, Josephine, I can scarce believe it. Is it really you?"

Suddenly she began to smile, a wide, delicately beautiful smile that transformed her face, lighting it with such incandescent happiness that the whole room seemed to glow.

"Grandpapa," she breathed, and her fingers excitedly squeezed Josie's arm.

"Oh, we must tell Grandpapa. Come, Josephine, we can talk later—you'll tell me everything and I shall tell you . . . how we came to be s-separated, and how frantically we searched."

"You searched for me?" Josie felt something thud deep inside her heart. "So you . . . they . . . *wanted* me. I wasn't given away?"

"Given away? No, good God, no! It was the w-war, Josephine, the War Between the States . . . I was only three, but I made it home to England while you, just a babe, ended up—"

She stopped suddenly. "I'll explain everything, I promise," she said quietly. "But Grandpapa has given up on f-finding you. He is old and no longer strong. We must tell him at once. He'll be beside himself with happiness. . . ."

"I have a grandfather. And a sister." Josie broke away suddenly, and paced to the mantel, feeling overwhelmed. She was shaken by all the information the girl was rattling off to her, and far too stunned to begin to absorb it all.

"Are you sure there isn't a mistake?" She whirled back toward Miss Denby, her lips dry. "I'd hate to tell him and get his hopes up if it wasn't true."

"You have the brooch. Our mama's brooch. And the r-resemblance . . . now that I know, it is easy to see. Come." Miss Denby, with surprising determination for one who had seemed so diffident, took her arm again and pulled her from the room. They ran through the hall to a music room, a wide, lovely chamber furnished with teal sofas and deep wing chairs, and an exquisite rosewood piano that gleamed in a place of honor beneath a gold-framed painting.

"L-look." Miss Denby drew her to the piano and pointed up at the painting.

It showed a man and woman, the same woman Josie had seen wearing the brooch in the portrait at Lady Cartwright's home. Beside her this time stood a lean, handsome man with a distinguished air and gleaming chestnut curls and a wide, strong-boned face. He was grinning at the artist with a devilish smile playing about his lips.

"You have our mama's eyes and our papa's hair," Miss Denby whispered, her voice thick with emotion as she gazed first at the painting and then at the beautiful young woman standing thunderstruck beside her.

"I've studied pictures of them all my life, I know exactly how they looked. And you are a stunning m-mixture of them both. I can see it now that I know. Josephine, it's t-true. We lived in Georgia on a plantation. Our family lost everything during the war . . . Papa was killed at the battle of Chickamauga, and Mama died before she could get you to safety . . . her efforts went amiss. You were lost to us for all these years. Josephine, Grandpapa and I—we despaired of ever finding you."

"But I found you." Josie clung to Miss Denby's hands, squeezing tightly, still feeling off balance, fearful of accepting that the search that had been fruitless for so many years had come to an end. "If it hadn't been for the holdup, and your letter—"

"Alicia, my dear? Forgive me for disturbing you."

Both of them turned to stare at the elderly man in the doorway. With the use of a cane, he came into the room, his gait slow and measured, but his shoulders very straight.

Josie's heart surged into her throat as she looked at him. Could this thin-faced, snow-haired gentleman with his erect carriage, sharp nose, faded, almost silver-blue eyes, and slow, beautiful diction be her grandfather?

"Grandpapa! C-come in! The most wonderful thing has happened. . . ."

The old gentleman moved forward with surprising grace, despite the fact that the blue-veined hand gripping his cane trembled. "Something has made you very happy, my dear," he said with a smile, and then, as his gaze shifted to Josie with polite interest, the blue eyes suddenly sharpened.

Josie felt herself examined swiftly, piercingly, saw something of hope and then doubt flicker in his dignified face.

"I want to hear, by all means. But first, won't you introduce me to this lady."

"Y-yes! That is what is so wonderful. She's Josephine, Grandpapa! Our Josephine! After all these years, she has found *us*!"

The old man's gaze swung back to Josie, locking on her. He stared at her as if he would dissect her with his eyes.

In the background, Miss Denby was saying something about the brooch, about an orphanage in the South, about years of fruitless inquiry. But Josie couldn't focus on anything but the awakening wonder in the old man's eyes.

"You look . . . like Winston, and like my . . . daughter. I thought I saw . . . something about you—can this be true? Alicia . . ."

He tore his gaze from Josie's at last to glance at the blond girl as she rushed to him and took his free arm.

"It's true. Your eyes tell you, and so does your h-heart, Grandpapa. Our Josephine has come home."

And as Josie watched, the elegant old man with his

beautiful carriage and immaculate suit and ivory-handled cane, held open his arms and began to cry.

❧❧❧❧

She spent three hours in the house in Belgravia discovering who she was and what had happened to her so many years ago. At some point, a footman sent Rupert and the carriage home, as Josie's grandfather insisted his own carriage would bring her home when she was ready. But, the old gentleman insisted, his eyes and voice strong again after the initial bout of emotion, she must stay as long as she wished.

This home was her home, he told her. And a shining-eyed Alicia ran to find photographs and letters of the parents Josie had never known.

Her grandfather was Hugh Althorpe, Duke of Bennington. Her mother, Charlotte, had been a great beauty, gently raised in London and at Bennington Hall in Kent. She'd fallen in love with an American plantation owner from Georgia, Winston Denby, and married him only a few years before the start of the War Between the States.

Alicia had been born first, lovingly ensconced in the white, pillared plantation house of Twelve Trees, where Winston's elderly father also lived. When the Confederates began drafting soldiers in 1862, Winston Denby had had to leave his wife and father and infant daughter. He'd joined the ranks of Confederate officers, had proved himself brave and cool in battle, and had received promotions.

"Winston went home to Twelve Trees on furlough. It was late summer of 1863," the Duke told Josie as he stared into his empty teacup. "He feared for Charlotte and for Alicia. Conditions were dreadful in the South and growing worse. He wanted Charlotte to go home to England. If only she had," he murmured sadly, "if only she had."

Before either Alicia or Josie could fill the silence that followed, the Duke began to speak again, his tone heavy. "But my daughter wouldn't leave her father-in-law, a stubborn, proud old man who vowed to die on Twelve Trees before he let the Yankees drive him away." He cleared his throat. "My daughter was stubborn too—or perhaps one might even call it courageous. She felt it her duty to remain on the land, to keep the family's plantation going as long as she could, to look after all their people there, and the livestock and crops."

"She had courage and loyalty," Josie whispered. She'd heard enough stories of the privations in the South during the war to know how difficult it must have been. Clothing, supplies, food, medicines, all had been in disastrously short supply. The women and children remaining behind had sacrificed their comfort and much more besides—giving all that they could.

The Duke shook his head. "At least Charlotte and Winston had the good sense not to want their little daughter to live in the midst of a war-torn land." He leaned back in his chair and sighed. "They didn't want young Alicia to suffer the hunger, deprivation, and fear afflicting everyone around them. And above all, they wanted her to be safe in the event the Yankees did get through."

The Duke steepled his fingers and glanced at Alicia, perched solemnly on the sofa beside Josie. "During his furlough Winston arranged for her to be taken north, to safety, and from there she sailed to us in England— accompanied by a slave couple devoted to her and to the Denby family. We were so relieved and overjoyed to have her with us. We thought it would be a temporary situation, an extended visit. Ah, but we were wrong."

His eldest granddaughter had tears in her eyes as she watched him turn his head away, to stare out the window at the garden, where the bird now was silent. She turned to Josie and continued the tale.

"During his furlough, when P-Papa visited Mama . . ." She took a breath and started again. "You were born some nine months after that."

Josie met her eyes and nodded.

"But Mama became ill only a few months after—she and our Papa's father took ill with smallpox—and General Sherman's troops were on the m-march. . . ."

Josie listened as the painful scraps of information the Duke had acquired over time emerged. News of baby Josephine's birth had reached them, and also news that Charlotte was ill and couldn't be moved—that the Yankees were closing in. . . .

Her mother and grandfather had died on the plantation amid the chaos of war, with Sherman's soldiers marauding and destroying everything in their path. By the time the dust had cleared and the war ended, and news could be sent and received, Charlotte's baby, Josephine Maud Denby, was missing.

The sun made gilded patterns on the carpet as it slipped westward, and as the brilliant afternoon faded and cooled, the clouds blew in. The words swirled around Josie as she sat with the Duke and with Alicia in the pretty room in Belgravia and heard how the Duke's hirelings had searched orphanages across Georgia, and in several other states as well, how a detective had made inquiries, how long and hard they'd struggled to find one tiny child in the wrecked and agonized South.

"We prayed you had been taken in by someone, that you would be found in a good home, or in one of the orphanages, but there were so many children orphaned by the war, it was impossible to find you. We tried, child," the Duke told her heavily, "for years we tried. And then, last year, Alicia sailed with me to America, determined to search for you herself—my shy, timid granddaughter who will not brave parties or balls, braved an ocean voyage and a strange new land in an effort to find her sister. We checked records, made inquiries in person, but came away empty-handed."

Josie's heart swelled with emotion as she met the gaze of the girl beside her. Now she understood the fragment of letter found in Alicia's stolen handbag, the reason her sister had been on the stagecoach that Snake and his boys had robbed.

Maybe it was all fate, destiny, that had enabled her to find her family at last. What had Ethan said last night? *You can't escape your destiny.*

One point struck her most forcibly. It made her grip her hands in her lap and swallow back tears. She had been wanted. Her mother had loved her, her family had wanted her. She had not been abandoned, tossed aside.

But for war, and circumstances, she would not have had to grow up alone and lonely, at the mercy of strangers. But for war, she would have grown up like Alicia—cared for, sheltered, loved.

She knew no resentment, no bitterness, of her fate. Josie was too much a survivor and realist for that. But there was immense relief and joy to know that she had indeed had people and a place, those to whom she belonged, if only she'd known. . . .

"If only we'd known . . ." Alicia murmured, tears in

her eyes when Josie related, at their urging, an overview of her own past, a sketch of her life—sparing them, for now, the harshest details.

"My dear, dear child, this pains me more than I can say. You never should have had to know such hardships." The Duke spoke hoarsely and passed a shaking hand across his brow. Instantly, Josie was sorry she had told him any of her past at all. But she was so tired of secrets.

"We'll make up for lost time," he went on, before she could speak. "There is so much to say, to know. You must return tomorrow, and dine with us. We're eager to meet Lord Stonecliff, to know both of you better."

At his mention of Ethan, Josie gave a start. A glance at the darkening sky beyond the window revealed the lateness of the hour. And the gold clock on the mantel read nearly five o'clock!

She jumped up from the sofa. "I must be going. Forgive me for having stayed overlong!"

"Child, you have stayed *away* overlong. You cannot now stay long enough to suit Alicia and myself."

Her heart trembled as she saw the film of emotion in the Duke's eyes. "You will return tomorrow?"

"Yes, oh, yes."

His shoulders relaxed at her reply and he nodded in relief. But Josie suddenly noticed just how weary he looked, how the afternoon's excitement and revelations had exhausted him and seemed to deepen the lines etched beneath his eyes.

"I'll send for the carriage and see Josephine on her way," Alicia said quickly, her anxiety mirroring Josie's as the two girls exchanged glances. "You must go upstairs and rest now, Grandpapa. I won't be long."

When the carriage came, Josie stared wonderingly into her sister's face. Her sister! She felt like shouting with joy. Instead she reached out impulsively and hugged this gentle girl who had welcomed her so openheartedly into her life. "You'll come back t-tomorrow?" Alicia asked eagerly. "Perhaps we could walk in the park? I d-don't go out much in society, as I told you. It's my stammer. People sometimes stare, or whisper. But we could ride, if you like."

"I'd like that very much." Josie glanced down at the opal-and-pearl brooch she now wore proudly upon her gown, and then at the matching ring Alicia had slipped onto her own finger. Jewels that had both belonged to their mother.

"I called your ring 'my treasure' all this time I had it. Because it was a clue, you see, it was precious to me. But now—now, Alicia, I truly have something to treasure."

"And so do I." Alicia clasped both her hands and smiled through a fresh shimmer of tears. "So do we all."

Neither of them saw the shadowy figure detach itself from the corner of the building as the Duke's carriage clattered away, carrying Josie toward Mayfair. And neither of them saw that same obscure figure cross the street and climb into another carriage, which immediately sprang off after the Duke's in brisk pursuit.

❄❄❄ ❄❄❄

When Josie sailed into the town house in excited search of Ethan, she was greeted by Edward, a footman, who informed her that his lordship regretted he must be away on business until later that night, but that he had left her a note.

"Will you be dining at home, my lady?"

"What? Oh, yes, Edward. I will." She struggled through her disappointment to answer distractedly as she tore open the missive he handed her from a silver tray.

Ethan's business regarding a seat in Parliament would keep him away until sometime this evening—but he wanted her to know that the meeting with Grismore was scheduled for the following day. He loved her, he wrote, in his firm, elegant black scrawl. And he would show her exactly how much when he was finally able to return to her from his damned round of meetings.

Grismore—tomorrow! Josie ignored the nervous flutters in her throat. It was time to get it over with, she told herself. She would pass inspection—for Ethan's sake, for both of their sakes, she would have to!

She ran lightly up the stairs, wondering how she could possibly wait another few hours to tell Ethan her news— that she had discovered who she was, that she had a grandfather and a sister living right here in England. She glanced down at her brooch once more, elated that now she could show it to him and wear it openly, that she could let the world know it was hers. No more hiding, no more wondering, no more searching . . .

She gave a little skip as she started down the corridor to her room, her lips curving in a smile of anticipation.

Suddenly a door flew open beside her. She glanced up, expecting it to be a housemaid, finished dusting one of the guest bedrooms, but instead a brawny figure lunged at her. A hand squashed her mouth, iron arms clamped around her in a death vise.

Before Josie could even try to scream, she was plucked from the corridor and dragged into the empty room. The door was kicked shut.

In total darkness she heard a laugh.

"Josie, honey, you didn't think I'd let you run off and leave me now, did you? Honey, I missed you somethin' fierce. And I'm going to show you how much. I'm going to show you so you'll never forget." Snake Barker chuckled in her ear.

And then something struck her over the head and there was blinding pain and blazing dots of light, and then nothing but cold—blizzard-white icy cold that snapped at her bones and dragged her down, down, down into a chilly river of blackness.

Chapter Twenty-four

She swam dizzily up out of pain and cold and darkness. Everything hurt. She couldn't open her eyes. The sound of rain beat against a window. Such a hard sound. Lightning flashed, hurting her closed eyes.

What's happened to me? Josie wondered groggily, and then she heard a door open, heard voices and the scrape of booted feet, and memory rushed back—and with it fear.

"Well, lookee here. She's comin' to. She's breathing hard now, not like before. So she's awake, boys. Snake, bet you twenty dollars she knows we're here."

Deck's voice. Josie tried to hold herself motionless, tried to slow her breathing. But suddenly she felt someone standing over her, and sensed Snake's presence the way she might sense a wolf baring its fangs in the dark.

"Wake up, Josie girl." Pain wrenched through her head as he knotted his hands in her hair and pulled.

Her eyes flew open. With a snarl she lunged at his arm and tried to break his hold, but he only laughed. He held her down with his free arm, and pulled harder.

"You been a real bad girl, Josie. I had to come all the way across the whole Atlantic Ocean to git you. And

Deck here was sick the whole way. It warn't too enjoy-
able, thet trip."

"I wish your ship had sunk," she gasped, tears stinging
her eyelids even as she fought not to give him the satisfaction of showing how much he was hurting her.

Snake roared with laughter and the others joined in.

But to her relief, he abruptly let go of her hair. "You'll
wish it even more, honey, by the time I'm done with
you."

There was a cruel glint in his eyes. Josie remembered
that glint all too well.

"Meantime," he said curtly, "we've got some business
to talk over. There'll be time for fun and games later."

She struggled up to a sitting position on the bed. Her
head ached. What had he hit her with? Gingerly, she
touched her fingers to the back of her head and winced at
the tender bump.

For a moment Josie just stared blearily at the four of
them, crowding around her in that dark, cramped room,
rain spattering the window, a jumble of noise coming
from somewhere beyond the door.

*Where was she? How had she come here? And did
anyone at the town house know she was gone?*

She was in a small, moldy-smelling room, which
seemed even smaller with Snake and the boys in it. An
inn, she guessed, and not one that served the aristocracy,
but one for the masses, those too poor for clean, well-
aired sheets and wholesome food. What furnishings the
room contained—the bed, a three-legged stool, a grimy
bureau—were cheap and garish. There was an ugly stiff
brown quilt on the bed and torn red muslin curtains at the
window, a bare floor that looked as if it hadn't had a
good scrubbing in decades, and a paraffin lamp in a tin

holder, which sent out a sickly yellowish glow that made Snake's fair hair look pale and greasy as butter.

"Something tells me this isn't the Grand Hotel."

"Not by a long shot, honey. Welcome to the rookery."

Snake's grin couldn't have stretched any wider if he'd just filled his belly with a slab of Texas beef. "You're in a corner of London where no one who don't live and belong here will ever find you. There's miles of alleys and gambling dens and brothels between you and that fancy house you been staying in, and every bit of it's crawling with rats—not to mention thieves and beggars and murderers who'd likely slit your throat just to get their hands on that pretty bauble you're wearing. Not to mention that shiny gold ring."

Before Josie could move, Snake clamped his fingers around her wrist and tugged off Latherby's gold ring, then ripped her opal-and-pearl brooch from her gown.

"No, you bastard! Give it back!" She hurled herself at him and tried to wrest the brooch from his grasp, but he flung her back onto the bed.

"This here is just the start of what you owe me, Josie girl. You took our loot, remember? And all them fancy jewels from the stagecoach passengers? Hell, I figger it's up to you to pay me back. For starters"—he nodded at Deck, who reached into his vest pocket and drew out a gray cloth pouch—"we cleaned out all the fancy jewels we could find in your bedroom—and in Savage's, too."

As Josie stared in horror, Deck fished out the ruby necklace she'd worn to Lady Tattersall's dinner party, dangled it in the air a moment, then with a grin fished out the matching earrings and a gold stickpin of Ethan's.

"These and the rest'll fetch a good price, but not near enough to pay back what you owe. It's going to take a hell of a lot more than money, and more than baubles to pay back what *you* owe, honey."

Josie barely heard the veiled threat in his words. Revenge, that's what Snake wanted. More than riches. His power over her, his ability to cause her pain and suffering, that would be the only payment that would satisfy him.

But she was far more concerned with the pouch Deck was now dropping back into his pocket. Those rubies had belonged to Ethan's mother. He'd entrusted them to Josie. And when Ethan returned home, he'd find her gone.

What if he saw that the jewels were gone too—as well as his own valuables?

Would he think she'd stolen them, and run off? That everything between them had been a lie?

"You have to let me out of this place." It wasn't a question, it was a demand she threw at Snake between gritted teeth.

"I don't *got* to do nothin', Josie girl," Snake growled, and grabbed her wrist once more. "And you'd best learn to quit all that back talk."

She glanced toward the window. The darkness of night now blackened the small slit of sky visible through the curtains. *Had Ethan returned from his meetings?* she wondered desperately. *Did he know yet that she was gone?*

She couldn't bear to think of how he would feel when he noticed all of the jewels that were missing as well. . . .

"It's not me you want, Snake." She jerked free of his grasp, then pushed her hair back, trying to speak clearly despite the pounding in her head, and the fear that tasted like sand in her throat. She forced herself to look into his wide, smarmily handsome face, hoping she appeared calmer than she felt. "It's money you want. Money to make up for the loot I stole. More money than these jewels are worth, money enough to buy you anything you want. I can get it for you. Take me back, and I'll—"

"You'll what?" Snake jeered, his mouth twisting with contempt. "You'll ask Savage to hand over a bag of gold? Or write out a bank draft? Just like that? You must think I'm a damned fool, Josie." Suddenly he leaned down and gripped her by the shoulders, wrenching her forward so sharply, her head snapped.

"I ain't. I got a better plan, one thet's goin' to pay you back and that son of a bitch would-be husband of yours too. And it's going to make me rich."

"It won't work, Snake, whatever it is. Ethan will find you and—"

"Find me, will he? Not till I'm good and ready to be found. Not till I've set my trap for him and he walks right into it, just like a squirrel tumbling down into a snake pit. Snake pit, honey, get it?" He burst into ugly laughter, and Spooner, Noah, and Deck joined in. They stood in a ring around Josie as she stared from one to the other of them with growing dread.

"You're too stupid to outsmart Ethan," she said, hoping to goad him into revealing his plan so she could figure out a way to stop it.

But she didn't count on Snake's whipcord temper. With a grunt, he lifted his hand and backhanded her hard.

"I ain't puttin' up with none of that smart talk of yours, you hear, girl?" Satisfaction glinted in his eyes as he watched her slam back against the pillows, the imprint of his hand showing first white and then red on her cheek.

"I masterminded my share of holdups back home, and since I got to London, you'll be proud to know I've done just fine. Matter of fact, me and the boys have made out real good. Got us some new pards, some new ideas. These here 'nobs,' as our new pards call 'em, they've got real money, and most of 'em walk around at night weighted down with more jewels than sense. It's easy as pie to lighten their load, if you know what I mean, honey."

Through the pain in her jaw, and her aching head, Josie tried to think clearly. "Ethan won't be . . . robbed so easily," she muttered. But she feared for him even as she spoke the words. The image of his being set upon to or from his club, or coming from some party, by Snake, Noah, Spooner, and Deck filled her with panic.

"If you know what's good for you, you'll stay away from him. All of you!" she cried. "If you don't believe me, ask Pirate Pete, the most feared criminal in all of London."

Snake just laughed. "Reckon I'll do just that," he grinned. As if on cue, Spooner loped to a door that adjoined the next room and yanked it open.

Josie's eyes narrowed as the other members of the gang each exchanged grins. Then she forgot all about them when the stout man with all too familiar slitted black eyes sauntered through that door, followed closely by a giant. From the second man's size and girth and those unforgettable blank wooden eyes, she had no doubt it was Tiny. And his companion was Pirate Pete.

"We meets agin, me lady," Tiny grunted, and gave her a low, clumsily executed bow. "Lady Stonecliff, me and Pete 'ave been itchin' to see you agin, we 'ave."

Her blood froze as Tiny closed in. But Snake held up a hand.

"You boys don't get ahold of her till I'm through."

"Through with what? What's going on?" Josie cried.

She couldn't believe that Snake had joined forces with Pirate Pete. This was worse than any nightmare. Only last night, she and Ethan had made love upon silken sheets in her beautiful bedroom, and only this afternoon she'd had tea with her grandfather and sister in Belgravia, and now . . . now she was imprisoned in some mean, damp hovel in the rookery, a captive of these animals.

"Tell me what you're planning!" She turned her gaze toward Snake. If her hands hadn't been clenched into fists, she'd have been tempted to rake him with her nails. When he didn't answer her, she peered frantically at Spooner, then at Deck and Noah. Only in Spooner's face did she see the faintest hint of sympathy.

"Tell me!" she pleaded with him, but he remained silent, and it was Pirate Pete who sidled forward to speak.

"None o' this would 'ave 'appened if yer Lord Stonecliff 'adn't killed Lucian and spoiled everything that night. Then he 'ad to top it off by offering that reward."

The lamp cast an eerie glow over Tiny's sallow flesh as he regarded Josie with satisfaction. "He's gettin' what's comin' to him, and so ar' you, me lady. Ye never should 'ave taken up against us. We 'ave our reputations to think of."

Feeling ill, Josie stared into both of their faces and then glanced at Snake. A sly, half-crooked smile curled his lips. He was happy as a coyote in a henhouse now that she was in this fix.

Damn him—damn all of them. She wasn't about to sit here meekly while they plotted against Ethan. There had to be a way out of this place, and if there was, she'd find it.

Snake hooked his thumbs in his pockets. "Boys, time

to leave me and my little wife alone for a spell. We got some personal matters to talk over. Noah, you'd best get yourself ready to ride."

"Sure will, Snake." He winked at Josie and stroked the ends of his reddish brown mustache.

"The rest of you boys," Snake continued easily, "go on outside and have a round of drinks on me."

Pirate Pete didn't budge. Those black eyes remained locked on Josie. "P'rhaps ye need a bit o' 'elp explaining things to 'er? I 'ave me a way with the ladies."

The glare Snake fixed him with left no doubt of his resentment. "I reckon I can handle my own wife," he snarled.

"That nob, Lord Stonecliff, thought she was *'is* wife." Pete's harsh gaze skimmed over Josie as if she were a morsel of pie he had in mind to swallow whole. "Seems to me she's a slippery one."

"Not slippery enough to get away from me again." Snake moved a hand to the gun holstered low on his hip. "Now leave us be before I throw you out myself."

"As if ye could." But Pirate Pete relented with a chuckle when Snake took a step toward him. "I'm a'goin', I am. Don't get yer drawers in a tangle, lad." He winked at Josie and followed the others to the door.

Snake frowned at her as the others shuffled out, closing the door behind them. The thud of their boots trodding downstairs died away before Snake broke the silence.

"You never should've left me, Josie girl." Beneath the quiet of his tone, she heard the deep, raging currents of his anger. It was there, too, in the pinprick of lust flickering in the center of his eyes.

"Now you and Savage are going to pay. No one runs off with my woman, makes a damned fool of me, and gets away with it, you hear? He's going to pay first with his money—and then with his life. And you . . . Hell, honey, I haven't decided yet exactly *what* the hell I'm going to do with *you*. If I oughta keep you awhiles just for fun or turn you over to Pete and Tiny as soon as this here job is done. Reckon it depends on how you behave."

Josie could only gasp in frozen fear as he reached out to cup her chin in his hand. But at his touch, she flinched, and instantly his smile widened and the strange light glowed brighter in his eyes.

"Easy, now, honey, don't be scared. I'm your lovin' husband, remember? And we've been apart for a hell of a long time. Too long, Josie girl. Way too long."

"You're making a big mistake."

It took all of Josie's willpower to keep the quaver from her voice, to hold his gaze with a modicum of calm. Only by digging her nails into her palms did she keep from shrieking in panic and hold the shreds of hysteria at bay.

"Think so, honey? Well, you're wrong." Snake's eyes narrowed as he sat down on the bed beside her. "I know exactly what I'm doing."

"You've gone too far. Taking me from my house. Ethan will have the police scouring for me day and night. You're going to be caught and locked up in prison—a British prison. I hear they're not too pleasant."

"The hell you say. Me and Pete have run circles around these London police. Them with their fancy inspectors, their constables and sergeants. We've outsmarted 'em all. They're tearing the rookery and half the English countryside upside down looking for Pete and Tiny—and can they find them? Nope." He grinned at her and leaned closer. She could smell the gin on his breath.

"We've got ourselves a real good hiding place here in

Beetle Bob's. No policeman's going to risk coming in here unless he knows for sure what he's after is in here—and none of 'em do. And no one's going to rat on any of us—in spite of that reward Savage offered—because they know they'd be dead before they could spend a penny of it. So, the boys and me and Pete and Tiny have been leading those constables on a wild chase. I've done some of the robberies, masked, and all done up like Pirate Pete—with Spooner passing himself off as Tiny. Yep, that's it," he chuckled as Josie gave a gasp. "Now you see.

"Pete and me, we look somethin' alike when we're wearing masks and dressed in the right clothes, and Spooner ain't as big as Tiny, but most folks we've held up are too scared to be exact in their recollectin'. We've got those policemen running around in circles, between pulling jobs in London and out in the country, and we've gotten ourselves a dandy pile of loot."

A crack of laughter burst from his lips. The rain outside the window began to pelt down even faster.

She had to keep him talking. As long as he was bragging about himself and his plans, he was too preoccupied to get any other ideas of how to spend this time with her.

"How did you meet up with Pirate Pete?"

"Hell, honey, that was plain luck. We came here looking for you—and for that varmint Savage. Found out he was called Lord Stonecliff over here. We landed in the rookery, got ourselves settled in a lodging house, met some folks, sort of got the lay of the land. And then we stumbled across Pete and Tiny under the eaves in the alley one night. Heard 'em making all kinds of plans. Plans to stick a knife in the ribs of some 'nob' they said—Lord Stonecliff. On account of he killed their pard,

Lucian, and offered a reward for them. Hell and damnation, honey, they were mighty burned up about that."

A knife in Ethan's ribs. Dear God. Josie fought panic. She had to get out of here and warn him.

But Snake had risen from the side of the bed and was swaggering about the hideous little room. He was never more than three paces from either the window or the door. "Well, soon as I heard that name I knew Lady Luck was smiling down on me. Because I'd heard all about how you'd up and married Savage—and then cleared out of Abilene."

Dry-mouthed, Josie met his glare. "Where did you hear that?"

"Don't matter none." He moved toward her again. "What matters, honey, is that you and me are back together. And I'm going to make that Savage feller real sorry he ran off with my wife."

Suddenly he hauled Josie up on her knees, dragged her against his chest, and clamped his mouth on hers. She fought, flailing her arms, twisting her body, but Snake held her fast and dragged out the greedy, sucking kiss until nausea swept through her.

"And you *are* still my wife, Josie girl. You'd best not forget it agin."

He ran a hand across her breasts, then pushed her away, slinging her down onto the bed with a laugh.

Josie frantically scrubbed the gin-flavored wetness from her lips. She rolled sideways and tried to dart off the bed, but Snake was faster and stronger, and he hauled her back.

"Don't you want to hear the plan, honey? Me and Pete came up with a real good one. Want to know what we're going to do?"

"No!" She tried to extricate herself from his grip, realized her struggles were only fueling his satisfaction, and abruptly went still. "Yes!" she spat, eyeing him from beneath the wild tangle of her hair. "I'm sure you're going to tell me whether I want you to or not!"

Snake, pleased by the paleness of her face, the fear staring from her eyes, continued with growing zest for his topic.

"First, I'm going to write Savage a nice little note. Tell him how you're going to die by noon tomorrow if he don't do what he's told. That if he wants ever to see you alive again and looking as pretty as the last time he laid eyes on you, he'd best show up with a wheelbarrow full of money, and no tricks."

"You bastard!"

"Noah's going to deliver it tonight. And"—he smiled, tightening his grip on her until she winced—"we're going to send along that gold wedding ring of yours since he'll recognize it and know we've really got you."

"What if he doesn't care?" she asked in a ragged tone. "What if he ignores your note?"

"Josie, honey, what man wouldn't care about getting you back? I did, didn't I? And besides, Pete told me all about how Savage fought to protect you that night he was robbed."

His face twisted, the outwardly handsome features becoming an ugly mask of hate. "He thinks you belong to him. So he'll come. But when he brings the money, he's going to get a little surprise. Not you, honey. You're staying with me—until I say Tiny can have you—or what's left of you," he added with a low-pitched chuckle. "No, Savage will drop off the money—and then he'll get himself a lesson he won't ever forget. Actually, he won't have a chance to. He'll be dead."

"No!"

Snake leaned down toward her, his eyes glowing as he brought his slick wet mouth within an inch of hers. "Yep, honey, and there ain't a damn thing you can do about it."

He watched the pain and the terror and the agony imprint themselves upon her face, and his smile deepened as he reached up to stroke her cheek.

"We're all of us going to get ourselves a piece of him," he promised. "A damn fine bloody piece."

Chapter Twenty-five

Heads swiveled to watch as the Earl of Stonecliff bounded up the steps of the Opera House at Covent Garden three stairs at a time. It was intermission, and the lights were up, the lobby filled with people. He nearly collided with several clusters of men and women in his single-minded haste to reach the private boxes.

"Good Lord, it's Stonecliff! What the devil has got into him?" Lord Cavenleigh muttered nervously to Lord Willowton as the black-haired earl, looking to be in an even blacker temper, lunged past.

"Perhaps he is looking for Lady Stonecliff?" the young woman on Lord Willowton's arm suggested with a sly quirk of her lips. "If what Miss Crenshaw told me is true, his lordship will have a time of it trying to keep tabs on *that lady*."

The way she sniffed and emphasized the final words made the two gentlemen smile, albeit nervously, but neither of them, knowing Lord Stonecliff to be in the vicinity, dared speak a word against the Earl's bride.

Ethan hadn't known such fear since the night Molly died, the night he'd heard of her accident, when he'd torn across town only to find her on her deathbed on that grim, cold hospital cot.

Nothing like that had befallen Josie, he'd told himself over and over on the drive to the Opera House, but the icy knot at the pit of his stomach said otherwise.

He'd returned from lengthy meetings with a group of reform-minded lords only to find his household in a tizzy. Lady Stonecliff had arrived home, yes. She had been given his letter; she had gone up to change for dinner.

And no one had seen her since.

Her room—both of their rooms—had been discovered to be in disarray. When Ethan had thundered up the steps and looked for himself, he'd seen at once that the jewels he'd given her to wear, which she normally kept in a velvet-lined ivory jewel box, were missing—and that the lid of the box had been left open.

Also missing were several items of his own—jeweled stickpins, a gold-handled walking stick, a snuffbox that had belonged to his great-grandfather. . . .

He'd stood frozen in the center of the floor until the housemaid, Brina, had tiptoed forward.

"I found this in the hall, my lord. It was lying on the carpet. I thought . . . it seemed to me . . . her ladyship may have dropped it there."

It was his letter—the letter stating that tomorrow they were to meet with Grismore.

That's when the rain had started, a faint but solid drumming that quite quickly began slamming against the windowpanes like coal pellets as he'd stared silently at the letter. Had Josie panicked? Had she fled, leaving him, taking all the jewels and valuables she could get her hands on in her mad dash to get away?

Had it all been a scheme, right from the start?

Ethan remembered the way she'd felt in his arms last night, the way she'd kissed him, moved her body with his, opened herself to him in every way.

"It was no scheme," he whispered.

"I beg your pardon, my lord?" Brina had twisted her hands together. "Were you speaking to me?"

"I'm going out," he told her as he turned on his heel. "If her ladyship returns while I'm gone . . ."

He didn't finish the sentence. He knew in his heart Josie would not be back—not until he found her. She hadn't merely gone out to dine without saying a word to anyone—and she hadn't run away. There was something sinister at work here.

His first thought was of Oliver Winthrop.

His second, of Ham.

❦❦❦❦❦❦

"Lord Stonecliff!" Miss Perry exclaimed when he stormed into the box where she sat with Miss Crenshaw, Mr. Winthrop, and Colonel Hamring. But her delighted smile faded as she saw the dark rage on the Earl's face.

"Whatever is wrong?" Miss Crenshaw fairly screeched.

Winthrop took one look and began backing away, nearly tripping over a gilt chair behind him, but Ethan grabbed him by the lapels of his tailcoat and wrenched him forward.

"At your lodgings they told me you were here. So where is she? What have you done with her?"

"Wh-who? I don't know what you're—"

Ethan's hands closed around his cousin's throat, but instantly Colonel Hamring was beside him, trying to pry them away. And on his other side, Miss Perry spoke in a low, breathless tone.

"My lord, this is unseemly. Only think of what you're doing, I beg of you—the scandal ... it will do Lady Stonecliff no good. In fact, she may suffer great harm ... irreparable harm."

The red fury ebbed from his eyes as her quiet, desperate words penetrated. He became aware of the countless faces turned to him from all over the theatre, the hushed silence, the shocked expressions, and he eased the pressure from Winthrop's throat.

"Outside, then," he snarled, and released his cousin, stepping back. But the ferocious expression in his eyes left Winthrop no hope of more than a temporary reprieve.

"Outside, you worthless piece of vermin," Ethan said so softly, only those in the box could hear, forcing a smile onto his face as he gestured toward the door. "Before I drag you out on your worthless knees."

When they had left the openness of the private box, he dragged Winthrop into a velvet-curtained alcove where it was dark save for one hissing gas jet.

"Now tell me what you've done with her before I end your stinking miserable life once and for all."

"If you mean Lady Stonecliff . . ."

"Who else?" Ethan shook him till his teeth rattled.

"I haven't seen her. Nor done anything—"

"Latherby told me you've been asking questions about her. That's right," Ethan sneered. "He came straight to me after you tried to bribe him into carrying tales of her to Grismore. You might be interested to know I gave him double the amount you offered him because he had the good sense and loyalty to toss you out on your ear. But you wouldn't know anything about loyalty, would you, Winthrop? You're loyal only to yourself."

"It's all a lie. I never—"

"And you've been spreading rumors about her—ugly rumors. Think you're going to turn London against her, don't you? And Grismore as well. But the way I'm figuring it, you weren't satisfied with that. You wanted to get rid of her—just in case she survives your nasty little whispering campaign."

"I will ask you one more time, Cousin, to unhand me or—"

Ethan slugged him and watched Winthrop slam against the wall.

"Or what?"

"You're mad!"

"I'm giving you until the count of five to tell me what you've done with her. And if she's been hurt . . ."

He advanced on Winthrop again, fists raised. Blanching, Winthrop cowered against the wall. "Nothing, I tell you. I haven't seen her. Or done anything."

"Hired someone?"

"No, by God, no! I was planning to meet with Grismore, that's all, and tell him what I know—and I know plenty," he added in a high, peevish tone, his temper getting away from him for a moment. "Enough to send that little tart packing. But I haven't done away with her, if that's what you mean. If she's missing, she's probably run off with the gardener or some groom, or—"

This time the blow sank him to his knees. Blood spurted from his mouth as, gasping, he fumbled for a handkerchief. "My t-tooth!" he sputtered. "You've knocked out my t-tooth!"

But Ethan Savage was already gone.

Colonel Hamring and Miss Perry were hovering by the stairway when he stalked in that direction.

"My lord, I don't know what the trouble is, but if there is any way I can help . . ." Miss Perry eyed him worriedly.

Beside her the Colonel spoke gravely. "I'm at your service, Stonecliff."

"You've both already been of help. You kept me from murdering that son of a bitch in front of hundreds of witnesses."

He wheeled away from them and started down the stairs without another word.

Miss Perry raised anxious eyes to the Colonel's face. He smiled down at her. "I'm certain everything will turn out for the best, my dear. At least I hope so. I like Stonecliff—and Lady Stonecliff, too."

"She is the dearest friend I've ever had," Miss Perry said quietly. "I wonder what has happened—and if there is some way I can help."

"You heard him. And it's quite true—you've already helped. If not for you, the situation might have become far worse. How brave you were to step up and speak to him when you did, Clara. Not many ladies I know would have dared approach a man in such a rage."

"I only wished to avoid a scandal. That wouldn't help either of them."

"Very quick thinking, my dear."

She blushed under his admiring scrutiny.

"I admire a woman who stands by her friends. Who is not afraid to act in their behalf. In the army, we learned the infinite value of loyalty, and how greatly it is to be cherished."

The intermission was drawing to a close. All around

them people in glittering finery were hurrying back to their boxes, and they could hear the expectant rustle and hush of the crowd.

Miss Perry smiled into his eyes. "Shouldn't we be going back?"

"Yes . . . no." Colonel Hamring found himself stammering for the first time since he was a very green young man, flustered at being summoned before his commander for a minor infraction. *This is not the time,* he told himself, but as he regarded Miss Perry in the now deserted lobby of the Opera House, he found himself oddly compelled by the questioning sweetness in her eyes, the very light way she rested her hand upon his arm.

His dear wife had died nearly fifteen years ago, and he had thought never to remarry. But Clara Perry was such a sweet, comfortable woman—and mightily becoming as well. And she had unexpected backbone for one who appeared so dainty. Odd that he had never noticed her before in these many years—they attended many of the same balls and dinner parties, though she was always compelled to stand in the shadow of that whiny Miss Crenshaw.

She deserved a better life than having to be at the beck and call of that selfish miss, he thought, his chest puffing out a bit with indignation on her behalf as he recalled the condescending way Miss Crenshaw had treated Miss Perry throughout the first half of tonight's performance.

He hesitated fractionally, regarding her as she waited for him to explain the delay. By God, she was a comfortable woman. Her image had popped into his mind countless times in the past few days—actually, ever since she had administered such anxious attention to him at Lady Tattersall's home.

"We'll go in if you wish," he said, his voice trembling a bit with excitement at what he was about to do. "But first, my dear Miss Perry, there is something I wish to ask you."

❈❈❈ ❈❈❈

A downpour slickened the streets of Mayfair as Ethan slammed back into the house. It was nearly eleven o'clock. He waved away the footmen who hurried to help him with his sodden coat and hat, and stalked into his library. The news that Josie hadn't returned held no surprise for him.

He splashed brandy into a glass and drank.

Where could she be? Was she hurt—frightened? What could have made her leave him?

The thought that she had wanted to leave, that this was part of some cruel plan presented itself to him once more. He finished the brandy and swung toward the window, staring past the heavy plum velvet draperies into the black, wet night.

For ten years he hadn't believed in anyone or anything. He hadn't allowed himself to feel, to care, to reach out— not to anyone, not since Molly. Not until now.

A tremendous weight seemed to press in upon him. He imagined Josie gathering up his mother's jewels, hurrying into his room, scooping up his stickpins, the snuffbox, sneaking off like some thief into the night. . . .

She isn't a thief. She didn't run off.

Ethan closed his eyes and searched for her with every particle of his being. If she was dead, he'd feel it. If she had run away, he'd know it. Wouldn't he?

Sweating, he downed another brandy. He'd always

relied on his instincts, and his instincts told him now that Josie was in trouble.

Bad trouble.

He slammed the glass down on the desk. He didn't know where to look for her, but he couldn't stay here another moment, warm and dry in this house while she was out there somewhere needing help.

He'd take the carriage and drive through every street in London if he had to. He'd start in Mayfair and branch out in gradually widening circles: the Strand, Trafalgar Square, Hyde Park, the Embankment. He'd search each area until—

The sound of crashing glass stopped him when he was halfway to the door.

He paused only an instant, and then sprinted forward.

"It came from upstairs," he shouted as the servants came running, their faces shocked and pale. He was already gaining the top of the split marble staircase and racing down the hall, every sense alert.

"A rock! Gracious me, my lord . . ."

"There's a note inside this pouch." Ethan tore it open. Latherby's gold ring tumbled out of the folded paper and landed on a shard of glass embedded in the carpet.

We've got her. You never should have offered that reward against us because now she's going to die. Unless you bring 25,000 pounds to Blackfriars Bridge at midnight tomorrow. Don't be late or she'll pay the price.

There was no signature. Ethan's hands clenched on the paper. Those bastards. He forced himself to keep the fury at bay, to concentrate on what he had to do to free Josie.

The letter had to be from Pirate Pete. Except that Ethan doubted either Pirate Pete or Tiny could read or write worth a damn—and the language of the note didn't reflect the cockney speech either of them used.

So someone had written the note for him.

It doesn't matter, he told himself as he stooped to pick up the gold ring. Turning it over and over in his fingers, he remembered how he'd balked at presenting the dark-haired pickpocket with his own ring to wear during their wedding ceremony, how he'd made Latherby hand over his ring instead. And now—now he would gladly give Josephine Cooper everything he possessed or ever might hope to possess.

No gift would be too much, no jewel too precious. She was the most precious treasure in his life.

The worried faces and voices of the servants swirled around him as he strode to his dressing room, tore off his finely tailored suit coat, and threw it on the floor. His mouth grim, he lifted his gunbelt from its hook. As he strapped on his guns, he struggled to take in the plot he had to contend with.

Josie's life was at stake. And where in hell was Ham?

Then, as if summoned by the sheer intensity of Ethan's will and need for him, there came a pounding at the front door, and even upstairs they could all faintly hear the low, gravelly voice raised in a frantic shout.

"Let me in, my lord. Ethan! Ethan, lad, let me in."

Ethan was already halfway down the stairs.

"I know!" Ham announced as the door swung open. He stumbled inside, a picture of disrepute, his clothes torn and dirty and soaked, his boots laden with mud. But there was triumph in his eyes as Ethan eagerly gripped his arms. And as he looked at the man whom he'd mentored as a young boy, there was also devotion—and a burning, frightening urgency.

"I got away as soon as I could. Ran into some trouble . . ." His breath was coming in heaving gasps. "Don't worry, lad, I'm fine, and so will she be if we hurry. But there's no time to lose. I been following her all day, just like you wanted, and you were right about those bloody bastards coming for her. But not to fear, lad, not to fear. I know! I know where she is."

Chapter Twenty-six

❦

The thunder had begun by the time Snake and Spooner returned to the room with a tray of food and a tin cup filled with ale. They'd left Josie tied to the bedpost, where she'd been struggling in vain ever since, trying to unknot the thick rope.

"Give up, honey," Snake advised, noting her flushed, disheveled appearance. Her hair hung into her face in damp tendrils, and the pretty gown she'd been wearing when they'd grabbed her was now hopelessly creased and wrinkled. "You ain't getting away again. This time I'm going to watch you like a hawk."

"Then I'll just have to kill you, won't I?" The words flew out before she thought, and she instantly regretted them for Snake's eyes began to glitter.

"You back-talking me again, girl?"

Use your head, she told herself, and lifted her eyes to show him what she hoped was a cowed expression. "I'm sorry. I didn't mean it," she mumbled. "But . . ."

"But what?"

"My arm hurts, Snake. And I don't feel so good." She watched Spooner set the tray down on a broken table beside the bed. It held a bowl of thin-looking brownish soup and a crust of bread. Both looked disgusting.

"I never had any dinner tonight. And you know how I get when I'm hungry." She tried to smile at him, hoping to pierce for an instant the armor of blustering pride and vengeance in which he'd encased himself.

"Then go ahead and eat your grub. Just quit complaining."

The dangerous glitter had faded a bit, and his voice was only irritable, no longer angry.

"Can you untie me for a little while so I can eat? I can't hardly get away with you and Spooner here."

Snake was pacing the room. "Go ahead," he told Spooner, as the broad-shouldered outlaw threw him a questioning look. "But only till she's done eatin'."

It took Spooner several moments to work her wrist free of the rope. "There you go, Josie," he said almost apologetically.

Josie rubbed her raw flesh. She'd tried to watch how he'd defeated the knot, but had a sinking feeling it would be too difficult for her to manage one-handed. She'd have to find another way.

Forcing herself to spoon up several mouthfuls of the vile soup, and to chew the chunk of bread, she studied Snake and Spooner thoughtfully from beneath her lashes. Snake had sat himself down on the stool and was trimming his fingernails with his knife. Spooner paced restlessly, glancing out the window each time thunder split the rain-soaked night.

At last Snake noticed that she'd finished eating and was simply sitting on the cot, cradling the ale cup between both hands and quietly surveying the dirty confines of the room.

He slipped his knife back in his pocket and stood, glowering at her. The din coming from downstairs in the gin house grew louder between rumbles of thunder.

"What are you up to, girl? Whatever it is, it won't work."

"I just . . . got a cramp in my legs. Before you tie me up again, can I just walk across the room, loosen up my muscles?"

Snake reached her in two strides. "Sure, honey," he sneered. "So long as I'm holding on to you."

Spooner backed away from the window, saying nothing as Snake slipped a heavy arm around Josie's waist. She teetered across the small room, toward the window. There wasn't much she could see in the inky night with all that rain slashing down. She thought she could just make out a maze of crumbling buildings and twisting alleyways, but she wasn't sure.

"Forget it." Snake's arm tightened around her waist. He spun her to face him, his breath hot in her face. "I know you're getting the lay of the land, thinking where you'd run if you had the chance. You're not going nowhere. You hear? We've got to settle our score, you and me. So you're staying put, right here in my arms where you belong."

"Like hell I belong in your arms," she muttered, pushing against his chest. His hold grew more restrictive. "That's enough, Snake. You're hurting me. . . ."

"You hurt me, honey. Hurt my feelings real bad when you ran off. Didn't she, Spooner?"

Spooner swallowed, looking at the floor. From the main room of the gin house came a roar and cheers and wild crashing and thumping.

"Snake, I'm thinkin' we should maybe get back out

there. Sounds like some fightin'—could be Noah and
Deck. They told me before they thought Pirate Pete was
cheatin' at cards and they weren't goin' to put up with
it—they've been drinking pretty heavy since Noah got
back. . . ."

"You go. I'm busy."

"But . . . they won't listen none to me. And you said
we all oughta keep a clear head for later."

"What's happening later?" Josie gasped, still trying
unsuccessfully to get free of Snake. He bent her slightly
backward and lowered himself over her.

"Nothin' that you need to worry your pretty head over,
honey." His breath reeked now of gin and onions and
tobacco. His mouth covered hers, wet and sucking. In
disgust, Josie tried to twist her face aside.

When he pushed her down on the bed and threw himself down heavily on top of her, she was filled with as
much repugnance as terror. This—Snake's painful groping and panting, the smearing together of mouths—was
an abomination, as different from the ecstasy she'd
known with Ethan as horse dung from meadow flowers.

"No . . . damn you! No, Snake—I'll never let you do
this . . . to me again."

His fingers closed, pinching over her breast. "I am
doing it, and I'll do it whenever I want to—you savvy?"

With all her might, Josie jerked her knee up. Snake let
out a yell. His heavy frame went rigid with pain, then he
doubled over and rolled off her with a tortured moan.

"Why, you . . . bitch." His face was purple with rage,
contorted with agony. "I'll . . . teach you to—"

Another crash from below, this one louder than the
first. "Snake, you'd better do somethin'." Near the door,

Spooner shifted from one foot to the other. "If those are our boys fightin' with Pete and Tiny . . ."

"Son of a bitch . . . all right." Snake took several deep breaths and grunted as he tried to stand. He was bent over, clutching his groin. The look of fury on his face made Josie's heart stop.

"Tie her up again—tight!"

His eyes pinned Josie as Spooner looped the rope around her wrist into a hard knot, then tied it to the bed-post. When Spooner at last stepped back, his shoulders drooped and he wouldn't meet her eyes.

Snake, still breathing hard but able to straighten up slightly, nodded with satisfaction. "I'll be back pronto."

Painfully, he lumbered toward the door. "And then I'm going to make that last beatin' I gave you look like it warn't nothin' at all."

Josie stared at the ceiling as she listened to the sound of their boots stamping down the hall. The rope was cutting painfully into her wrist, chafing the skin that was already tender.

"But not for long," she muttered between clenched teeth, and with her free hand, yanked Snake's knife from the pocket of her gown.

It was a good thing she hadn't lost her touch. She inched herself up into a sitting position, twisted around as far as she could, and began to saw at her bonds.

❧❧❧ ❧❧❧

At the mouth of the alley, Ham paused to drag in a deep breath. "It's this way." He wiped pouring rain from his eyes. "Down around that corner there, behind that wall, is the gin house. The very worst section of the rookery. She's in a corner room, upstairs. There's steps from the outside, broken ones. . . ."

A noise had Ethan spinning about, ready to strike. From the gloom a hunched figure materialized. But it was only an old drunken beggar, who glared at him with red, blank eyes and then hobbled away, muttering something indistinguishable. The stink of sewage filth, rats, unwashed flesh, urine, and liquor seemed to rise from the broken pavement. The crumbling buildings almost moaned with the echoes of human misery.

His stomach sickened at the thought of Josie trapped here in the bowels of London. "Show me where," he growled, his eyes narrowed against the rain.

As the downpour grew even more intense, they crept forward into the deeper darkness of the alley.

❧❧❧❧❧❧

Josie had only just freed herself when she heard footsteps in the hall. She dashed to the window and struggled to open it.

Before she could do more than throw one leg over the sill, the door burst open. "Ehh! What 'ave we 'ere?" Pirate Pete boomed.

Tiny didn't waste words. He hurtled toward her.

Josie threw Snake's knife. It struck Tiny full in the chest. She saw his eyes widen as blood spouted out.

"I'm goin' ter kill ye wi' me bare 'ands!" he roared, even as Pirate Pete dodged forward and hauled her back from the window's edge.

But Josie moved fast. She grabbed his pistol from his belt and gripped it in both hands, backing away.

"Stand back!" She cocked the gun. "I'll shoot you if you make a move!"

"The 'ell ye will. Ye don't 'ave the stomach fer it," Tiny grated, and yanked the knife from his chest with a grunt. Blinking, he advanced on her, the knife raised, blood pouring down his shirtfront and pooling on the floor with each step.

Without hesitation, Josie swung toward him and squeezed the trigger. The report sent pain ricocheting through her arm. It also sent Tiny whirling backward in a hideous explosion of blood and bone.

"Yer mad, girl!" Pirate Pete exclaimed, and then he dived toward her with a snarl.

She fired again. Pirate Pete doubled over and lay writhing on the floor, even as she heard more footsteps running down the hall.

She dashed to the window. Her whole body was shaking as she clambered over the ledge, gripping the gun as tightly as she could in hands that were slippery with sweat.

"Ye can't get away . . ." Pirate Pete gasped as blood seeped across the floor beneath his shuddering form.

"Watch me."

Even as she swung out the window and balanced precariously on the narrow platform, she heard the rumble of Snake's voice as he and the boys burst into the room.

"She . . . went . . . out the winder." Pirate Pete managed no more than a weak gasp. "She's got me . . . gun!"

"Damn her to hell! You boys git downstairs—head her off in the alley!"

Hugging the wall, Josie started down the crumbling outside stair. She risked one glance back and saw Snake shoving his burly frame out the window after her.

She raised the gun, letting go of the wall long enough to fire a shot. It missed, but the explosion shook her and almost made her lose her balance. Through the pouring rain, Snake's features were a mask of venom.

"You're dead, girl. Dead!" he roared, and started down the stairs.

Josie reached the bottom and hurled herself toward a corner, but suddenly she was seized from behind and pulled backward. She fought wildly and tried to point the gun.

"Easy, you wildcat," Ethan whispered in her ear. "Haven't you done enough for one night?"

"Ethan!"

His hand clamped over her mouth as she shrieked his name, then collapsed against him. Her arms coiled around his neck, clinging, inhaling the smell of him, feeling the strength of him. He was soaked and rain streamed down his coal-black hair into that beloved bronzed face. From beside them in the sodden darkness loomed Ham.

"Look out, lad, here they come," he warned, and suddenly the shadowy forms of Spooner, Deck, and Noah raced around the corner of the gin house straight toward them.

"Looking for someone, boys?" Ethan sprang in front of Josie so that she was shielded by his body.

Spooner froze. Noah and Deck went for their guns.

They never had a chance. Ethan drew like lightning and the dark alley rocked with gunfire.

Josie's shoulders trembled as she squinted through the rain. She could just make out Spooner wheeling around, running back up the alley, and Ham bounding through the shadows in pursuit.

But she suddenly heard the *zing* of another shot as Snake fired his Colt from the stairs. Her blood went cold as she heard Ethan's sharp intake of breath beside her.

He grasped her arm and dragged her around the corner and behind a stack of crates, breathing hard.

"Ethan, you've been shot!"

"Damn right, sweetheart. How about that?"

He was *grinning*, Josie saw incredulously. *Grinning.* And despite the blood that poured from a gaping wound in his arm, he sounded amazingly calm, almost pleased. "Always knew it had to happen sooner or later. Kind of a relief to get it over with."

"Winged ya, eh?" It sounded like Snake had reached the bottom of the steps. He was edging closer. "Next time you're going straight to hell, Savage. Hear that, Josie? Then it's just you and me gonna be left. The two of us . . . all alone. Just me and my no-good runaway wife."

Ethan clenched his jaw, whether from pain or anger she couldn't tell. "Did he hurt you?"

"No," she whispered, terrified by how pale he'd gone, and by how much his arm was bleeding. "I'm fine. . . ."

"Liar," he said softly, lovingly. Then he called out to Snake, his voice ringing through the alley like raw steel.

"She's my wife now, Barker. And you're going to pay for every bruise you ever gave her."

"Ha! Your wife! Not legally she ain't. Your marriage didn't mean squat, because all the time that lying bitch was still married to me!"

Flattened against the wall, Ethan spoke again, his hard voice clearly piercing the steady drum of the downpour. "Then I reckon I've got to make her a widow before she can be my bride."

As Josie watched in wordless terror, Ethan pushed himself away from the wall and swung around the corner. He swayed a bit on his feet as he faced the outlaw in the downpour.

"No!" she groaned, hugging her arms around herself, but even as the words left her lips, two gunshots split the night. Paralyzed, Josie stared at Ethan with fear raking her throat. When he swayed again on his feet, staggered a bit, and lowered the gun, she launched herself at him.

"My God, Ethan . . . no!"

Then she saw. Snake was dead, sprawled prone in the alley, blood oozing into the mud and sewage, a rat leaping over his bloodstained chest and disappearing behind a heap of refuse. Ethan was bleeding heavily from his wounded arm, but otherwise unhurt.

Snake's shot had gone wide.

"You . . . all right?" he asked her, looking into her face as she dropped Pete's pistol into her pocket and wrapped her arms around him, trying to take some of his weight.

"Me? I've never been better, Ethan, but we've got to bind your wound and get you to a doctor."

"Ham?" Ethan ignored her comment, detached himself from her, and started down the alley. "Ham!" he called sharply.

"Here, lad." The old groom swam out of the gloom. "The other one got away, but to bloody hell with him . . . you've been shot."

"You and my wife are so perceptive." With an effort Ethan managed to grin at Ham over Josie's head as she yanked his handkerchief from his pocket and wrapped it quickly around the wound. "She's a hell of a lot of trouble, this woman of mine, but she's worth it."

"Aye, I should think so." Ham frowned. "Can you walk, lad?"

"He won't admit it if he can't." Feeling queasy, Josie wiped her bloodied hands on her skirt and peered around the alley. "We must get out of here and get a hansom."

"Aye. Here, my lady, let him lean on me. Come along now." They started forward slowly, past Snake's prone form, veering away from Noah and Deck's blood-spattered bodies. "We've got to get you and the Countess out of here."

Their feet sloshed through oozing puddles. As several dark forms peered out of tiny windows or materialized like ghostly wretches in the shadows of the alley, Josie drew the pistol from her pocket—just in case.

"Ye . . . es. Damn right." Ethan's gaze met Josie's as she lifted anxious eyes to his. Love and worry twisted through her delicate features. For her sake, he smoothed the pain from his face and forced himself to grin at her, though weakly, and to walk more steadily between them.

"We'll send the police back later . . . for what those bastards stole. Right now, we've got to get . . . my Countess . . . safely home."

Chapter Twenty-seven

When the balding and bespectacled Mr. Grismore ushered them into his office chamber at precisely two o'clock the following afternoon, Josie braced herself for violence—Oliver Winthrop was present, waiting beside a deep green chair, his hands folded behind his back. Beside her, she felt Ethan stiffen.

"Don't hit him, please," she whispered as Ethan escorted her to a comfortable burgundy leather armchair that faced Grismore's desk.

"I'll just shoot him instead," Ethan replied loudly enough for both Grismore and Winthrop to hear.

Winthrop flushed. Grismore stared hard at the surviving son of his former employer, his gaze lingering on the sling that supported the Earl of Stonecliff's left arm.

"My lord, I trust this is going to be a civilized interview. No violence. It appears to me you have already been injured sufficiently.... I trust the accident was nothing serious?"

"It wasn't an accident, it was a bullet. But it's little more than a flesh wound," Ethan informed him easily. "Lost a bit of blood, but I'm fit enough to throw my esteemed cousin out of here in style if he doesn't mind his manners."

"This is outrageous!" Winthrop protested, then as Ethan turned toward him, his voice trailed off into a squeak. "Mr. Grismore, I demand you seize charge of this interview at once. I won't be intimidated."

"Won't you?" Ethan asked dangerously, a mocking smile curling his lips, and beside him, Josie had all she could do not to giggle at the terrified expression on Winthrop's face.

"Please—let us proceed, gentlemen," she said sweetly, but there was a silent plea in her eyes as she glanced at Ethan.

He kissed her hand and waited until she had slipped into the chair before seating himself beside her.

Mr. Grismore began by repeating the grave reservations the late Earl of Stonecliff had felt in bequeathing his fortune, his lands, his houses, and all of his worldly possessions to the son who had in the past showed himself to be an irresponsible hothead with no respect for his own noble birth or position.

"After the unfortunate demise of your brother, your father felt that you would benefit greatly and be much more likely to settle into your new position, if you had the advantage of a wife. The proper sort of wife," Grismore added. "A lady."

He looked expectantly at Josie and studied her over the top of his spectacles.

"Hence the rather unusual terms of his will."

"My father was always a damned tyrannical bastard," Ethan said, and Mr. Grismore's neck muscles bunched above his stiff collar.

"My lord, that is quite—"

"Quite true." Ethan cut him off silkily. "But I'm not here to talk about my father. He's dead, and the past is over. I can't change it, and I can't relive it. My wife has helped me to recognize that, and to give me some hope—and some enthusiasm—for the future."

Josie turned in her chair to arch a brow at him. "Only some enthusiasm?" she said softly.

And in her eyes, Ethan saw reflected the tender kisses and whispered words they'd shared last night after arriving safely home.

As always when he looked at her, when he saw her beauty, her vitality, her innate sweetness—which, thank God, had never been stamped out by the harshness of her life—he felt a jolt of desire, of pleasure and delight so strong, he wanted to snatch her into his arms there and then. And the fantastic tale she'd told him last night about having discovered the truth about her parentage, a matched set of jewels, a shy sister, and the Duke of Bennington's being her grandfather, only added to the odd enchantment of Josie Cooper Barker Savage.

Only the damned priggishness of their stately surroundings and the need to conclude this ridiculous stipulation of the will now, today, kept him from kissing her until her eyes darkened with a desire every bit as intense as his own for her.

"More than a little. Quite a bit more," he said for her ears only, and the truth was in his eyes as they exchanged glances. With an effort, he turned his attention back to Grismore.

"This meeting is now over. You've carried out your obligation to my father. You've met my wife, and seen for yourself that she is by all means a lady. Your responsibility in this matter is now at an end."

"I'm afraid it isn't quite that simple, my lord." Grismore fixed him with a regretful glance. The lovely young woman seated beside the succeeding earl was certainly elegant in her teal silk day gown with its cream-colored lace trim and tiny bustle, her hair coiled in shining ringlets atop her head, where perched a fashionable little ostrich plume hat. She moved gracefully, and her voice was beautiful, low and musical. It wasn't that he found fault with the brilliant sparkle of her eyes, or the outright provocatively sensual shape of her mouth, but he could scarcely ignore the report he had received from Mr. Oliver Winthrop. A report that, if true, would be utterly shocking and render her entirely inappropriate to the position of Countess of Stonecliff.

But he had to tread carefully. Should Mr. Winthrop's assertions prove untrue or exaggerated, he would be in an awkward position with the new earl. That would hardly benefit him. He was walking a careful line between his duty to the late earl, and his wish to win the patronage of the would-be new one.

"Mr. Winthrop has brought to my attention some information which is worrisome. I regret, my lady, that I must bring up these matters, but it is essential to get at the truth."

"I understand." Josie took a deep breath, bracing herself for the questions and accusations to come. Ethan had told her that Winthrop knew the truth about her and had been planting rumors behind her back, and that he would have certainly reported to Grismore.

Now she had only one choice. To lie. To lie well enough that Mr. Grismore believed her rather than Winthrop, so that he wouldn't pursue the matter with inquiries back to America.

If he did, all was lost. It would be easy for him to discover that Winthrop was right—not about her being a pickpocket, for who would know that—but that she was a nobody, an orphan who'd worked as a cook and in a dance hall, who was far, very far indeed, from the pampered and proper lady the late earl had dictated his son must marry.

Josie felt Ethan tense. She knew he was silently damning his father. He'd told Josie last night that if he had to choose between her and his inheritance, he would choose her without hesitation. They would return to America, he said, where they would build a life together free of anyone's restrictions or interference. To hell with Stonecliff Park and London and Parliament. . . .

But she knew that he loved Stonecliff Park. Why, she herself had felt it stealing its way into her heart, and she was almost a stranger. How easy it would be to love that house, that gentle emerald land—to call it home.

Home. She who had never had a home might now cause Ethan to lose the one that should rightfully be his.

She couldn't bear that. "I will answer all of your questions with pleasure."

She offered the solicitor the well-bred smile she'd been practicing before the mirror since the morning she'd sailed for England.

"If you don't mind, Mr. Grismore, I can clear this up with a few simple questions." Winthrop bustled forward, avoiding getting within range of Ethan's fists, skirting the desk, and coming to stand beside Mr. Grismore's chair.

"Did you or did you not find employment"—he uttered the last word with disgust—"in America working in a . . . *dance hall*?"

"I—"

Before she could finish the sentence, an imperative rap on the door interrupted.

Grismore frowned. "Come in," he snapped, but as he peered toward the door his expression of irritation changed to one of surprise and respect.

"Your grace!"

The Duke of Bennington walked slowly into the inner chamber, accompanied by Alicia Denby.

Stunned, Josie jumped up from her chair. She drew in her breath, but before she could do or say anything, Alicia sent her a determined, reassuring smile that bade her be silent.

When Josie glanced questioningly at Ethan, to whom she had confided all last evening when they'd returned from the rookery, he winked.

"Forgive the interruption, Mr. Grismore, but I understand you are interviewing my granddaughter this afternoon and I could not allow such an impertinence to continue."

"Your . . . granddaughter?" Grismore's mouth opened and closed several times, like that of a grounded fish gasping for air.

"That is correct." The Duke was frowning. "I won't have her interrogated like a common pickpocket apprehended by the police."

Josie made a small choking sound. Ethan turned to her with an expression of concern as he took her hand. "There, there, my love," he murmured while smoothing her brow with exaggerated care.

"My wife has suffered enough indignity for one day, Grismore, don't you agree?"

"Well, yes, my lord, I wouldn't wish to . . . that is . . . I say . . . you never mentioned that your wife was grand-daughter to the Duke of Bennington, my lord. I apolo-gize. If this is the case, certainly there is no need—"

"There is *every* need!" Winthrop shouted, staring from one to the other of them and fairly jumping up and down with frustration. "This dance hall girl is not your grand-daughter, sir! She cannot be, this is a trick . . . a lie. . . ."

His voice trailed off in the icy silence which followed. The Duke regarded him with cold contempt. The Earl's lip curled in mockery. Miss Denby walked over to take Josie's arm and tuck it protectively in hers. And Josie merely stood with shoulders straight and head held high, her eyes filled with exquisitely ladylike sadness.

"Oh, dear, Mr. Winthrop—I can't imagine why you've taken me in such dislike," she murmured. "I had so hoped we could become friends."

"It's obvious why, my dear." Ethan's gray eyes flicked toward Grismore. "*You* understand his motives for this nonsense, don't you?" he inquired scornfully.

Grismore met his keen, piercing gaze and winced. "Indeed I do, my lord." His voice was faint. He glanced at the Duke, who was still frowning imperiously at him.

"Indeed I do," he said more strongly.

Faced with the Duke of Bennington, who stated that the girl was his granddaughter, and the Earl of Stonecliff, who clearly intended to keep her for his wife, and the woman herself—a most uncommon beauty with delicate manners and elegance in every line of her bearing, in every nuance of voice and expression, the truth was obvious.

Vulgar greed had driven Winthrop to lie and vilify his cousin's wife and, in short, to go to desperate lengths to try to steal away the Stonecliff inheritance.

And I have almost let him draw me into his plot with this vile tale, Grismore realized in horror. *I've narrowly escaped a fatal misstep.*

He backed away as if saving himself from a deadly precipice.

"My lady, kindly accept my deepest apologies for any pain my inquiries may have caused you. I was only trying to do my duty by the late earl, to serve him as best I could—in the same way that I hope to serve *you* now and in the future, both you and Lord Stonecliff."

"Noooooo!" Winthrop, in frustration, snatched up the vase at the edge of Grismore's desk and flung it across the room. It shattered against the mantel with a crash that echoed through the austere chamber.

"Latherby!" Mr. Grismore called out, and Lucas Latherby appeared from the anteroom, his gold spectacles glinting upon his nose.

"Kindly escort Mr. Winthrop from the premises."

"You can't do this, you can't! It's a lie. . . ."

Latherby grasped him by the arm. "Come along."

His voice was cool and formal, but Josie saw the gleam of victory in his eyes.

"Need any help?" Ethan took a step forward.

"My lord, my lady." Latherby threw Josie a quick smile full of meaning. "Allow me. Nothing will give me greater pleasure."

If she hadn't been so relieved, Josie might actually have felt sorry for Winthrop as he was dragged, still shouting, from the office.

Mr. Grismore invited everyone to be seated. With Winthrop's fading cries still piercing the air, they accepted.

"Now," Mr. Grismore said, drawing a shaky breath as

he surveyed the impressive assemblage. "Only a few formalities remain—several papers, some signatures, my lord." He inclined his head apologetically to Josie and bestowed on her his most ingratiating smile. "Forgive me, my lady. You have my word, this will not take long."

Josie had waited her entire life to have someone care for her, want her, stand up for her, the way that Ethan, the Duke, and Alicia had just done. Her heart was soaring.

"It's quite all right," she informed the solicitor with a brilliant smile. Ethan's hand snugly encased hers.

"I don't mind the wait."

⊗⊗⊗ ⊗⊗⊗

Outside on the sun-dappled street, Josie kissed the Duke, and hugged Alicia.

"But how did you know to come today?"

Her grandfather smiled approvingly at Ethan. "We received a note from your husband early this morning, alerting us to what was taking place."

She threw Ethan an amazed glance. "You never told me. . . ."

"I didn't want to get your hopes up, sweetheart. I didn't know if the Duke and Miss Denby were otherwise engaged this morning—or if they would be willing to subject themselves to the interview. But I figured it was worth a try, better to have too much ammunition than not enough."

Her eyes shone. "It was very good of you to come. I can never thank you enough."

"It's the least we could do, Josie. You are our f-family."

"From now on, we will always be at your side, my dear." The firmness of the Duke's tone and the misting over of his eyes brought a lump to Josie's throat. "Families stand together and look after their own."

His keen gaze shifted suddenly to Ethan, tall and strong beside Josie, yet with a shadow of pain flickering across his face at the Duke's words. They all sensed what Ethan was feeling at this moment.

His own family had never stood behind him. Even in death, his father had put constraints on him and tried to control him, casting doubts upon his judgment, maturity, and sense of responsibility. That was at the root of this entire humiliating interview, an interview that might not have gone so well had not Josie's newfound family showed her the kind of support he had never known.

"Lord Stonecliff, you have brought my granddaughter home to me. And given Alicia here the sister she's always yearned to find. We are in your debt."

"I'm the one in your debt, sir. Your presence here today turned the tide. For that, I can never thank you enough."

"I see you're injured?" The Duke was eyeing the sling.

"A mere scratch."

"Much more than that," Josie interrupted. "So much has happened since I came to Belgravia yesterday. Ethan saved my life."

At their gasps, she tucked her arm through his good one, and nodded. "Yes—won't you come back to Mayfair for tea and I'll tell you all about it—and we can become better acquainted," she finished shyly.

"Oh, yes, we'd be delighted. We have a great d-deal of catching up to do, don't we, Grandpapa?"

"Yes, for far too many years apart." The Duke glanced at Josie then at Ethan, clearly including him in his words. "But we're all together now, a family," he said firmly.

"And there is much for which we need to be thankful. We will come to tea, granddaughter," he told Josie with a smile. "But this getting-acquainted time must be only the start."

Riding back to Mayfair in the carriage, with the Duke and Alicia following in their own, Josie leaned her head against Ethan's shoulder and thought she would die of happiness from the simple loveliness of this moment. She had the most wonderful man right there beside her, and at long last she'd found her family. The interview with Grismore was behind her, and so was the danger and uncertainty of the past.

And as the carriage pulled to a halt before the town house, Ethan grasped her hand in his. "Come on, sweetheart," he said softly, reading the emotion welling up in her eyes. His smile shook her to the core of her soul.

"We're home."

❧❧❧❧❧❧

It was a perfect morning for a wedding.

Sunshine bathed the tiny stone church nestled in a grove of shade trees less than ten miles from Stonecliff Park. Inside, its snug interior was bedecked with candles and flowers. A sense of peace clung to the sturdy old walls.

And the bride, in a gown of palest ivory satin, glowed with a radiance that put the sunshine streaming through the windows to shame.

Josie heard the vicar's voice as if from a great distance.

"My lord, do you solemnly take this woman to be your wife, to have and to hold. . . ."

To have and to hold. She and Ethan. Forever.

Happiness rocked Josie's heart. She was so caught up

in emotion that she couldn't even concentrate on the vicar's droning voice. All she saw was Ethan, handsome and elegant, smiling down at her, his hair smooth and black as coal, his eyes gleaming beneath those dark, aristocratic brows. She knew that the Duke and Alicia sat in the first pew, smiling, and that Clara and Colonel Hamring were beside them, holding hands—they had been married two weeks earlier. And Ham sat just behind them, stiff and straight in his Sunday-best clothes.

But after one quick glance at them as she'd floated down the aisle, she hadn't been able to see anyone but Ethan. Her heart—her husband.

This time it would be for real.

The five guests in the church—the only guests invited to this most private of ceremonies—all believed the couple was merely renewing their vows now that they were settled on English soil.

Only Josie and Ethan knew that this was truly their marriage ceremony—that the first one didn't count.

It had been Ethan's idea, his insistence, to have this ceremony.

"But Snake is dead," Josie had pointed out when he'd first told her of his intentions. "No one will ever know that I was already married to him when you and I got married in Abilene—"

"*I'll* know." He'd tipped her head back and stared fiercely into her eyes. "We're going to be married by the vicar—officially, legally, finally."

So here they were. Suddenly Josie realized that everyone was staring at her, waiting for her to speak those wonderful words.

"I do," she said in a clear, loving tone, and then Ethan removed her glove and slipped the ring on her finger.

For a moment she stared at it. Latherby's ring had been returned to him after the kidnapping. Since then, until today, she'd worn Ethan's grandfather's ring—at his insistence. But now he had given her a ring all her own. It was gold, set with a brilliant sapphire surrounded by a circle of diamonds.

She'd never thought anyone would give her something so beautiful. Never thought she'd have a fraction of all she now possessed: a family—a grandfather and sister— dear friends, and most of all, a husband who adored her. She'd never thought she'd have such a safe and lovely home, a place she would never, ever have to leave.

Before the vicar could continue, Josie lifted sparkling eyes to meet Ethan's gaze. "I know this part. It's time to kiss the bride," she murmured, an anticipatory catch in her throat. His answering grin heated her pulse as he pulled her into his arms. With joyous laughter bubbling inside her, Josie spoke so softly, no one else in the church could hear.

"First tell me, Ethan Savage, how many times in this lifetime do you plan to get married?"

Ethan's arms tightened around her, and there was no mistaking the tenderness in his eyes. His mouth slowly descended toward hers.

"That's easy, my beautiful little love. Just this once."

Dell's
Four of **Hearts**
Together
Again

Free book!

When you buy
Jill Gregory's
JUST THIS ONCE!

Purchase this Four of Hearts Together Again romance,
fill out the coupon below and send it to us along with
your original store receipt and you'll receive a free book
by any of our Four of Hearts Together Again authors.

(See back for details) Send to:

- -

D e l l

The Four of Hearts Together Again Romance Program
Dell Publishing
1540 Broadway, Dept. MF
New York, NY 10036

Name _____

Address _____

City _____ State _____ Zip _____

Telephone _____

Choose your
one free book from
the following list

The Four of Hearts Checklist

BOOKS BY MARSHA CANHAM:
___ ACROSS THE MOONLIT SEA
___ STRAIGHT FOR THE HEART
___ IN THE SHADOW OF MIDNIGHT
___ UNDER THE DESERT MOON
___ THROUGH A DARK MIST

BOOKS BY JILL GREGORY:
___ ALWAYS YOU
___ WHEN THE HEART BECKONS
___ DAISIES IN THE WIND
___ FOREVER AFTER
___ CHERISHED

BOOKS BY JOAN JOHNSTON:
___ CAPTIVE
___ MAVERICK HEART
___ THE INHERITANCE
___ OUTLAW'S BRIDE
___ KID CALHOUN
___ THE BAREFOOT BRIDE
___ SWEETWATER SEDUCTION

BY KATHERINE KINGSLEY
___ IN THE WAKE OF WIND

Dell